AZTEC ODYSSEY

Jay C. LaBarge

Characters and events portrayed in this book are fictitious. Any similarity to real persons, living or dead, is coincidental.

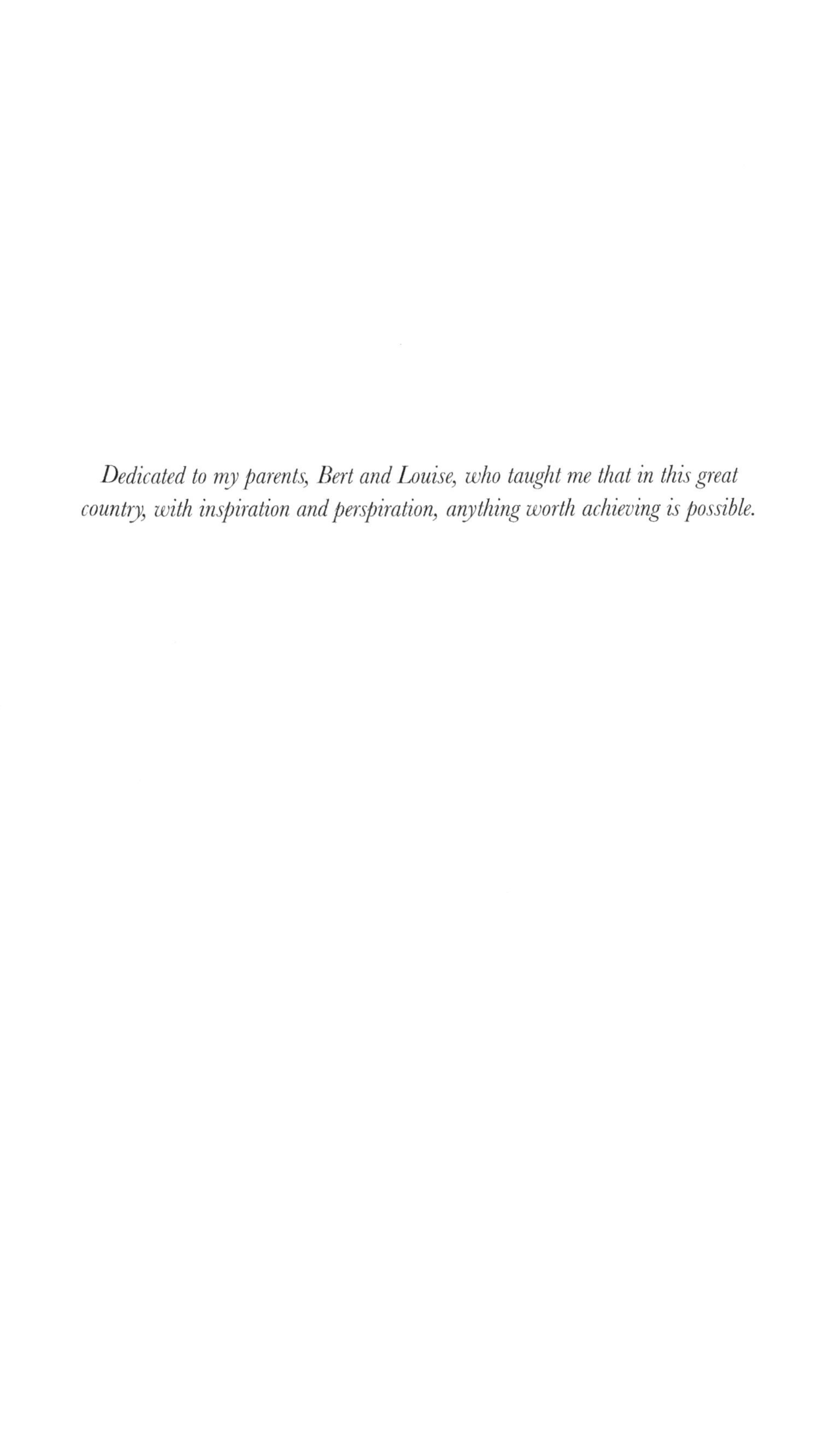

Dedicated to my parents, Bert and Louise, who taught me that in this great country, with inspiration and perspiration, anything worth achieving is possible.

I am bound to them, though I cannot look
into their eyes or hear their voices.
I honor their history.
I cherish their lives.
I will tell their story.
I will remember them.

—Unknown

CONTENTS

PART III

THE REBIRTH OF EMPIRE

EPILOGUE

PRINCIPLE CAST OF CHARACTERS

HISTORICAL NOTE

The Aztec Empire, or Triple Alliance, was the dominant civilization of Central America at the time the Spanish Conquistador Hernán Cortés set foot ashore in 1519. The fact that Cortés landed with approximately 500 men and 16 horses and toppled an Empire of over five million subjects still defies credible explanation and belief, yet it happened and ultimately changed the course of world history. As Mark Twain stated, "Truth is stranger than fiction, but it is because fiction is obliged to stick to possibilities. Truth isn't."

The initial part of this novel faithfully follows the conquest based upon as much historical evidence as was available. The principle protagonist from that time period is Asupacaci, third son of Montezuma and Queen Teotlalco. While Asupacaci is presumed to have died during the fall of Tenochtitlán (modern Mexico City) to the Spanish, there is no definitive proof of his demise. We have slightly more credible information on where and when Asupacaci's two older brothers died at the hands of the Spaniards, yet his exact fate is forever lost to the mists of time. Asupacaci's trek and subsequent adventure is where this novel delves from established fact, although it attempts to incorporate as much known history as possible in any references to the past.

Multiple languages are referenced in this book. For the sake of the reader, all dialogue is in English, even though much of it would have been spoken in the Nahuatl language of the Aztecs, Spanish, or Navajo. Where words from those languages are interjected for authenticity, a definition typically follows.

PART I

END OF DAYS

In the age of the fifth sun,
if the Aztecs failed to please
the Gods by not sacrificing
enough human blood in their honor,
the world would go black.

Tzitzimitl would destroy
all of humanity,
and an earthquake would
shatter the world completely.

CHAPTER 1 – APRIL 5, 1521

If they were followed and discovered, it would be the death of them all. It would be a lingering death, given what they were carrying. Of that he was sure. The fault would be his alone if the expedition wasn't warned. Indeed, it was a heavy burden for one man to carry. He pushed the thought from his mind and peered up over the rise, back along the trail. He struggled to hold his breath so his own labored breathing wouldn't hinder his hearing and squinted into the distance. Nothing, only cacti and scrub brush were visible. There was no telltale dust anywhere in the distance, not even the slightest sound carried downwind toward him.

Cholo carefully crept back down behind the rise, lay on his back and exhaled. It was an honor, he reminded himself, to have been chosen to ensure no one followed them. It was solely because of his remarkable endurance, and in a land of remarkable runners, he could run the farthest. Even his name reflected it, meaning *never tired.* For three rises of the sun he had stayed hidden after the caravan had trudged northward, surveying all possible routes that could have been used to follow it. Last night he jogged even further south while the air was cool and the darkness cloaked his movements, to this very vantage point. Finally satisfied their trail was growing cool, if not cold, he sat up and ate a bit of dried turkey meat and sipped from the gourd he carried.

As he stood to work his way back, a movement off in the distance suddenly caught his eye. Cholo stealthily edged behind a cactus and spied a poor *miltequitqui*, a simple field worker, putting down his load and examining the tracks that led northward.

Why now, you lizard eater, he thought. *You've endangered everything and gotten yourself killed.*

The old man touched the strange straight lines and animal footprints, then glanced at the sun. The lines in the trail were clearly visible, not yet worn down by wind nor rain. They seemed recent. Whatever had passed this way, he hadn't missed it by much. He grunted as he shouldered his load, and as he stood came face to face with a handsome Aztec warrior. The old man was startled but smiled, it was good to see a guardian of the empire, rather than any of the detested Spaniard invaders. His own daughter had been raped, his crops taken, and his wife felled by a mysterious and fatal illness. Perhaps this warrior had news of the great conflict to the south. Hopefully good news.

Cholo gently put a hand on the shoulder of the old man and a finger to his lips, *be quiet.* Before a word was spoken the warrior quickly slashed a sharp obsidian blade across the aged, leathery throat. Surprise registered on the elder's face, then a brief glint of understanding, as his life-giving blood pooled at his feet. Cholo grabbed him as he collapsed, then dragged the body well off the trail to a ravine. After burying it deep under heavy rocks so no animals would disturb it, he scattered the bundle and kicked the coagulated pool of blood off the trail. Satisfied no trace was left, he started jogging back northward. He had to report in, before he would linger behind the great procession and start the process yet again.

Ahead with the caravan, *Asupacaci* put a hand over his brow and glanced back southward, through dark green eyes that were an indelible mark of his lineage. A few others of royal blood had been born with the mark of jade eyes, but they were all gone now, either from the curse of disease or the ongoing war. Everyone else's eyes across the vast empire tended to be brown or black like obsidian, the sacred stone with which they made offerings to appease the gods. Jade or obsidian, a blessing or a curse, he was never sure which.

He alone had been chosen to lead this expedition, and while he knew that it was a journey from which he would never return, it was the only way to preserve for all time the heart of the empire. He had been entrusted with the most sacred of tasks, one that only a blood relative of the most holy ruler could undertake. It was truly a pilgrimage, and everything, in both this world and the next, depended upon it.

Letting his mind wander and thinking back, it all seemed like the fading mist of a bad dream. For some reason, the Gods were angry with the Nahuatl-speaking peoples the Spaniards called the Mexica, or more commonly, the *Aztecs*. According to the history in the pictographic codices the priests had recorded since the very beginning, the Aztecs were the last tribe to migrate to the great valley, and so had to take the worst of the land. They settled upon a desolate patch called Chapultepec, or hill of the grasshoppers. Here they gained the favor of the strongest of their neighbors, the city state of Culhuacan, by fighting for them as mercenaries.

When the ruler of Culhuacan demanded they submit to being governed by his daughter, the Aztec's response was defiance, and they flayed her as a sacrifice to the great god *Xipe Totec*, to ensure both a bountiful harvest and success in warfare. This incited the Culhuacan to gather their army to drive the Aztecs away from their desolate grasshopper hill. Defeated, they wandered until the favorable omen of an eagle with a snake in its claws alighted upon a cactus tree to show them where their true destiny lie. *Tenochtitlán* they would call the island city they founded in the center of Lake Texcoco, where the eagle had divinely landed in the year *Ōme Calli*, or Two House.

Asupacaci reflected on the irony that in serving Culhuacan and fighting their wars, the Aztecs should hone and perfect their martial skills. Alliances were formed, wars were fought, and territories were won, lost, and reconquered until a powerful empire emerged. It stretched from the great waters where the sun rose to the endless sea where the sun set and encompassed the numerous tribes and kingdoms that were allied or paid homage to the Aztecs.

Asupacaci's chest swelled with pride as he recalled the glory of Tenochtitlán, how tribute flowed in from vassal states, and captives to appease the gods were captured in ongoing wars. Warfare served to keep the Aztec warriors fighting skills honed, while also turning drought into life sustaining rain by soaking and enriching the earth with the blood of their enemies. Blood equaled rain, and rain made plants, beasts, and man flourish, so in the times of the greatest dryness, when lands wanted to become deserts, the most captives were sacrificed. Little did the Aztecs realize then, Asupacaci ruefully pondered, that in ruling with a firm fist and placating their gods with so much blood of their enemies, they were sowing the seeds of their own eventual destruction.

Why had the gods become so angry in the first place, Asupacaci wondered? What offense had his people committed that had caused the Aztecs to be abandoned to this new strange group of men, if he could call them that? *Coyoltlahtolli* were what he heard the nobility call the Spaniards, because they were all devious liars and cheats with the trickster tongue of the coyote. Why would the gods bring down such devastating disease, which affected only the people of this land, allies and enemies alike, and not the detested Spaniards? It killed them off in untold numbers in the most excruciating and lingering of deaths, spreading from village to village like wildfire carried on the breath of winds in the dry season. The disease wasn't even where the Spanish themselves had been. It preceded them like a reaper, killing the young and old, the healthy and feeble, wiping out entire villages, leaving no one to worship the gods or fight or work the fields. Why indeed?

The Spaniards sang the praises of their gods. They ate his body and drank his blood, yet they called the Aztecs savages? Why was their drinking the blood of the Christ right, while offering the blood of captives to placate the Aztec gods wrong? It made no sense, but the Spanish god had unleashed hellish disease that the Aztec gods had been powerless to stop, there was no denying that.

It all started when from across the waters, in huge floating houses with billowing cloth clouds, came the strange Spaniards and their leader Hernán Cortés. He was what their false religion called the devil, lying, deceiving and killing to gain what he wanted. Cortés first defeated and then allied himself with the *Tlaxcalans*, which swelled his little army into something much larger, more ominous, and threatening. Even the *Totonacs*, those traitorous dogs, rallied to his foreign banners. Some renegade tribes had never completely succumbed to living under the Aztec yoke, and Cortés cleverly played these shifting alliances to his advantage. Unrest was in the air, the edges of the Empire were fraying. Ill portents were in the wind.

Asupacaci remembered the day the Spaniards entered the sacred island city of Tenochtitlán, and how his father, the great Montezuma, had welcomed them. In the heart of the land of the Aztecs, in the middle of their impregnable island city fortress, how could so tiny a group of white, bearded, dog-faced men possibly present any possible threat? But they were devious, these coyote-men, and they had an unquenchable obsession with gold and silver. Their lust for it seemed insatiable, but why go to such extreme risks for something you could neither eat nor drink?

The Aztecs valued gold, silver, the bright stones the Spanish called emeralds, and the feathers of rare birds, but they did so only for the pure beauty of it, and as offerings to the gods. The Spaniards would do anything for it, even kill each other, they went *yollotlahueliloc*, crazy or loco for it. Once in possession they would erase the magnificent beauty the Aztec artisans had put into these offerings to the gods and melt it, all to make it easier to hide and carry away. Strange and vile creatures, the coyote-men.

The black day that changed the world of the Aztecs forever was so audacious that none could believe it happened. Cortés had taken the great Montezuma prisoner, and forced him to rule as a puppet of the detested Spaniards. The nobles and warriors had resisted, but the bearded ones had magic that no one had ever seen, hard swords that shattered the Aztec obsidian blades and spears, wore beetle-like coverings that were impervious to their thrusts, rode huge deer that could outrun even the fastest runner, and had vicious war dogs that devoured men. Most frightening of all, they had sticks and logs that made thunder noises and lightning flashes, killing at a great distance.

Montezuma appeared to do the bidding of the Spaniards, but was secretly encouraging resistance, and ultimately the overthrow of those who dared to defile his kingdom. The circle would be complete when Montezuma could stand on the top of the great temple of Tenochtitlán, overlooking his sacred domain watching the hearts of Cortés, his men, and his traitorous allies ripped out and offered to the gods.

The Aztecs used their own silent methods and of watching, learning, and waiting. They found that the great Spanish stags the conquistadors mounted were called horses, and while they were powerful and intimidating, there was a weakness. The Spaniards had gone to great trouble to kill and bury their injured horses, so that the Aztecs would think them immortal. But spies saw them do this, and the truth was discovered. The Aztecs secretly kidnapped two of the Spaniards, and saw that they trembled, bled and screamed like any creature of the forest when tortured, and died when their still beating hearts were cut out with obsidian knives as an offering to *Huitzilopochtli*, the great God of War. If these pale, hairy, repugnant coyote-men could be killed, then they could be defeated, despite their loud fire sticks, sharp long poles and horses. The Aztecs bided their time.

When Cortés departed from Tenochtitlán with many of his best men for the coast, he left Pedro de Alvarado behind with orders to guard Montezuma and keep up a show of strength. The great Aztec leader had eyes and ears everywhere, and had an established and sophisticated relay network of long runners who could provide news from either coast within two rises of the sun. He knew that the threat Cortés was facing on the coast was from another group of the pale, bearded Spaniards, led by a dog named Narváez. With Cortés gone, Alvarado and his men noticed increased whisperings and activity around the great island city, and it became impossible for them to leave the palace compound safely.

Alvarado decided to act at the annual Feast of Toxcatl. It was a festival day when all the Aztec nobility would all be in one confined place at one time. On that fateful day in May of 1520, the conquistadors hid and waited until the sacred temple square was so full of people it was hard for them to move, and they came in with their lances and swords made of what the Spanish called "good Toledo steel," and massacred everyone. The Aztecs had waited too long, paying for it with the flower of their nobility and leadership.

At nearly the same time, the cunning Cortés defeated his rival Spaniards on the coast, and then told them stories of the unbelievable riches and opulence that awaited them in Tenochtitlán. "Let us stop spilling Spanish blood and go and share in the spoils that Tenochtitlán has to offer. The wealth is vast, the people primitive, and by the grace of King Charles we shall extinguish their heathen religion and bring them into the light of Christ," Cortés exhorted. The defeated Spaniards couldn't believe their change of fortune, and while few wanted to partake in a religious crusade to convert ignorant heathens, they all believed in the intoxicating power of gold.

The vanquished Spaniards thus swelled Cortés' ranks, and he set off, back to the island city, confident in his destiny to overthrow an empire. Yet when Cortés approached Tenochtitlán, he saw the countryside was up on arms. While Alvarado had thought he had used the Feast of Toxcatl to preemptively cut the head off the snake, instead he had rallied the whole of the Aztec empire against their oppressors. Montezuma's courtiers had stealthily gotten word out across the realm, that the time for waiting had ended.

Asupacaci shook his head, coming back to the present and allowing himself a glance back at the slow-moving column, which was kicking up small trails of dust along its entire length. It was impressive, how this small detachment of the bravest of Aztec warriors had each set out on this most holy of quests. They all knew none would be coming back and that even fewer of their number would be chosen to reach the final destination. It was so secret, that after the porters had loaded the cargo before they left Tenochtitlán in the dead of night, each had willingly lay on the alter to make an offering of themselves. No one must know what they had or where they were going. Even Asupacaci, who was leading them, hadn't decided on the ultimate destination yet.

A military air surrounded the expedition, and it was as quiet and orderly as Asupacaci could have hoped for.

He breathed deeply and sighed, "Ayemo, *not yet, we still have much to do and far to go.*"

The tethered Spaniards looked around instinctively through dead eyes, listening through heightened hearing, yet disoriented, walking as though they had drunk too much *Octli*, made from the fermented sap of the agave plant. They had been chosen from among a large group of captives, stripped bare to reveal their pale and abhorrent skin, and then closely examined for any sign of the plague that had killed so many Aztecs. Those who bore no scars of what the Spanish called the pox were immediately offered as a sacrifice to appease the gods. For it was now known that they could be invisible vessels of disease. Those who had devil marks, the scars of the pox, and had survived the disease but could no longer transmit it, would prove most useful.

Even though there had been no real choice, the truth was it had given Asupacaci a certain amount of pleasure to have their eyes put out with red hot embers that served to both blind and cauterize. He needed the Spaniards to tend and manage their strange horse beasts, for they had so much of the heart of the empire to move, and they would be useful in proving to the Aztec's friends and foes alike that they had a common enemy. Behold, they invade Tenochtitlán today, tomorrow they will be at your doorstep. But should even one Spaniard escape, they must never be able to tell where they had been. If they couldn't see it, they couldn't tell it. If they made too much noise, he would take their tongues out too, but their voices seemed useful in tending the horses, at least for now.

The Spaniards held the bridles and led the horses and the

heavily laden carts blindly, while on each side a warrior jabbed them with an obsidian spear whenever they started slowing, crying, or praying to their false gods. Though the Aztecs were tempted to twist their spears in deeper, or coat them with *pocheoa*, animal dung, to cause a painful and fatal infection, they knew it wasn't the time. Not yet.

CHAPTER 2 – MAY 25, PRESENT DAY

Nick LaBounty felt the pounding in his temples even before he opened his eyes. *This isn't going to be good,* he thought. The dry taste of cotton in his mouth told him he had violated the cardinal rule of drinking too much, he hadn't bulked up on water before he fell asleep. *Damn it,* no wonder he had slept straight through the night, despite the relentless, recurring nightmares. He squinted at his wristwatch trying to figure out what time it was, holding it almost to his nose since he thankfully hadn't fallen asleep with his contact lenses in. *Been there, done that,* he mused. It was never a fun exercise trying to peel out a lens and not the cornea first thing in the morning.

It was 6:15 a.m. and the early sunlight filtered in through the open window. Lying on his back, Nick reached out to the nightstand and grabbed his glasses, sliding them on, he blinked hard and stared at the ceiling. He saw speckles of sunlight reflecting off the fine dust drifting in the air, moving ever so slightly. Blinking again, he focused on a small plastic solar system twisting lazily above him. How long ago had that been put up there? He could still see the white thumbtack his dad, Albert, used to hang it, back when he had first bought the camp on Lake Charlevoix, in the very top part of Michigan's Upper Peninsula, in the late nineties. The bunk beds were long gone, but like his dad had said back then, "two boys, one room, a lake, and lots of forest, what could possibly go wrong?"

Nick was only seven when they moved in, and his brother Charlie was thirteen, much bigger and tougher back then, but no more adventurous than his little brother. Dad had been right, it was paradise for two boys, and for his mom Josephine too. Summers as an outlet from their house in Muskegon, near Grand Rapids, had been everything a young boy could want growing up.

When his mom passed, far too young, at only 53, Dad had sold the house and moved to the camp in Charlevoix full time. Frankly, it was the reason Nick decided to do his PhD in Chicago, to be near his old man and offer what moral support he could, even if only through his occasional presence. The camp was the only place his dad could be truly content, because he always felt she was with him when he was there. Nick's eyes burned, and he fought back tears making his dull headache throb harder. He was still trying to get his mind around the fact that now his dad was gone too.

What had Winston Churchill described it as? Melancholy that was always in the background and surfaced occasionally like an old familiar pain . . . that heavy depression? *Oh yeah,* Nick thought. Churchill called it the black dog, and now it seemed to be Nick's constant companion as well. *I'd rather have a Labrador Retriever,* he thought. A dog would be less depressing and a whole lot more fun.

Coming to terms with grief over his Mother's death five years prior had been hard enough, but here he was thirty-years-old and now with no parents at all.

Charlie struggled with it as well, but he was in a different place in his life. Happily married to a terrific woman he had two great kids, a fabulous career, and he had been *their* child.

No, that wasn't fair, Nick and Charlie had both been their children, and they had always been loved and treated equally. After Al and Josie had Charlie, they tried for a larger family. Two miscarriages and many tears later, they adopted Nick, and he was forever grateful.

If anyone had ever won life's lottery, it was me, to have been so randomly brought into a household so selfless and so full of love, Nick reflected. *Enough of the self-pity, Mom and Dad wouldn't want endless mourning, time to face reality and get my ass up and face the day.*

Nick sat up on the edge of the bed—slowly—allowing his throbbing head to gain some semblance of equilibrium. The cool hardwood felt familiar on his bare feet, and he smiled at the memory of how he and Charlie used to see who could do the best Tom Cruise imitation from the movie *Risky Business* and slide the farthest across the floor in only their socks and underwear. Charlie always won, but Nick said he looked the best doing it. Charlie would scoff at him and say at least he had something in his underwear instead of Nick's skinny little butt and would give Nick a noogie for his troubles.

"Thank you, sir, may I have another," Nick would sarcastically yell and quickly scramble away before Charlie could grab him and administer it. Good times, those long-ago days.

He stood up and did a long, lazy stretch to unlimber his athletic six-foot frame, and walked over to the mirror above the dresser. Absent mindedly scratching the stubble on his face, he looked at himself, the striking pale blue eyes of a thirty-year-old who had already seen too much heartache staring back at him. In the corner he saw his old beat up yellow metal detector standing next to the closet. It was well used. "Got a lot of love," as his dad put it. Funny how that gift to acclimate a precocious youngster to the Upper Peninsula, Yooper's they were proudly called, led to what would be his passion in life.

Nick and Charlie took to exploring like ducks to water, and Albert found and researched the local history to find that a lot had gone on near here in pre-colonial and colonial times. Fort Michilimackinac had been recreated and was now a national park, and while there was no longer a Fort de Repentigny, exploring the trails and byways to both yielded a small treasure trove of artifacts, which Nick had kept in an old WWII machine gun ammunition case under his bed. Dad used to get genuinely excited on his "expeditions" with his boys, and always said that if he had gone to college, he would have been an archeologist, anthropologist, or historian. Instead life had led him to do what his father had done, continue to run the family business, a lumber yard that had done well for

Grandpa Jacques after the war, but was only limping along like the rest of Muskegon now.

Dad had always suggested that there was some family legend he was trying to unwind, and their summer trips were inevitably to the American Southwest. The boys would be packed into the back of an old rambling station wagon with air conditioning that never seemed to work quite right, and the adventures were fond memories to all. "Just one more stop," he would always say, while Mom rolled her eyes, and off he went to investigate some obscure trail with a goal only he could see. Everyone tagged along, Nick with his trusty metal detector in hand. More than a few artifacts from those trips, including arrow heads, musket balls, uniform buttons, the occasional belt buckle, and one treasured piece of eight were still in the ammo can.

Funny, where life takes you if you aren't paying attention, Nick thought. Following their dad's advice, who joked that the only college he had the chance to go to was the school of hard knocks, the boys followed their passions.

Charlie had a head for numbers and obscure concepts, along with the lack of personality and gravitas to go with it, Nick would jab. That had led to Charlie going to MIT for economics, where he also got his master's in finance. A logical steppingstone to his first job as a stockbroker and money manager, and to his current career in Chicago running a hedge fund.

Nick however never got over the thrill of the hunt or the find. He loved the research and history that went into it and ended up following Dad's unfulfilled dream of becoming an archeologist. He found an innate affinity for the mental as well as physical challenges it presented, the cryptology of deciphering the past, and the blend of both teamwork and solitude.

"That covered a lot of ground for me," Nick would muse, first to the University of Michigan for his Bachelors in Archeology, then to UPenn for his Masters in Historical Research & Methodology, and now working on his PhD focusing on Mesoamerican Migrations at the University of Chicago.

"Yeah," Charlie would laugh. "We'll be the highlight of any

party, me talking actuary tables and you with your Clovis arrow heads, we'll get laid every night!"

Nick laughed out loud, for the first time in a couple of days. It actually startled him. Based on his data sampling with his brother over the years and their relative successes or failures, evidently actuary tables *were* more exciting.

Nick walked out of the bedroom and scanned the scene. The cabin was neat and tidy, the way Dad always kept it. As neat as the day Nick came out to see his dad when he wasn't able to get a hold of him back in early March. Dad was always good about keeping in touch, maybe not right away, but he would always follow up when he got a voicemail or text message. Lots of dead cell phone space up here, which was always fine with everyone. Dad would spend his days out in the woods, or out on one of the many ponds, or even on one of the Great Lakes. He had two to choose from, Lake Michigan to the west, and Lake Huron to the east.

But he hadn't replied, despite Nick and Charlie calling and texting, and it had been three days. That was too out of character for Dad, to go dark on communications. Nick dropped the work he was doing on his PhD at the University of Chicago, jumped in his beat up, old Chevy pickup truck, and headed up the familiar west coast of Lake Michigan, past Muskegon, and up to Charlevoix. When Nick had arrived at the cabin, nothing was amiss, at least as far as he could tell. The front door was unlocked, nothing unusual there since it was never locked, and the wood stove was cold. Plates from what looked like breakfast had been washed and left in the dry rack next to the sink, the cell phone was gone, and a steak was thawing on the counter. Normal—except no Dad.

There was still a decent snowpack on the ground, and a cursory look around the cabin revealed only tracks of deer, squirrels and rabbits, and maybe a muskrat or two. No human footprints, which was puzzling since there had been no new snowfall for the last four days. Dad had to have gone somewhere, and while he was a talented outdoorsman, he wasn't Icarus and couldn't simply fly away.

Nick had wandered down to the edge of the lake and sat on the dock which had been pulled up on the shore for the winter. *Odd, this doesn't add up*, he thought, *too many things out of character.* Then Nick saw it, and his heart fell deep into an abyss. About 100 feet out on the lake, in a crease in the shifting ice, a frozen hand reached for the sky.

The funeral two days before had gone well, even better than could have been expected.

"I'm not even sure I would call it a funeral," Nick caught himself saying out loud. Charlie and Nick had followed Dad's wishes to the letter. They were simple and understated, like the man himself. Albert wasn't a particularly religious man, and never felt that he or anyone else had the right to cast judgment on what anyone chose to believe, as long as it wasn't harmful to others. He would joke in his folksy way that "religions are like ice cream, they come in lots of flavors that are all good, so who could choose one over another?" He couldn't buy into one religion, believing it alone had all the answers, and damning anyone else who didn't follow their doctrine, every honorable Christian or Hindi or Muslim or Buddhist, to some sort of purgatory or hell.

Over time he simply found that the pomp and circumstance of organized religion was not for him, certainly not since Josephine was taken from him. It wasn't bitterness, maybe simply numbing emptiness was a better description, yet he continued to be a spiritual man who believed in the inherent goodness in everyone, despite everything.

Albert's wishes were not that elaborate, but a part of them left Nick and Charlie confused. Since Mom had been cremated, there was no surprise with him having the same wish. But he didn't want any showing or gathering back in Muskegon, only a small one at the camp on Lake Charlevoix for those who chose to make the trip or neighbors already there. And like the mischievous guy he was, it wasn't to be a solemn gathering, but rather a sharing of the passions he had in his life, shared among his two boys, friends, and relatives. He wanted a B3 party, and the family was no stranger to it. Blues,

Brews, and BBQ's all around. The tv and some strategically placed electronic picture frames scrolled the life he and Josephine had built and shared with the boys through digitized photographs. What was anticipated to be a small crowd, given the distance, turned into a large one despite that.

Lives not touched in many years, even people who didn't show up for Josie's tribute five years ago, came by with well wishes. The day went off exactly liked Albert had planned. Nick reflected on the people laughing, reminiscing, telling old stories and lies, drinking the favorite drinks they had all shared, listening to Dad's blues collection, making some new memories, and at the end of the night one mass toast from the shore as the sun set. Nick and Charlie paddled out and scattered half of Albert's and Josephine's ashes as a gentle evening breeze breathed on the lake. It was serenely peaceful, the dust diffusing in the twilight, the echoes of the toast and laughter fading. Two lives, passionately lived, fading back into the world from whence they came.

Before Charlie headed back to Chicago the day after the funeral, along with his wife Sophie, their five-year-old son Julien and his mischievous three-year-old sister, Yvette, hugs and kisses were given all around, along with some playful tickles for the kids from their favorite Uncle.

"Hey, Julien, what was the most famous movie in Ancient Greece?" Nick asked. Julien made a face like he was concentrating hard, then looked at Charlie for help. "Troy Story!" Nick exclaimed.

Julien didn't get it, but it got a laugh out of Charlie and Sophie. Nick told them he would be fine. And he was, until he wasn't. He saw them off and went out and sat heavily on the front porch. Looking out on the lake, he felt the warmth of the toast from so many friends, and the companionship of his brother and his family, all begin to fade as the black dog of depression started to work its way back into his temples.

Hell, I don't even have Topaz around to keep me company, he thought, as his hand instinctively reached out below him to give the yellow lab a pet. Topaz, who preferred water to land, had been a gift from Charlie and Nick to Albert when he had moved to the camp full time after losing Josie. The dog, intended as the best kind of company, the kind that is always there, always ready to listen, was always ready for an adventure. Topaz was a rescue dog that had immediately bonded with Al, but he had to have been six or seven when they got him. He had four good years at the camp. Nick glanced over to his left and could see the little plaque on the tree his dad had put up when Topaz passed, and the telling rise of earth underneath it.

The shadows grew longer. A lonely afternoon turned into a lonely evening. Nick fixed himself a tall glass of ice, grabbed a good bottle of bourbon, put his feet up on the railing, and tried to make sense of his world slowly and steadily being pulled asunder. That had led to this morning's episode of cotton mouth, and he was actually surprised to find the bottle empty, not realizing he had gone so deep into his cups.

The thing that continued to puzzle Nick was Dad's second set of wishes. Which was for the two of them to go together to scatter the remaining commingled ashes in the Southwest, but at a place they had never been told had any special significance in all their summer wanderings. The refrain from one of Dad's favorite songs that they had played two nights ago at the B3 party, *Woodstock*, penned by Joni Mitchell but best performed by Crosby, Stills, Nash and Young, looped in his head.

> *"We are stardust, we are golden, we are billion-year-old carbon, and we got to get ourselves back to the garden."*

Yeah Dad, Nick thought, *like Chaco Canyon is the garden.*

CHAPTER 3 – APRIL 12, 1521

Asupacaci gazed ahead into the haze of the heat shimmering in the distance and knew from his scouts that they would soon be approaching the Pánuco River, the natural dividing line between the allies he knew and the wild, nomadic *Chichimeca* peoples beyond it.

The journey would now be more fraught with peril, as the long snaking column wound through the last of the lands of their northern allies, the *Totonacs* and the *Huastecs*.

There had been sporadic trade between them and the Chichimeca in the past, but never a formal exchange of dignitaries. The Chichimeca were simply too uncivilized. They had no dwellings worth mentioning, no permanent villages, moved with the seasons, and were savage about defending what they perceived as their territories.

Asupacaci stepped aside from the head of the column, and called *Cipactli* over, the warrior general who had been specifically charged with accompanying him on this quest. Cipactli looked at him quizzically. Asupacaci couldn't suppress a slight grin, knowing that Cipactli had been named after the primordial crocodile-like monster from Aztec legend. His large head and mouth showed a distinct likeness.

"Cipactli, in one more rise of the sun we will approach the

Pánuco, and we will need to find a ford to get all of this,"—Asupacaci gestured by opening his arms in both directions to encompass the column—"across safely. We will need to meet with someone of authority, and the sooner the better."

Cipactli nodded with a grunt. He had been girding his warriors for the moment they crossed into the unchartered territory. That moment was almost at hand.

"*Tlanahuatihqui*," he said in a deferential tone, meaning exalted leader. "Our long runners have already scouted the river and have found two places the horses and these boxes with wheels can make it across. But they haven't seen anyone yet, which is unusual. I expected we would have many eyes on us already."

Unusual indeed, Asupacaci thought.

"And the long runner from the south, what news of him?" he inquired.

"He arrived a few days ago and said there was no sign of anyone following us. As instructed, he hid and waited three rises of the sun to make sure," Cipactli replied. "The only person he encountered was some poor field worker. He killed him and buried his body under stones, and now trails us again watching for any pursuit."

Even Cipactli doesn't know, Asupacaci thought, *what lengths we have gone to to deceive the Spanish devils.* Other expeditions had been sent out, both discretely and in view of the Spaniards, in other directions. All in an attempt to put them off the scent of this one. And the only people who knew about this one—the only ones still alive who could tell the tale—were all right here. *The gods have favored us on our quest so far,* Asupacaci mused. *We have only had to kill two servants who couldn't keep pace and one injured warrior. Oh yes, and the Spaniard who went mad, who couldn't take the darkness.*

The Spaniard's pulsing heart had been offered to *Ehecatl*, the god of wind, whose breath moved the sun and pushed away rain, and would hopefully push them to their final destination.

The caravan continued along the footpath until before midday, then stopped at the signal from Asupacaci. The Spaniards, with their hollow eyes, were prodded to unhitch the horses and led to where the animals could graze. The Spaniards were tethered with rough rope about the length of two men to the horses and given a dry corncob to eat. Having traveled so many miles, they eventually worked their way to the shade side of the horses and sat down to eat and rest as best they could. A gourd of water was brought to them by the servants. It seemed they were never given quite enough to slake their burning thirsts, only enough to keep them alive.

Even the servants took the opportunity to discomfort them whenever possible, taunting in a language the Spanish couldn't comprehend but whose meaning was clear, pushing and tripping them when it wasn't expected, and spitting or putting a little ground chili into the water gourds they passed to them. But the warrior guards were worse and much feared, for they were proud and bitter. They had seen their way of life upended, their families decimated, and now they were being exiled from their homeland, never to return. Cipactli had made it clear that the Spanish were needed to tend the horses, as proof of an invasion, and as trade bounty. They needed to be kept alive, but not *too* alive.

The humiliations consequently continued, some merely demeaning, some nearly fatal. It was with much amusement that the captured leader of the Spanish, the one called El Capitán, was led to a little hill on the shade side of a horse to sit, given a corn cob, and left alone. The warriors quietly gathered a short distance away and elbowed one another, while a servant untied the tether from the horse and held it in his hand. For the little hill upon which he sat held a cruel surprise.

The snickering turned to laughter as the dance began, first with El Capitán slowly scratching himself, then jumping up and slapping, then his yelling turning to screaming as he danced wildly about as fire ants repeatedly injected their venom into his pallid flesh. The servant gave him slack on the rope, shouted, *"Oh Ley!"* in mimicking a sound he had heard the Spanish make when chasing Aztecs to ground on their horses, and followed him erratically about. Once the Spaniard could manically dance no more and fell exhausted to the ground panting, he was tied to the horse. The smirking crowd dispersed to their lunch of beans and corn meal wrapped in corn husks.

Two of the servants were playfully kicked by Cipactli, who pointed to the Spaniard, and they dutifully stood over his collapsed, sobbing form and pissed, taking away some of the sting, but only adding to his humiliation.

They would all rest here, in what shade they could find to avoid the worst of the midday sun. Scouts were posted outside the perimeter, ensuring no one would stumble upon them. The coolest spots were under the wagons, and in a militarized society like the Aztecs, heritage and rank took precedence, even here. The servants were put further out and had to constantly shift with the movement of the sun and shadows. The Spaniards had it the hardest, as the horses they were tethered to constantly shifted, and they were forced to scramble like exposed beetles trying to hide from the light.

Asupacaci dozed in his shaded spot under the middle of the biggest wheeled box, with everyone, even Cipactli, a respectful few inches away from touching his person. His thoughts wandered first to his father, Montezuma, then to his brothers *Chimalpopoca* and *Tlaltecatzin*. This quest was for them, for all of them, and his resolve stiffened in his half-conscious state. A dream started to play out in his mind, and though he knew he was dreaming, he felt that he was floating above everything, looking down on Tenochtitlán, a soaring eagle carried on the wind. He saw the city and its people in all their glory, the five causeways that led across Lake Texcoco into the city, the beautiful flags and pennants fluttering from the buildings, the smells of the markets drifting up to him, and the magnificent pyramid at the center of it all.

At the center of his universe, the *Hueteocalli*, dominated the landscape. He floated down closer, and saw it was no longer pristine or peaceful. He saw his people running in the streets, conquistadors riding their great horse beasts spearing two or three people at a time and holding them aloft, fire sticks belching smoke and lightning.

Aztecs were covered in spots, falling to the ground coughing, the skies overhead darkening, mountains erupting red and angry, a flock of ravens flying toward him, their numbers growing and obliterating the sky, their cries telling him to do something, do anything, to just save his people.

Asupacaci awoke with a start, his heart pounding, his hands out in front of him to ward off the ravens. He blinked hard, heard the gentle snoring next to him, and wiped the accumulated sweat and dirt from his brow. From the short shadows, he could tell the sun was still high in the sky. Very little time had passed. He shifted uncomfortably and pulled a small stone out from under his back. As he looked closer, he realized it was a broken piece of obsidian, an old arrowhead. It reminded him of how even their best weapons, their spears, arrows, and studded clubs, had all shattered when they met Spanish steel. Exactly like his people.

Trying fitfully to doze, Asupacaci's mind wandered back to when Cortés returned from the coast and approached Tenochtitlán, the resistance had become more fierce. The docile people he had first encountered had shaken off their awe of the Spanish. They no longer believed them gods and had been exhorted to resist with all their might to fight for their land, their ruler, and their true gods, to behave like real Mexica, like true *Aztecs*. They had, with renewed fury. And it was only with great difficulty that Cortés and his allies were able to rejoin Alvarado back at the palace in the center of the great city.

Once all together, they realized how precarious their situation had become. Despite the Spaniards they had added to their ranks from the coast, despite their Tlaxcalan and Totonac allies, despite their horses and guns and steel swords and lances, they were hopelessly outnumbered by a now determined foe. They had sat on the nest of fire ants too long.

Completely surrounded with their food supplies cut off, all non-essential servants were put to the sword to buy a little more time. Of course that didn't include *La Malinche*, that traitorous slave who was given to Cortés by Asupacaci's enemies when he first landed on the sacred shores. No one could have foreseen then that this lowly slave woman had the gift for tongues, could easily pick up and speak any language, and would become the right hand of Cortés as his interpreter, trusted advisor, and courtesan.

There were very few others who could speak both Aztec and Spanish, much less the languages of the various allies and enemies at the edges of the Aztec empire. But Friar Rodrìguez was one who could, and even though he was Spanish, Asupacaci had seen him take Cortés aside and obviously argue that what La Malinche was interpreting was not necessarily the truth. Evidently the woman with the gift of tongues could be manipulative in what she interpreted and spoke with two tongues, one true, one false.

The Friar objected to the systematic burning of the Aztec codices, which held their accumulated knowledge and history in pictographs. Such a man as Friar Rodrìguez, who could interpret these languages, who had shown he wanted to teach the Aztecs about the goodness of his god, who had openly defied Cortés about his treatment of the Aztecs, could prove useful with the northern tribes. He had thus been duly blinded and added to the caravan, and now sat unseeing in the shade of a horse, always kept close to Asupacaci in case he should beckon him. Even the warriors respectfully kept their distance away from this one.

Asupacaci sat up and glanced toward Friar Rodrìguez, hearing him humming something to himself, something he called a hymn. As the trek continued, Asupacaci had the Friar brought over to him to walk behind him at times, so he could converse with him. While he didn't have the gift of tongues that the Friar did, he found himself picking up a few words of Spanish, learning more about their world, their beliefs, their hopes and fears, and most importantly, their weaknesses. When he discovered something of significance, something that he thought would help the resistance back in Tenochtitlán, he was tempted to send a long runner back with the message. But he didn't. He knew he couldn't, because he didn't know if his people were still fighting, and he couldn't break his oath and risk discovery of his mission.

Even though his long runners were among the hardiest of warriors, the Spanish were true masters at torture, and every living creature had its breaking point. They had perfected their dark arts with what the Friar called the Inquisition. Asupacaci's eyes watered, and he leaned back down and forced them shut. He had witnessed it done to his own family. He couldn't let anyone see him in a state of weakness and tried to drift back off to sleep. After lying with his over wrought imagination keeping him awake, he admitted defeat and crawled out from under the wagon. Hearing the Friar softly chanting, he walked over and sat beside him.

"Tell me, do your gods hear you?"

The Friar jumped slightly, startled, as he was so deep into his meditations that he hadn't heard Asupacaci approach. He tilted his head slighted and looked at his questioner through shriveled eye sockets.

"Yes, I believe He does. Even when we don't say anything aloud, He can even read our minds, and so we must always be pure in thought," the Friar replied.

"Pure? Do you feel the actions of your people are pure? That killing, raping, and stealing are pure? What had we ever done to you to deserve this?" Asupacaci asked, in a rising voice that was loud enough Cipactli sat up under the wagon and watched them carefully. "Our world was a paradise before any of you came."

"You have done nothing to me, I am but a simple man of faith. But our soldiers believe they are instruments of our God and King and do what they must to spread the one true faith," the Friar replied in his calm, reasoned way.

Asupacaci arose and stood menacingly, glaring down. "Damn your God, and damn all of you. We'll see in the next life who is right. And that won't be long in coming for any of us."

CHAPTER 4 – MAY 29, PRESENT DAY

"C'mon Chuck, we don't need to go right away, but let's at least get a date on the calendar so we can both work around it," Nick implored his brother on the phone. He didn't want to say it, but better to take Al and Josie's ashes out to Chaco Canyon in New Mexico and get this done with, so it wasn't an unbearable task that became ever more daunting with the waiting.

Christ knucklehead, I'm fragile enough at this point, he thought.

"Alright, alright already. I'm thinking June 19th. I'll take a Friday off for a long weekend and be back with Sophie and the kids by Sunday night. Where the hell do we fly into over there anyway? Looks like Albuquerque might be the closest airport, that shouldn't be too hard to fly into from Chicago," Charlie noted.

"Hey, I'm not flying, I'm taking some time and driving, gonna hit a few of the old stops from the station wagon days." Nick wanted to ask Charlie to join him on a road trip, to be like old times, but he also realized Charlie had a household and career to answer to. He wasn't traveling light like Nick, whose faculty at the University of Chicago told him to take as much time as he needed. The thought of a road trip quickened Nick's pulse, and he realized he needed this, especially now.

"You sure you're doing alright, Nick? You and Dad were always a little too alike for your own good. You're the one who was adopted for crissake. I mean, you both have always kept the hard things inside, while smiling on the outside. Not like me and Mom. You *always* knew what was on our mind." Charlie knew Nick could be hard to read. He knew him better than anyone, especially now that their dad had passed.

"Naw, all good, or at least as good as could be expected," Nick assured him. "I actually think a road trip would be a great tonic, help me figure a few things out, or at least put them in perspective."

"Alright then, I'll make the arrangements to get out to Albuquerque. I'll text you the flight times so you can pick me up there. And instead of driving that rat trap halfway across the country, why don't you get something new? Dad left us a few bucks, what are you saving it for?" he said. But Charlie knew the reason, that the beat-up pickup truck had been Dad's, who had given it to Nick, and it was a part of him he refused to let go.

Charlie was joking, but only halfway. How many times had Nick's beloved rust bucket of a pickup broken down in some God forsaken, out of the way place?

I have to give him credit though, he turned into one heck of an improvisational mechanic, Charlie thought.

"No worries brother, just make sure *you* make it there. Dad said for both of us to do this, and by then I'll actually be looking forward to your company. What with all the snakes, tarantulas, scorpions, and such." Nick knew his brother was getting a bit citified, maybe a bit too comfortable as told by his waistline, and wanted to see him roughing it again, like in the good old days. And critters of that ilk could certainly provide some entertainment if properly employed to good effect—like in one of Charlie's boots. "See you on the 19th bro!"

Nick hung up and looked around the cabin, remembering the fond times they'd all shared right here. It didn't seem that long ago they were all playing board games, listening to baseball on the radio, making s'mores over an outdoor fire, staying up late catching fireflies and watching shooting stars. How his dad was the master of nicknames, and when Nick was a scrawny kid and Charlie a bit stouter, he used to call them Nicky Knees and Chuckie Cheese. Nick would add, "More like Chuck Wagon, if you asked me," which led to more chases and hijinks. *Those were the days.* Maybe they could make some new memories here yet, when this was all over.

Nick found himself wandering down toward the lake and sat at the spot where the dock had been stored before being put out for the summer. He looked out at the exact location he had first seen his dad's hand sticking out of the ice. "Tough times these, these last five years or so. Lost Mom, lost Dad, hell even lost Topaz, and somewhere along the line lost some of myself," he said to himself.

Mom's death was devastating, but for all the tragedy, it was understandable, discernible, tangible. They had all seen the results of the tests, the images clearly showing pancreatic cancer systematically spreading to the lymph nodes, then to her liver, and finally to her lungs and bones. Mom had no family history, so it wasn't detected until far too late. It had all seemed surreal, her going from a healthy, vibrant woman so full of life, to living in the hospital on comfort care, to dying at home, surrounded by the things she treasured and the people she loved.

Nick could still remember the warmth of her hand growing cool, then cold, being unable to let go, his grief only assuaged by the look in his father's eyes as he held his dear Josephine, a depth of love Nick could only admire, the resolute look that told they *would* be together again, and from this day forward Dad was only marking time.

But Dad had managed to carve out an existence that was surprisingly fulfilling. Instead of folding back within himself, he always joked he was still exploring, still learning, and until he gave up on those they could all stop with all the damn fussing and worrying about him. He certainly still had much to offer his sons, daughter-in-law and grandchildren. Hell, maybe one day he would even meet the future Mrs. Nick, if one of the blind dates Sophie and Charlie arranged ever worked out and Nick would stop looking for the perfect woman. Besides, Al had already found Josephine, and there was only one of those.

But Dad's death, the way it happened, still made no sense. Nick looked at the grass under his shoe, if grass was what you could call it. More like what you see under the forest trees, lonely sprigs of grass, lots of pine needles, roots exposed by high waves, a bit of gravel. The boys always joked that Dad should plant a lawn, but he would say, "It will all turn to this anyway, so I'll save the trouble and go exploring instead."

The police seemed satisfied with the events surrounding the accident. They seemed thorough and competent enough, but they didn't know Albert like Nick knew Albert. Charlie was right, Nick was like his dad. They were both in tune with each other, knew what the other was thinking, could communicate with just a glance, and handled things *exactly* the same. And how Dad had died, how he got into the situation that killed him, that was *not* how Nick would have handled it, nor was it a situation he would have put himself in the first place. When pressed he couldn't explain it, but there, behind the temples, behind the dull ache, in that deep part of the brain where thoughts go to work themselves out with no consciousness, it did not feel right.

The police had come, Charlevoix's finest, immediately after Nick had called them in a strangely, some would say clinically, detached voice. It took no more than twenty minutes for the cruiser to reach the LaBounty place out on the east shore of the lake. They treated it like an accident scene. Nick had already pulled Al's body from its ice encased tomb, set him off the side of the hole in the ice, with the ice around the middle giving the impression of someone in an inner tube. That would have to be chiseled or melted off later. When Nick had first seen the arm sticking out of the ice, he was tempted to run out and dig with his bare hands. But he knew his dad was already dead, rushing would only erase clues. His archeology training had kicked in and he immediately went into forensic mode. He had done this dozens of times on various digs around the world when coming across finds. It was only that this time the body was days old instead of thousands of years old, there were clues that had to be gathered before weather or the ignorant obliterated them—and the fact that the body just happened to be that of his father.

Nick had immediately stopped moving where he sat on the dock on shore, looked at the tracks he had made in approaching the edge of the frozen lake, and pulled out his iPhone. The good news was it was only a couple of months old and had an excellent built-in camera. The bad news was its predecessor was still in the bottom of an outhouse in the hinterlands of Michigan, destined to be ever further buried, inch by inch. Nick stood without shifting his feet, and started photographing his own footprints, then all markings on the ground in a 360-degree radius. When he was confident he had captured everything as best he could, he worked his way out onto the lake, walking obliquely in approaching the arm, careful to avoid making or obscuring any possible tracks.

The ice was thick and solid, and the surface hard and windblown. No markings anywhere, except for the striations from constant winds, with coarse hard snow pebbles beating the surface with the periodic gusts. He took more photos, including panoramas, and worked his way to the arm itself. Being the only thing sticking up, it had attracted birds, who had done a number on the exposed fingers.

Definitely Dad, I would know that wedding ring anywhere, but strange, no gloves. One thing that struck Nick was that the surface of the lake was smooth as far as the eye could see, except for a fault line in the ice right where the arm protruded. There were no ice shacks out, but that wasn't unusual, as there were other lakes nearby with much better fishing.

Something had reflected in the sun about 200 yards further out to the middle, and he wandered toward it. As he approached, he saw that it was a small frozen pile of ice from an ice auger that had been used to drill a hole. Well, maybe a couple of holes close enough to form a larger hole, it was hard to tell as it had all filled and frozen again. There was nothing around this, except for the same windblown striations on the ice surface. Nick snapped a few quick shots and worked his way back to the arm. After evaluating and documenting the situation, Nick got off the ice, photographed everything completely around the camp, then grabbed the tools he would need, and worked to remove the body. Nobody was going to see any of this before he did, and nobody was going to mess with *his* evidence.

Ultimately the police report and autopsy drew different conclusions than Nick did, and while he tried to convince Charlie about his intuitions, it was all just that, speculation. The police had ruled it an accidental death by drowning. He must have wandered out on the ice, maybe he got disoriented or had a small stroke, lost his bearings and then fell through.

"Dad would never just wander out on the ice, in the cold, with no gloves. Christ, he didn't even like to fish, much less ice fish," Nick had argued with Charlie. "And the coat on his left arm was pulled up, way up, where he bit himself. I'm not buying that gloves are somewhere at the bottom of the lake, his good gloves were in the cabin. And what about the tracks, he is in the lake, there are critter tracks everywhere, but no tracks out of the cabin or on the shore anywhere. I'm not buying that he bit himself in a panic while drowning, not there, right over his only tattoo, the only bite mark anywhere. And his leg was cut, like he was pushed down with something. I got a funny feeling about all this, and I think he was murdered, and he was trying to tell us something."

Charlie had held his tongue, lost in his own thoughts. He was as taken aback as Nick with his father's sudden death, but wondered if Nick was overly distraught, and if it was impacting his ability to see things clearly through the grief. He suspected neither of them would be seeing things clearly for quite a while. The best he could do was to walk over and hug his brother while they both sobbed.

"Enough of this," Nick said, snapping back to the present. He stood up, wiped the dampness from his jeans where he had been sitting, and walked back to the cabin. He put on the blues playlist his dad liked so much and smiled at the labyrinth of hidden speakers throughout the cabin, inside and out, now vibrating to the great BB King belting out *The Thrill Is Gone.*

He went through the familiar process of making two Old Fashions. The right amount of whiskey, bitters, simple syrup, a dark cherry, and a single, fat ice cube that would melt slowly, thereby adding only a little water at a time to release the hidden notes of the whiskey.

Back to the dock he went, listening to the King crooning from rock shaped speakers set in the ground.

"Cheers, Old Man, here's to unraveling some of your many mysteries," he said.

And with that Nick poured one Old Fashioned into the lake, and then sat, slowly and quietly pouring the other into himself.

CHAPTER 5 – APRIL 13, 1521

Asupacaci chose the shallower of the two fords the scouts had previously found across the Pánuco River. The water was only up to their thighs. While the other ford had been narrower, it channeled the water deeper and faster, and was deemed too risky. The scouts crossed before sunrise, screening the entire caravan. They were followed by one group of warriors, mostly the elite Eagle and Jaguar Knights, then the porters, seventeen heavily laden wagons, and all the spare horses.

Unfortunately, the last two trailing wagons got stuck in the sticky mud midstream, which had been churned to a morass by the prior wagons. No amount of manpower from the trailing group of servants or warriors could dislodge them, which seemed to sink even deeper with the handling. This is where the wisdom of bringing the Spaniards along proved its worth. They told Cipactli, through Friar Rodrìguez, what must be done. He in turn told the warriors, and they grabbed a few of the Spaniards, led them to the wagons already across the river, where they unhitched those teams of horses and double teamed them onto the stuck wagons. The Spaniards grabbed the traces of the horses, the warriors grabbed the sightless Spaniards to guide them, and with much yelling and exhorting of the horses, got the wagons released from the grip of the muck and safely to the other side.

A brief war council was called by Asupacaci. As they were now in the land of the Chichimeca, he wanted to proceed peacefully, if at all possible. But under no circumstances did he want to be surprised.

The leader of the scouts, *Huitzilin*, whose name meant Hummingbird and was appropriate for someone nervously flitting about as the eyes of the caravan, told him, with head bowed, that there had been no sign of anyone, only small abandoned villages.

Cipactli didn't find this odd, as the Chichimeca were known to be largely nomadic. But it gave Asupacaci a sense of foreboding, and orders were passed to proceed with caution, with the scouts and long runners screening the caravan checking in regularly.

Onward, they proceeded on the agreed-upon route, and the cadence of the march, the steadily rising heat, the familiar sounds of the wheels turning, horses neighing, and whispered chatter, all slowly dulled everyone's alertness. Asupacaci was shaken from his lethargy by a shout as they came upon one of the abandoned villages the scouts had told them about. It was just a cluster of fire pits, logs for sitting, and stick frames where the animal skins had hung.

A girl of about eight or nine *xihuitl*, or years, peered out from behind a tree at the edge of the clearing, her eyes wide in bewilderment. She lost her natural shyness and walked straight toward the column, directly past a warrior and up to one of the Spaniards beside a horse. It wasn't the beast that fascinated her. It was the hollow-eyed, bearded white face of the stumbling conquistador. The warrior next to him tapped him on the arm with his spear, and the Spaniard stopped walking and stood while slightly swaying, unsure what to do next. When he was tapped again on top of the shoulder, he knelt and felt small delicate fingers exploring his eye sockets, his face, his beard.

Asupacaci and Cipactli sauntered over and stood next to the young girl, who touched a pox mark on her face, while also touching one on the Spaniard's. The child showed no fear, only curiosity that was slowly hardening into something else, something far beyond her age and fair gender.

Friar Rodrìguez was summoned over, and in several languages he slowly asked the girl where her people were. She immediately turned to him with stormy eyes when she at last recognized some of his words, and asked him, "If we are all alike on the outside, with the same markings, why aren't we alike on the inside?"

As the Friar turned to translate, the girl quickly reached under her garment, grabbed the Spaniard by his filthy matted hair with one hand, and sliced deeply across his throat with a sharp piece of obsidian. The Spaniard's mouth opened, more in surprise than pain, but the only sound he could utter was a gurgling gasp. She stood her ground directly in front of his spurting neck, allowing the blood to pulsate on her and coat her, until he fell, lifeless to the ground.

The Friar couldn't see it, but she turned and glared directly at him with an otherworldly intensity and hissed, "An offering for the souls of my people." She turned defiantly around and walked slowly back into the woods.

Asupacaci, with no hint of surprise on his face, turned to Cipactli and said, "The plague precedes us, I didn't think the cursed Spanish god had the strength to blow it this far north, this far away from those who carry it. But here it is. The girl survives it, but there is no one else anywhere around to be found. Now we know why there have been no eyes on us, even from a distance. For all we know, they may think *we* are the bringers of plague, and want to avoid any contact with us. None of these are favorable omens, but a sacrifice has been made, let us hope it appeases Huitzilopochtli."

With that he raised his hand and the caravan lurched forward, past the desolate village, past the pathetic crumpled figure lying lifeless next to the trail, past the small bloody footprints leading into the dark, foreboding forest.

For five more risings of the sun they traveled, until they finally saw someone in the distance. Though they were still near the coast where the sun rose, the caravan had veered further inland. Asupacaci had not wanted to risk encountering any of the great floating Spanish log houses, which seemed to favor protected lagoons or what the coyote-men called "anchorages." This led them to a long fertile valley between low mountains on their left and rolling hills on their right. More and more signs of habitation had started to appear, and the scouts reported that there were now definitely eyes upon them, eyes of the Chichimeca.

Asupacaci called his scout leader in.

Hummingbird prostrated himself on the ground awaiting orders. "Rise. It is time we met with the Chichimeca. They will either avoid us because they think the Spaniards carry plague, will attack us to wipe us out and take what we carry, or want to trade and allow passage. I would prefer to trade, but we must be ready for all contingencies."

Asupacaci placed a hand on Hummingbird's shoulder and fixed him with a gaze from his piercing green eyes. "Choose one of your best Knights, have him wear his finest battle uniform, take this offering with him, and have him approach the Chichimeca alone. They will either torture him, kill him, or send him back with a delegation. But we will at last know their intentions." Hummingbird grasped the offering with both hands, bowed, and left.

Asupacaci climbed a small rise to the side of the column and could see Hummingbird choose a muscular Jaguar Knight named *Xicohtencatl*, or Angry Bumblebee, who was well known for his many brave exploits. He was especially noted for his ability to capture enemies for offerings to the gods during the ritualistic flower wars, but this time the tables were turned, and *he* was the offering. The other Knights at first looked dejected at not being chosen, but soon crowded around Bumblebee and reached out to touch him, wishing him luck, chanting him courage and their goodbyes. Bumblebee pulled his jaguar skin over his shoulders, affixed the helmet over his head so that his face was centered within its jaws, and straightened the feathers that protruded from the crown and made him look menacingly taller. He proudly held the gold ceremonial dagger aloft, intricately inlaid with jade, emerald, amber and obsidian, waved it to his comrades, and jogged down the path towards the Chichimeca, and the unknown.

It was past the setting of the sun when camp was made, new scouts were sent out in all directions to secure the perimeter, and a meal was quickly eaten. Asupacaci and Cipactli stayed up and greeted the relieved scouts as they came in from the changing of the guard, to let them know by their simple presence that their dangerous work was acknowledged. Morale wasn't an issue with the thirty knights and over one hundred warriors, they were all elite and came willingly when called upon. But the servants, many of them slaves, were becoming noticeably more agitated the further they traveled away from their homeland.

"Another example will need to be made soon, if our quest starts to be compromised," Asupacaci said to Cipactli, who had picked up on some of the same subtle signals. "And that one may be a good place to start," he added, as he glanced at a porter who was constantly spreading exaggerated rumors and exciting the others.

When Asupacaci took his familiar place under the wagon and rubbed his tired eyes, his thoughts drifted from the daily challenges of the expedition back to what had forced him on this journey in the first place. With a sigh and heaviness in his heart, he closed his eyes, and remembered how Cortés and his forces had fought their way back into Tenochtitlán and took refuge inside the Spanish compound with Montezuma as their prisoner. Asupacaci and his brothers Chimalpopoca and Tlaltecatzin were there as well and witnessed what happened next. Realizing how desperate their plight was, Cortés demanded that Montezuma address the Aztecs pressing in on them from all sides, to ask for safe passage for the Spanish to leave the city and pushed him out onto the terrace.

Instead, Montezuma exhorted his people to resist the Spaniards with all their strength and with their every breath. At that moment, he, the *Hueyi Tlatoani* of the Aztecs, the Emperor of all the Mexica, and his people were one. With the words still on his lips, he staggered backward and fell dead, run through by a steel sword in the back by the treacherous Cortés, as soon as La Malinche screamed what he was saying. An audible groan came from the Aztecs outside, and stones and darts started showering the terrace and the palace with renewed fury.

Being short of food, water, gunpowder, and supplies, Cortés decided they would have to make their escape at night. In order to buy time and possibly put the Aztecs off their guard, an emissary was sent to negotiate a ceasefire and ask for safe passage. In return the Spaniards would relinquish any treasure they had.

Asupacaci had heard that those Aztecs outside the compound elected Montezuma's brother *Cuitláhuac* as Hueyi Tlatoani to lead the resistance in his absence. He knew with his uncle in charge there would be no safe passage. Cortés issued orders to prepare to leave, to pack as much of the treasure as was possible, and for any Spaniard to load up with as much gold as they wished. He also told them to take the highest-ranking nobles as hostages, and to prepare a portable bridge to pass over the broken causeways which led out of the city.

On *La Noche Trist*, or The Night of Sorrows, the Spanish attempted to sneak out to the west under the cover of a rainstorm. They made good headway down the causeway, until they were noticed by an Eagle Warrior below and a priest on top of the Hueteocalli, or the Great Temple pyramid. As soon as the alarm was sounded, the Aztecs swarmed to all sides of the causeway, including hundreds of canoes. The vanguard with Cortés and the portable bridge made determined progress, but the middle and back of the column, in the dark, in the rain, and encountering increasingly broken sections of the causeway, struggled mightily. Conquistadors fighting for their lives, weighed down by their greed and on slippery ground, fell in increasing numbers. Many were simply grabbed by the Aztecs in canoes, and fell flailing into the deep water, unable to rise due to their armor and the weight of hidden gold.

Cortés couldn't see what was happening behind him and pressed ahead with his horses, fighting until they were on solid ground, away from the city. Asupacaci had heard that over 1,000 Spaniards and 2,000 of their allies had been killed, along with most of the horses and all of the lightning logs called artillery. But that did little to compensate for the loss of so many nobles, including his two brothers who were deliberately killed when they became too much to manage. Asupacaci had alertly used the chaos of the flight to dive into the water with his bound hands. Before he could be caught three warrior canoes shielded him from the vengeful Spanish and pulled him in, but he was hit by a crossbow bolt, the head of which he still carried inside of him. And even now, with every breath he took, its pressing against his shoulder and lung reminded him of his sacred task and hated enemy.

The Aztecs had chased the remnants of Cortés's army and whittled down their numbers, but they didn't succeed in destroying them. Exhausted and suffering their own losses, they gathered those Spaniards who were taken alive to be sacrificed, and subjects from all corners of the empire saw that these were indeed just men, who felt pain, prayed to their false gods, and fertilized the earth with their blood. Their heads filled the ceremonial skull racks at the base of the great temple pyramid, and a few were stuck on the tops of lances with their helmets on and made into torches, to show that they could indeed be defeated. One was even mounted on a skeleton of a horse, to show that these creatures too weren't invincible.

A special gold coated skull was kept separate from the rest and was placed on the very top of the temple, next to the sacrificial alter. This was the Spaniard known as the Inquisitor, that trained practitioner of the dark arts of extracting information from those who wouldn't tell or didn't know.

Asupacaci had seen him do his foul work on many, including his relatives, who were left to die a lingering death once the desired information was obtained. The Inquisitor had been left behind and surrounded on the causeway and dragged from the water when he tried to drown himself. He was bound and taken to the base of the temple, where he was buried in sand up to his neck. The gold and silver he'd had on him were melted before his eyes.

With Friar Rodrìguez translating, the Inquisitor was told that the gold would be poured upon his head, drop by drop, until he was encased in it, since he and all the Spanish had such an insatiable hunger for it. He would then be placed where he could look out and see every sacrifice the Aztecs would make, for all of eternity. When the screaming subsided and all movement stopped, the head was cleanly cut off the body, the molten silver was poured into the eye sockets, and a priest with much ceremony carried it aloft with two hands to the top of the great temple pyramid.

Cuitláhuac demanded to be kept abreast of every movement of Cortés and learned from his many spies that they were gathering strength, bolstered by more Spaniards, horses, fire logs and thousands upon thousands of traitorous allies. The day of reckoning would be coming, and only one way of life would survive.

As more allies deserted them, as their enemies gained strength, Cuitláhuac foresaw with great clarity the inevitable where others in Tenochtitlán did not. He devised the plan to save the heritage and legacy of the Aztec people, to send out token caravans in different directions and purposely let some overhear the false parts of the plan to spread rumors. He alone charged Asupacaci with leading the single, true expedition far away, far beyond the reach of the Spaniards. It had been with a sense of foreboding that Cuitláhuac told Asupacaci to choose the final route and destination and keep it to himself, so that no one in Tenochtitlán would know the location of the ultimate goal, not even himself.

The Aztecs dredged along the causeways. They recovered much treasure lost on La Noche Trist and gathered the vast hidden wealth that was never disclosed to the Spanish. And as the renewed army of Cortés worked its way back to the valley of the Aztecs, Asupacaci stole away in the night, leaving behind all dead who could tell the tale. All except Cuitláhuac, now the last great leader of the empire.

CHAPTER 6 – MAY 29, PRESENT DAY

Nick sat on the dock a long time, rubbing the stress out of his temples. He was feeling the slight buzz from the whiskey, letting his thoughts drift unguided, hoping for connections he might have missed. When none came, he stood up and stretched. He wandered along the shoreline, skipping a few rocks on the calm lake, like he had done so many times in his youth. He passed some stacked wood and smiled as he remembered a favorite saying his dad had, "Chop your own wood boys, it will warm you twice."

He followed the shoreline aimlessly, further down than he usually did, and turned to walk back up toward the camp. Not following any path, he nearly tripped on a couple of pine branches in the underbrush, and out of habit reached down to toss them deeper into the woods. As he picked them up, he noticed the ends weren't broken off or torn, but weathered and cleanly cut. The needles were still on them, not yet too dry and brittle, probably from last winter. That made no sense, not way over here away from the camp. His curiosity aroused, he walked toward the closest cluster of pine trees, felt around them at shoulder height, and found the corresponding branch cuts on the far side of one tree.

Now why would Dad cut off branches on the far side of a tree, and toss them into the undergrowth? Odd indeed, he thought. He tossed the branches to the bottom of the tree and worked his way to the side door of the cabin.

Like his dad used to do, and was now his habit, he went inside and grabbed the old guitar, and sat on the porch and started strumming along to the music emanating from the hidden speakers. *It Don't Come Easy* by Ringo Starr came on, and Nick easily slid into synching with the rhythm of the song.

"Got to pay your dues if you wanna sing the blues," Nick sang along softly. His thoughts drifted. His consciousness focused on the music, his unconsciousness seeking connections.

Abruptly he sat straight up, and said aloud, "It wasn't Dad, someone was covering their tracks!" It was only one little piece of a much greater mystery, one he wouldn't be able to prove, but it explained why he could find no human tracks in the snow or out onto the ice when he found Albert, despite the fact that there were numerous animal tracks onshore everywhere. He never came to terms with the circumstances of his dad's death, there were too many loose ends. Things just didn't add up. Somehow, he knew this was the thread he needed to pull on, to see where it might lead.

Nick's feet took him into the cabin until he was staring at a rustically framed photograph of Charlie, Mom, Dad, and himself standing proudly in front of the old station wagon on a deserted stretch of highway somewhere in Arizona or New Mexico. The barren landscape stretching out endlessly into the distance. It was faded from the passage of time and sitting where sunlight hit it, almost to a point of looking like an old daguerreotype. He carefully took the photo out of its frame and slipped it into his shirt pocket. It was going on the dashboard of his truck.

What was he missing? What was the link to all this? What could anyone have possibly wanted from his father?

Suddenly feeling nostalgic, Nick wandered into the master bedroom, and got on his knees in front of the old steamer trunk at the end of the bed. An old family heirloom, it had seen many a trip with his Grandparents and Great Grandparents. Weathered, dented, copper clad and reinforced on the edges, it was in remarkably good shape. Dad had used it as his catch-all for his adventures over the years, like Nick did with the ammo can under his bed.

He flipped it open and immediately smiled, seeing the visceral reminders of many journeys with his family. Nick unfastened and removed the top tray out of the trunk and put it on the bed. Still on his knees he started flipping through everything in the tray, small notebooks, photos and negatives of each trip still in the envelopes they were mailed in, old tour books, the occasional AAA TripTik, worn topographical maps with notations, all the memorabilia of past quests. Nick dug deep into the trunk itself, sorting through it, looking for something without really knowing what it was he wanted. Methodically, he removed all the contents onto the floor around him including a compass, gear sacks, old binoculars, a portable GPS, head lamps, various dig tools, bug spray and head nets, an older digital camera, sunglasses, a foldable cap, bandanas, and a set of logbooks, one for each year of their Southwest wanderings.

But one logbook was missing, and it occurred to Nick that that was what he was looking for. The hair on the back of his neck stood up. Dad had been meticulous, every trip was choreographed and planned out in minute detail. The logs were a chronological record of where they went, with small crudely sketched and annotated trail maps, key latitude and longitude coordinates, the soil and terrain conditions, the weather, people encountered with contact information, various photos taped to the pages, and what—if anything—they found. And the one logbook that was missing was one Nick distinctly remembered, because that was from the summer when his dad got his only tattoo.

The next morning, Nick drove the thirty minutes over to the Horizonvue Nursing Home, where his dad had placed Nick's grandmother, Grandma Ingrid. When his dad had moved from Muskegon to Lake Charlevoix full time, he was pleased to find this facility which catered to her increasing dementia, and the ease of access allowed him frequent visits. Nick and Charlie had decided not to tell their 96-year-old grandmother that her son Albert had passed, concerned with her ability to grasp the reality of it, deal with it, and to remember it. Nick recalled trying to convey information to her the past few years, and out of frustration had resorted to writing notes out in large letters so she could reference it, but she would simply forget there was even a note in the first place.

Occasionally she would have surprising moments of perfect recall, reciting events and facts that left Nick speechless, filling him on little known details of the family and their history. Grandma Ingrid had fallen for the handsome lumberjack who fluently spoke both French and English in Saginaw back in 1940, when she was only seventeen and he was twenty. One year later they were married, and one year after that he was off to the Pacific to fight the Japanese as part of the Army Air Corps. Grandpa Jacques came back physically unharmed, but like many of his generation he compartmentalized his wartime experiences, and set out to make a better life for he and his wife, and a better world to live in.

After a series of odd jobs, he was taken on at a lumber yard in Muskegon, proved himself, and worked his way up. He became enmeshed in the regional community, joined Rotary, the school board, and the Chamber of Commerce. As the business boomed in the postwar years, the widowed owner wanted to move to a warmer climate, and Grandpa Jacques bought the business. Jacques and Ingrid had a good life together, raised a family they were proud of, and had been very influential in the lives of their grandchildren.

The one thing that threw Nick off the most was that regardless of how lucid Grandma was or wasn't, she always thought Nick was Albert. *There is a certain irony in that,* Nick thought, since Charlie was a dead ringer for Albert. But somehow, even in her confused mind, Ingrid saw past the face and directly into the soul, where Nick was exactly like his dad.

"Hi Mémé, how have you been?" Nick asked as he rapped on the doorframe and let himself in. The room was bright and bathed in natural sunlight, comfortably furnished, with photos of the family on the dresser and a dream catcher in the window, which briefly reflected a bright glint as it turned lazily. Ingrid was propped up in bed, and her gaze shifted to Nick and she smiled, "Albert, how nice to see you."

Nick walked over to her bedside, gave her a kiss on the forehead, pulled a chair closer to her and took her hand. "I missed you Mémé. You're looking well today. The nurses said you have been staying out of trouble, not attempting any jail breaks lately."

Grandma Ingrid had developed a habit of getting up and wandering at odd hours, startling other patients by looking into their rooms to find her deceased husband Jacques. Several times she had sounded an exit alarm when the night shift was too preoccupied with their cell phones to notice the lithe figure silently shuffling down the hall.

Nick looked into her eyes and could see that she had already drifted off somewhere else, content. He had developed the habit of talking to her whether she was engaged or not and found that sometimes his innocuous updates of the goings on in his life, in Charlie's or Dad's, would trigger something and bring her back into focus. Ingrid had been the family historian, and fortunately she had taken on that task with a passion when she was still sharp as a tack, shortly after Jacques had passed.

With a great amount of love and devotion she'd put together a very detailed booklet tracing the family tree, including copies of old letters, newspaper articles, faded photographs, deeds, awards, civic recognitions, all of the flotsam and detritus of an ambitious, wandering, growing immigrant family making their way in a new world.

"If I don't document this for all of you, who will? I don't want our family history to fade with me. This is your legacy, and you can't add to it unless you know where you have come from," she had beseeched at a family reunion, and proudly gave out copies to everyone. When Nick ran out of small talk and updates, he would inevitably grab her well-worn copy of the book, and read it aloud to her. Even when she wasn't focused on what he was reading, he could see the corners of her eyes soften and a slight smile form on her lips.

Nick flipped to the post-it note he had in the booklet, which is how he kept track of where he left off, more for his sanity than Grandma Ingrid's. It was near the very beginning, and Nick shifted to get comfortable and started reading aloud. He started with very distant relatives who had arrived in New France, and noticed Ingrid sitting up slightly when he mentioned her great-great grandfather Alexandre LaBounty, who had been born in 1840, fought in the American Civil War, and then stayed in the cavalry after the war and was posted out west.

Nick's dad had tried over the years, via their annual summer trips, to visit every posting he had. The boys would pester Albert with questions about why go here or there, what was it that seemed to so obsess all his free time. Al would always allude to tales of family legends, of something Alexandre had come across in a remote desert, of trying to unlock a long-held secret. And what better way to have time with Josephine and his boys than with some high adventure.

Nick continued to read aloud on more details of Alexandre's life, the specific remote outposts he was assigned to, of how he befriended the native tribes in a time it wasn't fashionable to do so.

"Alexandre started this whole thing, you know," Grandma Ingrid said softly, and started humming to herself.

"Started what Mémé, how did he start it?" Nick inquired. The humming continued, but the eyes went somewhere else, and Nick knew he had had her for a moment, but the moment had passed.

Undiscouraged, Nick told her that he was about to take a little trip, to, perhaps, some of the places Alexandre had been, to places his dad had taken the family over time. He also was thinking out loud, wondering why his dad had never told the boys what the odd tattoo he had on his left forearm was, what it signified, and was always told that they would learn someday, when the whole puzzle came together. Until then it was just a fun curiosity, the butt of constant jokes, and they never thought too deeply about it. But that single, very distinct bite mark left around the tattoo continued to swirl in the back of his mind, gnawing at him, at some detail he was missing, some connection he couldn't make.

The humming then abruptly stopped. "Why honey, that was the necklace you had made for me, don't you remember?" Grandma Ingrid said, staring straight at him. Nick realized she was back, lucid, at least for the moment, but she was talking to her son Albert, not Nick.

"Yes, I remember. Whatever became of it? I searched your room high and low and can't seem to come up with it." Nick looked pleadingly at her, hoping she would stay with him just a little longer.

"Well, those lovely nurses took the necklace off me, said they didn't want it getting caught on anything, and you hung it over there, in the window." Nick glanced at the window, where he saw the dream catcher moving ever so slightly with the draft, and noticed a brief, bright reflection. "Bring it over would you, dearie, let me tell you all about where it came from."

Nick walked over and saw that there was a small necklace hanging off the dream catcher, but had never noticed it before, because it was so short and close to the same color. He lifted it to get it off, and then held it up to the light. The necklace was made of some type of thin rope or hemp, taupe in color, with what looked like a black metal link about the size and shape of an oversized zipper pull, hanging from the bottom. He held the link up to examine it closer, and saw it was covered in some type of heavy paint, slightly sticky, almost like tar. And on one part the covering had chipped off, revealing a bright glint underneath, the reflection briefly caught his eye.

Nick went back over to Grandma Ingrid and held it in front of her. "Here is it, where did you say this came from?" But instinctively he knew he wouldn't be getting an answer, as her eyes were now unfocused, and she drifted off somewhere else in her mind, hopefully with Grandpa Jacques. He leaned down and affectionately gave her forehead another kiss in farewell.

"Well, that makes it official then. If you don't mind Mémé, I am going to borrow your necklace and family history book with your blessing. Time for me to take a little road trip, and you better be here when I get back."

CHAPTER 7 – APRIL 14, 1521

Morning dawned in the cool, thin air, but it would be warm and then hot soon enough. The entire camp had slept in two shifts, so that half the warriors were always awake, alert, and ready. No word had come back from the scouts posted further out around the caravan in a protective perimeter. A sense of anticipation hung in the air since Bumblebee headed off alone toward the Chichimeca, and Asupacaci went to great lengths to betray no emotion or nervousness, at least on the outside.

"Let us hope our Bumblebee didn't end up in the soup pot of these savages," he confided to the ever present Cipactli. "If we hear nothing, we will move out prepared for battle. But we can't do that on empty stomachs. Have the men eat."

The slaves and servants went about their familiar rituals, bringing food out to the scouts on the perimeter first, then to the warriors, and finally to the Spaniards. The sun had crept up slightly in the sky, and the first signs of a warm breeze kicked up dirt devils on the trail. Suddenly scouts started shouting in the distance, and Asupacaci stood in anticipation, looking down the path. Soon a small group emerged at the far end of the trail. A fierce looking shaman broke away from the rest, ran forward, spinning around and around, and threw an object that landed with a dull thump and rolled slightly on its side, exposing the bloody stump of a skull.

An Eagle Warrior walked toward it, standing very erect while acting uninterested. He bent down slowly to examine it. He turned toward the Aztec camp, holding it aloft, and started shouting chants. It wasn't until he bowed in front of Asupacaci that it became evident it wasn't the head of Bumblebee, but that of a pox marked and bearded Spaniard. Asupacaci smiled slightly, relieved, and recalled the words with which his Uncle Cuitláhuac had advised in sending him on this journey.

"Remember, all we tribes quarrel with one another like brothers of the same family, but the Spaniards are true enemies to all."

The group of Chichimeca worked their way toward the camp, and Bumblebee emerged and prostrated himself in front of Asupacaci and Cipactli.

"I was taken to their leader, Lord," Bumblebee said, glancing over his shoulder at the tall older man, standing proudly in the middle of his savage looking warriors. "I presented the jeweled dagger to him, which he seemed pleased with. While I couldn't completely understand their language, we do share some common words, and with that and gestures I asked him to come here to meet you." Asupacaci tapped him on the shoulder to rise, called for Friar Rodrìguez, and nodded slightly at *Xólotl*, their striking leader with the red colored hair and tattoos.

They sat in the shadow of the wagons, in a tight circle, surrounded by the warriors of both groups, with the Friar, at first hesitantly and then more fluently, translating.

"I think you both spoke the same language sometime in distant the past," he whispered to Asupacaci. "As there are so many similarities." Through the verbal efforts of the Friar accompanied by the gestures of Asupacaci and his key leaders, communication was established and an understanding was reached. It turned out that the Chichimeca were not ignorant of the Spaniards, or their horses for that matter. Survivors of several shipwrecks had washed up on their shores, who had been rescued and treated with reverence, until the start of the spread of new, strange and devastating diseases. It hadn't taken the Chichimeca long to understand that the enemy of their enemy was their friend.

Xólotl cut a striking and slightly unnerving figure, even as he sat. To the Aztecs, Chichimeca meant red colored hair, which was from a pigment they used extensively to both give their hair its distinctive sheen, and to color their skin and clothing. All the Chichimeca were also adorned in silver, and Xólotl wore an impressive and very intricate necklace that seemed to be interlaced with human bone. The Aztecs practiced ritualistic cannibalism, but its purpose was as a part of a sacrifice to the gods, to show dominance over one's foe, and was traditionally practiced by priests. However, rumor had reached the Aztecs over time that these very fierce and nomadic red colored people to their north regularly ate human flesh, and not just for ceremony. Looking around at the increasingly barren landscape, Asupacaci didn't doubt that at times it was done for the mere sake of survival.

Xólotl noticed Asupacaci staring at his necklace. He reached up and touched it, returning Asupacaci's stare with a quizzical look. While the land of the Aztecs was rich in both gold and silver, the land of the Chichimeca had little gold but much silver.

"Friar, tell him of the Spaniards lust for silver, and if his land has it, then surely they will come to take it."

Xólotl indicated he understood the Friar's words, and then nudged the head on the ground between them with his foot, showing how his people would deal with anyone who took what was rightfully theirs.

Over the course of several hours, safe passage was negotiated, as were guides to lead them through the rest of the lands of the Chichimeca, to the borders of the next tribes, which the Aztecs knew even less about.

It had been barely perceptible, perhaps not at all to anyone but Xólotl and Asupacaci, but they had formed an unspoken and immediate bond, deeper than their alliance. As they looked at each other through eyes that betrayed little emotion but showed earned, common wisdom and mutual respect, they knew that despite their differences, their different gods and ways of life, their peoples had somehow grown from the same great tree. That their traditional way of life was being threatened to its core, that a great storm was coming that was alien and uncontrollable to them, that they had little power to avert it, and that their common tree with its deep roots grown in these grounds over the millennia might not be able to weather it. Asupacaci had never said what their quest was, he had only asked for passage, but he saw that Xólotl had internally discerned why this strange caravan of Aztecs, horses, wagons, and blind Spaniards dared walk through his land. He had accepted the necessity of it, understood that the Aztecs to the south were but a temporary bulwark to stop the spread to their own lands, and was pondering what he must ultimately do to ensure the survival of his own people and their way of life.

"These people may be savage in our eyes, but they are hardy to survive in a land which offers so little, and they are well-led. The Spaniards may defeat them in the long run, but they will pay dearly in the trying," Asupacaci confided to Cipactli.

Additional gifts were given to the Chichimeca, primarily in gold, since they had little of it. Two of the Spaniards were also offered but were refused, as it was conveyed that they had more of their own prisoners from the shipwrecks hidden deep in their lands and that when food became scarce, food they would become. Just before the chief departed, Xólotl gave a palm-sized silver cross to Asupacaci taken from one of the sailors, a talisman from their common enemy, from the potential destroyer of their worlds.

The sun was just starting its downward descent when Cipactli went ahead of the column with two warriors, a priest and a porter who was struggling to escape. Screams started echoing back and then stopped abruptly, and the caravan started its methodical forward movement. Past a moaning figure on the left side of the trail it went, the warriors not even bothering to glance, the eyeless Spaniards unseeing, and the servants and slaves wide eyed in horror, knowing it was a clear message intended solely for them. No one was above this quest, no one must impede it, they must all willingly lay down their lives to complete it. The troublesome porter, the one who had consistently excited his fellows, was tightly bound to a cactus, his tongue cut out, his arms and legs flayed, the insects already starting to swarm.

As the hot afternoon trek stretched on, Asupacaci beckoned Friar Rodrìguez over to him. In trying to understand the nature of the Spaniards, in what drove them to risk so much for what the Aztecs deemed of so little value. He was troubled that he could discern no clear, understandable motive. His meeting with Xólotl, of another people, yet one not so strange as the Spaniards, had crystallized his thinking and left questions.

Asupacaci turned to the Friar. "Why is it you believe your gods alone to be the only gods? Why do you seek to force your beliefs on anyone that doesn't match yours? Can't different peoples, who grew from this earth in different places and different ways, have their own beliefs that help them to make sense of their own worlds, to deal with it in their own ways?"

The Friar took a moment to formulate his thoughts, which was not his nature, as he was a highly intelligent man who usually responded both immediately and with conviction. Asupacaci knew he had struck at a fundamental conflict within him, something he hoped to leverage to his advantage.

"It is not only the Aztecs and your allies we seek to show the light of the Christ and the one true way. Even your enemies, those who have allied with Cortés, we will show them the error of their beliefs too. Our King, Charles V, and our most holy men, have decreed that it is our duty to save your souls from eternal damnation. That is why we baptized those on the islands off your shores, to save them from an eternity in hell. And in exchange for providing that salvation, the King gives a Spaniard land, and natives to work it. We call it an *encomienda*, and it works for the good of everyone."

Asupacaci slowed his pace slightly so the Friar could catch up and walk by his side, so he could talk in hushed tones for the Friar's ears only. "So you save the souls of those who didn't know they needed saving, by having them reject their beliefs and the beliefs of their ancestors? For the privilege of working for Spanish masters for no gain except their continued existence? Why don't you just call it what it is, slavery and bondage?"

A light smile formed on the lips of Friar Rodrìguez, who knew that in merely having this debate, it was reinforcing some of his own observations about the humanness of the Aztecs. These were indeed men with souls, albeit with a different belief system grown of their own environment and experiences.

"My spiritual leader, Bartolomé de las Casas, tends to agree with many of your views, as frankly do I. But it is not the policy of our government, nor King Charles, at least not yet. When last I heard, he was being petitioned to treat the natives more humanely. But human sacrifice must end, no religion that advocates the destruction of another human makes moral sense."

Asupacaci leaned in closer and intoned, "But that is exactly what your religion does, what your Inquisition has done. I not only saw it, we heard it from the slaves you brought with you from the islands. We sacrifice to ensure a bountiful harvest, or for success in war, and you call us savages. You sacrifice someone who doesn't believe as you do, and you call it the will of God. What truly is the difference?"

Friar Rodrìguez was silent, surprised to be in such a deep conversation with someone his people thought to be not completely human. Asupacaci used rational logic, and the Friar found he couldn't completely disagree with him.

"The reason I am having this conversation with you—am even allowing it to happen—is because I desire your help," Asupacaci said. "Not only to translate, I need you to believe in the quest we have set for ourselves. Because if you are convinced in the honor of what we undertake, the righteousness of our cause, that we are preserving not only the history of savages but of a whole culture who believes in their own gods and ways of life, then we both stand a better chance of accomplishing it." With that he placed the silver cross Xólotl had given him into the Friar's hands and walked briskly ahead.

For twenty-one more risings of the sun they traveled, through the heartland and to the far northern edge of the land of the

Chichimeca, following the trails best suited for the slow and ponderous advance of the heavily laden wagons. They had headed slightly inland, shadowed by the mountains to their west, slowed by the roughness of some of the trails and streams. They lived off the land wherever they could to save supplies, and even added to their stores when the guides conveyed the wishes of Xólotl, that they were to proceed unmolested, and to be given succor by those villages that could provide it. Asupacaci noted that these people didn't have many villages to speak of. They didn't plant many crops like the Aztecs. They moved frequently and lived off the land, gathering mesquite, agave, the fruit of the nopal, acorns, roots, and seeds. They showed the Aztecs how they survived in the harsher parts of their lands, how to live in caves and river ravines, how to find water, and how to use the juice of the agave when water was scarce. Even Cipactli, old crocodile head, the battle-hardened Aztec warrior general, had to give the Chichimeca his begrudging respect as both superb fighters and survivors.

At midday the next day, the caravan of wagons emerged onto a narrow plain which opened before them, the mountains to the west receding, giving way to smaller sporadic hills scattered on either side. The going became easier as the ground flattened and hardened, but it also kicked up more dust, especially toward the back part of the column. Going into the lands of the *Coahuiltecan* would not go unnoticed, and Asupacaci had the Chichimeca guides brought back to him. He was surprised to learn that they were not loaned to him, but given to him, a gift from the sage Xólotl. They were to do his bidding and advised that they had been chosen for their own linguistic skills, as they were versed in the language of their northern neighbors.

Asupacaci was thankful for this, as the further they trekked, the more foreign the languages became, although they still encountered random pockets of tribes that spoke a distant dialect of Aztec. But Friar Rodrìguez was a quick study, and he found that even Hummingbird, the leader of his scouts, was adept at picking up key words and signing with those he encountered. It was a barrier they were ever better armed to overcome, especially now that the Chichimeca guides would continue with them.

To Asupacaci, the Coahuiltecan were even more of an unknown entity than the Chichimeca had been, and that was not a good position for a leader to be in. He had always been taught to know your enemy better than you know yourself. At least the Chichimeca had encountered the Spaniards and experienced the disease that preceded them. Asupacaci unconsciously rubbed the scar on his chest, close to the shoulder, that hid the head of the crossbow bolt he carried inside of him.

Huitzilopochtli, see us through another unknown land, protect your people just a little longer. Soon enough, we will all be with you, he prayed silently.

CHAPTER 8 – MAY 30, PRESENT DAY

Nick rose early to a misty morning at the cabin on Lake Charlevoix, excited at the prospect of a road trip. His dad used to say to the boys, "you've got *fernweh*," a German word that meant an aching to travel to a distant place. It was the opposite of homesickness, rather a far sickness.

"Yeah Old Man, I've got fernweh fever again," Nick said out loud, smiling. He showered, packed quickly, taking a peek in the refrigerator to see if there was anything to fuel up on before he hit the road. Slim pickings, better to not risk ingesting dated foodstuffs and challenging his digestive system, especially when he would be only stopping at desolate gas stations scattered across the country.

Looking around one last time, he saw a favorite talisman of his father's on the desk, which he had used as a paperweight. It looked like a piece of an old decayed iron bracket, with two hand forged nails sticking out of the accumulated rust. This was one of the many random items they had found on their Southwest wanderings. For some reason, his dad had attached special significance to it. He said it sat on his desk as a constant reminder, and that although it didn't look like much, to him it was a key to all he sought. Nick instinctively grabbed it, putting it in his backpack.

He then grabbed his gear, plus the guitar, his old metal detector and the journals, locked up the camp, hung the camp key in its hiding place in the car port, and drove into town to his favorite greasy spoon diner for a little road trip sustenance.

"Nick, how you doing this fine morning?" Debbie called from behind the counter, looking up to see her old friend again. Debbie had been at the memorial party for his dad, wouldn't have missed it, and not only as a friend to Nick, but the whole family.

Nick smiled when he saw her, always did. He always had a bit of a thing for Debbie, who was four years older than him and had dated Charlie for a time. They used to joke that God got the dates wrong, Nick should have been the older brother. As happens so often in small towns after high school, those who stayed around kept changing dance partners until they found the right one to make a life with. Debbie had married an old friend of Charlie's who ran the local hardware store, someone Nick would have never guessed as a match. But they were happy, had three young rambunctious kids, and were the type of people who made up the backbone of the community. And damn, if she didn't still look as good as she did when she was nineteen, as wistful and charming as ever.

"Doing great Deb, about to take a long road trip and need to fuel myself up. The usual if you don't mind, my dear."

Nick sat down at a well-worn bench and table, tracing initials carved into the top with his fingertip. He could put the names to more than a few of them, and even found one he had etched himself back in high school. He pulled out a map and started calculating his way points, and how much ground he wanted to cover each day. He also put Grandma Ingrid's family history booklet on the table and started reviewing the different postings Alexandre had in the Southwest, and which ones his dad had taken him to.

Lost in his thoughts, he was surprised when a heavy spinning plate hit the table and slid down right in front of him, two poached eggs on top of a steaming pile of crispy corned beef hash with sourdough toast on the side. Debbie gave him her impish smile, poured him a large cup of coffee, and sang a song as she walked away. It wasn't until he was halfway through breakfast that Nick caught the joke. She was singing, "It's Hard to Belong to Someone Else When the Right One Comes Along," an old seventies song by England Dan & John Ford Coley. *Yeah, still a real firecracker, that one.*

When Nick walked over to the counter to pay his bill, Debbie reached down and put her hand lightly on top of his. "I meant to tell you the other night out at the lake, but there were so many people there and the timing just didn't feel appropriate. The day your father disappeared, two rough looking characters came in here for breakfast. Mexican or Tejano I think from their accents, but very loud and rude. Didn't exactly blend in with the locals round here, if you know what I mean. I didn't think anything of it, but when I mentioned them to my husband Don that night, he said the same two were in the hardware store and bought an ice auger."

Nick dug out his wallet, and said, "Nothing too unusual about that, especially around here for ice fishing season."

"That's what Don thought, but things just didn't add up. He was trying to be helpful, asked where they were going fishing, what they were using for bait, if they had tip-up's, or needed anything else. And they were completely clueless about fishing, like they just needed to drill a hole in the ice, and nothing else. I don't know if it means anything, but I wanted to make sure to pass it along. And before you ask, no, they didn't use a credit card to pay for anything, they paid cash."

Nick nodded a look of thanks to Debbie, gave her a genuine smile, and said, "Tell Don thanks for the insight, and you be sure to take care of yourself and that tribe of rug rats you're growing."

Nick considered stopping by the police department on his way out of town but decided against it. He had already been down that road once and been dismissed out of hand. His deepening suspicions about the cut pine branches he found in the woods, the missing journal, the new tip about two out-of-towners who bought an ice auger but didn't know anything about fishing, weren't much of an argument, at least not without filling in some more of the missing information, most crucially some type of motive. He had the better part of three weeks to do some digging into the old family history and mystery across the Southwest, so he drove out of the still sleepy little town, south along Lake Michigan, pushing his speed a little to avoid the choke point around the Chicago beltway before he headed southwest.

Rule number one of any successful road trip, take care of the entertainment first. Nick figured he had over thirty hours of driving before he was scheduled to pick up Charlie in northwest New Mexico, depending on what detours grabbed his attention. *That's a lot of windshield time* he thought. He was thankful for his lifelong obsession with great music.

He'd grown up in a household full of music, had a Mother who gave piano lessons to the neighborhood kids and helped with the local musical productions, and a father who had an extensive music collection and enjoyed playing the guitar and singing. Hell, Mom had even dressed him up and put him in all kinds of plays and competitions before he could even voice his dissent. The one residual of all of that was his abilities to play the piano, guitar, and to sing—and once he got past puberty his voice wasn't all that bad.

Nick's music collection centered around his dad's musical tastes, ranging from blues to jazz to classic rock. Even his grandparents with their big band and swing music had an influence. He veraciously digitized any music he could get his hands on, even exhausting the local library systems and all of Charlie's friends. Then his going to three different colleges had only broadened his exposure, and in a bit of serendipity he had a roommate named Eric who was as passionate a music fan as he was. Eric had a digital collection of the Billboard 100 for every year it had been in existence, back to 1955. It had been obtained through nefarious means which were never fully disclosed, although a liaison with a pretty radio station intern had long been rumored.

One challenge Nick had was that he drove an old Chevy pickup, but he found a way to jack his iPhone into the cassette player and still enjoy his digital music library on the road. A little bit of radio also broke things up and kept him current on the goings on in the world, which was usually depressing enough to get him to switch back to his personal music collection. With no built-in vehicle navigation, he still used a portable GPS unit in a cradle on the dashboard, which was also useful for hiking where there was no cell phone signal or if he was out of country. Completing the road trip ensemble, on his lap sat an old palm sized tape recorder, one that he would dictate random thoughts or bits of inspiration and insight to, the buttons so second nature he never needed to look at it while driving.

Nick got caught in traffic a little south of Chicago, right before lunch time, but it cleared out by Joliet and he went into long haul driver mode, partially turning off his mind to the driving and started daydreaming about the trip itself. First stop would be near Fort Leavenworth Kansas, one of Great-Great-Great-Great Grandfather Alexandre's first postings after the Civil War. In 1866 when he went through there, it had become famous as the base for the African-American soldiers who were to become known as the Buffalo Soldiers. The Apache gave them the moniker, because they had curly, kinky hair like bison, and out of respect for their tenacious fighting ability. Nick's interest was in taking a quick tour of the area to refresh himself on its history, because he hadn't been there since he was nine years old. And more importantly, it was close to Quivira, where the Spaniard, Francisco Vásquez de Coronado, had led a troop of conquistadors out of Mexico on a search for the fabled Seven Cities of Cibola. Quivira had caught Nick's father's attention, and they had all spent several days there the same summer they went through Fort Leavenworth.

Nick continued to cruise down the interstate, skipping lunch and only stopping to gas up and relieve himself to keep the momentum going. Around four in the afternoon he turned due west at Springfield and drove until hunger and heavy eyes compelled him to finally admit he needed a break. He decided to push himself a little further to get over the Mississippi River, and pulled off at Hannibal. As he wandered into the trucker's diner, he had a sense of déjà vu with his morning of seeing Debbie, in a very similar setting. He sat down heavily into a booth, ordered coffee and a meatloaf dinner from a gruff waitress right out of central casting, and attempted to clear his head. He glanced at a sign on the wall which proudly proclaimed Hannibal as the boyhood home of Samuel Clemens, better known as Mark Twain. As the muddy Mississippi rolled on by he saw some of the inspiration for Tom Sawyer and Huckleberry Finn.

Spread out in front of Nick were Grandma Ingrid's family history booklet, several of Dad's travel journals, and a map. As he tried hard to remember what his dad had told him of old family legends and his obsessive quest, he unconsciously rubbed the necklace he wore from the dream catcher in Grandma Ingrid's room. Dad had always been very cautious about what he disclosed to the boys, like he was guarding both a secret and the boys *from* the secret, like knowledge of it could somehow harm them.

Curious, Nick thought. *Because something had definitely harmed Dad.* There was something in the back of his mind, something he had heard a long time ago, that was a crucial piece of the puzzle, but he couldn't retrieve it out of the depths of his childhood memory. Which was why he was so excited yesterday when it seemed Grandma Ingrid was going to tell him about it, before she slipped back into herself and the moment was lost.

He pulled the necklace over his head and examined it closer in the flickering fluorescent light of the diner. The pendant was definitely covered in something, still tacky to the touch. It felt almost like the tar he had removed from prehistoric bones at the La Brea tar pits on one of his early field trips. Nick pulled out his iPhone, tapped the flashlight icon, and pointed the bright light directly at it. One part reflected a bright glimmer, and he scratched at it with his fingernail. No good, all he did was get his finger sticky, so he reached down to his belt, grabbed his multi-tool utility knife, flipped out the fish scaler, and scratched gently with that. A little flake came off, and then another. Holding it up to the iPhone's light, it reflected even more brightly. His pulse quickening, he grabbed his things, threw a twenty-dollar bill on the table for a ten-dollar meal, and ran out to the back of his truck. Fumbling with the key to unlock the cap on the back, he got it open and reached in to grab his metal detector.

Won't work here with a metal bed, he realized, and then unlocked the door to the cabin. He tried scanning the necklace on the front seat and laughed at himself because there were metal springs in the seats.

No good, this is just like when Alexander Graham Bell tried to find the assassin's bullet in President Garfield but couldn't because he was lying on a bed with metal coils. Great idea, bad execution, he thought.

Nick grabbed the necklace, took a deep breath, carefully placed it on the asphalt parking surface, and scanned it again with the metal detector. The shrill beeping made the heads in the diner window turn and look out at him. "Well I'll be damned," he said. He put on the necklace and tucked it back under his shirt, hopped in the pickup truck, and invigorated with the discovery that had been right in front of him this whole time, quickly got back on the interstate. Time to make some time.

CHAPTER 9 – MAY 5, 1521

The Coahuiltecan at first had confused Asupacaci. Here they lived in a vast land, yet they seemed to have no structure as a people. They survived in little bands, had no permanent dwellings of any kind, and moved frequently since the land provided so little, even less than that of the Chichimeca. In a harsh environment and with little organization, they couldn't survive if they stayed in any one place too long. The Coahuiltecan didn't seem to pose a threat, as their small bands didn't have enough warriors to challenge the caravan, not unless they united among themselves, which seemed unlikely. But that was also the challenge, as there was no central leader Asupacaci could meet with, no one powerful figure to negotiate with. The column had continued moving along much like a centipede does, with different parts moving forward, while others caught up and stopped, and then the process would start all over again. *Not very efficient,* he thought. *But we don't have real roads here, just worn trails.*

No longer able to live off the land, the Aztecs hesitantly dipped into their precious supplies of food. Anticipating this, Asupacaci had Cipactli decided who wasn't contributing enough to the progress of the group. This served multiple purposes, to save both on supplies and to appease the gods.

The sickest and injured were gathered, and under the light of the moon met one of two fates. Those that had done their duty were shown mercy and dispatched quickly, and with honor were offered to *Xipe Totec*, the god of life, death and rebirth. Those who had shirked their duty or were Spanish were bound and left behind for the Coahuiltecan to deal with as they saw fit. Small gifts were also placed around them, an offering to be allowed to proceed peacefully. And judging from the human remains placed strategically on the Aztecs' line of march, the shirkers wouldn't be meeting an honorable or merciful end.

Small bands of Coahuiltecan continuously spied on the column, and occasionally a few would approach to parlay or trade. The Chichimeca guides would translate, with Friar Rodrìguez listening in and learning, and eventually participating. Asupacaci even found himself picking up on some of the language and realized he had more of an aptitude for language than he'd known. It was evident that the Coahuiltecan were truly a poor and uneducated people, and the Aztecs were surprised at how little it took to appease them with what they considered insignificant trinkets.

Onward the expedition trekked through the high mesa, past dense thickets of what the Chichimeca guides called prickly pear cactus, the pads and fruit of which could be eaten, and were used to supplement their supplies.

In one particular wandering band they encountered, the chieftain seemed eager to communicate and trade with this strange caravan. He indicated a great river to their northeast, where the people lived a more settled life, the land more generous, with large beasts that wandered down from the north and provided a great bounty. He indicated they were even bigger than the horses, with horns on their heads and shaggy coats. Asupacaci and Cipactli asked about the great river, which direction it flowed, how fast was the current, and how deep. They had read each other's mind, with the thought that this may present an avenue for them to travel further and more efficiently, perhaps turning the wagons into rafts, as the Aztecs were expert at water travel and navigation. After all, the heart of their great homeland city, Tenochtitlán, was in fact an island. But it became evident that the current flowed strongly the wrong way, back out to the great sea that the Spanish controlled, and with the weight they were carrying it was deemed impractical. Ironically it would be the Spanish who would eventually give that river its name, the Rio Grande.

For another twenty-five risings of the sun they continued their journey until a pristine lake on the plateau was encountered, and Asupacaci called for two days of rest and refitting. The guard was kept up, and scouts were posted in a defensive perimeter, but the mood changed immediately. He had been driving them hard, and would have to do so again, but deep into their journey here was a place that seemed to be not *too* threatening, with a good unobstructed view in all directions. Long runners had come back saying that more of the same terrain and bands of scattered Coahuiltecan lay ahead, and thus it presented a good opportunity for the expedition to regroup.

The power of the little army was still strong, although Cipactli informed him they were now down to twenty-five Eagle and Jaguar Knights, eighty-six warriors, and the remaining servants, slaves and Spaniards. Having been forced to use some of their supplies and not live exclusively off the land, Asupacaci ordered that the wagon loads be redistributed, so that each team of horses was pulling less weight. Two of the weakest horses were killed to use as a feast and restore the food supply, and the wagon they had hauled was stripped down for spare parts and stored in the others. Asupacaci even ordered that the *octli* be broken out, that milk colored, sour tasting alcohol much beloved by his people.

In the midst of the celebration, Hummingbird, the leader of the scouts, came back excitedly and prostrated himself in front of Asupacaci and Cipactli. "Tlanahuatihqui, we have spotted horses in the distance milling about, but no Spaniards. The horses are naked and unadorned. They seem almost wild."

Asupacaci nodded, dismissed him, and said, "They must be survivors of the shipwrecks we have been told about. The land suits them, and they flourish. Let us give our warriors a good diversion and use this to honor *Tzitzimitl*." This Aztec deity was associated with the stars, and if at the end of a 52-year calendar the Aztecs could not start a bow fire in the empty chest cavity of a sacrificed human, then the fifth sun would end and Tzitzimitl would devour the last of men.

The warriors were broken up into separate teams and given until sundown to see who could kill or capture a wild horse. One by one the teams had returned as the sun set in the distance, empty handed and looking downcast. Then faint singing was heard, and with much fanfare the last team came into camp, lugging both a dead horse and a live, young one. The knight known as Angry Bumblebee had killed a mare with a skilled arrow shot as he crept downwind of the animal, hit it directly through the neck, and then hobbled its colt with a toss of a lasso made of three bound strips of raw hide with stones at the ends. The mare was added to the larder, the white colt presented as a gift to Asupacaci, and a Spaniard ritually offered to Tzitzimitl.

The next day they were all up early to resume the journey before sunrise, well before the heat of the day started to grow too much in strength. Some were still a little groggy from too much octli or a belly full of meat for the first time in weeks, but the steady pace of the march soon sweat it out of them.

For fifteen more risings of the sun they made good progress, finally reaching a place the local Coahuiltecan called *Chihuahua*, meaning dry place. Very purposely they didn't dwell in this area, and Asupacaci and Cipactli decided to press the expedition on even harder, having been told by those they traded with that beyond this lay a much more hospitable land, with good grazing for the horses and a bounty with which to replenish their supplies.

As he gazed about the desolate landscape around him, for the first time Asupacaci realized that they were facing the possibility of a catastrophic ending. Not that he hadn't believed this could happen, in fact he always thought there was a very good chance it ultimately would, he just never envisioned it being this early in the expedition. And he certainly wasn't ever going to let that gut feeling of intuition show to anyone, not even to Cipactli. Utter determination was the only thing he would ever show anyone. He purposely maintained his outer royal countenance, and wanted with every fiber of his being to put as much possible distance between them and any possible Spanish pursuers, or even future conquistador explorers.

The guides were sent out far ahead to pick the best trails, the scouts formed up in a protective cordon around the caravan, and the pace was increased, which made for more suffering of all those involved. But it was either short term duress with the hope of reaching a more fertile land, or a slower pace with longer suffering and possible failure of the entire quest. Asupacaci had started paying increased attention to his surroundings, with an eye toward deciding where and when to unload the wagons, and how best to secretly hide what they contained. Already he had seen *cenotes*, those deep subterranean water pools often barely visible from ground level. But not everything he transported would last under water, and he looked for other options, especially deep gorges, ravines, and caves.

He noticed some strange dwellings recently, dug directly into the sides of cliffs with formidable outer walls and accessible only by ladders. The stone surfaces around these had interesting symbols and designs on them, but their meaning was lost. Now abandoned, they were once easily defendable but not quite what he was searching for. There was no lack of deep gullies and ravines, and the farther north he went the more he saw ever larger canyons. If he could find a large enough one, far enough out of the way but still accessible to his caravan, perhaps that would meet his ultimate needs. It all depended on where the fates took him. Resigned that whatever was to happen would happen, he put his faith and his life in the hands of his gods and would simply react opportunistically to circumstances as they unfolded.

Twenty more risings of the sun were spent moving along at the quicker pace, which was wise given the sparseness of the terrain they encountered. They had been well informed and found that they exited the dry lands as quickly as they had entered. They stopped in a valley to let the horses graze and regain their strength for the next push forward. This place was called *Huápoca* by the regional tribes, and the Chichimeca guides had found a common dialect with one of them.

Asupacaci's Trek North

As the caravan rested, Asupacaci was taken to a local spring with bubbling hot waters, which was believed to offer healing properties to those who bathed in it. Given the arduous journey they had suffered through, Asupacaci and several others soaked in the springs, and found themselves cleansed and reinvigorated by the experience. They were also shown more of the cliff dwellings, expertly hidden and barely visible to the naked eye. Long abandoned, the extensive complexes gave Asupacaci a strange sense of foreboding of the fate of his own people. Climbing up ladders which could be easily withdrawn, Cipactli was amazed at how well these ingenious places could be defended, and yet they sat empty, desolate. In some of the crevices of rock within the small rooms, they were proudly shown several perfectly preserved mummies, the heat and dry air having stopped the decay.

Asupacaci took note, there were things he also wished to preserve for the coming ages.

Walking back into camp, they heard a commotion and saw many of the warriors had formed into a loose circle, yelling and cheering. Breaking through them, Asupacaci and Cipactli stood with open mouths, for there was Bumblebee upon a horse, at first moving slowly within the circle, and then breaking into a slight trot. He didn't ride with the practiced skill of a Spaniard, but he was learning, and obviously had been querying one forcefully for instruction.

Asupacaci noticed a Spaniard who had been brought to the edge of the circle, his face beaten, doing his best to provide insight to a powerful warrior to ride a horse he couldn't see, but only envision in his mind's eye. Upon closer inspection he realized it was El Capitán, the leader of all the captured Spaniards, a Conquistador who had been an excellent rider and much feared enemy.

"Greetings, Tlanahuatihqui," Bumblebee said upon seeing Asupacaci and Cipactli enter the ring. "There is no magic in these creatures, only strength and grace. They can be ridden by any man with patience and practice, Spanish or Aztec. I think the tribes around here will figure out how to tame the wild ones and will be ready if the Spanish *Coyoltlahtolli* ever come this way."

Asupacaci saw for a fleeting moment the grandeur of his empire, of the Aztec people, of the beautiful island city of Tenochtitlán with the Hueteocalli temple at its heart, all in the bronzed, heavily muscled figure of Bumblebee proudly and defiantly atop the horse. With everyone gathered about, Asupacaci, son of Montezuma, far from home and in a strange land, spread his arms out and said, "Behold, and witness Aztec mastery over the beast that serves our enemies."

Pausing for effect, he looked around and made eye contact with many, then continued. "Look around you brave warriors. What other people could possibly undertake such a journey, to travel so far and so hard to the other world, to save the best of our empire for all of eternity? No other people I tell you, not from here or from any distant place across the great sea. And certainly not from Spain!"

With that he spat loudly, and then nodded to the priests who held El Capitán. They led him to a nearby large stone, forced him on his back upon it, and each pulled an arm or leg downward to thrust his chest up. Asupacaci slowly walked over, tore open the rags of his shirt, and held an exquisite jeweled dagger of obsidian aloft for all to see.

"The gods have blessed our journey so far and they require blood in return. Not just any blood, but that of one who led many against us. Huitzilopochtli, accept this offering for your continued blessings."

El Capitán knew what was coming. He had witnessed it when he still had his eyesight and yelled that he had helped them get this far, that he could help them still. He fought with all his might, screaming out to his god for mercy, but he who had given none would receive none. The razor-sharp dagger was brought down heavily and landed with a thud, so hard that air was forced out of his lungs and he gasped. Asupacaci then expertly dragged it further, creating a larger opening, until he could reach in between the ribs and feel the pulsating heart. Pausing a moment to enjoy the agony of his sworn enemy, he placed his hand completely around it, clamped tightly on it, and pulled it out of the cavity, while simultaneously cutting it completely loose with his other hand.

Breathing deeply with excitement and blood lust, he smelled the cloying, coppery liquid of life running down his arm. Quickly stepping up, with one foot on the rock and the other on the collapsed chest of El Capitán, he looked intensely at his warriors and held the still beating heart aloft and shouted, "Behold, Aztec mastery over our enemies!"

CHAPTER 10 – MAY 31, PRESENT DAY

Nick awoke in the back of his pickup truck on a trusty air mattress he had tossed in, reasonably comfortable in his sleeping bag and a couple of pillows. The old cap on the back of the pickup gave him a little privacy, but the sun was coming up and starting to reflect off the aluminum inside into his eyes. He fiddled with the c-clamps he had scrounged to hold the cap in place, habitually double checking all of them to ensure he wouldn't see his cap sliding down the interstate after him. It had almost happened once before, but one of his friends who had been riding in back saved the day by pulling down on the window openings and banging against the cab with one foot until Nick pulled over. That was a close one but he still had the cap, even though he had lost touch with the friend over the years.

He sat up and had to think for a moment to recalibrate and, shaking off the cobwebs in his mind, realized he was in an abandoned parking lot near Fort Leavenworth. Driving hard and enthused, he had made good time and arrived there around 11 p.m. last night. It had taken a little while for the adrenaline to wear off after discovering that the piece on his necklace was actually made of gold. *Dad and Gram, you both have been holding out on me all these years, but I'm on to you now.*

He put on his glasses and held the necklace up, the sunlight glinting off where he had flaked off some of the black coating. Nick rummaged around and found his dig kit, and carefully pulled out a wrapped pack of all his go-to tools for any archeological site excavation. He put a headband on, flipped down the attached magnifier over his left eye, and grabbed what looked like a tiny jeweler's pick. With that he squinted through the magnifier and worked the rest of the sticky black substance off, which flaked off in small pieces that stuck to the pick. Once done he wiped it down with the bottom of a favorite t-shirt he was wearing, which his PhD mentor had given him and proudly proclaimed: *Archeology: Sift Happens.*

Nick crawled out of the back of the pickup, stood up and stretched to the heavens. Today was a good day to be alive. He was on to something, and there was nothing like the thrill of the hunt, of discovery, to get his blood up. And this one was personal.

Using the natural outside light, he examined the necklace piece closer through the magnifier, and saw it was indeed about the size and shape of an oversized zipper pull. It was solid gold, and had three small inlays, one above the other like tear drops, that he hadn't seen before, since they had been obscured by the sticky black coating. It appeared the inlays were made of what looked like emerald, obsidian, and jade, or maybe something else, but he could figure out all of that later. It was done with amazing craftsmanship, the detail and etching were intricate, almost feather-like. There were wear marks about a third of the way down, above the three inlays, and a small hook-like clasp at the top that the rope of the necklace ran through, which seemed to indicate it had been part of some larger piece.

Nick was about to take a photograph of the necklace on his iPhone to send to his brother, but an uneasy voice in the back of this head said, *don't do it, do nothing over the airwaves or internet, only communicate face to face*. That little voice had become progressively louder since his dad had passed and he had found various clues, none of which quite fit together.

The trained archeologist in him instinctively wanted to document any finding, so he grabbed his Canon Rebel digital camera—the good one he always brought along on digs and expeditions—and carefully put the gold link of the necklace down on a white index card, and photographed it from every angle, front and back. He also did close-ups of the coarse hemp like rope it hung on. Good to have copies digitally, just in case.

Seeing Fort Leavenworth again brought Nick's memory back to a more innocent time, back to seeing things through the eyes of a nine-year-old, back to having both parents and the cocoon of safety that came with it. It almost seemed he was seeing things through the lens of old home movies, and he enjoyed the temporary warmth of the nostalgia. Originally established in 1827, the fort was known as the post that opened up the west. It had proven instrumental in keeping peace between Indian tribes and the increasing number of intrusive settlers migrating westward via wagon train. Alexandre had passed through it about a year after the Civil War, and it served as a jumping off point for what would become a series of battles, pacifications and postings for him. Originally a part of the Michigan Brigade during the Civil War, his unit was affectionately known as the Wolverines, or more commonly as Custer's Cavalry, during the conflict.

When Alexandre headed west after the war, he was still a part of Custer's 7th Cavalry, but had been reassigned to fill out another depleted unit that needed experience troopers. "And a good thing too," Nick's dad had quipped. "Otherwise we would be visiting a cemetery up at Little Big Horn instead of having these great adventures in the Southwest." Queue the boys and Mom giggling and rolling their eyes at one another. Just one of those little twists of history that could have played out so differently, one where there was no necklace with a gold pendant, and perhaps his dad would be riding in the car with him instead of only occupying a place in his anguished memory.

Nick spent a couple hours taking photographs, exploring the fort, its cemetery, and the museum. Once he finally found Alexandre's name on a microfilm archive of the muster rolls, proof positive he had been through here, Nick snapped a last photo and started losing his interest, as it didn't seem there was anything else here relevant to his quest. He gassed up his pickup, grabbed a couple slices of pizza and an iced tea from the minimart and set out across the plains to the next stop on his traveling road show, to Quivira.

Back in the days of Nick's childhood, Quivira was one of many places that had caught his father's attention. They had all spent time there the same summer they went through Fort Leavenworth. It took Nick nearly four hours to drive to Lyons, Kansas, which was the nearest town to the supposed location of Quivira. He arrived in the late afternoon. Where to crash for the night, bed of the truck or bed in a hotel, was his big decision, but since he had just started his road trip, he opted for the truck. He used his smart phone to find a good local restaurant for dinner and thought some Tex-Mex at the El Portillo would put him in the right frame of mind. A fat burrito and a couple of Corona's later, he cruised the area to line up what he would do tomorrow, and to find a quite parking area to crash for the night. And crash he did, with the rain drumming on the aluminum roof of the truck cap lulling him into a deep slumber.

In Nick's sleep his mind wandered, uncluttered by conscience thought, until it focused on the kernel of something in his memory, something that had been nagging at him that he hadn't been able to quite pull to the surface. The memory sharpened, and all of a sudden he was five or six years old, sitting at the top of the stairs, peeking through the railings, listening to a whispered conversation between his dad and Grandma Ingrid. He crept lower, curious, since he rarely heard his boisterous Grandma whisper.

Grandpa Jacques had passed not too long ago, and she was telling his dad something important, something about a family legend passed down generation to generation. Alexandre, his distant relative, had befriended the Indians he was sent to fight. He had been given a gift by them, told of some type of hidden treasure, and given a hint on how to find it. Grandma Ingrid said that now her husband Jacques had passed, it was up to Albert to carry on the family quest. Just then lightning flashed close by, so bright Nick saw it through his dream and closed eyelids, and as the loud thunder boomed he sat straight up in a cold sweat. He reached for his voice recorder, carefully placed next to his glasses and watch, and spoke slowly and carefully into it before the memory faded. "So go and find the treasure Albert," she had said, "For Jacques' sake why don't you go and find it!"

Nick awoke early the next morning, a light rain still pinging on the aluminum cap and the sunrise obscured by fast moving, dark gray clouds. He instinctively touched the necklace he wore and tried to focus on a dream he had in the middle of the night, something he knew was very important, but it had faded. The dream he woke up to, about a small island covered in grasshoppers who flew in a swarm, morphed into the actual sound of the rain on the cap, and he couldn't get that one out of his mind.

He reached for his watch to see the time and found the voice recorder on top of it, and vaguely remembered dictating something during the night. He played it back, and heard his sleepy voice recounting the dream over the noise of the storm. The steady rain and thunder made it hard to hear, but the message was unmistakable, and the dream came back and clearly replayed in his mind.

Now that's the way to wake up, Nick thought, smiling to himself. He may have been missing one of his dad's journals, perhaps the key one, but he was methodically filling in the blanks. Like a deep lingering itch you couldn't quite scratch that finally went away, his mind found release in now knowing the memory he had so feverishly sought.

Nick grabbed a yogurt, some granola and an iced coffee out of his cooler, ate a quick breakfast, and drove over to the proudly titled, but somewhat underwhelming, Coronado Quivira Museum. *So typical,* he thought. *The oppressor who nearly wipes out the indigenous population now gets top billing.* If he felt a little bitter, it was largely a result of his education and chosen tradecraft. The more he learned and experienced over time, the more starkly evident it was that explorers the world over colonized in the name of God and King, and then proceeded to appropriate and exploit the natural resources, while raping, slaughtering, and enslaving the inhabitants. The old joke that rang so true was, "It was never good to be the natives when the colonizers came calling."

Nick paid the museum entry fee and got reacquainted with the history and relevance of Quivira. In 1540 Francisco Vásquez de

Coronado had set out from Mexico to find the fabled Seven Cities of Gold, also known as Cibola. Coronado was simply following what had been told to him by the survivors of an earlier ill-fated expedition led by Pánfilo de Narváez. Narváez had originally been sent by the Governor of Cuba to stop the invasion of Mexico by Hernán Cortés, who had overstepped his authority. Although he greatly outnumbered Cortés, Narváez not only lost an eye, he lost the battle, was taken prisoner, and held captive for several years.

Upon his release he returned to Spain, where Charles V authorized him to explore and colonize Florida, so named because it meant Flowering Easter, the Spanish name for Palm Sunday and the date of its discovery. They set out in 1527 with over 600 men in five ships, hopeful to find a civilization similar to what Cortés had discovered in Mexico. Florida proved to be anything but hospitable to Narváez, whose ships were damaged in a storm, and then landed near present day Tampa Bay with the remnants of his expedition. Unable to make headway and harassed by the natives, the survivors, including Narváez, built rafts and tried to navigate along the coast back to the Spanish province of Pánuco, so named from the river that ran through it. Narváez was carried out to sea, never to be seen again, and only four men made it out alive to tell the tale.

In one of the greatest documented feats of discovery, human endurance, and survival, Álvar Núñez Cabeza de Vaca and three of his fellows, over the course of nine years, traveled completely around the Gulf of Mexico, overshot their goal all the way to the Pacific Ocean, turned south again where they eventually met Spanish slave traders, and finally reached Mexico City in 1536. Stories were told by Cabeza de Vaca and the other survivors of the tribes and villages they had encountered, of rumors they had heard about even wealthier tribes and fabulous cities. These had excited the Spaniards, and soon more expeditions set out. Coronado's wasn't the first, but it built up the work of the others and the rumors that came back, which grew ever more fantastic with the retelling.

Coronado first worked his way to the Zuni Pueblos in western New Mexico. Not finding the riches they sought at the pueblos, Coronado's men viciously subdued those they encountered, and were told by an Indian called "the Turk" of a fabulous place where "trees hung with golden bells and people whose pots and pans were beaten gold." The Turk led them far afield, and when they found no treasure, they killed him and returned from whence they started. The furthest point the Spaniards reached was in Kansas, at a place Coronado named Quivira.

Nick wandered through the exhibits, taking photos of things that either interested him on a professional level, or might prove useful to his unraveling the family quest. There were reproductions of native lodgings, ancient Indian artifacts, a Spanish helmet and pieces of armor, and signs that pointed where one could pick up parts of the wagon rutted Santa Fe trail. He wandered outside and pondered the significance of Quivira, in and of itself and as it related to his dad's obsessive search.

While Alexandre had said he been through Quivira, where exactly it was located was open to debate. The Indians Coronado met there were described as living in thatched huts, which likely meant they were Wichita, and they hunted bison and moved with the herds from place to place. Regardless of where it was located, Coronado was disappointed in his quest for treasure, as all he found were iron pyrites and a few pieces of copper.

Nick deduced that Coronado had been duped, with the Indians he encountered always telling him that what he sought was just over the horizon, and they willingly provided guides to lead the Spaniards safely away from their own territories to that of their enemies, or to some desolate location from which they hopefully wouldn't return. Coronado glossed over his disappointment in his letters to the king, and even though the Spanish quest to find Cibola had failed utterly, it never quite died out.

On his drive out of Lyons, Nick pulled over at a historical marker that summarized Coronado's ill-fated expedition, which seemed to give too much credit to the Spaniards for essentially accomplishing nothing but wreaking havoc on the indigenous population. A bit down the road there was one last stop, at a marker to one Father Juan de Padilla.

Father Juan was a missionary who had accompanied Coronado

on his wanderings to Kansas and returned to save the souls of those who the Spaniards hadn't killed outright or through the eventual spread of disease. In an ironic twist of fate, he was killed by those he came to convert, yet was hailed as one of the first Christian martyrs of the New World.

Snapping another quick photo Nick was amazed at the gold lust that drove the Spaniards. Reflecting he had to laugh at himself for the irony that here he was, following in their footsteps, seeking the same thing.

But no, not the same thing, he thought. *They came to take; I come to answer questions. They enriched themselves to the detriment of others. I come to solve a mystery, and if I'm lucky, to share new knowledge with the world. And damn it, every legend in every civilization, no matter how far-fetched, always has at least a kernel of truth buried within it.*

CHAPTER 11 – JULY 2, 1521

Huápoca was on the edge of yet another tribe's territory, one the guides were told were much more aggressive and resistant. To the north, which was directly along their intended line of travel, was the land of the Chiricahua Apache. They had proceeded thus far without having been forced into any significant battle, but the indications were that one may now be in the offing. The foul breath of the Spanish gods and their disease hadn't blown this far to depopulate the area—at least not yet. There would be no free passage here.

Cipactli had instructed Bumblebee to ride a horse at the head of the column, dressed in full battle regalia. If the Apache were going to pick a fight, he wanted them to see a true Aztec warrior riding this strange beast into their midst, not walking along beside it. Eagle and Jaguar knights then deployed behind him, followed by warriors dispensed throughout and alongside the column. A screen was still deployed around the outer edges, in an effort to prevent their being attacked with no trip line for a warning. The day preceded uneventfully, the Apache never seen, and an uneasy calm settled over the column. Perhaps they would be like the Chichimeca and the Coahuiltecan and be appeased with gifts and offers of friendship.

Evening brought a halt to the day's progress, and a bivouac was made. The scouts were posted for the night and kept on high alert, just in case. Well before dawn the camp was awake, eating a light meal and preparing for the day's march. New scouts rotated to replace those who were out for the night, when word came back that not all was well.

Hummingbird reported directly to Asupacaci and asked him to accompany him out away from the camp. When they were well out of hearing distance he leaned in and said, "Tlanahuatihqui, we lost two scouts last night. At first we didn't know what had happened to them, and then we found this."

Cipactli was already standing there, looking down on the disfigured bodies of the two dead Aztec scouts. They were bound hand and foot, and their hair and the skin that attached it to their heads had been shorn cleanly off. They were left directly on the trail ahead, in sitting positions, facing the direction of the Aztec camp. Arrows riddled both their bodies.

Cipactli nodded to Asupacaci, adding, "It appears they made a *tlamanalli* of them," meaning an offering. "And it is odd, their hair is nowhere to be found, perhaps they view it as the taking of their souls, much like we take hearts. Or perhaps they view it as a trophy of some kind."

Asupacaci looked closer, he recognized one but couldn't place the other, not with the blood that had run down and obscured his face. "They were placed here on purpose, this is a warning to us. But we will have no secrets from our people, keep them both in place. When we march by, everyone will see them, and realize that they must always be on guard. We have met an enemy more like us than the Spanish, but an enemy nonetheless."

The order to start was given. The caravan began its centipede-like movement forward, and eventually came upon the two bodies. The pace slowed slightly as everyone trudged by, directly observing the ingenious methods of their new enemies. There wasn't a reaction of fear, but rather a communal girding for battle on the part of the warriors. Fear had been of the unknown, but now they at least had a sense of what they were up against, and an enemy that shot arrows was one they were happy to take their chances with. The outer ring of scouts and long runners reported back increased sightings and glimpses of the Apache, but they were merely being harassed, not attacked.

For three more settings of the sun they continued in this manner, the pace kept as brisk as possible. The inevitable consequence was that more of those with marginal endurance saw their strength ebb until they could go on no further. In keeping with the firmly established protocol, those who had served well were ritualistically and quickly dispatched with honor, and those who didn't were left to a lingering fate, tied to a cactus with their tongues cut out, without even gifts around them as an offering to the Apache. Everyone knew what that implied, that when they were discovered still alive, they were likely to meet a lingering end.

On the following day, the trail through the valley narrowed, still wide enough for the horses dutifully pulling the wagons, but it necessitated the scouts and long runners to pull in closer to the column. The screen around the edges became more constricted, the buffer between the Apache and the column ever closer.

Asupacaci called a quick council to decide on the best course of action, and it was decided to send out a strong scouting party to determine what trail presented the best route with the least possibility of ambush. Hummingbird picked only the best among his scouts and long runners, along with a dozen warriors. Bumblebee was the first chosen, but they decided to leave his horse with the column, not wanting to lose the element of stealth. Also accompanying them were the two Coahuiltecan guides that had joined the expedition shortly after the Aztecs first entered their territory. Their knowledge of the terrain and the regional language might be useful. Late at night, when the clouds drifted over the moon and made detection less likely, the party set out.

As had been agreed upon, the column set out early the next morning, working their way toward a place called *Paquimé*. The plan was for the scouting party to do a reconnaissance in force and meet back up with the column already in motion, with the intention of keeping the initiative and not simply react to the forays of the Apache. By late morning the trail started narrowing further, with the walls of the surrounding hills steadily encroaching, forcing the outer screen of scouts to draw ever closer to the column. Eventually they were skirting the heights above, within eyesight of Asupacaci, not offering much of a buffer to any potential threat. But by now it was too late to change the plan, turning back would only invite chaos and certain disaster.

Suddenly shouts and war *whoops* were heard ahead, and Cipactli quickly summoned some of the warriors on the edges of the caravan to form in front to face the threat. He purposely didn't bring them all, anticipating that what was happening in front might be merely a diversion, and didn't want to leave the flanks of the caravan exposed. He called for the scouts on the hills above on both sides to prepare for an attack and took his place at the head of the column, next to Asupacaci. Soon they could see figures in front of them through a cloud of dust, kicked up by the wind that funneled through the valley. At first they couldn't tell if it was friend or foe, but as the wind died slightly they saw it was the scouting party, with their backs to them, fighting off the Apaches farther away.

Asupacaci motioned forward, and the warriors let out a shout in unison and sprinted to reinforce their exhausted comrades. Stopping in back of them, they let loose with a volley of spears with their *atlatls*, a wooden shaft that gave them extra leverage and greatly increased the effective distance. Scattered screams could be heard in the distance, and the surprise and accuracy of the massed volley broke the momentum of the attack, and the Apaches retreated to the hills in the distance.

As the column worked its way up to the front line of the conflict, Asupacaci sought out Hummingbird, who had led the scouting party out the prior evening. He noticed that their numbers were much reduced, as they had obviously met bitter resistance.

Bumblebee heard him and prostrated himself at Asupacaci's feet. "In the hills further ahead we were ambushed Lord, they must have seen us coming the entire way despite our stealth. They had surrounded us but we finally broke out and fought our way back to here. Hummingbird fell, along with many others, fighting gallantly." Even as he spoke, a few war whoops could be heard in the surrounding hills, slowly spreading in a widening arc around them.

Asupacaci tapped him lightly on the shoulder and Bumblebee rose, bleeding from several wounds and obviously exhausted.

Looking around, Asupacaci asked, "Where are the Coahuiltecan guides who went out with you last night? Did you see them fall?"

Bumblebee looked directly at him, replying, "It all happened so fast, there was so much confusion, I can't say for sure. They were with us when we first ran into the ambush. After that, I know not."

Asupacaci felt a hollowness and churning in his gut and wondered of a possible betrayal leading them all into a trap. The cacophony of shouts and whoops from the hills increased, echoing all around them, until it became obvious that they were now completely surrounded, by a formidable foe whose numbers were only increasing.

The sun had risen to its zenith, beating down mercilessly, creating heat ripples that distorted views in the distance. Even the slight breeze radiated an unnatural heat, like the breath of a coiled jaguar before the killing blow. A sporadic harassing fire of arrows fell among them, an occasional one finding its mark. The Apache, natives to this land and hostile environment, appeared to be content with letting nature do the heavy lifting for them, sapping the strength of the entire expedition. Advancing slowly and deliberately, the Aztecs came to an even narrower part of the trail and found that boulders had been pried loose and rolled down the hills, creating an impassable barrier.

Asupacaci held a quick council with Cipactli, and it was decided to prepare what defenses they could and await the inevitable onslaught. Bumblebee spoke for all the warriors when he said, "It is better to die standing in battle, than to waste away and lose their hair lying down."

Looking at all gathered, Asupacaci gave them a proud look of satisfaction, and defiantly raised his sacrificial dagger in one hand and an obsidian studded war club in the other. No quarter would be offered, and none would be accepted. *It would be prophetic,* he thought. *For a people who believed the gods required blood, to give all of their own as the final offering.*

As the day wore on with no immediate battle, Asupacaci sat in the shade of a wagon and summoned to have Friar Rodrìguez brought over to him. The Friar appeared and seemed to be holding up reasonably well, no doubt because of the special status he enjoyed as an increasing confidant to the Aztec leader, but also perhaps due to his strong faith. Faith which his remaining fellow hallow-eyed Spaniards had lost the deeper the journey progressed.

"*Tetotopixqui*, so did we fatten you up a little with our endless wanderings?" Asupacaci inquired, calling him the Aztec name for a holy man or priest as a joke.

"Yes, I feel like the prodigal son who, when he returned, feasted on a fatted calf at a celebration his father threw," Friar Rodrìguez replied.

Asupacaci patted the ground indicating he should sit and noticed that the silver cross he had given him was now tied around his neck, tucked under his coarse tunic. "This land is vast, even bigger than I had ever envisioned, and as a member of the house of Montezuma I saw much of the empire. You say you came across the great sea from a land as large, it almost makes one feel, how do you say, insignificant."

The Friar paused for a moment, and then said, "I felt that also, in sailing across the great sea, not knowing if we would ever see land again, and prayed for deliverance. But our gods work in mysterious ways do they not? For here we both sit in the shade, brought together in a land strange to both of us."

Asupacaci smiled. "And a land we may never leave. If it all is to end here, I have a last question, to better understand your world."

Friar Rodrìguez bowed his head. "At your service."

"I had been wondering Tetotopixqui about your *requiremento*, which your people say gives them the right to take any lands and enslave or kill the people. You read it in a language nobody understands, often with nobody of the land even present. This makes your quest legitimate and holy?" Asupacaci inquired.

Friar Rodrìguez tried to choose his words carefully, to defend the actions of his king and country, but found that, like his spiritual superior Bartolomé de las Casas, he could not in good conscience. "Alas, I cannot justify all of it. Even Las Casas tells us all humankind is one. While I disagree with your acts of human sacrifice, I find that I don't disagree with you choosing what you want to believe. I think my people would say I'm going native, and I suspect I would be burned at the stake for it."

Asupacaci grunted to himself, he had won a small victory here. He'd had a meeting of the minds with a man from an alien place, in a vast, dry land his people had never been, on his way to an unknown destination at the end of all their endurance.

"Well, how do you preserve the soul of your people, your collective knowledge, your history, for generations unborn?" Asupacaci inquired.

"We hand it to the next generation by the telling of it, by the singing of it, by the living of it, and by capturing the words in books so that those more eloquent and educated can make their voices heard forever," the Friar replied.

Asupacaci looked toward his unseeing eyes, fighting back the tears which started trickling down his dusty face. "Ah, but that is the problem my people face. You Spaniards and your greed, your stealing, and your disease may not leave us a next generation to hand it down to. And then what are we, who will know of us, who will keep us and our ancestors and traditions alive in their memories?"

Friar Rodrìguez was about to say something but stopped, for once no appropriate words coming to him. Asupacaci closed his eyes, it seemed the world was collapsing in on itself as the prophesies had foretold, that the Age of the Fifth Sun was about to end, and Tzitzimitl would descend and devour the last of all men.

In the momentary silence, the sound of a young horse whinnying could be heard. Asupacaci raised his head, the dark spell suddenly broken, a slight smile forming on his lips as he saw it was the colt that had been presented as a gift to him, prancing about at the end of its tether. This wild yearling was the offspring of horses that had survived a shipwreck all the way from the other world. He took it as a sign, that despite everything life continues, life always finds a way. He stood, shook off the momentary self-pity, weight of the task he was undertaking, and the battle he was in, regaining his regal composure. He realized that enough blood had to have been sacrificed to Tzitzimitl already. How could it not be with nearly all of his race dead? The realization that the world was not going to end, at least not yet and not on these terms, gave him renewed strength and determination.

He jumped up on the wagon, in full view of everyone, including the Apache, and raised his voice. "We will not fail, and that is why we are here, in this strange land, on this sacred task. What we have brought with us will outlast us all, will tell future generations the story of a people who left grasshopper hill to found a great city, and then a great empire, and in doing so changed the world, long before the world ever changed them!"

His men raised their weapons and shouted and chanted back at him.

"A great people mustn't simply fade away, erased from history forever by a strange invader and disease. We will shout across all of time that we were here, that we lived and breathed and prospered and raised great temples to our gods. We were Aztec!"

CHAPTER 12 – JUNE 2, PRESENT DAY

Nick spent the next few weeks carefully following the trail of his great-great-great-great grandfather, Alexandre, as told across the journals of his father Albert. While they had spent parts of several summer vacations in his youth visiting these places, now he was doing a condensed revisit of most of the sites his dad had systematically explored. And he was seeing it through the eyes of not only an adult, but as one educated in history and archeology, with a very personal mystery to unwind.

From Quivira he had journeyed to Fort Larned and then to Fort Wallace, both in Kansas, chronologically following where Alexandre had been posted. Fort Larned billed itself as the "Home to the Guardians of the Santa Fe Trail," and had a superbly preserved sandstone fort that Nick spent several hours exploring and photographing. He could find no records of Alexandre having been there, but that wasn't unusual in the tumult of troops coming and going during the Indian wars. Fort Wallace, named for a general who died at the battle of Shiloh, no longer existed, but it had a small museum Nick found interesting. Ever the archeologist, he also found time to visit nearby Monument Rocks, a stunning formation of chalk monoliths used as a landmark to the passing prairie schooners, rich in fossils and formed by the erosion of what had been an ancient seabed.

Alexandre's Postings

From there it was on to Beecher's Island in Colorado, where, according to one of the journals, Alexandre was recruited to be on a specially selected force of fifty troopers who had participated in a pitched battle against Cheyenne and Sioux warriors. They were only able to survive due to their Spencer repeating rifles, and a relief expedition eventually sent from Fort Wallace. Nick then went to Summit Springs, where Alexandre had his second blooding, again against the Cheyenne, but this was more of a massacre than a battle, with the Pawnee Scouts doing most of the killing. From copies of his letters home in the journal, it seemed something in Alexandre changed after this, that he didn't quite agree with Philip Sheridan's philosophy that "the only good Indian is a dead Indian." It was an unpopular stance to take given the times and his chosen profession, but it was evident that his moral compass was inexorably shifting.

Alexandre had then been posted to Fort Garland in the New Mexico Territory, which was eventually abandoned after the natives were forced onto scattered reservations. As Nick drove through, it was gearing up for the annual Jam Band Music Festival. And judging from the crowds around the recreational marijuana shops, it was going to attract a bit of a psychedelic crowd. One brightly colored t-shirt in particular caught his eye, and proudly proclaimed *Long Live the Dead*. While there were a couple of preserved buildings from the fort on the outskirts of town, there were no records he could dig into, so he motored over to a much more substantial and interesting site, Mesa Verde, located in the southwest corner of Colorado. This is where the journal cut off, having ended at Fort Wingate, and Nick was now going by memory in recreating the places he had been on those hot summer trips, so long ago. It wasn't hard to remember Mesa Verde, it being so indelible that he reflected his passion for archeology very well may have started there.

Its stunning pueblos were sheltered under the lips of imposing cliffs, and the main settlements and the surrounding scattered dwellings had influenced a large area until abandoned sometime in the late thirteenth century. It was speculated that drought and over-population had forced their abandonment and the inhabitant's migration south to locations in Arizona and New Mexico.

Dad had visited it several times over the years with the boys and Josie, as if something there was reaching out to him, somehow drawing him back. But one trip to the magnificent ruins seemed more significant than the others, more time had been spent there, Dad immersed in it more deeply. That was the trip detailed in the missing journal, its secrets now beyond Nick's reach and memory.

After driving up the plateau to 8,500 feet, he paid his entrance fee and arranged with the park rangers—who were happy to accommodate a professional archeologist—to camp out in a restricted area and see a sunset and sunrise in the astonishing vista it afforded.

Appropriately named, Nick thought as he surveyed the plateau and surrounding area. On the ride up he had seen a variety of vegetation, much of it sun-scorched and stunted. Here up on the flat top there was more virility and wildlife. The Spanish translation of Mesa Verde literally meant *green table.*

Sequestered that night in an out of the way place with an outstanding vantage point, he crawled out of his sleeping bag to look at the stars, reflecting this would have been a great place to have a dog for a companion. *You would have loved this Topaz,* he thought. He blew in his hands to warm them, and carefully screwed his camera onto a tripod, set the image to wide screen, cranked the aperture setting, and coded in a long exposure. Photos of the night-time sky, with no ambient light interfering and the pinpoints of the stars rotating as the earth revolved, never ceased to provoke a sense of awe in him, somehow making him feel very small in the universe. Tonight in this setting he wanted one for posterity.

Nick awoke early the next morning to the sweet and bitter scent of the creosote bushes, feeling refreshed and invigorated, relishing having had the chance to spend some unrushed time in such a transcendent place. "Food for the soul, exercise for the mind," as his dad would have said. The view of the iconic Cliff Palace and the Montezuma Valley to the north took his breath away. He spent the cooler early morning hours playing tourist, crawling up ladders and squeezing through small openings on both guided and unguided tours. As the heat rose and the tourists started multiplying, he decided it was time to hit the road. He had only one more stop before meeting Charlie, in what was Alexandre's last real posting, at Fort Wingate in New Mexico.

The drive was pleasant, unhurried, and when the Eagles happened to come on and play *Take It Easy*, he found himself belting out the lyrics along with them.

"Well I'm a-standin' on a corner in Winslow Arizona, such a fine sight to see,
it's a girl my lord in a flatbed Ford slowin' down to take a look at me."

He laughed at himself and continued singing as he spied a roadrunner skittering off in the distance. *Wile E. Coyote and an Acme anvil can't be far off,* he thought.

Nostalgia of the places he had been with his family, of a younger and more innocent time he missed, of the loss of his parents, and of the anticipation of seeing his brother, all conspired to make him start to feel a bit lonely, almost melancholy.

Yeah, one of these days I'm going to take someone special on a real road trip to this part of the beautiful earth. But first I have to find her, he mused.

He glanced out the window at a passing convertible with a beautiful young woman driving, her golden hair flowing in the breeze, her hand out the window, dipping with the wind.

"Any volunteers?" he asked as she zoomed past.

Route 66 took him right to Fort Wingate, which back in the day had played a role in the pacification of the Indians in the area, mainly Navajo. As later efforts against the Apache to the south increased, many found themselves incarcerated at the fort. Two notable figures from history who had been here included Douglas McArthur, who lived here as an infant, and Black Jack Pershing, who served as a lieutenant at the fort. "And Alexandre LaBounty," Nick added, "Though in what capacity I know not." What he did know was this area was a favorite haunt of his dad's, and the kids had been to the fort, and to the nearby Canyon De Chelly and Chaco Canyon, on multiple summer trips. Nick did his usual thorough checking out of the fort, but there wasn't much there to see, and he remembered his dad being much more interested in the nearby canyons.

His road supplies nearly exhausted, Nick decided to dine at the aptly named Badlands Grill, which was as good as billed, with good food cheap. As he ate, he flipped between the two journals in front of him, those that bookended the one that was missing. Nothing indicative of anything that seemed consequential in either of them, no meaningful threads he could pull on, no hints as to why the one journal was gone. He then opened Grandma Ingrid's well-worn family reunion booklet, and a small piece of paper fluttered out of the back of it, narrowly missing his almost finished meal.

It was the corner of an old envelope, with a stamp and faded postmark dated September 20, 1870, from Fort Wingate in New Mexico. His pulse quickening and intrigued as to where it could have come from, Nick thoroughly examined the entire booklet and found a small, thin pocket attached to the inside back cover, something that an old 5¼" computer floppy disc would have gone in. He had never noticed it inside his own booklet and guessed Grandma had put it in her copy to put random thoughts, ideas, and missing information into. Within the pocket were several notes with Grandma's distinctive cursive writing on them, notes to herself of various forgotten facts to weave into her booklet. There was also a well-worn, faded sheet of paper inside, which he unfolded carefully. Seeing its contents, he shoved his plate and silverware away, wiped down the table in front of him, and carefully laid it out. It was a letter addressed to Alexandre's Mother and Father, written by a very rough hand on the front and back:

Deerest Parents,

I writ you today from a vry hot and dry place called the Teritory of New Mexica. Finnly got promotd to Sargent, now in carge of a bunch of the men. I bin posted to Ft. Wingate these past 4 months, seems the werst of the heat is finly breakin. My helth is gud, cept I keep gittin the trots. Seems most do round here, spect it is the food and watter. Things ben setlin down at the fort but let me tell you board solders sur makin for dangerus solders. Like I wrot befor, I caint get over how badly we treet the injuns here. Most my unit ratter shoot em as look at em, supose sum of the batles we had makes the men bitter, but the injuns aint no more cruul den us hve ben to them.

I stoped anothur bad beeting the uther day, and hve tried keepin ur solders offin ther womn folk. Just taint right, tretin em like dogs we do, or wors. Well dis old medisin man sees wat I bin doin, n he culdnt do enuff for me. Gave me a litle necklace wit wat he sed was made frm the sun, was part of n old tresure of the Mixica, sumthing hid fur yeers frm the conqurors. Sed ifin I ever git back ere, to look fur the sign of the outsa nd a taleys nd eyeteden in the peeblo. Not sur whatin hell they all is, but he was dam spfic I undrstaand it. Sed many yeers from now, whn dar is peece twixt us all, hav gud peeple put the

Mixica soles in a saf place forevr. He was so pleedin to me wit teers in is gureen eyes I sed coursin I wud, or my kin folk ventully wud.

The letter went on about more mundane things, how little he could wash, the quality of the food, wishing his brother and sister well, when he hoped to get out of the cavalry and get home, but Nick's mind was already locked on that one key paragraph, re-reading into it, deciphering it. This letter was the little Rosetta Stone into his family history that had been handed down to his dad and probably was copied in the missing journal. It explained the whispered conversation between him and Grandma Ingrid, his obsession with an unknown mystery, made it tangible, and perhaps provided the solution to finish fulfilling his quest. It didn't all make sense, at least not yet, but as Churchill had said, "It was a riddle, wrapped in a mystery, inside an enigma, but perhaps there is a key." And he felt like he had at last finally found the elusive key.

Instinctively Nick looked around the restaurant to see if anyone was observing him and felt foolish when it became obvious no one gave him a second thought. Since his dad died, he had a case of paranoia. *Which can be a healthy thing if properly deployed,* Nick thought. An idea struck him, and he went out to the truck, grabbed his camera, and carefully laid the letter out on the front seat, adjusted his flash, and took a series of photos of both the front and the back, as well as of the stamp and postmark. He then cut off a small piece of a loose end of the rope of the necklace he wore. Nick grabbed the small digital card out of his camera, wrapped the cut piece of rope and some of the scrapings from the pendant in acid free paper, and put it in a pre-stamped envelope he had in his backpack. He addressed it and walked across the street to a mailbox he had spotted, and dropped it in.

Can't be too careful, not now that I finally have a real thread to pull on, Nick thought as his heart rate increased. *Let's see what some real professionals make of all this.*

PART II

THE GOD OF THE HUNT

Mixcoatl, the god of hunting
and lord of the chase,
was father of seven sons who were
the founders of the seven cities
speaking the Nahuatl language.

Human sacrifices were made
to him to ensure a successful
hunt of whatever was
being pursued.
Be it man or beast.

CHAPTER 13 – JUNE 18, PRESENT DAY

It had been a while since Nick had slept in a real bed, but more importantly had a real shower. Biting the bullet, he checked into an Econo Lodge outside of Albuquerque that was running a $39 special. *Clean sheets and hot water, life is good,* Nick thought as he stretched out in bed after taking an extra-long hot and steamy shower, washing off and sweating out the accumulated dirt and grime, and then falling asleep so quickly he wore only the necklace.

Nick awoke the next morning with a start, excited to see his brother, to be reunited with him, to download him on all he had so recently learned. While he wasn't necessarily looking forward to spreading his parent's ashes at Chaco Canyon in fulfilling his dad's final wishes, he did have a sense that it would provide some of the closure he had been so desperately seeking. Nick turned in his room key and grabbed a cup of coffee in the lobby and headed off into the traffic to the airport. He sat in the long-term parking lot, sipping on the tepid brew, looking over everything he had discovered on his road trip out.

His cell phone buzzed, and Charlie cheerfully greeted him. "The eagle has landed. I didn't check any luggage, so see you out front in ten." Nick pulled up among all the double-parked cars frantically picking up people. Charlie hopped in and leaned over and gave him a sincere bear hug. "Missed you little brother, so what mischief you been up to?" he inquired with a wide grin.

"Plenty, we'll catch up on the drive out to Chaco Canyon," Nick replied seriously as he dangled the necklace in front of him and then handed it over.

There were no hotels anywhere near the canyon, and the only way to stay close to there would be to sleep in the pickup or pitch a tent. The boys instead opted for the Rim Rock Lodge, which was about a 40 mile drive out. They still had over two hours to reach the hotel, and Nick brought Charlie up to speed on both his recent discoveries and the trip out.

"So there it was, in front of us all this time, hanging in Grandma Ingrid's window. The pendant was covered in something black and tacky, so none of us ever really noticed it, with the rope blending in perfectly with the dream catcher. I'm not sure what it was on it, but am guessing some type of tar, probably to keep it from catching the wrong person's eye. Just before I left, Gram was about to tell me the story of Dad's obsession, and then I lost her again before she could get it out. For a moment she had perfect clarity—you know, like she does sometimes, so very close, and yet so far. But hey, the pendant is undoubtedly gold, and from the clasp and the wear marks, I think it was a piece of something larger," Nick excitedly disclosed.

Charlie grabbed the magnifier Nick offered and squinted as he took in the fine detail of it. "Whoa, this is so intricate. I see what you mean about the wear marks. And what did you say it was inlaid with, emerald, jade, and obsidian? What is that, like amber? Maybe that means we have Aztec DNA in here, you know, like in Jurassic Park?" Charlie joked.

"Ha ha, spoken like a true actuary Chuckles, or at least a hedge fund manager. No, it's not amber, although they used that for ornamentation too. Its obsidian, a volcanic glass-like rock, which while decorative could also be used in weapons. Some used to call it Apache tears. Chip it just right, and you have the sixteenth century equivalent of a razor blade. Sharp as anything, but brittle against the steel the Spanish brought over with them," Nick said.

Charlie let out a little whistle, examining it closer. "Unbelievable. So intricate."

"I know, right? Before I forget, I had this wild dream that jogged my memory, and I finally remembered a conversation I overheard Gram and Dad have a few years after Grandpa Jacques died," Nick continued. "She was imploring him to take up the quest, that it was up to him to not let it die with Grandpa, to do it for his sake. And Dad obviously took it to heart, I think he was grooming us to follow in his footsteps if he didn't solve it, but he never got the chance to pass it on. Not only is that why we spent our summers chasing the footsteps of a dead relative, it is why he was so meticulous in recording it in his journals. And I think it is no coincidence that the most important journal is the one that came up missing. But you won't believe what I just found!"

Nick now had Charlie's full attention, and he was expectantly waiting for Nick to finish the thought and tell him more. Instead Nick reached down into a cubby hole in the pickup, grabbed the old letter from September 20, 1870, and gently put it on Charlie's lap. They drove on in silence, Nick giving Charlie time to read and reread the letter and discern the significance of what it implied and disclosed.

"Wow, that's unbelievable bro. That's what we were doing, every summer, following Alexandre's wanderings, eliminating the dead ends, looking for the clue that he had been given with the necklace. Dad was working his way through it, with us in tow, getting ever closer to it. But why the hell didn't you call me when you found all this out?"

Nick turned and held him with an intense gaze for a moment. "Do you remember when he stopped taking us along, and started going by himself? I know I thought it was just the timing of things, with you well out of the house by then, and I had just started college. But the more I think about this, I think he was getting close to something, something dangerous, or maybe something desirable to others, which could be the same thing. I tell you I think he was killed back home, that somebody grabbed his journal, and we have some competition in finding the sign Alexandre tells of in that letter you are holding. I suspect that if we find what Dad was looking for, we find his killer too."

They drove on in silence, each lost in their own thoughts, the mood having completely changed, with the initial joy of seeing each other having turned to anger as the reality of events settled upon them, now slowly turning into a steely resolve.

"Remember what Sherlock Holmes told Watson," Nick finally said, "When you have eliminated all which is impossible, then whatever remains, however improbable, must be the truth."

More silence followed, until at last Charlie reached over and gave Nick an affectionate punch in the arm. "Well, at least we know why Dad wanted their ashes scattered in Chaco Canyon. That's as far as his search ever got."

The brothers reached their hotel in Farmington later in the afternoon, checked in, and asked where the best local places to eat were. It had always been a family quest to never eat chain food, and always find the kind of places off the beaten path the tourists never went but the locals called home. Experience taught that there was never any better barometer for the quality of the food or the fun factor of the entertainment. Charlie wasn't up for Mexican, never was, and Nick joked that his constitution was too delicate, damn that city living. Off to the Spare Rib BBQ Company they went, and it was even better than they both expected. After a great meal of gorging on ribs, beans, coleslaw and corn bread, and having downed a couple cold frosty ones, the brothers were in rare form. Having been through so much lately, they were enjoying blowing off a little steam.

Nick eyed a bottle of his Dad's favorite bourbon whiskey, Blanton's, on the back-bar shelf, and Charlie caught the look in his eye and said, "Oh no, here we go."

Shot glasses in hand, Nick toasted, "To Al and Josie, who both left us far too soon, but gave us so very much, and truly showed us how to love and live. You will be forever missed." As Nick raised the shot glass to the heavens, he caught a glimpse of a dark haired, dark eyed beauty across the room, who briefly returned his gaze and raised her own shot glass back at him. With a brief clink of glasses, Nick and Charlie toasted a heartfelt Santé, and downed their shots.

Suddenly the lights dimmed and with a blast of sound so loud you could feel it in your gut, a band in the far corner started playing through the smoke of a fog machine, their light show suddenly illuminating the bar. It was a bluesy cover of *Hold On, I'm Coming*, and conversation became almost impossible.

Nick yelled to Charlie, "I feel like I'm listening to blues at Kingston Mines back in Chicago. Dad would have loved this!" Which of course led to a few more beers and another shot or two. The band caught the vibe of the crowd, and slowly worked them up until everyone was belting out the words to songs they all knew, ending their set with a rousing rendition of *Soul Man*.

The brothers made room at the bar for a couple of the band members who came by looking thirsty, bought them a drink, and started chatting with them earnestly about blues in general and their band in specific.

The musicians were all Native Americans, and the leader introduced himself as *Bidzii.* His buddy joked that it was Navajo for "Strong One, so don't take it too seriously." Bidzii, a genuinely carved specimen who was aptly named, playfully pushed him away, and explained they really played for the joy of it, and banged around the edges of various reservations, enjoying a strong regional following. The next thing he knew, Nick found himself trotting out to his pickup and grabbing his old Fender guitar for a little impromptu jamming. Enjoying himself immensely playing in the background for the second set, Nick found Bidzii giving him a nod at the midpoint of *Dear Mr. Fantasy*, and Nick seamlessly took over the guitar lead and joined in the vocals. Now the crowd was not only singing along but dancing too and erupted into a loud ovation right before the song ended.

"Name your song white boy," Bidzii told him.

Nick replied, "*Sweet Home, Chicago,*" his choice immediately getting the whole band smiling, as it was the quintessential blues song to feature each doing his own improvised solo. Nick rocked out on lead guitar and vocals, completely lost in the music, his troubles fading for the moment. As they finished the set with *Spirits in The Night,* Nick smiled out at Charlie, who was dancing by himself with a beer bottle in each hand, obviously caught up in the communal mood of hedonism at the Spare Rib BBQ Company, outside of Chaco Canyon, on a crystal-clear Friday night.

Nick carefully drove back to the hotel, having stopped drinking as he played the second and third sets with his new friends in the band. Charlie sat with happily glazed eyes on the ride, humming one of the tunes and playing drums on the dashboard. *He obviously didn't get to unplug very often,* Nick thought, realizing Charlie was fighting his own demons with this whole situation too.

"Hey numb nuts, tomorrow is the summer solstice, the longest day of the year, and I'm getting up early to photograph it. Should be pretty cool out here to see in the desert, think you want to join me?" Nick asked.

"Yeah, sure, wake me up when you want to go," Charlie dreamily replied, as he did a big finish to the song in his head on the dashboard.

Well before sunrise, Nick was up, making sure he had all the equipment he needed for this once in a lifetime photo shoot. The weather looked like it was going to be perfect, but that seemed to be the norm around here.

"Hey Chuckles, grab your gear and move your rear," he said, giving Charlie a hard shake for good measure. He smiled in saying it, as that had been their dad's favorite rallying cry on many a trip.

"Oh my freaking head, do you have a mute button? I'm tapping out, too many last night," came the not so surprising announcement from Charlie.

"Ah, me thinks my big brother haveth a tiny set of balls. You stay here and play with them and nurse your little headache, and I'll bravely venture out into the darkness and unknown by meself!" Nick teased and slammed the door several times on the way out, just to make sure the latch wasn't sticking and the mute button wasn't on.

Having done his homework well beforehand, Nick knew exactly where to drive and park, and where to hike for the perfect view of a summer solstice sunrise. He was initially surprised at the number of vehicles already there, but then he remembered Bidzii had told him the summer solstice was a significant event to the Native Americans in the area, which is why the bar was so packed, and why they decided to play there last night. Fajada Butte, located within Chaco Canyon, was his destination, and was known for having solar markings for the solstices and equinoxes. It also had a number of small dwellings dating from the tenth to the thirteenth centuries. Nick turned off the headlights and got out of the pickup, and as his eyes adjusted he saw that a lot of people had slept in their vehicles out here.

Not at the luxurious Rim Rock Lodge, like me and my brother with the soft city hands, he thought. He put on a headband with a headlamp, slung a backpack over his shoulders, put in one ear bud connected to his phone, hit random play on his tunes, and started trekking toward the butte to find the ideal vantage point.

The pitch darkness began to fade, with a slight brightening over the eastern horizon, revealing a sublime vista. Nick double-checked his equipment, deciding to use a tripod again for longer exposures. Despite a fair number of other people about, his spot was isolated, he had framed the butte to maximize the sun rising next to and then over it, with some cacti nearby to break up the horizon. A sense of anticipation hung in the silent and cool pre-dawn air. Once the sun finally broke the plane of the horizon, it appeared to rise quickly, an illusion aided by the lack of any clouds to give it perspective. Nick heard native singing carried in the wind around him. He was enchanted by it, all the while being engrossed in shooting away. How many others had been at this very spot, looking at this exact view, on this very day of the year, for untold centuries? All in this timeless place, in a timeless time.

With the sun now well above the horizon, Nick knew he had a couple hours to kill until the three large stone slabs on top of the butte would funnel the sunlight onto a famous petroglyph on a cliff wall, exactly bisecting it only on this one day of the year. This was a shot he was excited to get and was playing out the best angle and approach in his mind. He reached into his backpack, pulled out a thermos filled with coffee and a granola bar, and leaned back to enjoy the view. As he did so he heard a loud humph, a deep sort of releasing breath, and saw a large dog had lain down right beside him, which then proceeded to put his massive head directly in his lap.

"Well, hello there, big guy. What's your name?" he rhetorically asked, instinctively stroking deep behind its ears. He enjoyed the moment, sipping on his coffee, quietly soaking in the view, but when he tried to lean over to grab his granola bar, he got nudged until he gave up on it and resumed stroking with his free hand. He took another sip of his coffee and a longer look at the head in his lap and saw this was no ordinary dog. Too big, head and coat looked like a husky but all white, but something more feral about it, a deep underlying strength.

"Well, if you're not going to tell me, I'll just have to call you—" Nick was just about to make up a name, when he heard someone shuffling in back of him.

"Nanook. His name is Nanook. It's an Inuit name, meaning polar bear. Well, more exactly, master of bears," said a soft female voice. Nick still had one ear bud in and one out, and a new song came on. Indigenous, a Native American blues band Nick had latched onto, had started playing *This Place I Know,* an ode to the broken promises and challenges all too familiar around the reservations.

She crouched down and put the other loose ear bud in her own ear, above her gently tinkling silver and turquoise earring, and laughed then started humming. "I can see I'm going to have a hard time not liking you."

Nick turned over his shoulder and looked at her, and realized he had seen her last night, that she had raised a shot glass up from across the room to him. Dark hair, dark eyes, bronzed skin, a beautiful Amerindian if ever there was one. She took the ear bud out and stood, smiling down at him. Nick stood, or tried to stand, but

Nanook wasn't letting him up, not until she clicked her tongue and he lifted his head.

"Hello, I'm Nick. I believe I saw you last night, across the room at the bar," he awkwardly stammered.

"Oh, I know who you are, Nick LaBounty. I know all about you."

CHAPTER 14 – MORNING, JUNE 20

"You have me a quite a disadvantage," Nick said and smiled, after regaining at least some of his composure.

Having such a large dog hold him in place with a head that seemed like it should have been on a horse had thrown him off his game. He just wasn't feeling quite as debonair as he wanted to come across.

"Well, first off, for some reason my wolf likes you. Well he's not all wolf, but mostly. At least the good parts. The rest are husky. To be honest with you, Nanook doesn't like too many men, especially *Bilagáana*, I mean white people.

"He's an impressive animal, where did you get him?" Nick inquired.

"He was a gift to my people at a Tribal Council gathering of clans from all over the Americas. And my people gave him to me, for some work I had been doing, sort of as my bodyguard."

Nick laughed as Nanook came up behind him, nuzzled his head between his legs and started walking right through him, like he wanted to take him for a ride. Nick hopped on one foot and side-stepped him, but Nanook simply reared up, put a massive paw on each of his shoulders, gave him a deep sniff in the ear with no ear bud, and followed up with a wet chin to forehead lick. She started laughing so hard she doubled over, losing her composure too, unable to even tell Nanook to get down. Finally catching her breath, she snapped her fingers and pointed down.

"I've never seen him do that with anyone, white or Indian. You must be the wolf whisperer, or just smell like bacon."

Nick staggered backward, caught himself, and self-consciously tried to smooth his hair but ended up rubbing a sticky ear.

"And why exactly is it you're going to have a hard time not liking me?" Nick asked, finally able to look directly at her. She was immediately beguiling to him, with a slightly exotic accent he couldn't quite place, like someone who speaks many languages but English isn't native to them. She was definitely 100% Native American, with dark, almost black eyes, and tall for her race with a lithe, athletic figure. Nanook had to outweigh her by at least 50 pounds, no wonder he was the bodyguard.

"Oh, maybe it is because anyone who plays Indigenous, my all-time favorite band, on their headphones at sunrise on the solstice is OK with me. Did you know they were all Nakota? Their music struck a nerve with tribes across the country, one of the first Indian bands to make it in the white man's world. And of course they had to make their mark with the blues, because they touched on all our struggles."

"My dad was a huge blues fan, and I grew up with it. I actually saw Indigenous play outdoors at Millennium Park in Chicago when I was young, and got hooked. My dad said their lead guitarist was the Native American version of Carlos Santana. The more I learned about music over the years, the more I realized he was absolutely right. As they say: long live rock!"

Nanook sat down next to Nick, shimmying over until he was positioned directly on one of his shoes. "Interesting, he is marking you in every way possible," she observed as Nick reached down absent mindedly and gently rubbed him. "I liked your little performance last night. You obviously grew up around music and know your way around a stage. My brother thought you were quite good, even had a little rhythm for a white boy," she teased.

"Ah, so that's how you know my name. I have to tell you, I had a ball playing with Bidzii and his buddies. We got to know each other a bit between sets, great guy. Jams the blues and likes bourbon too, my kind of wing man."

"Yeah, well don't get too cocky. I didn't think you were too bad either, but you're no Clapton."

Nick looked at her and smiled. "So, you're Navajo too then. Tell me, does this mysterious creature who raised her glass to me last night have a name?" Nick inquired with a raised, slightly sticky eyebrow.

"Altsoba, but my friends call me Soba. Pleased to meet you Nick LaBounty," she replied, taking an offered cup of coffee from him.

"Nice to meet you too, Soba. I heard what Bidzii means, what about your name?"

"You'll laugh, but it means 'at war.' Turns out it wasn't so far off, the way my life has played out. I guess that's why I ended up with this big hunk of canine following me around," she replied.

Soba sat and pulled her knees up under her chin, sipped on the coffee, and quietly admired the view. Nick took a couple of tries to finally get his foot out from under Nanook, then sat as well, the dog between them. Nanook stretched out and lay down, put his head heavily back on Nick's lap, and grunted and nudged until he got Nick to resume his deep tissue, behind the ear massage.

Soba looked down at the dog, shook her head and said, "You're just so needy," then glanced at Nick with her piercingly dark eyes and smiled.

They sat in silence, watching the other hikers pack up and scurry off to other places, and saw an eagle and a couple of falcons riding the thermal updrafts surrounding the butte. Nick had a hundred questions he wanted to ask her, was eager to get to know her better, but he didn't want to break the calm, peaceful aura that had settled around them. Not just yet. Finally, he couldn't stand it any longer and was about to speak when she beat him to it by a beat. "So what brings two outlanders to Chaco Canyon on the summer solstice? One who obviously can't dance, and one who has some magical spell on my wolf?"

Nick paused before answering, thinking he could get lost in the pools of those deep, dark eyes. "It's a long story, but one quick part of it is my brother and I came to scatter the ashes of our parents this evening. We were all here as a family in our youth, and my dad found it a sacred place, for a lot of reasons. What about you? What brings you here? Why do you need such a large, furry bodyguard?"

"Hmm," Soba thought. "That's a long story too, but the short answer is I am here because of the solstice, because I am a medicine woman, a shaman to my people, and because we too find this place sacred." With that she slowly got up, stretched, handed him back an empty cup and held his hand briefly for a moment, and then said, "Goodbye for now, Nick LaBounty."

Turning on her heel she walked briskly away, clicking her tongue once. Nanook cocked an ear and then immediately got up, looked at her leaving, then looked back at Nick, wagging his tail. He gave the side of Nick's face a quick tongue bath, and then bounded happily after her. Without looking back Altsoba smiled inwardly, this unpretentious Bilagáana was growing on her. Nick watched her drift into the distance, grabbed the bottom of his shirt and wiped the side of his face with it and thought, *Did that all really just happen?*

Nick sat there for a while, contemplating everything that had transpired, getting his mind around it, while looking out into the timeless beauty that surrounded him. Glancing at his watch, he finally gathered his things, careful to leave no trash behind. Having been trained so meticulously by his father, he picked up even what he hadn't brought in. Over to Fajada Butte itself he meandered, working his way up to the petroglyph on a cliff wall, where he found a small crowd likewise waiting for the sun to hit it just right. His camera lens was so powerful he didn't need to be in front and found a comfortable place in the shade to get the postcard shot he had in his mind, along with a quick video clip. After a night of drinking he carefully kept himself hydrated, consciously sipping on the water bladder in his backpack.

He looked at his watch and then through the camera lens and started shooting away. An audible gasp came from those gathered, as a distinct shaft of light formed on the petroglyph, and then quickly moved like an arrow shot through the center of it.

Ingenious minds to create that in any time or place, especially with the primitive tools they had, Nick thought, inspired at what he had just seen. He worked his way back down, glancing at the pueblos built into the sides of the butte, and wandered over to see the remains of one of the strategically located *Kivas,* large structures partially built into the ground, used for religious ceremonies and oriented on a celestial axis.

On the floor of the Kiva and astride the fire pit was a small hole that Nick knew was called a *Sipapu,* which was a symbolic passageway to the underworld. It was believed that as the first ancient peoples had emerged from it they changed from lizard-like beings into humans who split into the various tribes. The *Anasazi,* more commonly known as the Pueblo Indians, who built this and all of the surrounding complexes, definitely had the archeologist in him firmly impressed.

When he arrived back at the hotel, Nick found Charlie showered, refreshed and ready for the next great adventure, whatever that might be. "Funny what an extra four hours of sleep will do for one's disposition," Nick cracked when he saw him. They checked out of the hotel, found a convenient greasy spoon diner, and settled down for a late morning brunch to get caught up on last evening's and this morning's events. While they waited for their order, Nick flipped through photos on his camera, and would show Charlie one when something of note came up.

"Here is the sun rising off the side of the butte. Here are some of the ruins, and oh, get a load of this guy," Nick chuckled.

"What the hell is that, a white St. Bernard, or a polar bear?" Charlie asked.

"No, that's Nanook. From what I understand he's mostly wolf. For some reason he seems to have adopted me. Oh, and check out his owner, she didn't see me snap this one."

Charlie let out a low whistle, which was his habit when something impressed him. He grabbed the camera away, held it closer, and cracked, "Maybe she'll adopt you too. Does she know you have a better looking, more established older brother?"

Nick grabbed the camera back. "Easy whiskey, she knows one thing about you, and that is that you can't dance worth a hoot. She was at the bar last night and personally witnessed your epileptic fit out on the floor. And maybe that other subtle little detail, you know, you have a wife and two kids, that might get in the way too. By the way, she's Bidzii's sister. We had a nice little visit this morning after sunrise. I gotta admit, there is definitely something about her. And you know, she can't help it, chicks dig musicians."

"Well let's hope she doesn't meet one, for your sake," Charlie teased. "My little brother could use some romance."

"Yeah, as always thanks for the moral support. What was the line from that Bob Seger song?" Nick remembered it and started singing.

"She was a black-haired beauty with big dark eyes
And points all her own sitting way up high . . ."

The song *Night Moves* was now in his head, and he hummed it as he gathered his things.

The brothers discussed where they would scatter the ashes at sunset, the rub being that doing so around here was not officially sanctioned, so they would have to do it on the sly, within the context of a sunset photo shoot. The best bet seemed to disperse them from the west wall of the canyon, overlooking Pueblo Bonito, where the wind would blow over the greater canyon. It was a good spot, a little more discrete with fewer visitors. There were also several kivas and a lot of beautiful petroglyphs in that area, so it was decided to make a trip out later in the afternoon.

"If his quest ended here, if this was as far as he got, then having their ashes scattered here was intended so we would pick up on the trail. I distinctly remember being here, more than once, but man, it's a big place. Without that one journal, this is challenging, maybe too challenging," Nick said, watching Charlie devour his food like he hadn't eaten in weeks.

"Well, if you asked me bro," Charlie said between veracious bites, "I'm not sure there is a simple way to unwind it. While we at least now have a few clues, they are pretty vague. Alexandre was posted at a fort near here, there is some type of marking somewhere out in the big, wide desert that might or might not point us in the right direction, but it is goddamn hard to decipher even his writing, much less the meaning of it. Yup, no problem at all, at least for someone with as finely honed an intellect as yours."

The boys sat in silence for a while, and Nick pulled out a copy he had made of the letter, not wanting to handle the original any more than necessary.

"Well, my supposed intellect did pick up a few things, and I have been doing more than a little research. Alexandre was at Fort Wingate when he wrote this. The necklace I'm wearing has to be the same one he references, based on what Grandma Ingrid said to me, and the mere fact that she still possessed it. He said it was part of an old treasure of the *Mixica*, hid from the *conqurors*. Well, Mixica, in his garbled English and spelling, probably meant Mexica, which is distinctly different from our modern Mexican. The Mexica were the indigenous people of central Mexico, and they spoke a distinct language which was the main dialect of Nahuatl. Meaning if we go back in time, the old medicine man talking with Alexandre was probably referencing some type of treasure of the Aztecs."

Charlie put his fork down long enough to look up and let out a "whew," then tucked back into his plate.

Nick traced a passage on the sheet. "I'm not sure whether *conqurors* means conquerors or conquistadors, but if we are truly talking about Aztecs from that timeframe, it would pretty much mean the same thing. A couple of details continue to throw me off. First, this area is a hell of a long way from the home ground of the Aztecs, and while there are lots of documented expeditions of the Spanish from around that time frame banging around the Southwest, there is no record of the Aztecs ever coming anywhere close to here. They were being decimated by war and disease and then subjugated, and frankly I don't know what the hell they would be doing around here anyway. Just way, way too far from their home base. The second thing is the description of the clue he gives, he calls it an outsa, a taleys, and an eyeteden. I cannot for the life of me decipher or translate any of those. And trust me, I've tried everything."

Nick tapped that part of the letter with a nervous fingertip. "Just makes no sense, none at all. And the rub from a greater historical perspective is that the Aztecs left so little of their own documented history. The Spanish tell their version, but how accurate is that? Churchill said it best, 'History is written by the victors.' And the victors always had an agenda, whether obvious or hidden. Hell, the Spaniards, driven by their clergy, eradicated any written history the Aztecs had.'"

Charlie let out a satisfied belch, pushed his plate away, and said, "I didn't know the Aztecs could write, or even had any kind of written language."

"That is exactly the point, nobody could contradict what they wanted history to believe. Maddening, it's like George Orwell in his book 1984. They just keep erasing things and changing meanings until people don't remember it ever happened. The Aztecs did have their own written language, sort of like the Egyptians did, also based on pictures. We call the Egyptian writing hieroglyphs, and the Aztec's pictographs. The Aztec's in fact had a beautifully documented history in pictographs on codices, which were long folded sheets of deerskin or plant fiber. But of course, the Spanish and their priests and their missionaries systematically burned the codices on a massive scale. Couldn't have any conflict with their own precious religion. Frickin' worse than the Nazis. That and the fact that any of the few codices that survived didn't preserve well, especially in a tropical environment. And of course you've got all the conspiracy theorists who figure since the Aztecs and Egyptians both wrote with small pictures, and both built pyramids, that it took aliens or the lost tribes of Israel to tie them together."

Charlie started laughing at him and said, "You know, you tend to get just a little too worked up talking about dead things. You should consider becoming an archeologist or something. I'm sure that'll get Bidzii's sister all worked up."

Nick flicked a straw at Charlie and gave him a mock look of disgust. "You know, here I am working things out way beyond your pay grade, pouring my soul out to you, and all you can do is take a shot at the first girl I've found remotely interesting in, like, forever."

Charlie made a pained face but couldn't keep it and started laughing again. Nick gave him a kick under the table. "Seriously, I think instead of looking at everything around here and trying to pick up a singular clue, I could cover a lot more ground doing some real research. I think what I need to do is go to the National Museum of Anthropology in Mexico City. I know people there, and can triangulate things better with their resources, along with access to some of the Spanish archives."

Charlie pulled himself together and finally got a little serious. "Well bro, sounds like a plan, you follow Pedro south of the border and go play Indiana Jones. I on the other hand gotta fly back home tomorrow, you know, to those little details like a wife and kids and a real job. Maybe I'll even work out my epileptic dance moves with Sophie under the sheets."

Nick rolled his eyes, that was a visual he just didn't need, and said, "Let's boogie, we've got a date with some ashes." With that Charlie paid the tab on the table, put his arm around Nick as they got up and left, and gave him a noogie for old time's sake.

A short, swarthy man who had been sitting in the booth directly next to them, with his back to their table, patiently waited until he saw both walking across the parking lot. His sunglasses and pulled down ball cap hid his wandering eyes, his long sleeve shirt hid his gang tattoos. Once he was sure they were leaving, he pulled out a cell phone and hit a number. "Yeah boss, both of the gringos are here. They were whining about having to dump some ashes off some fuckin' cliff somewhere. Yeah, I'll keep an eye on them here, but I won't need to for long. The older one is headed back to Chicago mañana, the other rock hugger is going to be a pain in the culo. But the good news is he's saving you the trip and coming directly to you."

CHAPTER 15 – AFTERNOON, JUNE 20

"Come on, we'll camp out like old times, it will be great. I've got all the gear, and if you are still feeling too citified you can sleep in the back of the truck, you wuss," Nick needled his brother.

Charlie made a pained expression and held the small of his back. "The last time I camped with you, you gave me an air mattress that went flat during the night, I woke up with roots going up my ass and had black fly bites in places no bug has a right to go."

Nick laughed easily at the memory, Charlie wasn't exaggerating. "I love camping with you, no matter how bad the bugs, they always go to you and leave me alone. You're like bait man, every hiker needs one of you. I should patent your sweat and sell it. We'll call it something with a good marketing ring to it, maybe a little esoteric like 'Clogged Pore of Fat Ass White Man,' I'd make a million I tell you!"

The decision reached by default, the brothers grabbed food and beer for the night and set off for an afternoon of exploring, with the goal of being at the west rim of the canyon overlooking Pueblo Bonito before sunset. The first stop was to the *Wijiji Trail*, a mile and a half hike to see a series of petroglyphs popular with the tourist crowd. Not too hard of a pitch on the trail, at least until the end, so Nick thought it was something Charlie could hack. Later they stopped for the same view Nick had of Fajada Butte at sunrise, but now the sun was high in the sky with no shade in sight.

Then it was on to *Peñasco Blanco*, or White House, at the far western edge of the canyon. This was a fairly arduous hike, but Nick intentionally wanted to push Charlie a little, and they had both the time and the rare opportunity to do it.

"Alright, billy goat, no need to keep showing off," Charlie huffed, pausing to catch his breath. The trail from the parking lot to Peñasco Blanco was just a under four miles in length, with little elevation gain and plenty to stop and see along the way. Mother Nature was turning up the thermostat.

"I see what city living, sleeping in and eating a big breakfast has done for you. Dad would have loved to have hiked that desk-jockey belly fat right off of you brother," Nick taunted.

"Yeah, I know, and I wish he were here to do it too."

They stopped at a bend in the trail, Charlie starting to sweat heavily, Nick's pulse barely even picking up yet. Nick pointed to a series of clearly visible illustrations on a sheltered rock surface.

"Get a load of the pictograph here, rumor has it this is of a supernova that was clearly visible in the sky back on in the year 1054, when this area was still inhabited."

Charlie took a deep drink of water and caught his breath. "If this is a pictograph, then what the hell is a petroglyph?" Nick smiled inwardly, he liked it when he possessed knowledge his brother lacked, which had always been the other way around growing up.

"Good question. A pictograph is something painted onto stone, using some type of pigment native to the area. A petroglyph is when something is etched or carved into the surface. Obviously petroglyphs hold up better if exposed to the elements, and pictographs do better if they are in some type of sheltered environment."

Charlie grimaced, he knew more information than he wanted was coming his way.

"Probably the most famous pictographs are in the Lascaux Cave in France, over 17,000 years old. You see that, and you know our ancestors thought more deeply than most people give them credit for. But take a good look at this one, they saw something unusual in the nighttime sky, a supernova that they couldn't comprehend in today's terms, yet they assimilated it into their own way of thinking. And a few days later it was no longer visible in the sky to them, but here it is, over a thousand years later, for us to see. Pretty amazing when you think about it."

Charlie let out a low whistle. "Some of the pueblos around here look like they could still be used today. How long ago did they abandon this area?"

Nick held up a finger indicating wait a moment, finished taking a photograph of the pictographs and the surrounding area, then grabbed Charlie around the neck and extended his arm for the obligatory selfie.

"Say whiskey," he said, taking a quick snap before Charlie could give him a backhander where it hurt.

The ongoing contest between brothers, whenever the situation called for a nice smile or a straight face, had always been to see who could get the other to laugh out loud, or failing that, give them a shot in the nether regions to double them over. Their mother would feign disgust and tell them to act their age, but Dad would just laugh and say, "Boys will be boys," and then prudently cover himself up too.

"The thinking today is that an extended period of drought hit the area sometime in the early eleventh century, which led to gradual emigration out of the region. A similar dynamic was happening much further south about the same time with the Maya in the Yucatán peninsula, although for both it is still educated conjecture. Some think it was the encroachment of more aggressive tribes, or some combination of that plus the drought. Whatever it was, they certainly left their fingerprints on this whole area for eternity."

When they reached the end of the trail, Nick walked over to a particular viewpoint and yelled to his lagging brother, "Hey bubba, get a load of this. Tell me if this rings any bells."

Charlie finally caught up, took off his sunglasses and wiped down his brow, then squinted into the distance for a moment. "Ha, you're kidding me. I forgot all about this, but there it is. All that's missing is the four of us standing in front of the ruins right there."

Their Mother, Josephine, always made a big production out of taking the perfect photograph in some obscure, out of the way place each year for their annual Christmas card. The more exotic the locale or outrageous the picture, the better. He could feel her playfully pinching his earlobe even now to get him to smile. One year when the boys were young, it had been taken right there.

Nick turned melancholy for a moment, the black dog of depression peeking through, and thought, *I seem to remember things most vividly in snapshots, like the actual memories are already fading away. It just wasn't that long ago, all of us here laughing, exploring, and reveling in just being together. And now just Charlie and I are left, and I'm losing details of the memories of Mom and Dad I hold most dear. If I don't take a picture now, will I forget we even did this? Charlie has a legacy, will always be here through his kids, or their kids. Maybe I should find some ocher and outline my hands on the cliffs. At least when I'm gone, that would still be here.*

He looked up and saw Charlie talking to him but hadn't tuned in on the words yet. ". . . I said are you doing OK man? You looked like you were somewhere else for a moment. I know, I feel it too. You know they wanted us together here, now. For a good reason too, and not just to scatter their ashes. And yes, let's take a photo and recreate the old Christmas card for old times' sake, Mom would have wanted it that way."

As the sun finally started its inevitable decent, Nick and Charlie hiked back out, pausing to look at some of the sites they had hurried past on the way in. Reaching the truck at the trail head, they jumped in and drove over by the Visitors Center for a quick shower to refresh and recharge. After an exchange of wet towel whip snaps, Nick getting the larger welt on the buttock of the two, they drove back toward Pueblo Bonito.

Charlie chuckled when Nick hit a bump and grimaced. "Yup, that's gonna leave a mark," he wryly commented. The loop of the roadway took them almost directly there, and they went past it and parked the truck at a nearby trail head and hiked above to an overlooking plateau.

With the sun slowly setting over their shoulders, the brothers sat, cracked open a beer, and clinked them together. The view was stunning and looked out to the northeast, with nature's sunlit kaleidoscope slowly turning the landscape different hues before their eyes.

"It wasn't all about the search, although that was a big part of it. They wanted us together, bonded, doing something worthwhile together. I guess that's the difference between being smart and being wise," Charlie reflected.

Nick nodded his head, took a long pull on his beer and added, "There were just so many lessons, the best ones were when we never knew we were being taught. Integrity and moral compass are overused phrases you hear bantered about everywhere today, but they just set the example by living it. Really all their closest friends too, if you think about it, just a very impressive generation. Dad would say, 'No, your grandparents were an impressive generation, the greatest generation.' Mom and Dad both always said, 'You boys know right from wrong, you know it innately, there was never any gray area.' They set tough standards to live up to, but great ones to aspire to."

Nick pulled the ashes out of his backpack and set the small urn between them. There were still a few hikers and campers milling about below them, but the crowd was thinning, people headed back to a campfire and dinner, kids worn out and finally settling down, marshmallows coming out.

"Yeah, they would have loved this, knowing we were together here, actually both living in the moment, remembering them. After Mom passed, I asked Dad why he had her cremated, why he couldn't just bury her like everyone else did, so we would have a specific physical place to go to remember her. He said, 'There are seven billion people alive out there in the world today, plus all those who have ever lived, and all those yet to be born. What will happen if we have to make space to bury them all? We came from this earth, your Mother and I want to go back to it, and if you scatter our ashes in the wind in our favorite places, we will always be there for you, and perhaps everywhere else too. We're all just stardust, who could ask for more?'"

They slowly drained their beers, each lost in his own thoughts, letting the sun settle a little lower on the horizon in back of them. Finally deciding it was time, Charlie got up first, dusted himself off, and reached in his backpack. Nick grabbed the urn and walked to the edge of the plateau. Charlie ambled over behind him, with a small flask in each hand. He gave one to Nick, who slowly rubbed a finger over the engraving.

Albert, Josephine, Charles, Nicholas
Family is nature's truest masterpiece.

"Thanks man, this means everything to me," Nick said, genuinely and deeply touched by the gesture. They each opened their flask and took a sip, then held it out in a silent salute. Charlie, as the older brother, felt obliged to say something fitting. He started, but with tears welling could only stammer, "There are no words."

Nick looked him directly in the eye, and said in a steady voice, "You're right, and all worth saying has already been said. The lives they led said it all."

With that he opened the urn and heaved the ashes into the wind, which grabbed them in an updraft and swirled them away, out over Pueblo Bonito, out farther and farther into Chaco Canyon, the sun setting behind them, reflecting ever so briefly off the windswept pieces of stardust.

CHAPTER 16 – JUNE 21

The desert sky put on a show the prior evening that had been ethereal, the view crystal clear with no ambient light, bands of the Milky Way galaxy distinctly visible, punctuated by the occasional shooting star. Sitting out on the plateau by themselves, it was one of those nights Nick and Charlie could almost perceive the earth slowly turning underneath them, a sense of awe and wonder about their place in the vastness of the universe washing over them. The conversation had been lighthearted, the mood buoyant, a weight lifted off their collective shoulders. Lives had ended, but life would go on.

The night had passed with no incidences, the brothers sleeping deeply like in their youth safely ensconced in their beds back at camp on Lake Charlevoix. When morning came, Nick was suddenly awakened by the sound of Charlie screaming. With a sleepy grin on his face, he grabbed his camera and slowly poked his head out of the tent to watch the commotion unfolding. Outside Charlie was jumping about on one booted foot, shaking the other boot until something fell out of it, losing his balance and falling over awkwardly with a heavy thud.

Sitting unceremoniously in the dust he yelled to Nick, "It's a damn scorpion, I'm lucky it didn't sting me!" Nick finally couldn't keep it in any longer and burst out laughing, having taken a video of the whole escapade. Charlie looked at him quizzically, then realizing he had been had, leaned over and picked up the 'scorpion.' Long dead and just a dried husk, Charlie tossed it at a hysterically laughing Nick, hitting the side of the tent. "Yeah, real funny dumb ass, it's all fun and games until somebody loses an eye."

They broke down camp quickly, with the long-practiced efficiency of brothers who had done this a lot growing up, taking down the tent, stowing the gear, and packing everything back into duffle bags and coolers. The camp site itself was more pristine than when they arrived, just like they had been taught. Dad would have been proud. As Nick drove out of Chaco Canyon and back to the airport, Charlie commented on how much they had accomplished in so short a time. "That was a productive 48 hours bro. We did some good work there. Last night was fitting, couldn't have been more appropriate, just the two of us." Nick nodded, obviously feeling the same way, an echo of sadness overcome by the release of a collective weight they had carried.

"I feel like one chapter has closed, but for us, and especially you, another is about to open," Charlie continued. "I know you are going to dig around to do some research, just promise me you won't get caught up in anything you can't handle. I know that look in your eye, you look just like Dad when his determination sometimes overtook his judgment."

Nick looked over and raised an eyebrow, and replied, "Sure, OK Mom, I promise to be good." But he knew Charlie's intentions were sincere, and added, "Hey, I'll be in regular touch, and I'll be discrete. This is an academic exercise, but if it sheds light on what happened to Dad, so much the better. South of the border I go." They drove on in silence, enjoying the last bit of time they had together, a steady stream of blues playing in the background, the songs reassuringly familiar.

Suddenly Nick looked down at the dashboard, tapped it, and said, "Crap, the oil light just came on again. I swear this truck burns more oil than gas." He patted the dashboard and pleaded, "Come on Mable, you're able."

Charlie just shook his head and advised, "Seriously, why don't you just get a more dependable set of wheels? Or if you can't part with this, get it really refurbished? Lots of places specialize in customizing old rust buckets like this. You've got the coin, quit being so tight."

Nick looked off in the distance, his mind already somewhere else. "Yeah, yeah, I know. Someday, when time allows and I'm not chasing any more mysteries. Someday."

At a gas station just outside the airport Nick pulled over, filled up with gas and added a quart of motor oil. He also picked up three more quarts of oil and put them in the back, doing rough calculations in his head of how much he would need on his drive down to Mexico. That should get him there, he'd worry about the trip back later. Nick eased into the departure parking area of the airport and got out and gave Charlie a big bear hug.

"Sophie works tomorrow too, she's got a charge shift on the maternity floor. Back to the city of broad shoulders and the rat race for me brother," Charlie said, finally loosening his grip.

Nick smiled at him, he thought Sophie was a terrific match for Charlie, a dedicated wife, wonderful mother and a damn good nurse too. Not a bad person to have in the trenches with you, especially when raising a young family. Frankly there were times he envied Charlie and the organization and discipline of his life, the stability he had so carefully crafted for Sophie and the kids. But that all seemed counter to his wanderlust and insatiable curiosity, at least at this juncture of his life.

"Hey, give Sophie and the kids my love, would you? I'll be in touch in the next couple of days with an update of anything I uncover," Nick said, shaking hands with Charlie as he broke away and waved one last time.

Nick sat heavily back into the seat in his faithful Chevy pickup, deciding on his next immediate move. He could grab a few supplies and start to head south, or he could hang out here one more night and see if anyone was still around—and anyone meant Soba. Now that he was past the emotion of scattering the ashes with Charlie, his thoughts had immediately returned to her. He was bewitched by her, by that graceful and exotic shaman, he knew it, and wondered how he could even begin to track her down. "I don't even have her number," he ruefully reflected.

He checked his phone and saw that he had missed a text when seeing Charlie off. He grinned and his pulse immediately quickened when he saw it was from Bidzii, who was still in town with his band mates and a few friends. It said, "If you boys are still around, stop out in the evening at the Gallo Campground in Chaco Canyon for a cookout and a campfire."

Nick's stomach fluttered like a teenager asking his first date out. He wanted to inquire if Soba would be there, but didn't know how protective her big brother would be and decided not to.

Man, he thought. *Mom would say I'm smitten. I'm too old for this type of reaction, aren't I?* He sent a text back to Bidzii saying he would be there, but that Charlie had gone back to the white man's world of materialistic obligations, and that was his loss.

Nick made time from the airport along the now familiar route to Chaco Canyon, to the aptly named Gallo Campsite which ran along Gallo Creek. It was just past dinner time, dusk settling in, and he wandered through the campsites looking for his new group of friends. Packs of giggling kids ran past him, the smell of toasted marshmallows and smoky campfires hanging in the air. Seeing plenty of people but not any he recognized, he was about to call Bidzii on his cell phone when he heard singing and laughter carried on a slight breeze toward him. Instinctively he followed the sounds and saw that the Navajo band and their little entourage had taken over the large campfire circle in back of the campsite. Many other campers were joining in the fun, sitting on coolers, fold out chairs, or on the benches which formed a small natural amphitheater around the large fire pit. Just beyond the fire pit was a little ledge, forming a perfect stage often used for camp theater, now being used for some impromptu moonlight dancing.

Nothing like some good live music to draw a crowd out of nowhere, he thought.

Bidzii looked up and saw him and yelled, "Hey Vanilla Ice, come and join the party!" Nick grinned and waved back and worked his way through scattered coolers and chairs to the inner circle around a large bonfire. A couple of the other musicians saw him too and made room, Bidzii patting the ground next to him.

"Incoming," one of them shouted, and Nick looked up just in time to catch an icy PBR tall boy that came sailing his way. "Good catch," he heard.

As Nick sat down, he replied, "Nice spiral." Bidzii draped a muscular arm around his shoulder and gave him an affectionate crush and tapped beer cans with him.

"Welcome, Outlander. Glad you could fit us into your hectic schedule," Bidzii said through a mischievous grin.

"Hello, *Shik'is*, glad I could make it work, thanks for the invite," Nick replied, butchering the pronunciation of *my friend* in Navajo. With that he took the top off a bottle of bourbon he brought and handed it to Bidzii.

"Ha, you're pretty fly for a white guy, let's drink to it!"

A game of musical guitar was being played, with anyone who sat on the inner circle being passed an acoustic guitar to stand and sing to the whole gathering. If the crowd liked it, they would join in and sing the courses and often break into dance. If they didn't there would be raspberries and cat calls until the player did a shot of booze to pay their dues, at which point they could try again or tap out and pass the guitar along. *Atsa*, whose name meant Eagle and was sitting to Nick's right, had just gotten booed and dutifully did his shot. Nick laughed and looked over at Bidzii.

"Tough crowd tonight. Don't forget to tip your waitresses," Bidzii warned.

But Atsa was determined, and started banging out another song, this time singing *Midnight Rider* by the Allman Brothers. The crowd clapped and whistled its approval and sang along and danced. Before he could even pick a song, the guitar had been passed to Nick. He had been so preoccupied with wondering if Soba would show up, and with getting his courage up to ask Bidzii of her whereabouts, that he had no song idea, his mind completely blank. He looked over to Bidzii, hoping for him to throw a lifeline and offer a suggestion.

Bidzii, obviously sensing his discomfort and enjoying it, leaned in and whispered, "Hey, no pressure. It's like Indiana Jones when he had a table full of grails in front of him. Choose wisely."

Nick slowly stood, still searching for an idea, when he felt a heavy thump against his leg. He was about to protest that he needed just one more moment to think, when he saw it was Nanook leaning heavily into him, almost knocking him over.

"Aha, I've got it," he said, knowing that Soba couldn't be too far away. With that Nanook sat territorially next to him, and he played the first strands of *Mustang Sally*. The crowd murmured, unsure if this was a winning choice or not for the mood of the evening. Indecision wafted in the air, until he looked over and made eye contact with Soba dancing on the ledge by herself and sang out *Mustang Soba*. With that the band members started laughing. The crowd gathered and started to cheer and sing, and more people got up and joined in the dancing. The moon came out from behind a cloud, the gathering suddenly bathed in a soft lunar glow, the bodies swaying to Nick singing *All you want to do is ride around Soba*, with the crowd in unison shouting back *Ride, Soba, ride!*

"Well played, Eminem, now the pressure's on me," Bidzii said as he high fived Nick, taking the guitar for his turn. Nick cracked another beer, slowly catching a buzz between that, the bourbon, and the intoxicating vision of Soba dancing. She didn't dance quite like anyone he had seen before, she used her long lithe figure exquisitely, gracefully moving to the music in her soul, her eyes closed, unencumbered by anyone's perceptions. Even among the other Navajo she stood out, taller than most, swaying rhythmically, an elegant island of tranquility in a sea of herky-jerky foot stomping movements.

Nick was about to wander over to where Soba was dancing, when Atsa tapped him with the guitar again. *Wow, already?* he thought. It seemed he had just passed it along to Bidzii moments ago. It was turning into one of those nights, primal spirits were stirring under the moon, something was definitely in the air.

Bidzii looked at him while grinning ear to ear, and shouted, "Let's see what you got for us this time, maybe some Bee-Gee's?"

The song choice came to him easily, and he continued to watch

Soba dancing by herself, even after the music had stopped. He strummed the first few notes to get his chords down, and then broke into an old favorite of his parents that seemed perfectly appropriate to this time and place, *Dancing in The Moonlight* by King Harvest.

Soba opened her eyes and looked around until she found his, the smile on her face crinkling the corners of her large dark eyes. Nick sang as he walked, working his way around the edge of the fire pit, then stepped up onto the ledge, and shimmied through the crowd and over to Soba. She turned to him, her arms making elegant movements above her, her hips swaying gently to the rhythm, an unbreakable force field between them, both moving perfectly in synch, never touching, with the crowd chanting out:

"Everybody's dancin' in the moonlight
Everybody's feelin' warm and right
It's such a fine and natural sight
Everybody's dancin' in the moonlight"

After he had finished, Nick held the guitar up over his head. Bidzii jumped up and grabbed it from his outstretched hand, looked over at them both and said, "Oh, you crazy kids."

Soba's arms finally came down and rested gently around Nick's neck, all while never stopping her swaying. Making a pout face she playfully refused to make eye contact with him and asked, "What took you so long, Nick LaBounty? I thought I would have to dance the whole night away all by myself. What's a poor girl to do?"

Nick even found her voice enchanting, an accent that wasn't quite pure Navajo, the lilt of a sing song cadence in everything she said. Nick put his hands around her hips and pulled her a little closer.

"I was unavoidably detained by some renegade Navajo blues band nobody ever heard of and a bottle of bourbon. I have to confess there also may have been some bad singing involved."

Nearly his height, Soba raised her head and looked directly into his eyes and sighed. "Likely story. If only I had a dime for every time I heard that one." She turned her head away and closed her eyes and snuggled into his shoulder, Nick breathing in her dark hair deeply, smelling piñon pine, dry desert herbs, and light campfire smoke. They slow danced while Bidzii finished his song, not really hearing it or even being conscience of anyone around them. Finally noticing that the song had ended, she turned and nibbled his ear.

"What say we get out of here?" she whispered.

CHAPTER 17 – NIGHT, JUNE 21

Taking Nick by the hand, Soba grabbed a bottle of mezcal and a couple of blankets and headed out away from all the commotion. Nanook pranced out in front of them, constantly circling them at a distance, the ever-vigilant sentinel. The moon was bright, outlining everything in sharp focus, small paths and trails easy to discern. The cacti cast strange shadows, looking like ghosts with their arms raised in mock salute to the wandering couple. With no real destination in mind they meandered hand in hand, enjoying the sudden quiet and solitude. Away from the fire the air had a chill to it, and Nick unrolled one blanket and put it around Soba's shoulders. They continued in one direction, as if drawn to it, sharing occasional sips on the bottle, which tasted like a sweet tequila. The path wound around and rose for some time until it suddenly ended, revealing a part of the canyon below, one wall of which was directly illuminated by the moon. Built into the cliff wall was a distinctly visible pueblo, the colors cast so sharply black and white the whole area looked like an old photograph, a glowing lunar landscape.

Nick found a large boulder to sit and lean against, allowing them to take in the surreal vista spread out before them. Nanook crawled up above it and lay down, with only his two front paws and snout visible directly above them. He let out a huff to let them know he was there, and all was safe. Nick put one blanket under them, and when Soba crawled into the nook of his arm, pulled the other over them. His restless soul was at ease for the first time since he could remember, he thought he could easily stay here, just like this, and let his worries and obligations melt away. He had made a complete nonverbal connection with someone, an entirely new concept to him. But he knew in the brief time he had with Soba there was a deeper connection here. He didn't want them to just have a brief fling and then go their separate ways, a random encounter. He wanted to know more about her, the night was perfect, his senses were heightened, there would be no sleeping tonight.

Nick gave her a light squeeze around her shoulder. "Hey, I want to get to know you, I hope you don't mind, but I have so many questions."

Soba sat a little more upright, still leaning into him, and said, "I know, me too. How about we play a game, we each ask one question, back and forth. By morning, if we don't fall asleep first, both our curiosities should be filled." Nick smiled inwardly, this vexing creature always seemed to be one step in front of him.

"I'll go first," Soba said as she sat straight up, pulled the blanket down, playfully unbuttoned his shirt, and spread it apart to reveal the undershirt. The gray t-shirt had a "Life's Good" cartoon caricature on it of a man with a pickax and a rock, which said, "*I dig, therefore I am.*"

She looked at it quizzically and then at him. "So, what exactly is it you do for a living?" Nick gave her the long version answer, how he and his brother grew up on a lake in the woods in northern Michigan, how their dad loved travel and exploration, how they spent so much time in the Southwest, and how it led to him working on his PhD on Mesoamerican Migration Patterns.

"Publish or perish, that's the mantra in academia. But I found it is the field work I really enjoy. The one thing I knew was I didn't want to just be an armchair historian. I didn't just want to read about history, I wanted to be in it, to live it, to decipher it. Don't you want to know how you, how your people, came to be here, to this very place of all places?" he asked excitedly, his obvious passion bubbling to the surface.

Not waiting for an answer he continued. "I am interested not just in how things were, but on how things came to be, and what undercurrents in time influenced them. I am driven by the pursuit of knowledge, the hunt to uncover something complex and incomplete and hidden by time, to shed light on it, to unravel the unknown."

Nick noticed Soba perked up when he revealed his passion for solving mysteries of the past, and his love of the blurring lines between history, anthropology, and archeology. But he didn't tell her about the family mystery, at least not yet.

"OK Altsoba, Miss *'At War,'* my turn. You said you were a shaman to your Navajo people. Is that your full time calling, or what exactly is it that *you* do?"

Soba buttoned his shirt, patted his chest and sighed, "You want the long answer too?" Nick nodded and took a sip of the mezcal, he had all night and no place he'd rather be. Looking off into the distance with her dark, luminous eyes, Soba took a deep breath and then slowly released it. "I belong to the tribe, and yet I don't. I am a shaman, yet I am an outcast. I am the last of what you might call a tribe within a tribe. My parents have passed, and I try to preserve the knowledge they handed down to me, especially by my father, as best I can."

Soba sat up, and pulled her knees tightly to her chest, as if to gird herself. "But even we Indians have our own caste system. My father, and his father before him, and many more going back in time, were of another decimated tribe that the Navajo sort of adopted. It wasn't unusual for tribes, as they fought off unknown disease and encroachment by the white man, to band together and consolidate. What else can you do when you have no one to mate with, no warriors to protect you? After the wars all Indians were herded onto reservations, often side by side with their traditional enemies. When you face extermination as a people, you do desperate things, and so long ago we became part of the Navajo nation. But we were never completely accepted, that's what I mean by a tribe within a tribe. Somehow, we always managed to carry on *our* blood line, never quite dying out, but in our tradition that always meant a male of ours mating with a female of the Navajo. The women like me were considered valueless offspring, they always wanted a male heir to carry on the blood line, to be the shaman. And now there is no male heir, my father was the last. Bidzii is my brother in spirit only, my Navajo guardian. I am the last of my line, and that is why I am now the shaman, as my forefathers were before me."

Nick saw her face reflected in the moonlight, tears steadily streaming down it. "Valueless. Let's be truthful, that translates to infanticide. The tribes themselves were facing genocide from the outside, and within it practiced infanticide. Frankly I was only allowed to live because there was no son. Up until now my little tribe never had a girl that was allowed to survive. Well, that changed with me. My father wasn't an educated man, not by your standards. But he was very knowledgeable in the traditional ways of his tribe and of the Navajo, and he passed that all on to me. He said he would die before he let anything happen to me, and that's exactly what he did, when I was just sixteen. By the hand of his supposed 'own' people, for letting me live. After he was killed, the tribal elders finally realized the error of their ways, and decreed that anyone who touched me, including their families, would be shunned and banished. That was when Bidzii and a few of the others befriended me. They became my protectors on the reservation."

An outcast looking for her roots, a parent killed too early, these were things Nick could relate to on a personal level. He ached for her sorrow, and yet barely even knew her. But somehow he felt completely connected to her, two very different people from very different worlds, yet with so many common threads.

"I guess I am starting to get the 'At War' meaning of your name," Nick gently said. "Healers sometimes need healing too. Some day you will be stronger in all the broken places."

Soba hugged his arm and leaned deeper into him. "I'm telling you things even Bidzii doesn't know, but for some reason I feel I can trust you. You are removed from it, you have no agenda. You are a kind sounding board. I think you have what my grandmother would have called a *pure soul*."

"So I took what my father taught me, and I took what the Navajo taught me, and I decided to go outside the reservation and do something useful for my people. I took advantage of an education grant and went to college, majoring as a linguist, focused on the preservation of native languages and traditions. The traditions are dying, the elders who remember those who knew the old ways are passing. If nothing is done, in another generation we will lose many of the languages and tribal history of the lesser tribes. I have devoted my life to capturing the stories of the elders wherever I can, videotaping the conversations, building the archive, documenting and learning the language, before they are all no more than just dust in the wind. That is how I ended up with that big hunk of wolf above us. The Tribal Councils appreciated what I had been doing, and gifted Nanook to me for those efforts."

Nick stroked her hair and leaned his head against hers. "That is no easy calling, helping those who rejected you. And from what it sounds like, condoned the killing of your father. We share similar lives in different worlds somehow."

Soba leaned back into him, drying her tears. "All I know is it is the right thing to do. If I am not of one tribe, then I am of all tribes. And I will not let our history fade into oblivion." She suddenly sat upright and turned to him. "I think that is why we connect, because you peer into the past, want to understand it, want to preserve it. You have no ulterior motives, you just want to get the truth out."

Nick laughed softly to himself and passed her the bottle of mezcal. "How can someone who really doesn't know me at all, know me so very well?"

Soba took a drink from the bottle, a little trickling down her lip. "That's because I am a shaman and can see into your soul Nick LaBounty." Nick leaned over and kissed her deeply, the sweet taste of mezcal on her lips, the intoxicating smell of her hair, the radiance of the moonlight almost overwhelming him.

Suddenly without warning Nanook sat upright on the top of the boulder and let out a long, deep and hauntingly lonely howl at the moon. Nick was startled and started to pull away, but Soba pulled him closer, not allowing him to break the kiss. "Does he always do that?" Nick mumbled, a hint of wonder in his voice.

"I don't know, he's never really had to share me with anyone before," Soba softly replied. After a lingering moment she pulled away and looked deep into his eyes, their foreheads still touching.

Nick smiled at her and then sighed, "Well get comfortable then, I've got more I need to tell you."

With that he stood up, looked at Nanook, and let loose a long howl of his own. Nanook gave a confused look and tilted his head to the side, then wagged his tail like he was in on the joke and looked back at the moon and joined in the chorus. Off in the distance a few scattered replies echoed off the canyon walls, slowly joined by more even farther away. Truly, primal spirits were loose this night, drifting in the ether.

CHAPTER 18 – EARLY MORNING, JUNE 22

I am no longer going to call you the wolf whisperer. I think from now on you will be known by the Navajo name of wolf howler, *mąʼiitsoh nahatʼin*," Soba said with a laugh, in her sing song accent. Nick grinned and stood listening to the far away wolf cries carried on the breeze, cascading farther and farther away until they couldn't be heard.

"If that doesn't tug at the soul of your being, I don't know what will," he said, looking off into the distance. Soba got up, threw a blanket around his shoulders and used it to pull him closer until they were face to face, then nose to nose.

"I think you will," she purred, and rewarded him another mezcal-flavored kiss.

The moon was just starting to fade, the slightest hint of dawn on the horizon to the east. The air was cool, they had become stiff from sitting, and decided to walk and talk to warm up. Nick thought it was time to finally take a chance with completely trusting someone other than family, and if he couldn't do it with Soba, he knew he never would, and be a social cripple for life.

"I've got a couple of things to disclose to you too. Like my parents said, if you want a real relationship, it comes with warts and all." Soba leaned into him and clasped his hand a little tighter.

"I could never claim to have been an outcast like you, but I have at times felt like an outsider. I was adopted, by the best two parents anyone could have ever asked for. But maybe that's why I'm always searching for something, why I always have this undecipherable longing, and it seems to go deeper than just wanderlust. They had Charlie first, and tried for years to have another. It wasn't in the cosmic cards, and frankly I won the embryonic lottery when they adopted me. My dad used to say 'Blood is a tie, but it's not the only one. Look at me and your Mother, we're not blood, but we couldn't be closer. There are some who use blood ties as an entitlement, as a right, and don't invest in it. But then there are those who choose one another, whether with their spouse or their closest friends, their intimate inner circle, and really invest in it. The common denominator is they share a restlessness of the soul, a common yearning, a want of bettering one another and their world, a reason for being.'" Soba listened intently, she knew this was new ground for Nick, that it was cathartic for him, that it was drawing them closer.

"I believe in that, that we make our own tribes by who we choose to invest ourselves emotionally with, by who we choose to let in. The clock is always ticking, we only have so much time to spread around to everything we want to fit into our very finite lives. So why live an ordinary life? Everyone's got one of those. I yearn to do extraordinary things with extraordinary people. I want to learn everything I can about my passions. I want to leave this world a better place than I found it. And, I think most of all, I yearn for unraveling the past, because I have yet to unravel my own."

Soba nodded, reflecting, "Nietzsche felt that it takes self-realization for the exemplary person to craft their own identity. I'm no philosopher, but I think you've got the self-realization thing down pat."

"Nietzsche? When the heck did you pick up on his musings?" Nick inquired.

"We all had our pre-req's to kill in college," Soba smiled. "I thought it would be good to expand my horizon's a little."

They continued walking back the way they came, Nanook happily bounding around them, flushing rabbits and the occasional armadillo, batting about those that had rolled into a protective ball. Nick put his arm around Soba and pulled her in a little closer.

"An outcast and an adoptee, both looking for greater meaning and a deeper sense of something to belong to. Strange happenstance, that in all the cosmos, we happen to stumble on each other right here, right now."

"Maybe not so strange. Maybe the fates preordained it," she replied, batting her lustrous eyes.

They wandered in silence for a while, Soba absentmindedly kicking a stone out of the path. "Did you ever seek out any information on your birth parents? Did you ever want to know where you came from, what you are made of?"

Nick paused before answering, his thoughts on this were deeply held, not even Charlie dared go there. "Of course I was curious, any adopted kid is. But I held the parents who raised me as sacred, sacrosanct. I never wanted to insult or demean their memory by seeking roots that didn't tie to them. Maybe someday, when old wounds heal. But I'm satisfied for now, and I know what I'm made of. The same stardust as you."

They reached a slight rise overlooking the desert and threw down the blankets to watch one last sunrise together. "So what about your parents, you always talk of them in the past tense," Soba asked, almost afraid to broach the subject.

"Ah, now that's a long sad story, almost like yours." Nick told her how his Mother had died too young of cancer, how he believed his dad had been killed recently, and the series of clues that had aroused his suspicions. And he went into great detail about the necklace and clues Alexandre had left, how they had been handed down generation to generation, and that he was now on a quest to unravel or disprove the family mystery, once and for all.

Soba turned the pendant of Nick's necklace in her hand, holding it up to the dawning sunlight. "It's beautiful, the craftsmanship is stunning. So, what do you do now?" Nick had been thinking about that, had been completely focused on his next steps, when Soba had so care freely drifted into his life. Now things were not quite so clear, maybe even a little complicated. Or so he hoped.

"I left it with Chuck that if I really wanted to get serious about doing this correctly, forensically and archeologically speaking, then I needed access to better information, and not just go out on a wild goose chase. I need to go down to Mexico City, to the main archeological museum there, and do my research. I have contacts who work there, deep access shouldn't be a problem. And that might in turn dictate referencing some original Spanish archives, but I won't know until I get there and dig deeper. But I'm not so sure I want to leave here, not now. What about you, what's next for this beautiful woman who always seems to be at war, and who has so vexed me?"

Soba sat there serenely smiling, peering into the sunrise, her long black hair drifting over her shoulder. "Your personal shaman wants to know if you believe in kismet. Do you think our fate is really written in the stars? Otherwise why would we both be in the same small town, at the same bar, at the exact same time? A linguist trying to save obscure Native American languages and traditions, an aspiring archeologist trying to solve a mystery between the white and the native worlds. One of us arrives at that bar a couple of hours earlier or later, we're not having this conversation. Our lives would have gone on, unknowing."

Nick nodded, chance was a dicey proposition at best. Chance had already taken two people he loved away from him too soon. He didn't believe in chance, he believed in choices made and direct consequences, actions and reactions. No gray areas.

Soba stood and rolled up the blanket. "It just so happens I have a First Nations Tribal Council coming up that I am to make a presentation at. That is why I came down here with Bidzii, to this gathering in Chaco Canyon on the summer solstice. It was on the way to my ultimate destination, Cuernavaca, which is about 90 minutes south of Mexico City. Maybe there is something in the stars."

She turned to Nick with an impish grin, showed a little leg and stuck her thumb out. "Think I could catch a ride?"

The campsite was slowly waking up, tents unzipping, kids stirring, a few early souls up making coffee for the rest. The smell drifting in the air was a strange mélange of stale beer, sweaty bodies, fresh coffee and campfire smoke.

Bidzii, the rest of the band, and their friends, were showing no signs of life yet. It must have been a late night for them too. With the adrenaline of the night finally wearing off and all the raw emotions drained, Soba led Nick by the hand to her tent. They were not feeling quite as frisky as when they had wandered off the prior evening. Nanook followed and lay down protectively outside the tent door. Nick crawled into the sleeping bag behind Soba and extended one arm under her head, the other across her chest. He looked at the dream catcher twirling lazily above him, casting dull, early morning shadows. He touched his necklace and smiled inwardly at the irony. Soba burrowed backwards into him, interlocked her fingers with his and released a contented breath, as they both fell into a deep, cozy, peaceful sleep.

Nick awoke and carefully pulled his arm out from under Soba's head, feeling the pins and needles of it being asleep. As he made a fist and released it to get the blood flowing, he looked at her, sleeping angelically beside him. He was falling hard and knew it. Glancing at his watch he saw they had slept for over four hours, despite the bright sun and rambunctious noises reverberating around the campsites. He shook his head to get the cobwebs out, amazed at all that had transpired since he picked up his brother just four days ago. Already it seemed like a lifetime ago.

He ducked down and exited the tent quietly on his hands and knees through the low opening. As he emerged he was greeted by a heavy head to head nuzzling from Nanook, and as he looked up an obligatory face lick. "Hey boy, good to see you too. I know, it's been so long."

He heard laughter and guitar chords, and looked over to where Bidzii, Atsa, and several others were sitting in the shade. "Hey Kemosabe, over here," Bidzii yelled, a cigar in his mouth, the almost empty bottle of bourbon in one hand.

Atsa hollered, "Incoming," and arced a graceful spiral of a beer can toward Nick, who was squinting into the sunlight. Nick reacted quickly, turning his back toward them, and caught the beer back-handed. Catcalls, whistles and laughter greeted him as he made his way over and sat down.

"I can see that the festivities continue." As he opened his beer, those next to him leaned away as it exploded and doused him with foam.

Atsa doubled over laughing, adding, "I may have given it a little shake first."

Nick smiled back easily at him as he wiped his face with his t-shirt, "I'm sure Nanook will be happy to clean it up."

Bidzii flipped him a Cuban, and Nick deftly cut the end off with his utility knife and lit up. He wasn't a smoker, but he was never one to turn down a fine cigar when proffered. The conversation drifted in and out from the fun of last night, to what everybody was doing next, and inevitably circled back to music. The bourbon made one last lap around before Nick declared it a "dead soldier." Everyone suddenly cheered and high fived, and Nick realized that the saying had a whole different meaning with this group. Bidzii looked at him, still laughing and gave him a slap on the back and said, "I swear, you crack me up McFly."

The conversation drifted to their shared love of the blues, which led to a fun argument on syncopation, whereby the regular rhythm was unexpectedly shifted by stressing the weak beat. But then the alcohol fueled discussion shifted to who was the best Native American band of all time.

"Redbone? You can't be serious," said *Yas*, the drummer whose name meant Snow. "I mean they were good, but they weren't the best."

"Come on man, no Redbone, then no Blackfoot, no Blackfoot, no Indigenous. You can't tell me *Come and Get Your Love* and *The Witch Queen of New Orleans* weren't great songs," argued Bidzii.

"Blackfoot rocked man, *Highway Song* and *Train, Train* kicked ass," Yas replied.

Atsa threw in his two cents, asking, "Really dudes, what are you guys smoking? What about Kansas? *Dust in the Wind* is the all-time classic, and *People of The South Wind* rocked too."

Tahoma cracked up at that one. "Get real Atsa, Kansas didn't even have a single Indian in the band. They just wrote songs like they did."

Nick took it all in, the barbs and witty repartee, and then jumped in. "Alright, guys, I've got to call bullshit. I'm not even Native American, and I gotta tell you Indigenous is one of the best rock bands I have ever heard, period. And I heard many. Their best album was *Broken Lands*, and their best song was . . ."

"*This Place I Know*," chimed in Soba, having wandered over with Nanook by her side, while everyone was intently arguing.

"Ah, welcome, Mistress Shaman, practitioner of the dark arts. I say cheers to that," shouted Bidzii, raising a beer to her, to which everyone cheered and joined in.

Breakfast having been spontaneously drunk instead of eaten, people started wandering off to prepare some real food to refuel. Now it was just Nick, Bidzii, and Soba sitting together in the shade, lounging contentedly in the afterglow of the prior evening and a mellow morning. Nanook glowered at any outlanders who wandered too close, keeping the gathering intimate.

"Yeah, we've got another three or four gigs lined up, hitting places on our way back home. Maybe another one or two will fall in our lap on the way," Bidzii disclosed. "What about you?"

Soba kicked Nick's foot playfully and said, "Slight change of plans. You know I've got a presentation down Mexico way, turns out Nick needs to do some research in Mexico City. I'll catch a ride with him, and keep you posted."

Bidzii looked at Nick, this time with a more critical eye, appraising him. "You know what Soba means to me, to all of us here. And I suspect you now know all about her too. We Navajo don't take our obligations to one another lightly. You're like a tumbleweed man, one that just blew into our lives, and maybe will blow right on through it. But I know one thing, Pocahontas over there is a good judge of people, can see deep into them, and for some reason seems to like you. Hell, I like you. Even her damn wolf likes you, and he doesn't like anybody. But if you two want to run off on some traveling road show together, as her self-appointed guardian I have to ask you to pass one simple test."

Nick knew he was being challenged, with the best of all intentions. *If she were my charge, I'd be the same way, probably even worse,* he thought.

"OK, bring it on Tonto." He was finally catching on to the wordplay that Bidzii liked to banter about.

Bidzii put a hand on his knee and looked him straight in the eye. "I'm being serious here Peckerwood, you are either in our tribe or out of it. And I gotta know your level of commitment before you take her off to somewhere I can't reach her. But before I tell you what the test is, you have to agree to it. Like right now."

Nick glanced over at Soba, who suddenly looked uneasy and shifted about. The look on her face was inscrutable. She refused to make direct eye contact with him, he just couldn't read her. He paused, reflecting that he had spent a lot of time these last few years being relentlessly restless, searching for something, and that something had turned out to be a someone, someone who understood him, grew him, completed him. Like Dad had said about his mother, "There's only one of her son, and she's taken." With that he slapped his hand down hard on top of Bidzii's, and said, "I'm in. Bring it on Geronimo."

"I was hoping you would say that Opie, otherwise Sacajawea here would be doing some weird type of incantation on my ass and blaming me for you're getting away." Soba gave Bidzii her best Bambi eyes, obviously imploring 'be gentle.'

"Seeing you are so anxious to join our little tribe, you need to do a *Vision Quest.* Nothing too elaborate, we'll even let you do the abridged version. But instead of making you fast for four days to see your vision of how best to help our people, we'll accelerate the process. Ever hear of Peyote? For those of you in our studio audience that are unfamiliar with it, Soba told me it is Nahuatl for *Devine Messenger.* And I'll want to know exactly what message it is that you receive."

This time Soba's eyes met Nick's, and he could see tears just slightly welling in the corners, a silent thank you whispered on her lips.

"We gotta run, no time to waste." Bidzii put a powerful arm around Nick and then put him in a playful headlock, calling out to his friends, "We've got a live one here," and headed out to the desert accompanied by cheers and cat calls. "Come on Bueller, you've got a date with the Green Fairy."

CHAPTER 19 – AFTERNOON, JUNE 22

Nick looked back over his shoulder as he was being hustled away. Obviously Soba wasn't going to be a part of these festivities, but she gave him an apprehensive wave anyway. *Come back with your shield, or upon it,* he thought. A few of the band members trotted out, always up for some spontaneous entertainment.

"Green Fairy, really? I thought that was Absinth," Nick asked.

"Just a figure of speech, but I suspect the end result may be similar. You're going to see some strange stuff, man, better fasten your seatbelt. And remember, we want a full postgame report," Bidzii replied.

Atsa caught up and handed Nick a hamburger fresh off the grill. "You're gonna need something in your stomach dude, chow down."

When Yas gave him a water bottle, Nick wryly commented, "At least it isn't sour wine on a sponge before you nail me to the cross."

Nobody got the joke, and Atsa merely raised an eyebrow and mimicked what he heard Nick say yesterday, "Tough crowd."

Bidzii, who seemed to be the self-appointed master of ceremonies for the festivities, introduced the one person Nick hadn't met yet. "Hey Forrest Gump, this is Tohoma. His name means *Water's Edge*, we all think that's where he was conceived, but his mamma ain't saying. He's with the band but can't play a damn thing. But if you ever need anything scrounged up or fixed, he's your man."

Nick looked over at him and nodded, "Good to meet you, but why the hell did they name you after a pickup truck?" That got a few chuckles and elicited a "beep beep" from someone.

The man-pack wandered a little farther to a slight rise, where Bidzii announced, "Okay, this should be perfect." The Navajos cleared a space, removing loose rocks, and set a large traditional blanket down in the middle. There was an unobstructed view in every direction, the occasional cactus poking up, some cliffs visible in the distance. A warm gentle breeze kicked up a little dust.

"You'll get a nice light show with the sunset and a clear sky for the stars. Should make for an interesting trip, all without ever having to leave the blanket or buy a ticket," Atsa advised.

"Alright guys, you've obviously been down this road before. What exactly am I in for?" Nick asked, a little trepidation coming through his voice.

Bidzii sat down cross legged on the blanket and motioned for Nick to join him. "Here's the drill Custer, I've got a tasty little treat for you, and we'll all witness you eat it. After that we vamoose, the next ten hours or so should be an interesting experience for you. What you are about to ingest contains mescaline, something my ancestors have been using ritualistically for, like, forever. Turns out they all really liked the Grateful Dead." He chuckled at his own joke. "It will take you on a trip in your mind, probably distort some reality, maybe reveal something within yourself you never really knew. But it will definitely go into some dark corners and peer behind some doors you've never opened. At least not yet."

Nick looked over at him, and said, "Really, all this so I can give Soba a lift?"

Bidzii leaned over and punched him in the arm. "Come on man, I see how she looks at you. And that's not a look I've seen her give anyone else, ever. I've known her since she was sixteen, and now she's like twenty-five. She's my adopted little sister. I'd do anything for her. And that includes making sure the guy she's taking an extended road trip with is the real deal. Now open up wide and have a taste of the *Devil's Root.*"

Nick took what was offered, chewed it down and swallowed,

thinking it tasted like eating a cactus, which it actually was. He chased it with a big swig of water. When he opened his mouth and stuck his tongue out and said, "Ah," Bidzii rose, mussed Nick's hair, and walked away. As everyone else left they tossed their water bottles onto the blanket, regardless of how much was in them.

Tohoma let him know that, "We'll peek in on the show occasionally from a distance, to make sure you aren't running naked into a cactus or anything."

Just before they were all out of site, Yas turned and yelled back, "And remember, no leaving from the blanket. For anything!" He then made a motion that his eyes would be on Nick, no wandering allowed.

Nick sat back down, patiently waiting for something, anything, to happen. He looked around in every direction, enjoying the view. Still nothing. Time passed, a warm breeze blew through his hair, his palms started sweating. Seeing the scattered water bottles, he thought it prudent to place them out of the sun, under a corner of the blanket. He then set the stopwatch function of his watch, so he could see how long things might take. *Tick.* He looked at the horizon, the sun setting just above it, not yet touching, an eagle screeching and swooping down on some unseen prey. *Tock.*

I wonder if his peyote was old, maybe not that potent, Nick thought. He felt a slight chill in the air and buttoned his outer shirt up. *The sun must be going down, that's why I'm chilled.* He looked up at the sun, but it seemed like it was higher on the horizon, not lower. *Tick.* Suddenly he realized he was thirsty and reached for a water bottle. But there weren't any. "I can't believe they wouldn't leave me any water out here in the frikin' desert," he said out loud. "That's insane." *Tock.*

Feeling stiff from sitting too much, Nick stood up and stretched. It felt good to stand. He felt a thud, and realized he was lying on the carpet face down. He rolled over and squinted at the horizon to take in the sunset. The sun looked like it had melted through the horizon and into the landscape. *Tick, tock.* The carpet was moving, what the hell was under it? He moved to get away from it, but felt like he was falling, not down, but up. He grasped the carpet hard with both hands. *Tick, tock.* He felt like the ashes he and his brother had just scattered, could taste them in his mouth, was blowing about, stardust caught in the wind, twirling, higher and higher. He saw the entire canyon from far above, could see the blanket below, a figure sprawled out on it. *Tick, tock.* He drifted away from the desert, higher and faster, over the Plains states, over the Midwest, the landscape changing to snow and ice. He flew over Lake Michigan, over the town of Muskegon, and started to descend toward Lake Charlevoix. *Tick, tock.*

It's winter, there is ice on the lake, snow is gusting and it's freezing out. It makes Nick so cold he is shivering. He is hovering over his dad's camp, sees two men knocking on the door. His dad answers, they force their way in. *Tick, tock, tick, tock.* The two men go out the back door, one dragging a body, the other dragging an ice auger. Far out onto the lake they drill a hole, then drill more around the edges to make it bigger. *Tick, tock, tick, tock.* They take the body and force it into the hole headfirst, pushing it in deeper with the tip of the auger. Then they hastily push snow and ice on top of the hole and go back to the cabin. *Tick, tock, tick, tock.* Nick flies down through the hole in the ice, into the bitter ice-cold water. He sees his dad drifting and then suddenly revive, a scream escapes in air bubbles, he is moving frantically about, swimming back up to the ice, pressing it, looking for a way out. *Tick, tock, tick, tock.*

Nick follows his dad, sees him swim for a bright spot, a fault line in the ice. He reaches for it, and punches it, but there is no strength to the blows, no leverage. *Tick, tock.* His dad slowly stops thrashing about, and pulls up one sleeve, and bites down deeply on his tattoo. Blood swirls in the water. With a final bust of energy, he punches an arm through a crack in the ice, can feel the air on his hand. *Tick, tock.* The body suddenly goes limp, hanging by the arm stuck through the ice pack. A last few air bubbles waft upwards, caught under the ice, and escape through the hole by the arm. *Tick, tock.* Nick bursts up through the ice gasping for air, and is now hovering back above the cabin, sees two men leaving it, carefully covering their tracks, one holding a journal aloft, a high five exchanged. *Tick, tock.*

He is flying higher and higher again, back the way he came,

across Lake Michigan, through the Plains states, the landscape changing from cold winter to desert heat. Chaco Canyon comes in focus below. He is so very hot. *Tick.* Freefall. Pushed out of the sky, arms and legs flailing, the ground rushing up to crush him, tensing for the impact. *Tock.* Nick lands directly on the body sprawled out on the carpet far below. He crawls into its skin and sits up, sweating and chilled at the same time, the skin conforming tightly to his body. He holds a hand out in front of him to make sure the skin feels right and flexes all his fingers. Good, perfect fit. *Tick.* Now I understand, I see how all the loose ends tie together. It was always there, right in front of me, so obvious. And they will pay, they will all pay—plus interest. *Tock.*

Nick resumed sitting as he had started, cross legged in the middle, and calmly lifted a corner of the carpet for a bottle of water. He felt around the inside of his mouth with his tongue, tasted sand, and spit it out. He drank the whole bottle, still felt dehydrated, and grabbed and drank another. His hands weren't shaking anymore, he had perfect control of them. He looked up at the sky, it was still night, probably a few hours before the dawn. A glance at his watch confirmed it, he had been gone in his mind for a little over eight hours, but it felt more like eight minutes. That was definitely some very strong hallucinogenic stuff, with a wild type of time warping effect. The back of his eyes hurt, his mouth still tasted gritty. He gingerly got up, stood there and stared at the horizon until he regained his internal equilibrium, grabbed another water bottle, and then picked up some rocks and made a design off to the side in the sand. Then he covered his tracks and started walking slowly back to camp.

About halfway back Nick heard a thumping on the ground that sounded like a horse approaching and stopped to look up. There on the far edge of the trail stood Nanook, ears alert and surveying the area, the white sentinel, silently waiting for him. Nick paused and again put down additional rocks, way off the path. As he approached, Nanook turned on heel and quietly led the way back to the camp, back to Soba's tent, where he sat patiently to one side of the door. Once Nick unzippered it and crawled in, Nanook resumed his spot directly outside the entrance, the ground still warm from when he lay there last. He tilted his head looking at a few rocks Nick had just laid right outside the tent, then huffed and put his head down.

Early morning came, and Bidzii jogged through the camp back to where Atsa, Yas, and Tahoma sat gathered around a smoldering fire pit. "He must have wandered off, I don't see him anywhere. When did any of you last check on him?" Bidzii breathlessly asked.

They all looked at each other, and Tahoma said, "A little after midnight. Anyone go later?"

Atsa just shrugged his shoulders, and Yas added, "I slept like a baby, man. I was taking a little trip of my own."

Tohoma started chuckling. "I gotta tell you, when I last saw him that white boy was sprawled flat on his back, holding onto that carpet for dear life. Flying off somewhere like a bat out of hell."

Bidzii frowned, starting to get really worried, and decided to act before this little escapade got too far out of hand. Soba would *kill* him if anything happened. "Alright guys, the wide-open desert is no place to just wander off when you're trippin'. We've got to spread out and track him down, let's get moving, *pronto!*"

In the tent Nick pulled Soba a little closer to him, and whispered into her ear, "Think I should let them know I managed to find my way home?"

Soba rolled over and rubbed noses with him. "Naw, I think a few morning calisthenics would do them all some good. Such naughty boys, teach them a little lesson." With that she curled up in the nook of his arm, and they both drifted off back to sleep.

CHAPTER 20 – EARLY MORNING, JUNE 23

Bidzii circled around where the blanket was on the rise, looking for signs of tracks in any direction. He couldn't find any, and yet Nick couldn't have just disappeared. He might have flown away in his mind, but not with the body too. "Anyone see anything yet?"

Atsa, Yas, and Tahoma were all circling around farther out, looking for clues, calling for Nick. The sun was creeping up in the sky, the air dry and dusty, a warm breeze starting to stir. In their haste no one had eaten anything or thought to bring water, and they all started to get hot and thirsty. But most importantly, no one had seen anything of Nick yet.

Bidzii squatted down to gather his thoughts for a moment, and then saw a rock *cairn,* a small pyramid of rocks often used to indicate direction, nestled at the foot of the tallest cactus in sight. In the smooth sand in front of the cairn small pebbles outlined a hand, with the middle finger extended. Bidzii couldn't help himself and laughed loudly. "A clever one, this *Bilagáana.*" He called his posse over, showed them the cairn, and said, "We need to find the next one, but I think I know where they are leading." One by one they found them, irregularly spaced but zigzagging back toward the camp, not a footprint anywhere near them.

Outside of Soba's tent they saw the last cairn next to Nanook, with small pebbles in the sand in the shape of a happy face.

Together the sweaty group started slow clapping until Nick stuck his head out and smiled at them all. "This probably would have been a good place to start, don't you think?" He chuckled as he got out to join them.

"Alright everyone, since you worked so hard this morning, a nice traditional Navajo breakfast is on me." Soba shooed them all away and went over to the fire pit. There she made small cakes of flour, which she cooked directly in the embers. While those were toasting, she ground piñon pine nuts with corn meal to create a nut butter paste for the cakes and finished with goat meat grilled over the fire. Being favorites of any true Navajo, everyone was lined up and looking famished as she finished cooking.

Plates of food on their laps, everyone dug in hungrily and waited expectantly for Nick's Vision Quest download. Maybe he would disclose some Salvador Dalí type of melting cacti or landscapes, a Jimi Hendrix hallucinogenic charged dream, or perhaps a visit by his true spirit animal. Some had seen things even stranger than that.

Atsa couldn't help himself and blurted out, "We heard you meet your spirit critter, and it turned out to be a dung beetle. That had to be disappointing!" A chorus of guffaws followed all around.

Soba looked at him and grinned, "Nothing like dining with the *Diné*, eh?" Diné was the Navajo word they had for themselves, which simply meant *The People*.

Nick smiled back at her, relieved to finally be feeling completely like himself again. He held one hand out in front of his face and flexed all the fingers. "No, nothing like it anywhere in the world."

"OK, Lawrence of Arabia, time for the play by play," Bidzii said, anxious to hear what the currents of the cosmos had revealed last night to Nick's psychedelically expanded mind. Nick sat there silently for a while, composing his thoughts, amalgamating them back together into a cohesive narrative.

"I wasn't sure what to expect, and at first I thought it would be nothing at all. That you just gave me some shitty tasting cactus to eat as a gag, to see if you could make me stay up all night. An initiation ritual, a little hazing for the gringo, for the Navajo wanna be.

And frankly that would have been pretty funny. Hilarious actually. And then time actually changed, I never even had a chance to realize anything differently, I was already swept up in it. It wasn't different experiences, it was only one. And it was so vivid I knew it wasn't made up, not my rambling imagination turned loose, but rather my unconsciousness suddenly and profoundly focused. With laser like intensity, on something I had all the disconcerted pieces to all along. I was there, *right there,* and I saw how my father was killed."

Nick recapped first all his suspicions about his father's death, and how the police had thought them unsubstantiated conjecture, how he had started to doubt them himself. He told how he then found more clues, the cut branches which could have covered tracks, that Debbie at the diner told of an ice auger sold to strangers in the winter who didn't know how to fish. And how one journal had come up missing, *the key* journal.

Pausing and taking a deep breath he calmly comported himself. Looking only at the fire he launched into a recounting of the peyote induced trance, the mescaline activated dream. He recounted the flight, the arrival of the two men, the struggle, the death, and his return. "I know what they did and how they did it, I saw all that with great clarity. But I still don't know *who* they were and *why* they did it."

Nick paused for a moment, struggling internally with what was right to do, and what he needed to do. "But even if my dad had somehow stumbled onto something they had to have, they didn't have to kill him for it. I am going to find them someday, I promise you that."

When Nick finished he looked up, and saw that everybody had stopped eating, and were sitting with open mouths, incredulous.

Bidzii slowly shook his head and finally broke the silence. "Over time, many unexplainable insights have come out of our people fasting and doing a vision quest or doing peyote like you just did. The accuracy is often inexplicable, there is simply no rational explanation. My grandfather did it in his youth, saw himself in a foreign land he had never been with black sand and explosions all around him, yelling into a strange box with a stick coming out of it. Ten years later he is on Okinawa, he had become a *Windtalker*, and was almost killed by artillery fire off Mount Suribachi. He found himself calling in reinforcements, then counter battery coordinates on a walkie-talkie to destroyers offshore in Navajo code, because the Japanese could never decipher the language."

"And I have to tell you," Soba injected, "that the grandfather Bidzii is talking about had a big influence on me. His knowledge of the traditional ways of the tribe, his war experience with language as a Windtalker, all influenced me in my pursuit of linguistics. He was one of those fountains of knowledge I wanted to make sure were captured for the posterity of our people."

Nick nodded his head, appreciating the insight they both provided. "I can't explain what I saw, I won't even try. But I have you to thank for lifting the veil from my eyes. I now have a quest of my own to complete."

Nick looked at Bidzii with an upturned eyebrow. "So what do say Sitting Bull, do I have your blessing to drive Soba south with me?"

Bidzii paused, his brow furrowed, wrestling with conflicting emotions. "You are headed into troubled times. I do not know where your path ultimately leads. But keep Soba from harm, remember that this is your path, your quest, not hers."

With that he rose and offered his hand, which Nick stood and accepted. The two then exchanged a man hug, with Bidzii whispering in his ear, "Be careful out there my friend, I want *both* of you to come back safely. And remember, my posse is always just a phone call away."

With that Nick looked over Bidzii's shoulder at Soba and winked. "Road trip!"

CHAPTER 21 – MORNING, JUNE 23

As Soba threw her things in the back of the old Chevy pickup, she realized she had never even asked Nick if Nanook could accompany them. Before she could he patted on the tailgate, and the large animal nimbly jumped into the back bed, the shocks squeaking audibly in protest.

"Sweet ride for man and beast alike," she teased. Nick crawled in and made sure the side windows of the cap on back were opened for circulation, and that the c-clamps that held it in place were secure. There was a window in the front of the cap and in the back of the truck cab, which were both opened. Nanook immediately figured out he could just barely squeeze his massive head through to see what was going on in front or give Nick's ear the occasional sniff and lick.

As they jumped in and sat in the front, Nick turned and asked, "So we've got a little time to kill before you have to be in Cuernavaca, right?"

Soba looked at him and smiled, batting her dark eyes playfully and nodding yes.

"Then it's off to Hawikuh with my voodoo medicine woman." Nick pulled out of the parking lot and gave a honk on the horn. Soba leaned out the window and waved and shouted, "*Hágoónee,*" to Bidzii and her friends. "See you later!"

"You know he really likes you, don't you?" Soba asked.

"Yeah, Nanook's a great companion," Nick replied, as he felt a cool nose and a huff of breath in his ear.

"No, Bidzii, I mean, silly," she said, petting the big snout of Nanook. "I've seen him tolerate white folks, even make some friendships, but you he really seems to like on a different level. That's why he's always busting on you."

Nick glanced over and smiled. "I gotta tell you, Bidzii is a rock-solid guy. You can tell the water runs deep, much deeper than he lets on. I think he uses his humor to cover up a lot of scar tissue."

Soba looked out the side window at the view, listening but softly humming to herself. "You have insight Nick LaBounty, you would make a good shaman."

They drove on in silence for a while, enjoying the excitement of the start of a road trip, and the serenity of being alone. "You know why he's so quick witted with obscure pop culture trivia?" she asked rhetorically. "It's because there isn't a lot to do on the reservation, few meaningful opportunities. Not everyone wants to work at a casino or do menial jobs. Subsidizing just creates a cycle of dependency that's hard to break. Young men with time on their hands usually end up in trouble, going down a dark path and then not coming back."

"Bidzii doesn't strike me as someone seeking cheap thrills. He is a lot of fun, but I catch a serious undercurrent within him, a deeper purpose," Nick observed.

"He definitely wasn't like the others, he wasn't easily influenced. On the res you work on your English by watching television, old movies and the like. Cable TV doesn't reach everywhere, and cable and satellite TV costs money. DVD's are cheap, especially older ones. So you watch them, again and again, and then quote them with your buddies, again and again. That's where a lot of the raw material he uses on you is from, from some dark days in a trailer with nothing to do but watch reruns of the same handful of old movies and shows everyone passes around."

"And then he found music," Nick said.

"And God saw that rock was good," Soba laughed. "Bidzii

always had a way about him, people were attracted to him even when he was young. He and his gang saw a few acts back in the day and started banging around and playing little gigs. So of course he enjoyed the white girl groupies who found him kind of exotic and following an Indian band kind of trendy. But then something happened. They actually started getting pretty good. Bidzii decided to stop screwing around and trying to be everything to everyone and said, 'this is what we're going to do guys, we're going to do the blues.' And of course they all went along with him, and now they are slowly working their tails off and their way up. Maybe something will come of it or maybe not. But even if it doesn't, it kept them out of the dark places all these years."

Nick glanced sideways and saw that her own words were painful to her. There was more to this story.

They continued cruising, the breeze of the open windows feeling good on them, Nanook now sound asleep to the monotonous drone of the engine. At a truck stop Nick gassed up, and Soba let Nanook out of the back to relieve himself. He spotted a pay phone and went over and dialed Charlie's office phone. Nick got voice mail and told Charlie he was avoiding using cell phones. He was a little paranoid and disclosed all that had unfolded the past few days, especially the details revealed to him from his peyote induced trip. And of course, the fact that Soba and Attila the Hound had accompanied him.

The drive to Zuni would be about another two hours, with the Hawikuh Ruins just down the road from there. There was time for some deeper conversation between them, and Soba let her natural curiosity show.

"Mesoamerican Migrations, pretty fascinating stuff, at least to me. But I'm Mesoamerican. That couldn't have made you popular with the ladies back in the upper peninsula of Michigan," Soba playfully kidded.

Nick's Trek South

"Mesoamerican Migration *Patterns*, actually. Yeah, I was always the life of any cocktail party. Thank goodness for Charlie, I could always look good, at least in comparison to him."

"What compelled you down that path, of all possible paths?"

"Well, I was already hooked on history and adventure, thanks to my dad. That led to archeology and anthropology, just dialing the clock back a little further. And as I started to dig digging, my mind started wrapping itself around bigger issues and patterns."

With that he pointed to his t-shirt, which read "Archeology 101 – Rock, Tool or Relic?" Soba could only grin and shake her head, it took a true archeology nerd to have such a collection of outwear.

"Not that unearthing a wooly mammoth skeleton isn't exciting, it is, it's a real rush. But when you find a precisely crafted arrowhead imbedded in the rib cage, cut marks on the bones, it sets your mind to wondering who killed it, what skills they had to orchestrate bringing down such a big animal, and where they came from in the first place. Which, if you follow the logic trail backward, would ultimately lead to where you came from, where I came from. Ultimately it was all from one original group on an ancient savannah in Africa, we have just been doing a lot of migrating and splintering all these millennia since."

"Big questions, so does your path to enlightenment lead to a scientific or religious answer?"

"I am the first to admit my path is incremental, my knowledge and beliefs evolving. I can't say that science and religion exclude one another, it is more a matter of interpretation and time span. I only have one lifetime to solve pieces of what to me is the mystery of being human, and the piece I am currently focused on is Mesoamerican migration patterns. That in turn seeks to answer how people first came to North and South America, who were they and how they mixed to form pre-Columbian civilizations. All well before the European's ever 'discovered' them."

Soba furrowed her eyebrows. "You know that is a sore spot with my people, with any of the tribes. The Spanish didn't discover a new world. It was already here, with all of us in it. That is why so many origin stories of native tribes deal with coming from the earth. *We* discovered it an epoch ago, when there was not a single human upon it. They didn't discover anything, they bumped into a continent they didn't know existed."

Nick couldn't help himself and smiled at her passion. "And ironies of ironies, Columbus thought he had landed in the Indies, and henceforth and evermore you were all known as Indians. By the way, did you know Columbus Day is October 12th this year?"

Soba rolled her eyes at that one. "So educate me, Nick LaBounty. Defend your thesis to me, where did we *Indians* originally come from?"

"Well, not from the earth as your Hopi cousins believe. At least not the earth of the Americas. First, let's agree to a couple of assumptions. That there was at one time a single supercontinent, called *Pangaea.* That the forces of plate tectonics broke apart our jigsaw puzzle of the world and caused the continents to drift to their current approximate positions. And that ice age glaciers soaked up a lot of water and brought about lower sea levels, which created a land bridge between Asia and North America, near the Bering Sea Strait. With me so far?"

"We concede to you your assumptions for the purpose of this exercise. Please continue with the defense of your position," Soba joked in her best serious, academic voice.

"There are two primary indicators which reinforce each other, with additional evidence that continues to accumulate. The first is following the fossil record, including the trail of *spear points. H*ow they were made, how they evolved, what animal remains they were found in, and even the protein preserved within their porous surfaces. Clovis is a term used for a particular type of spear point, characterized by grooves within it. You can follow the spread of these and other types of spear and arrow heads like trails across the continents. Combine that with remains of camp sites, butchered and discarded bones, cave habitations and the like, and you get a reasonable migration map across North and South America."

"And the second indicator, what might that be?" Soba inquired, batting her dark eyelashes in his direction.

"Why you, of course," Nick stated, thinking it was obvious.

"I think I follow, but please expound on your position."

"*DNA*. DNA doesn't lie. And the science behind it has only gotten better, more refined, more conclusive. Plus, there are ever more ways of recovering it, things that a decade ago didn't exist, and ones we can't imagine today that are yet to be revealed. Then melt the ice sheets and bring all kinds of new samples to light. We find Wooly Mammoths preserved in permafrost with spear points in them, and preserved hunters with mammoth meat in their stomachs."

Nick was warming up to his subject. "Toss in mummies well preserved by accident or by certain cultures like the Inca, and we have access to lots of tissue. The soft tissue record compliments the fossil record. And all this accumulated data shows Siberians and related Asians walked or boated the kelp highway along the Bering Strait to Alaska. Pacific Islanders island hopped and drifted to South America, Hell, even some wayward Europeans far back in time somehow drifted over, as evidenced by trace amounts in the blood lineage. All these went into an empty continent and mixed into the pre-Columbian man. Or woman."

Nick was on a roll, his tempo picking up. "In conclusion, the ice sheets formed and melted multiple times, allowing people to cross from Asia and Siberia to North America more than once. So there were multiple migrations from there. And DNA evidence shows others arrived at different times from different points of origin. This was a *melting pot* of ethnicities even before the Europeans made that claim much later. You had to get those high cheekbones and striking good looks from somewhere. It's just too bad they didn't all come out looking like you."

His eyes on the road, he listened for a response and thought he heard a gentle snoring. He looked over at Soba, curled up against the window, rhythmically breathing, obviously fascinated by him pouring his heart out on his academic passions. As he let out a sigh of disappointment, Soba suddenly sat bolt upright, laughing out loud. "Real edge of your seat stuff, *mąʼiitsoh nahatʼin*," she said, teasing him again with her nickname of the wolf howler.

"And maybe a bit drier than our origin stories. Frankly I think the myths have more flair. Well look at the bright side, at least it did create one of me!" she giggled playfully.

With that she leaned over and gave him an affectionate kiss on the cheek. At which time Nanook poked his head through the back window and gave his ear a lick. Good times, these.

CHAPTER 22 – AFTERNOON, JUNE 23

As they approached the Visitors Center in Zuni, Nick nudged Soba awake to let her know they had arrived, as well as give her some interesting news.

"I have some colleagues back at the universities I attended who are well aware of my quest and sworn to secrecy. They have been keeping a steady eye out for anything which may be of interest popping up on the news front or in academia. And I've done the same with some web crawlers and my personal news feeds. There is a Pueblo just down the road in Hawikuh which was well explored over time. Turns out a part of it just recently disintegrated, which was a false back wall. Some artifacts were found behind it, still *in situ*, but what was most interesting were some petroglyphs etched into the cliff wall hidden behind it. Nobody knows about this outside the tribe except for my old mentor, Dr. Storm. One of his old students is a member of the tribe here, and he was the one who came across it. He reached out to Dr. Storm, who arranged for us to have access."

"What does in situ mean, I haven't heard that term before?"

"In situ just means something has been left as it was found, that it is still it its original place. It helps in dating artifacts, since the detritus around it may provide clues. Like if you can't date the artifact itself, perhaps you can use carbon 14 dating on a biologic item like a seed, bone or piece of wood found with it. Frankly its archeology speak for making the simple complicated."

"Do you think it reveals anything relevant to your search, or is it just something new related to the Pueblo Indians?" Soba asked.

"I don't know, but timing is everything. Definitely worth checking out while we are here, you never know what thread it may provide now or later."

A quick run through the Visitors Center showed that the area was rumored to have been one of the 'Seven Cities of Gold' that originally tempted the Spanish to venture north. In due course it was overtaken by them, and Coronado made it his headquarters. Later the Pueblo revolts eventually led to it being abandoned by the Spanish. The subtext was that the area had been occupied, not subdued, with no love lost for the Spanish in the process.

This was on Zuni Reservation Land, and the wisdom of having Soba along became immediately apparent. As they finished browsing around the Visitors Center they were greeted by a deeply tanned and wrinkled old man named *Lonan*, a tribal elder whose name meant Cloud in the Zuni language. He was in charge of the access to restricted areas and spoke jilted English but could make himself understood. Soba immediately replied to him in Zuni, which was a language isolate, meaning not related to any other known language. Lonan was immediately enchanted with this pretty young Navajo who spoke his unique language so eloquently.

"Lonan said that your Dr. Storm has contacted him to arrange for us to examine the newly discovered room and its contents. He would be delighted to lead us there and asks if there is anything you need."

Nick looked him in the eye and held out his hand and said, "Pleased to meet you Lonan. I have everything we need, and a willing apprentice. I look forward to sharing anything we discover with your people, just show us the way."

Lonan indicated they were to follow him and drove off in an old Willy Jeep with no doors and a tied down hood that had seen better days. They followed, and fifteen minutes later pulled up to a compound of buildings that were broken down from a cycle of

Spanish occupations and tribal recapture, and the inevitable erosion of time. Lonan led them through the compound, to a nondescript partial building adjoining a low cliff. The collapsed wall was marked off with little more than duct tape and sticks. It wouldn't have been noticeable to anyone passing by. But Lonan knew these ruins like the back of his well weathered hands, and proudly showed them to his new guests.

"I know you good rock digger. Take as much time you need. Just ask you keep finds secret with tribe only." With that Lonan smiled, bowed slightly toward Soba, and left. Nanook accompanied him back to his Jeep and sat quietly as he drove away.

When Nick crawled into the bed of the pickup for his tools, he saw an acoustic guitar had been placed there, covered by a tarp. There was a hastily scrawled note between the strings. "In case of campfire, break out immediately." A little drawing of a wolf howling at a full moon was at the bottom. He smiled and shook his head at the heartfelt gift from Bidzii. The water did indeed run deep with his Navajo friend.

He grabbed his kit and his camera and walked out to the site. Nick proceeded to photograph and document the site exactly as it was before he even stepped into it. He asked that Soba make sure Nanook did not enter the area, and carefully worked his way in. A glance back showed Nanook had taken an instinctual defensive position, protectively positioned in front of the only access point, looking out. Soba saw what he was thinking, smiled, and shrugged her shoulders as if to say, 'I didn't teach him that.'

A very old wall within the building remains had partially collapsed, evidently from nothing more than time and deterioration. The area it occupied was small and somewhat triangular, angling away from the low cliff face, only 18 or 20 square feet.

Nick immediately set up a grid with strings and stakes, and pulled out a folded portable sifter, a couple of tarps, and a box of boxes and packing out of the back of the pickup. After continuing to carefully photograph everything, he started investigating, square by square. Immediately evident were a decayed Spanish helmet, a sword pommel, part of a bridle, obsidian arrow points and a war club of some kind. Nick put labeled index cards near each and photographed them in position.

After the larger items were removed, dirt was taken out square by square and sifted. Soba was enlisted, and this tedious process revealed a small silver cross and a broken necklace a little under the surface. The necklace looked to be gold, with some type of amber or obsidian within it. Everything was meticulously chronicled and documented by grid and placed in their corresponding position on the tarp. Further digging revealed nothing more, and eventually hit the hardpan surface.

"Why do you think they went to such trouble to hide this, it doesn't seem like it would have been a substantial treasure to them?" Soba asked.

"Hard to say. There are both Spanish and native artifacts, it is almost like it was a talisman of some kind. Or a warning. I was hoping there might be more clues, let's take a closer look at the wall."

The etchings on the wall were faded, barely visible. Nick grabbed a camera lens duster and used it to puff air on a portion of the etching, and a fine dust came out. It didn't change the coloring, but the etchings became more pronounced. He proceeded to do it on all the etchings he could see, and then stepped back to let the dust in the air settle. When it was evident it was still too hard to see and it wasn't painted, he patted over it with a damp cloth.

Even damp it was still difficult to discern the etchings, so he grabbed his camera and took shots with and without the flash, at different exposures. When he looked at the viewing screen on back, he edited one photo in particular to jack up the contrast. With that the image finally came distinctly into view.

"That makes no sense, not all the way up here, halfway up New Mexico." Nick mumbled to himself in astonishment.

Soba looked at him questioningly. "What makes no sense?"

"These are petroglyphs, etched symbols and artwork. As you well know petroglyphs are common around the Southwest, except these appear to be Aztec symbols. They had their own written language, mostly in picture form, like hieroglyphs were for the

Egyptians. The Aztecs kept extensive records on folded deer skin or their own form of agave paper. What they record are called codices. Almost none survive, and the most extensive ones were created after the conquest by a few somewhat renegade Franciscans who wanted to save the Aztec history. But this far north, and possibly pre-conquest, to be etched like this, it makes no sense."

"Were they accurate, I mean the depictions the Franciscans created?"

"History is written by the victors, not by the vanquished. So I always take it with a grain of salt, there is usually propaganda or someone's agenda masked within it."

Soba watched silently as Nick gently ran his fingers over the etchings. "This wasn't written by the victors. Perhaps they didn't even know they were vanquished yet. I suspect it is in stone to stand the test of time."

"I can speak Nahuatl, several dialects actually. But I haven't seen but a couple codices reproduced in old history books. They almost look like each picture tells a story," Soba replied.

"They do, and I know from personal experience sometimes you can come up with the right story to accompany them, but not always. This probably has nothing to do with my quest, but it is significant if the Aztecs were actually this far north, before they were defeated and subjugated. I need to get these images to Dr. Storm, he may know someone who can decipher them."

Nick finished his work at the site, carefully removing his grid along with the original sticks and duct tape and threw them all into the back of the truck. He made sure to cover any signs that he, or anyone else for that matter, had ever been there. All the artifacts were carefully wrapped and marked, and they headed back to the Visitors Center to see Lonan.

He wasn't there when they arrived, and the center had just closed for the day. Soba saw someone about to drive away and went over to talk with her. When she returned she said, "Lonan went home, and it is not easy to get to from here. I was asked to bring the findings back in the morning. She said there is a nice camp site over that ridge."

"Tent or truck?" Nick asked, not wanting to make Soba feel uncomfortable with spending her first night on the road with him.

"We're getting a late start, I vote for truck," she replied as Nick drove over to the ridge. "I suspect we'll have plenty of chances to tent it."

Soba wandered off and said she would be back shortly. Nick gathered some dry sage brush and scraggly loose wood and got a small fire going in the fire pit. They had been told accurately, this definitely was a nice camp site, with a panoramic vista spread out from the small ledge they were on. In the quiet of dusk, Nick heard a joyful shout from Soba, and soon saw her wandering back with a rabbit over her shoulder. Nanook was carrying something large and prancing behind her.

"Nanook get the rabbit?" Nick inquired, tossing her a folded hunting knife.

"No silly, I did with a snare. We live well off the land because we are in tune with it. We need nothing more."

When Nick looked more carefully at Nanook sitting between them and the road, he noticed he was crunching hard on something with his powerful jaws. Nanook's eyes reflected in the dusk briefly, his white face wearing a mask of red. Seeing a hoof shaking in the air, Nick was glad to call this wolf a friend.

Darkness was closing in, the stars just starting to show as pin pricks of faint light high overhead. Content with a full belly of rabbit and beans, and lulled by the glow of the embers, Nick pulled the acoustic guitar out of the truck. When Soba saw it she immediately recognized it as Bidzii's, her eyes welling up. She looked to the sky, said something in hushed tones under her breath, and bowed her head.

"I didn't know I even had it, that he had given it to me. Mom said when you receive an unexpected gift, the best thing you can do is accept it graciously. But I never even got the chance."

"You will. All in good time," Soba replied through damp eyes and a grateful smile.

"OK, I keep having songs play in my head that make me think

of you. So for the rest of the trip, whenever I think of one, I'm going to play it to you that night. Here goes nothing."

Nick strummed a few notes, tuned the guitar slightly, then cleared his throat. He concentrated for a moment to remember the lyrics, he wanted to get it just right. "An old favorite by Atlanta Rhythm Section called Spooky, for you my bewitching sorceress," he began.

In the cool of the evenin'
when ev'rything is gettin' kind of groovy
I call you up
and ask if you'd like to go with me and see a movie
First you say no, you've got some plans for the night
And then you stop, and say, all right
Love is kinda crazy with a spooky little girl like you

Soba sat with her eyes closed for a moment, smiling until she recognized the song. Then laughingly she sang the refrains along with Nick, their eyes meeting and never straying. She threw out a half dozen song requests to him, and he played them all, some well, some struggling to remember the words or chords.

When he finished the last one, Soba walked over and took the guitar from him, placed it on the front seat, and took him by the hand into the back of the truck. Nick left the tailgate and back window open so they could see the stars. Nanook stood momentarily with his snout on the tailgate, ears alert, and saw them spooning in the sleeping bag. He then circled several times before laying down directly under the tailgate. By the time he let out his usual huff of a releasing breath, they were both already fast asleep.

CHAPTER 23 – JUNE 24

Lonan greeted Nick and Soba when they arrived early morning at the Visitors Center, obviously pleased with the artifacts and documentation provided. He told Soba in Zuni that they would make a nice addition to the local *A:shiwi A:wan Museum*. He was also curious as to how the items came to be hidden behind a false wall. And that if they ever found out what the strange markings on the wall said, please let him know. For now, the markings would continue to be their little secret.

Lonan looked over at Nick and spoke in Zuni to him while Soba translated. "We have mysteries both here and in our past. Our histories handed down tell of many of our people who left even before Spanish came. We call them the *Lost Others*. It would be good to know what became of them, if ever possible. Over time our people are like so much chaff from corn tossed into a great wind, scattered all over."

Soba gave Lonan a hug and kiss on the cheek goodbye and detected a slight blush on his face. He smiled and said, "Many years since young woman kissed old face," and couldn't help but laugh at himself.

"*Ahéhee'*," Nick said: thank you, in his first attempt at speaking a word of Zuni. Lonan knowingly winked at Soba, suspecting her of a little coaching.

Standing more than a full head taller than the age-stooped Lonan, Soba impulsively gave him another kiss on the top of his wrinkled bald head and saw that turn crimson too. "Now they match," she said in Zuni and winked back at him, waving as she left.

"How can you not love the elders, the keepers of legacy and tradition? They are truly the best of us," she mused as they drove away. Nick nodded subconsciously as he looked ahead at the horizon, a lonely trail of dust rising in their wake.

They had decided on just one more stop before they crossed the border into Mexico, at the Gila Cliff Dwellings near Silver City. Further south than the territory of the Anasazi or Pueblo Indians, this was on the northern edge of the area of *Mogollon* influence. They were contemporary societies, flourishing and fading at about the same timeframe. Illustrating how well these and similar cliff-dwelling ruins were hidden, Gila wasn't seen by a white man until 1878—or at least one who lived to tell about it.

It was about a six-hour drive to get there, and Nick was looking forward to seeing an old classmate who now worked at the site. He called ahead and arranged to see him tomorrow. They had time to kill on the drive, some time to find a diversion for a little fun, and a chance to peel the onion back one more layer on each other.

"My turn today. Genesis tells us that, after the great flood, a united mankind spoke one language, and in their vanity tried to build a tower to reach heaven. God saw this and confused their single language into many and scattered them across the land. So exactly how many of these languages do you speak?" Nick inquired.

"All that I have set out to learn. My father spoke Navajo fluently like everyone in the tribe did, as well as a stilted version of Nahuatl. As I learned more over the years, it struck me as odd that he was insistent that I learn Nahuatl, a language with roots so far from home. What was most interesting was I came to realize he spoke a very distinct dialect of Nahuatl, a somewhat more ancient version. As peoples who spoke the base language scattered back in time, pockets of them evolved slightly different versions of it."

"Who else did he ever even speak Nahuatl with?"

"With his grandfather and father while they were still alive, and then with me. My mother never learned to speak it, although she could understand most of it. The other tribal elders ignored it, they were having a hard-enough time keeping their own Navajo language alive with the young people."

Nick looked over at her with a bit of a look of wonder in his eyes. "From what I understand, Nahuatl is not an easy language to master. Neither is Navajo. But you grew up bi-lingual with both, so that I understand. But your English is impeccable, I just heard you speak Zuni, what else do you have up your sleeve?"

"When I tested for university, I found I had a real gift for language. I didn't even know I had it, it just was. My undergraduate advisor said I was a phonetic prodigy, that I should go even further in my studies, but I wanted to help my people, not languish in a classroom. The language isolates, those languages that are unrelated to any other like Zuni, are a little more work to learn. But they are rare, most of the rest are spin offs of something else somewhere down the line, like the romance languages to Europeans. If you know one, you have the keys to the next, and then the next in turn. Like you, I like to solve puzzles. Yours are abstract in time and place, mine are abstract in people and communication. If you asked me, I think we make a pretty good team, because underneath it all we both seek the same thing. Truth."

The afternoon was sweltering, the heat reflecting off the asphalt pavement and distorting the horizon, the stifling breeze through the truck offering little relief. They didn't want to close the back of the front cab off because Nanook would get little air flow, so they drove with the side windows cracked and the air conditioning on full. After a couple of hours they stopped and gassed up, Nick adding the obligatory quart of oil, Nanook marking some virgin territory. When they found a hose off the side of the gas station, they sprayed the wolf down until he was drenched, which perked him back up a bit. A glance at an old map thumb tacked to the wall showed the

Gila River ran by where they were going, and the irresistible idea of taking a swim took hold. Just a few hours more.

By late afternoon the heat was finally breaking, and Soba used Nick's cell phone to locate the best part of the river for a dip. His phone was newer and more powerful than hers, although she had some difficulty in initially figuring it out.

"Why are smart phones so stupid?" she finally exclaimed in exasperation.

"Sure it's the phone?" Nick grinned.

After driving since the early morning from Hawikuh, they were both relieved to finally pull over for the day. The bend of the river Soba selected was a little off the beaten path, and as the turn off to a dirt road eventually became more of a path, Nick put the Chevy in four-wheel drive and slowly crept down it. They pulled up around a corner, and a glistening bend in the river spread out before them. Here the water slowed slightly, the encroaching hills blanketed by ponderosa pines, the banks giving way to shorter piñon pine and scrub brush, ending in a pebbled stretch of sand.

Soba immediately started to gather edible pine nuts and scattered berries. Nick opened the tailgate so Nanook could get out, and he stood stiffly on the edge, sniffing his new surroundings. Nick gave him a swat on the rump, and he took off with a bound to explore the perimeter as Nick pulled out some camping gear.

"*Baa shił hózhǫ́!*" Soba shouted, translating roughly to *about me there is joy*. Nick looked up, and saw her clothes strewn in a trail leading to the river, a brief glimpse of her naked figure diving gracefully into it.

"Yeah, that's a great idea," he excitedly yelled, and ran toward the water. He kicked off his shoes, pulled off his shirt, and wiped out as he tried to peel off his shorts, his feet tangled in them. Soba watched it all from the water and giggled as he tried to maintain his dignity, with little success. The new bloody scrape mark on his buttock mirrored the black and blue one Charlie had snapped into him a few days—or was it a lifetime—ago. He stood on the water's edge, looked at Soba, and shrugged as if to say, "It's all I've got," and dove into the river.

"Graceful disrobe and dismount, you never fail to impress a girl," Soba mewed as she tread water, holding her position in the gentle current.

Nick swam to her, touched noses, and added, "I notice it's not just my ego that seems to take a beating around you."

They kissed eagerly, twisting in the current, drifting downstream until Nick's feet touched the murky bottom.

"So what song will you serenade me with tonight, Nick LaBounty?" Soba asked softly in her sing song cadence.

Nick was about to reply, but felt something bump his calf, and then his thigh. He let Soba go and jumped back when something hit his nether regions. "What the hell is that?" he yelped.

Soba had been staring into the water, put both her hands slowly under the surface, and then lunged completely into it.

"That's dinner," she said as she emerged, holding a fat catfish tightly in her hands. "Pucker up buttercup, kiss it for good luck!"

She chased Nick out of the water with it, giggling until he relented and she planted the catfish's mouth and whiskers on his lips. "Thank him for the nourishment he provides, some day it will be our turn to return the favor."

"Great, I am really looking forward to being worm food," Nick chuckled.

"What was it I heard a white priest say at a funeral I attended, ashes to ashes, dust to dust? That's not so far from what we believe, we all eventually have our turn," she replied.

Nick smiled at her, watched as she went over and placed stones in a circle, then gathered wood for a fire. He was a modest man, not used to being naked outdoors except for the occasional skinny dip. He looked at her, completely at ease in her own skin, utterly unconcerned about her nakedness, wearing only silver and turquoise earrings. He found he felt comfortable around her, his own preconceptions and hang-ups about a lot of things somehow melting away.

Soba walked up behind Nick and started rubbing something gently on his scraped hip. "What is that?" he asked.

Soba put a dab on his nose. "Piñon pine salve. It will help you to heal quicker."

As they started to cook, Nick slipped back into his shorts, naked for as long as he could stand it. He caught Soba smiling and staring at him and said, "Thought I would dress up for dinner."

"You're a good sport, you lasted longer than I thought you would," she jabbed back, and pulled a long, loose fitting black gauze dress over her head.

As was becoming usual, the meal was outstanding. Simply prepared, with wild accompaniments Nick didn't even know were edible, they both ate their fill. And it didn't escape his attention that when Soba had handed him his plate, the head of the catfish was in the middle, looking up at him with long whiskers that draped over the edges.

"Pucker up," she laughed.

"Buttercup," he replied.

There were two 50-pound bags of dog food in the back of the truck, but Nick noticed Soba had yet to use them. Nanook seemed perfectly capable of providing for himself when in the wilderness, but he tossed him the fish head anyway.

The sun set over the river, the reflections shimmering in the gentle current. Soba went to the truck and brought back the guitar to Nick, and started gently dancing around the fire, like the first time he had seen her dance. Her arms gracefully moving about her, her hips rhythmically swaying. She playfully asked, "What song strikes you as appropriate for tonight?"

Nick watched her, her movements in and out of the firelight, the sparks rising, the darkness falling, an ephemeral moment. The inspiration hit him. "Got it," he finally said.

A few practice chords, then he broke into a song that had made Stevie Nicks and Fleetwood Mac famous, a song about a witch, love, desire, and fleeting moments. Soba immediately shouted, "You're kidding, that's what my roommate in college used to call me!" She loved the song *Rhiannon*, knew every word, and sashayed her long black sleeves and hair to the acoustic beat, singing the refrain with Nick as she twirled around and around him.

She is like a cat in the dark and then

She is the darkness
She rules her life like a fine skylark
And when the sky is starless

All your life you've never seen
A woman taken by the wind
Would you stay if she promised you heaven?
Will you ever win?
Will you ever win?

Rhiannon, Rhiannon

Nick took a few more song requests from her, and then with a mischievous smile Soba grabbed the guitar away and put it carefully on the front seat of the Chevy. Grabbed by the belt, Nick followed her and climbed onto the air mattress in the back of the pickup. She smelled like the first time he met her, all piñon pine, desert herbs, and smoky hair. When they felt a heavy thud on the truck, they both peered up and saw Nanook with his two front paws on the tailgate, staring back, ready to play. They laughed and pulled the sleeping bag over them, anxious to get to the bottom of at least one mystery this night.

Later they lay resting in one another's arms, the rising tension of the past days finally finding its release. Soba softly hummed *Rhiannon*, and couldn't help singing the refrain, *"Dreams unwind, love's a state of mind."* They lay intertwined and listened to the sounds of the night, staring out the back at the fading fire, the moon slowly working its way across the endless blanket of stars, until they drifted off to a blissful sleep.

When morning came, Nick rolled over and saw Soba open her eyes and look back at him, a gentle smile on her face, the taste of wild berries in her kiss.

"Funny, somehow you know the songs that bare my soul. I guess that's fair, since I can see into yours," Soba said softly.

It took him a moment to focus, to see that something was different, and then he realized what it was. She had deep, dark green, jade colored eyes. He blinked hard and stared and felt like two luminous emeralds were looking back at him.

Soba saw the confusion on his face. "Colored contact lenses. Remember I said my tribe thought I was different? I couldn't hide my height, but I could hide my green eyes. There were only so many ways I could try to blend in."

Her dark, almost black eyes had captivated him. But these were something else entirely. "They're stunning, why couldn't they just let you be who you are?" Nick asked, feeling defensive for her against a past he couldn't protect her from.

"My dad and his forefathers before him, going back hundreds of years, were all shamans, and yet outcasts. We Diné are a superstitious people, and those who are different, like with green eyes or physically taller, they were considered loco, useful but never quite embraced, the crazy medicine men. Not all of my forefathers had green eyes, but enough did to cause trepidation in the greater tribe. So when I came of age and grew taller than the boys, all I could do to try to fit in was change my eyes."

"Did your father have green eyes?" Nick asked, unable to take his off of hers.

"No, so perhaps that in its own way made it harder for me. The younger kids had never seen them, and you know how cruel kids can be. But the elders remembered, they never let us forget anything."

"Well do me a favor, would you? Around me and away from the tribe, skip the contact lenses. I want an unobstructed view into your soul."

CHAPTER 24 – MORNING, JUNE 25

Killian Yudhisthir, how the hell are you?" Nick asked as he embraced his long-lost friend, both of them immediately laughing and punching one another.

"Soba, I want you to meet Kill Devil, I mean Killian, a dear friend of mine from college days."

Killian offered his hand, but Soba ignored it and gave him a hug too. "Any friend of Nick's is a friend of mine," she said warmly. "You both look like you've been up to no good. So how exactly did you two meet?"

"Introduction to Archeology with old man Laing. We got paired up on a field project, and I could never get rid of him," Killian replied, laughing. "Not that I wanted to, those were some fun years running with this guy."

"So how did you end up here, of all places?" Soba inquired.

"Ultimately, I felt the pull of wanting to learn how to preserve the history of my people and this area, and archeology seemed the best path to it. So I work for the Park Service here, building up the collection for the museum and interpreting and preserving the dwellings you see."

"What Killian isn't telling you is what a hell raiser he was. That's where the *Kill Devil* comes from. But that isn't what is most interesting about this wild man. Tell her about your lineage buddy, and the meaning of your name. You two have a few things in common," Nick said.

"Not that much to tell. You go back far enough, a little Irish girl got kidnapped by my tribe, the Chiricahua Apache. Lots of that going on as the sod busters pushed west. She was adopted and raised by them, and down the line you get me. Irish name and a little Irish blood in an Apache body. All good except I sunburn like the blazes and like whiskey!" he said, slapping Nick on the back and cackling with his infectious laugh. "*Yudhisthir* is Apache for 'Firm in Battle.' I know Nick's story," he said, faking a yawn. "What's yours?"

Soba looked at Nick with an upraised eyebrow, and then turned to Killian. "Soba is short for Altsoba, Navajo for 'At War.' If I remember correctly, a lot of that was fighting the Apache. I also have devoted my life to my people, specifically by preserving their languages and traditions. Through some quirk of fate we both somehow ended up attached to this guy."

"Ha, sounds more like fate is a cruel mistress, if you asked me. C'mon, let me show you the lay of the land."

Soba looked at Nick and grinned. "Or the gods have a twisted sense of humor."

There were many ruins in the area, but Killian proudly showed them around two of the major sites. The first was five cliff dwellings interconnected by natural caves above the aptly named Cliff Dweller Canyon. They climbed and crawled through the impressive shelters, Killian narrating and providing remarkable insight, Nick asking questions and taking pictures. The second site he showed was called the TJ Ruins, named for a former rancher the greater sprawling mesa was named after. It was perched on a bluff overlooking the Gila River below. When Nick caught a glimpse of the river, he nudged Soba and said, "Care to go for a skinny dip later?" Her eyes sparkled as she replied, "Only if we don't get caught."

"Amazing what they built here," Killian observed. "My Apache ancestors wandered into the area after it had been abandoned. The scientific community is still trying to definitively determine why this and so many other similar locations were vacated during about the same timeframe. Let me show you the museum, it contains both Mogollon and Apache artifacts."

After walking them through, Killian pulled both Nick and Soba aside and whispered, "Did you know there were mummies found here? Most were looted and sold to private collectors. But in 1912 another was found and put in the Smithsonian, where it sits to this day. And you know what is even cooler? I *found one* last month. Very unusual since this area has all been so well explored. But it was hidden in one of the connecting caves I was exploring, purposely tucked into a crack and concealed with stone to make a false wall, which eventually crumbled. Want to see it?"

"Are you kidding? I'd love to!" Nick said a little too loudly in his excitement.

Killian put a finger to his lips and gave a conspiratorial grin and led them down to the end of a hallway to a locked door that said, 'Park Service Employees Only.' He fiddled with a key and got it opened, turned on a light switch and led them in. Bathed in cold florescent light, he pulled back a tarp and revealed a large plastic container, and then carefully removed the lid. Checking the hygrometer for a humidity reading he said, "Meet John Doe, or as we're calling him, the Misplaced Padre."

Nick and Soba peered closer, looking at the naturally mummified remains of a man with his knees drawn up to his chest, with his arms crossed, as if in a sitting position. A woven bag was around him, though badly decayed and showing what was underneath. It was evident why Killian called him Padre, as he was wearing the coarse dark tunic of the order. And clasped in his hands were a cross and chain made of silver.

"This is an incredible find, remarkably well preserved. But why would a Spanish missionary, or whoever he was, be preserved here, hidden in a place sacred to the tribes? And what will you do with him?" Nick asked.

"Good questions. As of yet we don't know how he got here. Right now my job is to make sure to stabilize him and thoroughly examine the area around where I found him. Have to establish proper provenance, you know the drill. It was important to get him out of there once found, the looting has only become more endemic, so we're keeping this hush hush for now. They're sending a forensic archeologist down from Albuquerque to examine him in more detail. I suspect they will x-ray and CAT scan him before all is said and done. Maybe I can find something we can carbon date too."

As Nick and Killian wandered away talking, Soba leaned over the table and gently put her hand on the head of the mummy. As Nick glanced back at her, her eyes were closed, and she was silently reciting something to herself, some type of incantation. Killian noticed it too and stopped talking to listen and looked at Nick questioningly.

"There is more here than meets the eye. He is part of a greater something, he has a story to tell across time. I don't know what it is, but I can sense it," Soba said when she opened her eyes and looked back in their direction. "And somehow I am tied into this."

Nick clapped Killian on the back. "She is a tribal shaman, with both Aztec and Navajo roots. It's a long story. But if I've learned anything about Soba, it is that she can see into things no one else can, and to trust her intuition."

Nick snapped a few photos on his phone of the mummy, with a couple of close-ups including the cross he held. Then they took Killian out to meet Nanook and say goodbye.

Killian was slightly taken aback when Nanook was let out of the back of the truck and came up to him and sniffed. With an indifferent air, Nanook then ignored him and sat next to Soba. "That is one big animal, do you think you will have any problem getting him over the border?" he inquired.

"No, I've got all his papers, his record of shots. Just another large canine going through customs, I expect. He's been across before." With that Soba led Nanook away so he could stretch his legs and relieve himself.

Nick put his arm around Killian and said, "Great to see you man. It's been way too long. I appreciate you showing us your little discovery too. Let me know if you find out anything else about your

Padre. You know you still owe me a visit back up north, be good to get a few of the old classmates together."

They said their goodbyes, and Soba leaned in for one more hug with her new Apache friend. Nick looked at them both and said, "Glad to see your tribes have finally buried the hatchet after all these years." That got a laugh out of both Killian and Soba, as the phrase had multiple connotations.

It was about a four-hour drive to El Paso and the border, and they settled into the familiar rhythm of the road. Soba picked the music this time, shaking things up a little with a random selection of jazz tunes playing in the background. She shook her head at how he had his iPhone connected via a cable into an old cassette deck in the dashboard.

"Old school meets new school," she commented.

"Old school is still the best school," Nick replied. "Hey, I've been meaning to ask you, it sounded like Bidzii was able to keep his buddies away from the dark side, from what you were telling me. But I got the sense there was something else going on with it."

Soba sighed and looked out the window. "Too much time, too little work, people out to make a quick buck. Alcohol was the drug of choice for most on the reservation, even though it was illegal. But drugs were always an issue too, a constant undercurrent. Especially around the young people. Bidzii lost his brother to an overdose when he was young and swore he would never affiliate with anyone who did or dealt drugs. The friends he kept all knew this, and they avoided that path, both for their own good and because of their respect for Bidzii."

"That explains it, the vibe I was getting from him now makes sense. Hey, I was no angel, I toked occasionally in my rebellious phase, but that was never my thing. Frankly that element was something I went out of my way to avoid. I could never understand the psyche of someone who could only feel something by feeling absolutely nothing at all. It seemed a lot of them ended up aging well before their time, if they even got that far. How does he deal with it now?" Nick asked.

"If you're his friend and you want to drink, he's with you all the way. I believe you've experienced that firsthand already. You smoke a little pot, he'll give you the silent treatment. You do harder drugs, he'll pick a fight with you. You deal drugs, he'd like to kill you," Soba said, surprised at the matter-of-fact conviction in her own voice.

It was early evening when they reached El Paso, and Nick pulled into a large truck stop for a bite to eat. Soba walked Nanook, while he put a call into Charlie from a pay phone and caught him at the office this time. They talked for over twenty minutes, and Nick brought him up to speed on the artifacts and wall etchings he saw at Hawikuh, and the interesting mummy Killian showed them at the Gila Cliff Dwellings.

"Was that Kill Devil Killian from college?" Charlie asked. They had met when Nick brought him home over one break, the three of them becoming fast drinking buddies.

"One and the same, although I think he has settled down a little bit. Hard to tell in the brief time I saw him. Anyway, I doubt any of what I saw at Hawikuh or Gila is relevant to Dad's quest, but it sure as hell fascinates the archeologist in me."

"Also sounds like Soba fascinates you too. I'm jealous, that's quite the road trip you've got going brother. Be careful and keep in touch. If what you said was true about the way Dad got killed, you don't want to tangle with those hombres," Charlie warned.

As they sat down to eat, Soba said she had also called Bidzii to give him an update. "All good with him, they are playing gigs and working their way back home. But he said it was more fun when the two of us were around," Soba said as she leaned into Nick playfully. "I think he misses you too. Should I be jealous of your bromance?"

Stomachs and gas tank full, they headed for the border crossing, the lines much shorter going into Mexico than into the states. As they pulled up for their turn, the agent glanced down at a computer screen, and then took a call on his cell phone. He asked for their documents, and slowly reviewed them. Looking nervously about, he told Nick to pull over off to the side.

Nick did as he was told, and they sat waiting for several minutes. With no warning, the doors were opened, and they were both told to get out of the vehicle. One stiff looking Mexican Border Agent went to open the back but saw Nanook glaring back at him. "Get your dog out, and keep him with you," he instructed. Soba grabbed Nanook but could sense the hair on his back slightly raised and heard a low growl from deep within. She and Nick looked at one another with raised eyebrows, neither knowing what had prompted the spontaneous inspection.

Sitting on a bench to the side, they saw two agents go through the vehicle thoroughly. Once that was done, one agent brought back a German shepherd and had him sniff everything. The second agent looked under the Chevy with a mirror on a telescoping pole. For a final check, he crawled under and examined it directly. When he was sure no one was looking, he slipped a small device out of his pocket and attached it securely. He then turned it on and waited to see a faint red-light blink to know it was active. With that he rolled out from under and nodded to his companion with the shepherd.

Nick and Soba were allowed to get back up, and Soba put Nanook in the back of the truck. They noticed where they had sat on the bench was now being examined as well. With no explanation they were curtly told to be on their way, and pulled out, relieved that they must have been misidentified in some way. As they drove away lightheartedly laughing at their good fortune, a faint red light continued to blink, unseen under the truck frame.

PART III

THE REBIRTH OF EMPIRE

Xipe Totec, Our Lord the Flayed One,
was God of the spring, of planting, and of rebirth.

He wore the skin of a sacrificial victim,
eventually shedding it to symbolize
the continuous renewal of the earth.

Like maize that sheds it skin
when the seeds are ready to germinate,
so too new life grows from the old.

CHAPTER 25 – MORNING, JUNE 25

Esteban González sat alone in his elegant private museum, protectively set beneath his sprawling mansion in the affluent Polanco neighborhood of Mexico City. Known as the Beverly Hills of Mexico, it was home to the wealthiest of the elite of the country. His mansion was probably the most secure building in all of Central America, and he preferred it that way, for good reason.

Esteban took a puff on his Regius Doube Corona cigar, and another sip of his Ultra-Premium Pasion Azteca tequila. They were the most expensive money could buy, but what did he care? Money was no object at this stage of his life, only the consumption and collection of the finer things. Things meant to be savored by someone with his refined taste and appreciation of history, someone who had the will and means to actually *shape* history.

He put down his cigar and turned in his hands a skull, coated in gold, with pure silver in the eye sockets. Purportedly this was the very skull that sat at the top of the Hueteocalli, or Great Temple Pyramid, at the heart of Tenochtitlán in 1521. Legend had it that it was the skull of a particularly hated Spaniard taken prisoner by the Aztecs during the fight for their homeland, coated in precious metals as he breathed his last, as a punishment for his greed and cruelty. It was to sit on the very top of the temple, to see the glory of their empire for all of eternity.

Eternity certainly didn't last very long, Esteban thought. The Aztecs were overwhelmed, subjugated and humiliated when Hernán Cortés returned from his worst defeat to conquer them. *La Noche Trist*, or The Night of Sorrows, should have been the end of the Spanish occupation. But the Aztecs let them escape, and it proved to be their ultimate undoing.

A different kind of Mexico could have emerged, one with a prouder heritage of independence, one with a purer native blood line, one that didn't bow to colonial powers then or the Norteamericanos now. Different oppressors, same yoke over the people. But the Aztecs didn't have the leadership, nor the will, to finish them off when they had the chance, he ruefully reflected.

He felt his anger rising, his face flushing. "I would have ground them all into dust, I would have flayed Cortés and pissed in his skull and offered his heart to the gods," Esteban said to no one in particular, his words echoing down the corridors. And he meant it and had done worse. Much worse. Nobody became a man in his position without earning it, without proving himself to anyone and everyone who crossed him or got in the way of his far seeing and grand ambitions.

He ground his cigar out, took a last sip of tequila and stood and stretched. He looked out over his domain, down the rows upon rows of exquisite display cases and intricately decorated walls and was pleased. For stretched out before him was the largest collection of pre-Columbian artifacts from the Central American region anywhere in the world. What the Louvre, British Museum, and Smithsonian had in their paltry collections paled in comparison. Even the Museo Nacional de Antropología, or National Museum of Anthropology in Mexico City, offered little that he would consider worthy of adding to his private collection.

Over many years and at phenomenal expense he had acquired priceless artifacts on the black market. Artifacts that museums could only dream of, and frankly some had been pilfered from the museums themselves. He laughed at how long it even took some of the museums and private collectors to notice a key item was missing. So meticulously his duplicates were fabricated. Some might never be discovered, and, from embarrassment, some might never be reported.

Establishing *provenanace*, or the precise location an item was found and its chain of ownership, proved trickier in the murky backwaters he and his minions utilized. When something desirable was brought in from a place such as the deep jungles of Guatemala, it wasn't always possible to trace exactly where it came from. Esteban no longer personally got his hands dirty with acquisitions, he had a small army of very well paid, highly educated and specially skilled professionals fronting for him. This network was extremely well connected to both legitimate and black-market opportunities. Little ever became available anywhere in the world that he didn't have the opportunity to consider.

And while he would always gladly pay top dollar or outbid an Arab oil sheik for something he desired, his organization was one to never cross. Those few times a well-made forgery came into his possession, a very public example was made of the provider. And of his family, and his relatives. Esteban González was never a man to cross, and he made sure the world knew it.

His network was completely attuned to anything that was discovered that might be of interest, or anything new that became available on the antiquities market. He discretely funded scholarships to the best archeology programs, not just to hire new and indebted blood into his organization, but also so that he had eyes and ears in all of the major centers of learning. Places that would be the first to know of any new discoveries, sponsoring expeditions, sending students to sites to train, conducting meticulous research. He even had his tentacles into archeological, anthropological, and historical magazine publishers and web sites. These generated insight, gossip, and tidbits of information that occasionally paid off.

And of course he sent out his own well-financed and equipped teams to actively and preemptively explore sites of interest. The latest technology was utilized, including satellite imagery acquired from well-placed and well-paid informants in various agencies. Investments in recent innovations such as LIDAR, or Light Detection and Ranging, a form of radar which was especially useful for penetrating the dense jungle canopies of the tropics, paid off handsomely. Even Ground Penetrating Radar was effectively deployed, revealing subsurface anomalies, structures and caches. Coupled with his payoffs to various governments and military leaders, whole undiscovered villages and trading routes were coming to light, well before the public sector could even discover them or react accordingly.

On the nautical front, Side Scan Sonar had also been further perfected, allowing detailed mapping of the deepest recesses of the oceans. This proved most useful in the quest for finding lost ships not already discovered, from the Spanish treasure fleets—especially those far off the shores, in deep international waters with no local government interference or jurisdiction. The sheer expense of researching and mounting such undersea expeditions limited his competition. And in the event payoffs were ever needed, everyone had their price, or, failing that, their weak spot to exploit or family to protect.

Farsighted and ambitious with his goals to an extreme, he would utilize his network to feed information to certain organizations to get them off the scent of something he was actively pursuing. A continuous stream of false leads were proffered to various, possibly competing, entities. In a favorite example he liked to brag about, the National Geographic Society went off on a proverbial wild goose chase to a site he knew to be mostly barren. It would keep them busy for years researching, fundraising, and mounting an expedition. And then ultimately drain their finite resources for little gain.

Esteban González was a complex man, the polished veneer of sophistication and scholarly insight hiding the soul of a hardened career criminal and pathological killer. He started life as an abandoned child on the mean streets of Ciudad Victoria, whose claim to fame at various times was being the homicide capital of all of Mexico. Street smart and tough, Esteban made his bones hustling as a kid, as a drug mule in his teens and eventually as a hired *Soldado*, or Soldier, for the local drug ring. He came to the attention of a drug lord when he intervened in a shootout and took a bullet intended for him.

Brought within the cartel, he learned the organization intimately from the inside out, rising within the ranks to the position of *Narco-traficantes*, a fully-fledged drug trafficker. After paying his dues over time, he became an *Oficial*, or Made Man. Once achieving that he went through an initiation ritual, which included being tattooed with Aztec symbols and given his Aztec cartel name. Within the organization he would henceforth be known as the Blood Prince, or *Eztli Príncipe.* But the name was shortened over time to one word, such was his growing notoriety and fame. He became known as simply *Eztli*, or Blood. It was a moniker that even those who bestowed it upon him would soon have reason to dread.

Having hired and trained most of the Soldados, and as a senior Oficial and consummate backstage player, he was the replacement when his boss met an untimely end. Mysterious circumstances surrounded his death, but Esteban was now the local drug lord, and a member of the *Junta Directiva*, or Board of Directors. These were the executive members of the greater cartel, who only answered to the *Jefe de Jefes*, or Boss of Bosses.

Fifteen years later, through a relentless trail of bribery, extortion, intimidation and a pogrom of murder, Esteban González, now known simply as *Eztli*, was the Boss of Bosses. Blood had flowed freely, an incomprehensible fortune had been amassed, and an idea took hold. Eztli would fade into the background and run his empire silently and discretely from his opulent mansion in the Polanco neighborhood of Mexico City. He would become the king maker, ensuring those in political and military power were favorable to his interests, until the time was right for him to emerge from behind the curtain. Slowly he would grant more freedom to his Junta Directiva to run the day to day operations. He still ruled with an iron fist, and periodically went out of his way to make an extreme example of some overambitious cartel, political, or military member. But his focus shifted to other, farther reaching ambitions.

Eztli became a student of the history of the cartels, and what ultimately befell them. Hubris, overreaching greed, conspicuous displays of wealth, becoming users instead of just dealers, in short falling to mortal whims and urges instead of methodically implementing any kind of visionary long-term plan. Even the Arabs knew that oil, or at least the need for oil, wouldn't last forever, and they anticipated it and diversified their holdings accordingly. It was a very useful analogy for the drug world, and there was a lesson to be learned. Eztli would not make the mistakes of his predecessors. Not only would he build on his empire, he would construct it in such a way as to outlast them all.

Most passionately, Eztli became a student of the history of his ancestors, the Aztecs. He was interested in cultivating something far beyond a simple drug empire, he knew that it would inevitably rise and fall despite his best efforts. No, better to utilize the vast resources at his disposal to restore the pride of his people, and their proper place in the world. The chaos and instability of the political situation in Mexico worked to his advantage, and he contributed to the carnage to perpetuate the uncertainty, to raise the noise level. Because beneath that cover he could operate with impunity. As he liked to say about using bloody news, turmoil, and false innuendo to his advantage, "People are sheep, and media is the shepherd. And nothing is easier to manipulate than the media."

He wandered to the front of his vast underground museum, where there stood an original Aztec Sun Stone. It wasn't as big as the 12-foot carved basalt one found buried under Mexico City in 1790 and now displayed at the Museo Nacional de Antropología, but it was in better shape. And even more amazing, it was made of solid gold, meticulously crafted by Aztec goldsmiths before the conquest.

In front of the gold Sun Stone sat a replica of a skull rack that had been recently discovered in 2017 in the archeological zone of the Hueteocalli Temple in Mexico City, which contained an astounding 650 human skulls. While this one only contained 60 skulls, they were each personally known to Eztli, each and every one a small steppingstone to the position of power he now held. He smiled smugly to himself and thought, *There is always room for more.*

But most of all, he considered himself a direct descendant of the Aztecs, a Mesoamerican patriot, a modern-day reincarnation of Montezuma. One who had the will power, the vision, and the means to achieve his grand ambitions. The scattering of countries and arbitrary borders in Central America made no sense, vestiges of colonial rule that no longer existed. Small regional internecine rivalries bled the area of its strength, depriving it of any synergy in gaining greater prominence on the world stage.

This was his vision, his quest for the remaining time he had on this earth. No longer would he allow petty political or military leaders in Mexico or any banana republic to manipulate and divide the masses. Nor would he allow the greater region to continue to grind under the heel of the Norteamericanos. That was why he took such great satisfaction in flooding North America with illicit drugs. It not only financed his greater mission, it also took a measure of revenge, Montezuma's revenge, one ruined life at a time.

With his financial war chest secure, Eztli would devote himself to his life's one true quest. He would personally see to it that the Aztec Empire would rise to world prominence once again. And the world would tremble.

CHAPTER 26 – NOON, JUNE 25

That was interesting. What do you think it was all about?" Soba asked Nick. "I know they let us pass through customs, but I felt kind of violated."

"I've really no idea. Maybe we just have that look about us, a dusty gringo, a pretty Indian, and a beat-up pickup truck with a wolf in back. I would have expected it more getting into the states, rather than getting into Mexico. I had that experience once when I was 17 or 18 going to a concert with my friends in Canada, but we probably deserved it back then, not now."

"So how far are you thinking of going tonight? I'm in no rush," Soba playfully inquired, her hand tickling his inner thigh.

Nick thought for a moment, he really hadn't planned it out yet, he was just aiming to get south of the border today. "Let's shoot for Chihuahua, that should get us in around eight. I think I'd prefer a motel tonight, we can shower and clean up a bit, then grab a bite." What he didn't tell her was he was feeling a little more paranoid and vulnerable than normal and wanted to be around people until he got comfortable with his surroundings again.

It was Nick's turn to pick the road tunes, and his selection was a psychedelic collection from the late '60s and early '70s. He grinned at Soba and said, "These are from my dad's radical youth days, I think I know them as well as he did." Soba recognized many of the songs, and unconsciously hummed along when she heard one she particularly liked.

After a half hour of no conversation with each lost in their own thoughts, she asked, "What ultimately became of Alexandre? You're on a quest that ties back to him but you never told me his whole story." The Grateful Dead came on and appropriately played *Truckin'* in the background as Nick kept steady time on the highway.

"Certainly not what he had hoped for, and some of this will ring true with you. He had a son, Victor, born before he went off to the Civil War. Just after the war he went home before he headed out to Fort Leavenworth, and his daughter was born while he was away. But ultimately he died far out west, and you know what the irony of it was?"

Soba looked questioningly at him and asked, "I have no idea. Do I really even want to know?"

"He was killed by his fellow soldiers, for being a friend to the Indians he was sent to pacify and then protect. He left a wife and two children behind. Never even had the chance to meet his own daughter. He was killed by his own people, just like your father was."

Soba sat unmoving, contemplating the uncanny parallels in their lives, the many filaments of happenstance that had brought them together. And which now seemed to be bonding them ever more tightly together.

Nick reached over and held her hand. "I have a copy of a letter, written by an obscure Civil War soldier named Sullivan Ballou, to his wife just before he was killed at the Battle of Bull Run. It is one of the transcendent pieces of literature the English language has ever produced. Ken Burns featured it in his famous documentary on the Civil War, and like it did to millions of others, it made quite an impression on my dad. He said it always made him think of Alexandre serving in the war, and he was so moved by it that he hand wrote a copy and gave it to my Mother. She framed it and kept it by her bedside. And now that they are both gone, I carry it on me." With that he somberly passed his wallet over.

Soba fumbled with the wallet until she found the well-worn copy tucked in a small compartment behind his credit cards. She carefully removed it and read the poignant letter from a distant battlefield and time, a heartbreakingly beautiful ode to the love of family, freedom and devotion to cause, with a premonition of death. One passage toward the end particularly moved her:

> *But, O Sarah, if the dead can come back to this earth, and flit unseen around those they loved, I shall always be near you in the garish day, and the darkest night amidst your happiest scenes and gloomiest hours always, always, and, if the soft breeze fans your cheek, it shall be my breath; or the cool air cools your throbbing temples, it shall be my spirit passing by.*
>
> *Sarah, do not mourn me dead, think I am gone and wait for me, for we shall meet again.*

She slowly touched the handwriting of Nick's father and shook her head and looked away out the window at nothing in particular, hiding her tears. "Why is it that the good ones, those who take the moral high ground, not just in words but with deeds, always seem to end up below ground?"

"I wish I knew, I truly do," Nick grimly replied. "I have to believe that there is justice ultimately meted out for any great misdeed, that there is a sort of cosmic balance to be maintained. You know, the 'nature abhors a vacuum' type of argument. And if I have to be the instrument to achieve it in my dad's case, so be it."

There was a coldness and edge in Nick's voice Soba had never heard before, and it chilled her.

Later they pulled into a cheap motel in Chihuahua, tired and grimy from the last few days' travel. Nick paid cash, he had made sure to load up on it before crossing the border, wanting to leave a less traceable path. They each took a hot shower, and, feeling refreshed, grabbed an outside table at Los Mezquites, a hopping local roadhouse he had noticed on the drive in. They purposely took a table on the edge, with Nanook quietly sitting away from the crowd, alert and intimidating as ever. Soba quizzed the plump, fast talking waitress in Spanish and ordered for them both, a couple of local draft beers arriving first.

She raised her glass and proposed a toast, clinking his mug and adding, "To tilting at windmills."

Nick couldn't help but smile at his enchanting and insightful companion who quoted Don Quixote. "To fighting injustice through chivalry," he replied. Some day he would be one thought ahead of her, but evidently not tonight.

He sipped on his beer, contemplating things. "If only the Spanish conquistadors were as honorable as Don Quixote was. Did you know what the Incas called gold and silver? Sweat of the sun, tears of the moon. Descriptively poetic, isn't it? The Incas and the Aztecs both had the same world views of precious metals, that they were beautiful and useful as adornment and offerings to the gods. But they weren't obsessed with it like the Spaniards were.

Nick glanced up as a couple was about to sit at the table next to them, and then thought better of it when Nanook emitted a low growl under his breath. "Two different cultures, two completely different value systems. There was a mountain in Bolivia called Potosi, it literally was a mountain of pure silver. By the time the Spaniards had conquered the Inca and forced them to mine it, the Inca had given it a new name. They called it 'The Mountain That Ate Men.' Not quite so chivalrous on the Spaniard's part."

Soba kicked him gently under the table. "A quest can be an exuberant pursuit, or it can become a dark obsession. I can clearly see you are coming to a fork in the road Nick LaBounty. Are you going to go off joyously tilting at windmills, or are you going to have to dig two graves?" she asked. Nick understood the reference, that before embarking on a journey of revenge, plan on digging two graves because you will inevitably be damned by the process as well.

"I'm not sure yet," he answered honestly. "In trying to rid the world of an evil, I am worried about becoming that which I hate. But I suspect I'll know how many graves to dig soon enough."

It was still a substantial drive to Cuernavaca, which was south of Mexico City, and to Soba's conference, so Nick put the pedal to the metal. They made about half the distance with a nine-hour drive, arriving at Zacatecas in the early evening. Up before dawn the next morning they had a similar distance to cover, and the conversation drifted to what drove the Spaniards to such levels of zealousness and what they were ultimately after.

Nick & Soba's Trek South

Soba sat watching the scenery pass by, the rise and fall of empires and the fate of the impacted tribes on her mind. "It still amazes me that a people like the Spanish were so determined to crush civilizations instead of learning from them, or even partnering with them. It seems there was so much more they could have gained with an olive branch rather than the sword," she reflected.

Nick sighed heavily as he looked down the roadway. "The Spanish conquered the Aztecs in 1521, and the Inca starting in 1532. They poured untold resources into conquest and then colonial administration, all under the flimsy veneer of the justification of saving the souls of the native population. But there was a constant undercurrent of further exploration, always looking for the next fabulous empire to exploit. It kind of became a part of their national psyche, no matter how their rulers whitewashed it."

"But at such a cost, at least to all those already here in the Americas. What turns a whole society into that?" Soba innocently asked.

"After the Spanish finally kicked the Muslims out of the Iberian Peninsula in 1492 via the *Reconquista,* you had a whole class of professional warriors with no war, no new cause, no way to improve their lot in life. And then just a few months later Columbus bumps into the New World thinking he's in the Indies, and its game on. The Spaniards may have been obsessive and overly zealous, but they were also damn methodical. Most of their explorations built upon prior ones, pushing known boundaries quickly. Map makers couldn't even keep up. Did you know how America got its name?

Soba smiled and looked at Nick with an arched eyebrow. "Is it possible to get the short answer?"

"It was named after *Amerigo Vespucci*, the first to figure out that it was part of a whole new continent unknown to any European."

"Maybe if the lands had been poorer, didn't have gold and silver, they would have left the people alone. I'm guessing just wishful thinking on my part," Soba reflected.

"I'm not so sure. Even when they didn't find riches, they exploited whatever resources they could find. Slavery was big business early on during the conquests, they extracted labor whenever they couldn't take advantage of natural resources. And when they struck out on treasure, they were especially cruel to the inhabitants, taking their frustrations out on them. Symbiotic they weren't, more parasitic in nature."

The ride droned on, the landscape turning slightly greener as they worked their way further south of Zacatecas toward Guanajuato, about halfway to their day's destination of Cuernavaca. A bit after noon Nick pulled into a large dusty truck stop to gas up, and Soba let Nanook stretch his legs and relieve himself. As they were about to leave they noticed a line of truckers standing beside a roadside stall, smelled what was cooking, and immediately drove over to get fresh authentic tortillas to go.

Nick pulled the Chevy out and laughed as Soba dived in, the only words she could mutter being: "Wow, so good." He patiently waited as he drove onward, wondering when she would notice that he too might be hungry. Two tortillas later Soba finally looked up, the homemade salsa dripping from the corners of her mouth, a little perspiration from the heat of the hot sauce forming on her forehead. When she realized Nick had been waiting and watching her, she caught herself and started laughing so hard a little of the hot sauce went up her nose, making her eyes water.

"Yeah, yeah, yuck it up. Nobody's hungry over here, they don't smell good at all. I swear you look like Nanook the night he was munching on that deer, with that sauce all around your mouth," Nick sarcastically observed. That only made her laugh all the harder, the tears from the laughter and the hot sauce running down her cheeks.

Nanook stuck his head in through the back window to see what all the commotion was about and being puzzled gave Soba a lick to make sure she was OK. All he got for his efforts was the taste of salsa and hot sauce, which he tried to wipe out of his mouth with a paw. Having no luck with that and now foaming a little, he licked the back of Nick's head and shirt to get it off his tongue. To which Soba squealed so hard she snorted, which got Nick laughing out loud too.

Having never heard this surprisingly heinous sound emitted from Soba, Nick asked, "Did you really just snort? Or is that the pork in the tortillas talking?" After unsuccessfully attempting to stifle another snort, with watery eyes she held out one for him to finally have a taste. Nick took a big bite and smiled.

"Yeah, so good. Damn tough for a gringo to get any service around this joint."

After cooling the spice with iced tea and now with full bellies, they settled back into the rhythm of the road. Soba sat humming to a song playing, leaning into Nick's shoulder, a look of contentment on her face. Finally she asked, "So what exactly do you think it was that your father sought, what was the treasure he was told about?"

"I've spent so much time concentrating on the where of the quest, I haven't allowed my mind to wander too deeply into the what of it. It's hard to read into the old letter from Alexandre with his broken English, it leads to a lot of supposition."

Reaching over Soba rubbed the link on his necklace. "But you must have a theory, or believe this link implies something,"

"If they were hiding something from the Spanish, one would think it was what they so feverishly sought, namely gold, silver, and precious gems. But Alexandre also said, 'to put the Mexica souls in a safe place forever.' That would make me think it has something to do with remains or urns. And then there is this pendant, definitely part of something larger."

Soba sat back up, stretching the stiffness out. "You do know this could all lead to nothing, ambiguous clues lost in the sands of time."

"I've thought of that, that this might be a wild goose chase, or what was there might have been pilfered already. Not much of any substantial discovery has survived the grave robbers and thieves over the millennia. Tut's tomb was certainly the exception. But Charlie and I need closure, and whether I find anything or not, I'm going to give it the college try."

By early evening they had run afoul of traffic around Mexico City, and slowly worked their way south. Soba turned to Nick, and with a pout face and sad eyes said, "I see they haven't improved the air quality since I was here last. Amazing that people have to live like this here."

"I know, the first time I was here for a field trip and dig it amazed me. The city literally has three strikes against it."

Soba couldn't help rolling her eyes, there was another scholarly lecture coming.

"First it is surrounded by mountains, so nothing disperses easily. Second, the city is over 6,500 feet in elevation, so pollutants tend to stay near the ground. And third, there are just way too many people with cars." They both shook their heads as they passed a couple of older tractor trailers, angrily belching dense diesel fumes as they struggled up an incline.

The traffic let up and the air started to clear as they got south of the city. The route eventually took them through El Tepozteco National Park, where they decided to find an out of the way place to camp for the night. There was no need to press on to Cuernavaca tonight, they could get there easily in the morning. As he impulsively turned onto a promising looking dirt road, Nick put the Chevy in four-wheel drive. After about 10 minutes Soba pointed out an *Arroyo*, or dry creek bed off to the side. Nick followed it until they came around a bend to a clearing. The stars were bright to the south, and a little more muted to the north, partially obscured by the glow of Mexico City.

Soba let Nanook loose, raised her arms to the sky and breathed deeply. Surrounded by cacti and agave on a warm summer evening, she filled her lungs with fresh air. "Finally," she exclaimed, "I can breathe again!"

The air was so heavy with warmth Nick decided against sleeping in a tent or in the back of the truck and spread out sleeping pads and bags to sleep under the canopy of stars. Out of a cooler came dinner and two cold bottles of Modelo, which they raised and clinked together as they smiled at one another. Nanook came back and took several victory laps around them while prancing with a large *coatis*, or native raccoon, dangling from his jaws. When he wandered off to devour his prey, they tucked into their dinner as well. Once finished, Soba pulled the acoustic guitar Bidzii had given Nick out of the truck and gave it to him.

"You owe me a serenade," she said seductively in her sing song accent, playing it up because she knew how it enchanted Nick. "Time for you to earn your keep, señor gringo."

Nick grinned and took a moment to tune the guitar, allowing his mind to wander for something appropriate for the evening. He closed his eyes to concentrate and smiled when the insight hit him. He strummed a few notes to synch his chords, and then belted out:

Well, I remember every little thing

As if it happened only yesterday . . .

Soba gleefully rocked back and forth in her sitting position, exclaiming, "*Paradise by the Dashboard Light*, I love it!"

Nick did a rousing acoustic rendition to his audience of one and to the nighttime sky, the animal spirits in them both stirring, Soba enthusiastically belting out the female part of the lyrics. The song ended with a flourish, and Soba immediately sat atop Nick and wrapped her legs tightly around him, kissing him eagerly. As passions flared, clothes flew off in heaps, some landing on the surrounding cacti, slowly dancing in the slight hint of an evening breeze.

Giggling and now naked, Soba pounced on top of Nick, her dark hair shimmering from the barely visible crescent moon. Pinning him down, she swayed her long hair over his face, tickling him back and forth.

"*What's it gonna be boy? Yes or no?*"

Nick laughed out loud as he grabbed her by the shoulders and rolled back on top, mesmerized by those dancing, deep green eyes. Later, their passions finally played out, he lay down beside her. Still gently panting, he closed his eyes, perfectly content. He felt like he was floating in space, but there was no peyote required this time.

"*Let me sleep on it*," Nick gently sang. "*And I'll give you an answer in the morning.*"

Soba softly chuckled. "Figures."

They lay, hand in hand, letting the heat dissipate, until the nighttime air cooled their shimmering bodies. Finally chilled, Soba pulled the sleeping bag up under her chin and lay across him.

Nick looked dreamily at Soba in the nook of his arm, then turned and gazed under his truck into the distance as he drifted off into a deep sleep. In an endorphin fueled dream he and Soba were driving wildly in his pickup, chased by some unseen, ominous foe. He couldn't quite make it out, but the dark foreboding presence was drawing ever closer, gaining on them, about to overtake and descend upon them. The words to the song he had sung were now screaming in his mind, looping faster and faster. *Paradise by the dashboard light, by the light, the light, light, light, light.*

Down the road they went, rapidly accelerating and picking up reckless speed, veering around slower cars, screaming toward an intersection with a bright red flashing light and traffic flowing everywhere. Just as he was about to blow through the intersection and crash he instinctively put his arm out to shield Soba and closed his eyes tight.

When he awoke with a start, he realized it was still night, the cicadas softly singing in the cottonwood and willow trees by the stream bed, and it had all been just an intense Technicolor dream. But he couldn't shake off the vision of the flashing red light, nor the song ringing in his head.

As he closed his eyes again to compose himself, Nick could swear he still saw the flashing red light. He slowly opened them and turned his head slightly. There it was, a slight red reflection blinking off one of the struts of the running boards of the Chevy. Nick gently pulled his arm out from under Soba, put on his glasses, and carefully edged his way under the truck.

"I'll be damned," he whispered to himself, as he reached out and pulled off a small black box with some type of antenna and a faint LED activation light, blinking red. "That sure as hell isn't paradise by the dashboard light."

CHAPTER 27 – JUNE 28

It was early Monday morning, and they were only about an hour drive from Cuernavaca. Soba wanted to get there and register for her conference before noon, so she was up gathering wild edibles for a quick breakfast. No need to kill anything this morning, this would be a simple harvest meal.

Nick debated in his head whether or not to tell her what he found the prior night under the truck, but ultimately decided not to, or at least not yet. No sense in worrying her until he knew more.

Nanook was playfully following Soba around, nipping at her heels, looking for a little attention. He proudly dropped the coati's skull at her feet and backed off and crouched down, the universal sign for wanting to play. Viscera hung where the neck had been, and the one unblinking eye looked back up at her. Soba deftly put her toe under the other empty socket, flicked it up in the air and in one smooth motion caught the skull and then sent it spinning wildly into the distance.

"Funny," Nick remarked to Soba as he shook his head in bewilderment. "You sure don't throw like the girls I knew back home."

In a bound Nanook was off after the crazily twirling skull, his heavy feet kicking up dust and thumping on the dry stream bed of the arroyo. Nick smiled to himself as he watched, thinking how idyllic the scene was, except it was an oversized white wolf instead of a dog, and a desiccated skull instead of a ball. *Oh well, when in Rome.*

Nick carefully hid the still blinking device in back of the front seat of his pickup, a nascent plan evolving in the background of his mind. If someone was tracking him, better to not let them know he was on to them. The little voice in the back of his head had been right all along, he would do well to heed it in the future, for all their sakes.

On the quick ride to the convention center in Cuernavaca, Soba gave Nick the background on why she was so excited to attend this First Nations Tribal Council gathering.

"Not only will there be representatives of tribes from the states, but also from Canada, Mexico and Central America, and right on down through South America. There have been smaller gatherings over time, but I am so excited to have so many different peoples together at once!"

Nick could feel the passion in her voice and couldn't help but get caught up in her enthusiasm.

"So if this all goes well, if you as a group accomplish what you set out to, what exactly would that be?" Nick inquired.

Soba excitedly patted his leg, as she obviously wanted to rehearse this pitch on someone.

"Well, we can share best practices, build on what works, and enable one another. And that will take a common agenda, something we have struggled with. We need to take small steps first, but we all suffer from the legacies of colonial division. We didn't make the borders, but the tribes live in isolated pockets scattered across continents, sharing common problems."

"Yeah, you can thank the Pope for that shortly after Columbus landed. He divided the *Orbe Novo*, I mean the new world, into spheres of influence between the Spanish and Portuguese. Couldn't have the Christians tripping over each other and fighting, instead of enslaving the natives," Nick sarcastically observed.

Soba rolled her eyes at that one. "Well, what we found in the smaller gatherings and by video conferencing was we tended to share the same challenges, regardless of location or former colonial master. That is why we need to get on the same page, to come up with a common agenda. And if we can achieve acceptance and recognition of that, then we can perhaps gain some momentum. Our collective voices will ring louder than any one tribe, and we can then really work to preserve our languages, our stories and legends, our collective heritage. I feel being able to pass that down to our descendants would be a noble endeavor. That is *my* quest, Nick LaBounty."

A short time later they arrived in Cuernavaca and made their way slightly south of it to the Congress Center Morelos, the site of the convention. Nick smiled as he pulled up, suddenly feeling his battered pickup truck fit right in among the Volkswagon vans covered in hippie graffiti, the rusted Toyota trucks, and other various vehicles held together with equal parts Bondo and duct tape.

"Not exactly Monaco, is it?" Soba smiled cheerfully. "But it's not how you got here, it's that you *are* here."

Suddenly a high-pitched call from across the parking lot, one that would have made a Conquistador shudder, made Soba jump out and run to its sender.

"Colel, how are you? It's been too long!" Soba yelled as she embraced her friend and picked her up and twirled her around and around.

Nick parked the truck and let Nanook out. He waited patiently for the white wolf to mark his new territory, and then looked up to see Soba and Colel laughing like schoolgirls and come trotting towards him.

"Colel, I want you to meet Nick, and of course you remember Nanook. Nick this is Colel, whose name means *goddess of the bees*. Usually it's the boys who are buzzing around her."

Colel meekly put out her hand, which Nick reached for. But once she grasped his hand, she pulled him in tight and gave him a surprisingly hard hug, giggling. Then she abruptly pushed him away with both hands and looked up at him appraisingly.

"Hmm, didn't sting you, did I? So what do we have here Soba? I see you're not going native, you're turned to the dark side. Or should I say the lighter side?" Colel raised a conspiratorial eyebrow to Nick and smiled, then kneeled down and gave Nanook a deep hug as well, which earned her a nuzzling and wet face lick.

Soba grinned and looked at Nick. "I think you're meeting my counterpart to your friend Killian, my hell raising alter ego. If you couldn't tell Colel is Mayan, we met at one of those earlier, smaller council meetings I was telling you about."

Colel stood up next to Soba, noticeably shorter than her Navajo friend. Putting her arm around Soba's waist and pulling her tight, she looked at Nick and said, "Ah, the stories I could tell you. Two young girls, sneaking away from their elders and chasing two-legged game, those were the days!" At which she did her high pitch shout again, to which Nanook raised his head and howled along.

"They sure were," Soba enthused. "Turns out not only is this one good at climbing out of windows and an expert at evasion, but she also has the gift of tongues. We could always find a mutual language no one else knew to come up with our schemes in private." They giggled knowingly between themselves, with Nick shaking his head in amusement.

After Colel said her goodbyes, Soba gathered her things to review her presentation for the conference, and Nick grabbed his backpack. He made sure he had Grandma Ingrid's copy of the family history, and instinctively touched the link on his necklace, a habit he was forming, like rubbing a worry stone.

Soba looked at him expectantly, reminding him of a kid whose friends were waiting outside for them to come play. "I don't present until tomorrow, but I have a full agenda for this afternoon and a group mixer after. I'll keep Nanook with me, he won't lack for attention. More likely he will be the center of it. What will you do, think you will be able to survive without me?"

"Oh, I'll manage to muddle by. Think I will find the business center, all I need is an internet connection to get some research rolling."

Nick absentmindedly gave her a peck on the cheek, which she returned with a hardy slap to his backside and a laugh as she waved to Colel across the parking lot and scurried away.

"See you tonight," she called over her shoulder, which Nick barely heard, already lost deep in his own thoughts.

The sun was now at its zenith, the sky cobalt blue, the air devoid of any trace of humidity and searingly hot. Nick wandered inside to the business center, an air-conditioned oasis of dark wood and cubicles with sleek computer screens and was greeted by a well-dressed attendant who correctly guessed Nick was American.

"Welcome to the City of Eternal Spring, sir," he said in perfect English. "How may I be of service?"

Nick pondered the nickname given to Cuernavaca by Alexander von Humboldt in the nineteenth century for a moment. It certainly was appropriate given how temperate the area tended to be, although the current heat wave belied it. He procured the password for the wireless network and thanked him.

He then noticed an elegant bar across the hallway, and self-consciously dusted himself off before grabbing a tall Dos Equis draft in a frosted mug and a bowl of tortilla chips and salsa. Nick then made his way out to the empty veranda and sat in a well shaded corner near a power outlet, shielded by the beamed terracotta roof. A series of elegant ceiling fans, all artfully interconnected by pulleys and gears, provided a welcomed breeze. There were not many people around on a Monday, save for the conference attendees that continued to trickle in. Nick connected the power to his nearly drained laptop and logged onto the network.

Time to catch up and then break things down into an executable plan before I hit Mexico City, he thought.

First, Nick sent an email to his old professor, Dr. Storm, at the University of Chicago, to see if he had received what he had mailed to him earlier in the month. His insight was always perfectly objective and welcomed and tended to keep Nick centered and able to see the forest through the trees. More than once he had gotten lost in the details of a research project or dig, and the good doctor had shown him that with professional methodology and good deductive reasoning the answer was often right in front of him, hidden in plain sight.

He also realized it had been a while since he had talked with Charlie, and dialed him at his office, his call immediately going to voice mail.

"Hi brother, just touching base. Made it to Cuernavaca with Soba, we're here for a couple of days for her First Nations Tribal Council. I'm going to get some research done while she is presenting and hobnobbing with all the natives. I'm a little outnumbered here man, I feel like Custer riding into Little Big Horn. Anyway, give me a call back and we'll catch up in real time, hope all is well with Sophie and the kids. *Buenos días hermano*, talk soon."

Nick hung up and smiled, envisioning Charlie at work at his hedge fund, diligently making people's retirements a little more secure, bit by bit. "I shouldn't complain," he mused. "He's managing my future too."

Nick took a long slow drink of his beer, the frosted mug perspiring onto the ceramic tabletop. If he was to maximize his research time at the archives in Mexico City, he needed to formulate a plan here, while he had the time to focus with a clear head. But where to begin? Ever since the Spanish had subjugated the indigenous peoples of the Americas, untold adventurers had sought treasures, both real and imagined. A pang of doubt started sounding in the recesses of his mind, gnawing at the depression hidden just below the surface. What did he possibly possess to unlock one of these undecipherable mysteries that they had lacked, was his even trying just hubris?

He again rubbed the pendant that hung around his neck, seeking inspiration. After another pull on the beer with his eyes shut tight in contemplation, he shook his head slowly and opened them, a look of steadfast determination now etched on his countenance. He realized he had everything any conquistador or adventurer had lacked, especially the purest of motives. His wasn't gold lust or treasure for his own benefit, it was to solve a long-held family mystery, now inextricably intertwined with solving the murder of his father. He had the professional training and experience of an archeologist, cutting edge research tools and the latest in technology, and most importantly the conviction of his cause. But now that he knew others also had an interest in his quest, he also had competition. The clock was ticking, louder and louder. He was determined to get to the bottom of this, come what may.

There was only one place to start, and that was at the beginning. Right in Tenochtitlán, immediately after the conquest. *Maybe even before*, he pondered. While Nick knew others had gone through the exercise he was about to undertake, he wanted to do it himself, from ground zero, with a virgin perspective. He didn't want to fall into the trap of missing what others had missed by simply following their footsteps and research and wandering down the same dead ends. Because all of that had led to very little new discoveries or knowledge being added to the academic record. "Ah, the definition of insanity," he smiled. "Doing the same thing over and over again but expecting different results."

He opened a spreadsheet, titled it *Known Southwest Expeditions*, and started labeling a series of columns with Date, Legend Pursued, Expedition Leader, Origin, Destination, Artifacts Recovered, Provenance and Where Now. Nick sat back and scratched the stubble on his chin, contemplating. In one long slow pull he drained the rest of his beer, and then added a last heading, Documented Research Links, to the spread sheet. Finally satisfied with the template, he spent the afternoon fleshing it out and filling in the blanks with detail.

Completely engrossed in his task, Nick didn't notice the slowly dimming sky, cooler evening air or the soft cadence of the singing of the cicadas. It was only when Nanook's damp nose nudged under his elbow that he looked up and saw Soba sitting across from him, an impish smile on her face.

"Miss me gringo? Or did you not even notice I was gone," she inquired in her sing song accent.

Nick took a moment to come back to the present, stretched out the stiffness in his neck, and found the favorite spot behind Nanook's ears and stroked deeply.

"Buenas noches, señorita," Nick lazily replied. "Frankly I'm not sure how I ever got through the day without you."

"Yeah, yeah, likely story. I see you're still tuning up your Spanish, best not to quit your day job," Soba teased, gently kicking him under the table. "Did you make any progress during my painfully prolonged absence?"

"Yeah, I've framed things out," Nick replied, the focus in his thinking sharpening. "To decipher anything complex in archeology, you first need to deconstruct it. That's what I am doing, so I can reconstruct things in a way that makes sense. I'm not trying to solve every hair brained, wild assed treasure quest in northern Mexico and the Southwest States. I just want to narrow it down to those that pertain to the trail Alexandre, and eventually my father, left. So I am working out what I know, but more importantly, what I don't know. And that is where the archives in Mexico City will come into play."

Soba closed her eyes and fake snored, obviously not too engrossed in his academic ramblings. "Fascinating, really edge of your seat stuff. I guess I'm just not convinced you really missed me. Well I gotta go to the conference mixer, it's a great chance to mingle with those I didn't get to talk with this afternoon. You sure you're good for the evening?"

Nick smiled at her and leaned over to give her a real kiss. "Yes ma'am, I'll be just fine." His stomach grumbled, and he looked down at the empty bowl of tortilla chips, not even remembering eating them. "I'm gonna grab a bite, do a little more research, and crash. Give me a nudge when you get in."

Soba gave him a room key with a wink, tussled his hair, and got up and waved over her shoulder as she walked away, hips swaying, Nanook trotting at her side.

"*If* you get in," Nick called after her, laughing. "And stay away from that Colel chick, she's nothing but trouble." He heard Soba giggle at that one in the distance, and then she was gone.

Nick thought of eating right at the convention center, which would have been convenient and allow him to get back to researching. But instead he followed his instincts and his nose, and wandered across the street, through a maze of shops and to a back-alley street with a cantina and a line of hungry patrons snaking out the door. He knew instinctively he had hit gastrointestinal pay dirt.

He skipped the line of people waiting for a table and went directly to the bar and found a just vacated seat toward the middle. To his left a handsome local couple were having an animated conversation in Spanish, the woman gesturing wildly with her arms, poking a large man sharply in the chest. To his right sat a disheveled looking *aventurero*, judging from the smell of the trail on his clothes, the pack at his feet, and the tattered topographical map in front of him on the bar. A line of overturned shot glasses sat in a neat row along the top of the map. He glanced over at Nick, raised a full shot glass to him and nodded with a slight smile, then swigged the tequila and slammed the shot glass down, looking away, his eyes focusing on nothing.

Nick nodded to the bar keep, pointed to his mouth like he was hungry and then to a shot glass on the bar and held up two fingers. The bar tender, an older man with a paunchy beer belly and hard lines on his face, pointed to a chalk board in the corner with the menu scrawled on it and poured two shots of tequila. Without a smile he put them unceremoniously in front of Nick and wandered off to tend other customers.

"Fortuna favorece a los atrevidos," Nick said in stilted Spanish as he passed a shot glass to the hiker to his right. The man came out of his daydream, his eyes refocusing as he grasped the shot, and raised it back toward Nick.

"Indeed, fortune favors the bold," he replied with a Mexican accent, and with a clink downed it and looked back into oblivion.

Nick sensed the hiker wanted his privacy, and respectfully gave him his space. He ordered a Tecate draft and the house special, pork enchiladas, which he had smelled as he approached the cantina. When they arrived, he was pleased to see they came with a large side of black beans and rice and doused them with hot sauce and eagerly tucked into them. As he took a drink from his beer to wash the first bites down, the woman on his left was suddenly flung onto his lap, hitting his elbow and tossing his glass of beer straight up, drenching him.

"Tu puta, como pudiste?" her male companion shouted, slapping her sharply across the face. She jumped off Nick's lap, and started hitting the large man in the chest, yelling at him in Spanish too fast for Nick to comprehend. Before Nick could even react, the bar keep tossed a towel at him, and placed a fresh beer next to his food.

"Lover's quarrel," the hiker to his right laughed, and slapped Nick on the shoulder. "Never a dull moment when somebody wanders, si amigo?"

Nick glanced at the hiker, and then back at the couple, where the man now had the woman in his broad arms, laughing as her punches became softer, her words less loud, their lips finally embracing. A few of the indifferent crowd gave a brief cheer and raised glasses toward the couple, and then went back about their own noisy business. Nick noticed the hiker briefly glancing at two men sitting off to the side in back, who looked like they were in some type of uniform. It was hard to tell in the darkness and through the haze of smoke across the bar.

Nick wiped his head and face off, and looked more closely at the hiker, who was now looking back with a bemused expression. Self-consciously smiling at himself, Nick tipped his glass toward him and said, "Salud," and took a long deep drink.

"Salud, and bienvenido," the hiker replied, extending a calloused hand. "Chico Martinez, at your service."

Nick shook his hand, surprised at the firmness of the grip, the hardness of the calluses, and the sudden clarity he saw in someone he initially thought was off on a drunken bender.

"Enough self-pity," Chico said mostly to himself, and then ordered food to sober up. Turning back toward Nick he asked, "So what brings an Americano to the mean back streets of Cuernavaca?"

For some reason Nick found himself taken in by this solitary figure, intuitively feeling there was a kindred spirit lurking underneath all that tequila. Nick told him how he had come south with Soba to her conference, that he was an archeologist by training, and was enjoying some free time to explore and take in the local culture.

But he purposely didn't tell him anything deeper about his own hidden agenda. Nick pointed to the map Chico had out on the bar and raised a quizzical eyebrow.

"Si, this should be interesting to you. I work for the Department of Antiquities, and I'm just back from some newly discovered—how you say—*ruinas toltecas*," Chico enthusiastically replied.

Nick jabbed at a location on the map and grinned. "I spent a whole season working on Toltec ruins right near there, we uncovered some fantastic artifacts. That is why I can *habla un poco de español.* I'm going to show Soba what we found at the Museum in Mexico City after the conference."

Chico smiled and slowly shook his head. "You're right, a little Spanish is all you can speak my gringo amigo. We weren't so lucky at the new ruins we found, and that's why I drink the tequila. We made the discovery using LIDAR to see through the vegetation in the hills, and before we could even begin to excavate, looters ransacked it."

Chico sat back and observed Nick and saw his face flush with a little color and the veins on his neck start to stand out. Obviously this was someone more interested in pursuing the truth than monetary gain.

Nick composed himself and spoke quietly, so only Chico could hear. "Too many countries around the world are slowly losing their heritage to the greedy few. The stories that need to be heard by everyone are being sequestered so selfish men can stoke their egos and flip off the rest of humanity. Looters are a plague I wish we could eradicate, but it is the goddamn collectors who entice them that are the real menace. But money trumps hunger, and if even the Egyptians looted their own tombs, then I suspect looters will always be with us."

Chico leaned in closer to Nick and spoke in a voice barely above a whisper. "Down here, honesty doesn't pay amigo. In fact, it can get you *delicado*—how you say—killed. Invisible men pull all the strings, and they have infiltrated every part of every agency, like ghosts. We have a leak in ours, and that's why the best pieces go missing, and they leave us crumbs, almost like they are taunting us."

Looking at Chico through fresh eyes, Nick inquired, "So why are you so vested in all this, my Mexican friend?"

"Ah, I am indeed Mexican, but also Spanish blooded. I am *meztizo*, the worst of all and the best of nothing," he joked, laughing loudly at his own witticism. "But we can still be proud of *all* our roots, can we not? Can't we take pride in our heritage and the great accomplishments of our ancestors?"

Nick caught the eye of the bar tender and put up two fingers. "Just for the record, you're English is a whole lot better than my Spanish. Where did you learn it?" he asked as he passed a shot to Chico.

Chico fingered the chipped shot glass for a moment, then looked up. "I was lucky, I got sponsored and accepted to the Archeology and Archaeometry program at Rice University in Houston, and while I could speak a little English before then, I got *mucho fluido* while there."

Nick was duly impressed. Archaeometry focused on utilizing scientific techniques in analyzing archaeological materials to assist in dating them. This was no footloose treasure seeker he had bumped into. Chico was an educated patriot, trying to do the right thing from within the system, however imperfect that system might be.

"Then *toca fondo* friend, and to fighting the good fight," Nick toasted.

"Yes, bottoms up, camarada. To the buena lucha."

Nick spent the next hour in an animated conversation with Chico, becoming slightly buzzed while Chico maintained the equilibrium of his evening binge. When Nick decided it was time to leave, Chico stood and gave Nick his card, a boozy hug and a pat on the back. As he walked out Nick saw a pretty woman immediately sit in his just vacated seat, and Chico glanced up and gave him a sly smile and a wink.

Stepping fully outside Nick looked up at the stars and stretched his arms high, breathing in a refreshing lungful of fresh air. He had lost track of time in the smoky bar, and it felt good to move about and limber up. Twisting his torso back and forth to stretch, he was startled to hear someone right in back of him flick open a lighter, kindle something and take a deep drag, followed by two brief coughs, a smoker's cough. He was tapped on the shoulder and smelled the expelled smoke even before he turned.

"Beware of that one. We've been following him for some time now, and he is not what he appears to be," said a sallow faced policeman in a dark uniform. His English was clipped, his barely visible eyes unflinching. His larger companion, who Nick hadn't initially noticed because of the glare from the cantina, gave an acknowledging grunt in the background.

A shot of adrenaline coursed through his veins, focusing him, and Nick asked, "And what exactly does he appear to be?"

"Harmless. And it would certainly be a mistake to think otherwise. Too many valuable artifacts have come up missing, too many coincidences. I think you could understand how we have our suspicions when the same person keeps turning up in the middle of missing items."

Nick rubbed his hands together and frowned, thinking back, trying to decipher the evening's conversation with Chico. They had covered a lot of ground, the exchange between similar professional minds expansive and invigorating.

"He seemed sincere to me. And knowledgeable. Like he really understood antiquities, and the science behind them," Nick protested.

"This is not a safe place for Americanos señor, sniffing around antiquities is not a safe profession in Mexica. Be careful who you befriend," came the ominous reply.

Nick was about to ask another question when his phone rang, and as he reached down to silence it he saw that it was Charlie returning his call. He clicked it to voice mail, and expectantly looked back up to continue the conversation. But no one was there, just a little swirl of cigarillo smoke wafting away in an evening breeze. Nick squinted and looked all around, then shrugged his shoulders and headed back through the alley to the hotel.

In the parking lot he stopped to grab a few things out of his truck, and then let himself into the hotel room. *A real room,* he thought when he saw it. It was way more luxurious than he had anticipated. Feeling grimy from the evening at the bar, Nick slipped out of his clothes and jumped in the shower, and let the pulsating hot water ease the stress away. He dried off and slipped under the soft quilt comforter on an oversized bed and was asleep before he even hit the pillow.

Later, still slightly buzzed and in a deep slumber, he awoke with a start when something hot blew in his ear. "Awe, cut it out Soba," he mumbled, "I'm just so beat."

"That's not me silly," she whispered to him, gently stroking his lips with her finger. A lick and a huff in his ear confirmed it was Nanook, who nudged harder and harder until Nick rolled over and made eye contact and gave him a rub. Satisfied, the wolf wandered off, sniffing around the room for any signs of prior inhabitants.

As he lay there regaining his bearings, Nick closed his eyes again until he briefly tasted a delicate mescal flavored kiss, and then heard Soba purr in his other ear.

"Mą'iitsoh nahał'in," she softly crooned in Navajo, teasing him with her new nickname for him. "We have this lovely room and clean sheets, it sure would be a shame not to mess them up."

CHAPTER 28 – JUNE 29

S*he certainly is an exquisite creature, even when she sleeps,* Nick thought as he lay in bed across from Soba.

He gazed at her in the soft morning light that streamed in around the edges of the curtains. He wouldn't call it angelic, that wasn't her nature, more like mischievous and strikingly attractive. She gave no more pretenses of early dating decorum here, just good deep breathing, up from the toes, enough to make some of her black hair wave up and down.

Nick grinned inwardly. This wasn't like in the movies, where people woke up and rolled over and kissed intimately as if they had just brushed their teeth and gargled with mouthwash. No, this was reality, where you kind of covered your mouth until you could sneak into the bathroom and then crawl back under the covers, ready for that kiss.

He thought he had heard Soba get up a little while ago, so Nick had just done his own sneaking, and was back under the covers for the first kiss of the day to remember a memorable night. He leaned in and kissed her deeply, then quickly sat back up. Soba mumbled, "Sorry," put a hand over her mouth and stumbled to the bathroom. Nick laughed and went over and rubbed Nanook.

"Now you wouldn't do that to me, would you boy? You would never eat something really nasty or put your nose where it shouldn't have been and then lick my face, no, not you," Nick murmured. "Cause you're a good boy, that's what you are, a good boy."

Nanook rolled over and enjoyed the stroking, then suddenly tilted his head when he heard a gargle that sounded like a lawn mower starting. He thumped his tail hard when a sassy looking Soba emerged from the bathroom, loudly smacking her lips.

"Now where were we, white boy," she called, playfully creeping over the bed until she had Nick cornered against the wall.

She wrapped her long arms and one leg around him and leaned in and gave him a long, wet kiss, with a tease of a flick of the tongue before she lay her head on his shoulder. Slightly smoky hair that smelled like piñon pine and desert herbs, it got him every time.

"And just for the record, I didn't eat anything nasty last night," she sighed. Nick raised an eyebrow and was about to offer a wisecrack, but prudently thought better of it.

As Soba showered, he listened to the voice mail from Charlie, and took a chance and called him. Charlie immediately picked up while he was driving in from the suburbs to his office in downtown Chicago.

"Hey man, sorry I missed your call last night. I was getting some regional intel from a guy who works for the department of antiquities. He was complaining about all the corruption, and then a couple of local *policía* chat me up and say this same guy is the common denominator on stuff coming up missing. I tell you it's the wild west down here south of the border, Pedro," Nick informed him.

"Good to hear your voice bro," Charlie replied. "You would do well to stay out of the crosshairs of any turf battles going on down there. With your white ass you don't exactly blend in with the locals. And regardless of what you do or don't find, always remember, all that glitters is not gold."

The brothers chatted for fifteen minutes, getting caught up on Nick's latest adventures, and his work to frame out his upcoming search of the archives. Charlie offered not just his own help, but that of his firm, which was skilled in investigating international businesses and money trails. The hedge fund had to do due diligence on all its investments, both domestic and abroad, and some countries were notorious for graft and corruption. Like those in Central America. Charlie readily admitted their methods and sources could be unconventional, but he found them both very discrete and very effective. More than once they had saved tens of millions by steering away from bad investments, corrupt politicians, and lawyers and judges on the take. Finally caught up, they said their goodbyes as Charlie walked to his office.

Nick had toyed with telling him about the black box transmitter he found under the truck but decided against it. He had an increasing feeling he was being watched, and impulsively unscrewed the ear and mouthpiece of the hotel room phone. Nothing, it all looked normal, maybe his imagination was just getting the best of him. But this was real. You couldn't be *too* paranoid with a blinking black box sitting in your truck.

Soba wandered out of the bathroom, her hair wrapped in a towel. She gathered and organized her things for practicing her presentation, which she would give tomorrow. She was a little nervous, but also excited and wanted to fine tune it. There would be a series of breakout sessions today for the conference attendees, and hers tomorrow was near the end of the general session. Nick had teased her she must carry a lot of weight for one so young to be presenting just before the conclusion by the tribal elders.

"Well, it's all in here, for the good or the bad," Soba said as she held up a small thumb drive. "I'm going to go over to the business center and do one more dry run through it, and then go to the other sessions."

"I've heard it three times already, you've got it down pat. You'll do just fine," Nick reassured her with a wink. "It's well constructed and passionate. Just like you."

"Thanks, but the message I want to convey isn't the one you seem to keep picking up on," Soba said with a sly smile. "Stay out of trouble, would you? I'll see you later tonight."

After Soba and Nanook left, Nick gathered his things and wandered over to his now favorite spot on the veranda outside the business center. He filled his insulated mug with iced cucumber-water from a dispenser and sat down determined to flesh out more details in his *Known Southwest Expeditions* research spreadsheet. Engrossed completely in his task, several hours passed before he hit the proverbial brick wall. The information he was finding was varied, the level of detail for some of the prior expeditions well researched, and for others no more than myth and conjecture. If he was going to crack the code, he had to get into the right mindset, and to do that he had to get out of the present, away from the air conditioning and the internet. He somehow needed to put himself in the shoes of those he was seeking to follow. Sitting here staring at a computer screen sipping flavored water at a modern resort just wasn't cutting it.

Nick typed into Google a search for places of historical interest around Cuernavaca and scrolled down the list. Immediately one caught his eye, the *Palacio de Cortés.*

Of course, he thought. *That is the one place that can get me in the right frame of mind.*

He had remembered hearing about it when he was down here years ago digging on the nearby Toltec ruins. But he had never had the time or means to visit it back then. That would have been a luxury an indentured servant like an archeology student simply didn't have. Nick beamed inwardly at the fond memory of his little band of brothers scraping, sifting and sweating through a dry hot summer, all under the sagacious gaze of Dr. Storm. Fun nights were had too, camping out near the dig, with the help of the locally made tequila and mezcal. A fair amount of research had gone into discerning the subtle differences between the two, and he had to admit that all these years later, he still liked the sweetness and smokiness of the mezcal better.

Nick put his things into his backpack, punched the address into his portable GPS, snapped it into its cradle on the dashboard, and drove away from the resort toward town. Almost to his destination, he pulled up to one of the many roadside food stands and wolfed down a quick lunch. Today food was for fuel only, he had an agenda to get to.

Reaching his destination, he parked and gazed at the exterior of the Palace of Cortés, reading that a former tribute palace of the Aztecs had stood on this very spot. Located in the heart of downtown Cuernavaca on the Francisco Leyva, it had been constructed between 1523 and 1528. Cortés himself had lived here with his second wife in the fortress-like structure, and he purposely chose the location to assert his authority over the conquered populace.

"Gotta love the Spaniards, always conquering for God and King," Nick ruefully reflected. "Never missed an opportunity to consecrate, dominate, or subjugate."

He walked fully around the exterior to take it all in through his practiced and critical eye. A fortress indeed, it had been designed not just to impress but to provide safe haven if needed from a resentful populace. A cylindrical tower stood on the northwest corner, seemingly out of place with the original architecture of the rest of the building. The clock within it was especially incongruent, a callous relic from a more recent time. The tower had been added about a century before, after an earthquake had damaged a part of the original structure.

As he walked around he noticed a covered dig in progress, although no workers were at the site yet. Nick paused in front of a large carved Aztec stone set on a pedestal before the palace entrance. His fingers moved along the etchings, tracing grooves made by skilled craftsmen over 500 years before. Craftsmen from a now extinct civilization.

He entered and paid his fee, and slowly and methodically started exploring the nearly empty building. It was exactly what he needed, a time capsule to transport him back to an inflection point of a civilization in chaos, decimated by war and disease, ruled by an alien culture who wanted to exploit the native population and force their religion upon them. He felt himself drifting away from the present, his mind's eye sifting backwards through the layers of time to when this had truly been a very different place.

The museum had nineteen halls covering the history of the area and peoples from prehistoric to contemporary times. He purposely concentrated on the periods of just before, during, and after the conquest, ignoring the mammoth fossils, the murals glorifying the revolution, and samples of the modern-day output of the region. He lingered over the artifacts of the Aztecs and those related to Cortés, trying to gain a glimmer of insight into the psyche of both the conquerors and the conquered.

As Nick pondered over suits of armor, obsidian war clubs and religious artifacts, he had no immediate epiphany, but rather a gradual increase in awareness that slowly synchronized him with the era. For three hours he went from exhibit to exhibit, pausing to take photos and read the placards, and touching where the bare interior original walls showed through the modern resurfacing. The echoes of the past were louder in his ears now, the whispers clearer, what he must do now crystallized in his mind.

He was jolted out of his contemplation when a janitor dropped a mop handle on the floor, which sent a sharp loud crack reverberating down the empty halls. With his mind finally full, Nick went outside to where an archeological excavation was taking place, which had been covered when he first arrived. He spotted a small man with a pencil mustache in a neat suit coat holding a clip board, who was directing the work crew. His name tag said he worked for the *Instituto Nacional de Antropología e Historia*, the caretakers of many important historical sites, including the Palace of Cortés. Nick introduced himself as a professional colleague and asked if they were having any luck.

"Ah señor, it is most intriguing," replied Alejandro Diaz, who was flattered to have anyone at all interested in his work. "Not only are we finding remnants from our Aztec cousins as we dig but buried deeper under that is proof of the *Tlahuicas* who preceded them. These grounds are alive with history."

"And have much to say," Nick commented. "It is so good to see that you are bringing it to light. My specialty is in Mesoamerican migrations, and I can tell you this area was an ancient throughway to all of South America." He paused thoughtfully for a moment, and then asked, "You don't per chance know a Chico Martinez, do you?"

Alejandro discretely led Nick by the elbow away from the work site, away from open ears and wagging tongues. "Chico? Of course

I know Chico, anyone in this field knows him. A good hombre, an honest hombre señor. No *soborno* with him, no bribing him. He and I have both been at this a long time, long enough to know when to keep our heads down. But I sense he is getting frustrated and hope he can take the long view. Me, I have a wife, children, I have to be patient. I want to win the war, not just a single battle. But Chico is single, thinks he is Che Guevara, you know, more of an agitator. But we both love our country and want the right thing." Alejandro furrowed his brow and looked down, then spat on the ground in frustration. "It's not easy señor."

"Doing the right thing never is, Alejandro," Nick replied, shaking his hand. "It never is."

It was nearly 3 p.m. when Nick drove back to the conference center, inspired by what he had seen and learned. To have been in the actual palace fortress built by Cortés, right on top of a tribute gathering place for the Aztecs, was ground zero for his quest as far as he was concerned. And stumbling across a knowledgeable archeological patriot like Alejandro, well, that was just serendipity.

He went to the bar, grabbed a tall Corona draft, and set up shop in his favorite corner of the veranda. He was barely conscious of his surroundings, almost in another place in his mind, as he added more and more information into his research spreadsheet. His fingers flew in an outpouring of pent up creative thought, back and forth to online resources, the gaps in the historical record becoming starkly evident. He worked until he was too bleary eyed to continue, his impending task in Mexico City becoming ever clearer.

Nick awoke early Wednesday morning, well before the dawn. He had never heard Soba come in the night before, and she hadn't disturbed his rest. He leaned over and gave her a kiss on the cheek, then left a short note. He had been a little too sedentary with all the driving and researching and slipped into running shorts and went outside with Nanook. The starry pre-dawn air was crisp, just the slightest hint of an imminent sunrise hanging off the far horizon. He slowly stretched out and spotted a rough outline of a trail leading away from the parking lot to the east. Nanook finished marking his territory and looked at him expectantly.

"Let's go see what trouble we can get into boy. I think we could both do with some exercise," he good naturedly whispered. He then smiled at himself, realizing there was no one around to possibly disturb.

Nick headed down the barely visible trail, and once Nanook discerned where he was headed, the white wolf took the lead. The outline of Nanook was easier to follow than the trail itself, and Nick fell into an easy rhythm as his lungs acclimated to the temperature and pace. The trail meandered away from the last vestiges of civilization, out toward rougher country, as the dawn slowly brightened from black to dark blue, to finally a hint of orange. Nick squinted as the first glimmer of sun sparkled on the horizon, glad to be sweating out some of the beer and tequila of the past few days.

They trotted on for a good 30 minutes, toward a sun that was now fully above the horizon. Pausing to put his sunglasses on, he noticed Nanook had stopped and was sitting up ahead. Catching up he sat next to Nanook, who turned and gave him a quick affectionate lick, then stared straight ahead again, unblinking. The trail had led up a gradual incline, to the top of a ridge with a clear, unobstructed view in all directions. The trail continued down in front of them, until it faded away in the morning mist. A gentle breeze brushed their faces as the air was warmed and rose up over the ridge, a few birds of prey starting to drift lazily on the thermals in front of them.

"Stunning, eh Nanook? This is the land the Aztecs ruled over, where they built fantastic temples and prayed to their gods, where they celebrated life and honored death. Their voices are loud in the wind, their history rich in this soil. I can feel their presence here, why they wanted so badly to preserve their legacy. You know what I think ol' boy? It's time for us to see if they managed to pull it off."

Soba gave her presentation later in the afternoon, and after the elders came up with a common resolution and communal prayer, the conference wrapped up with a banquet dinner open to all. She dragged Nick along, insisting that he come to meet more of her friends and colleagues. He agreed reluctantly, since he was on a roll with his research. He typically liked to work when the inspiration flowed, which it didn't always do, but it was now. However, upon walking into the main hall he was instantly glad he was there. This didn't transport him back in time like his visit to the Palace of Cortés had, but it immersed him in the diversity of the original peoples of the Americas, an altogether different experience.

Soba was noticeably relieved, the pressure of her presentation behind her, which had obviously been well received. Numerous delegates came up to her with compliments and promises of keeping in touch. She graciously accepted their praise and introduced Nick to indigenous peoples from as far north as the Inuits of the Arctic, to Central American descendants of the Aztecs and Maya, and to those from the far south with pure Inca bloodlines still coursing through their veins. To Nick it felt like things were somehow coming full circle to a logical conclusion, whatever that conclusion might be.

Deeply engaged in an introduction from Soba to a regal looking Incan speaking *Quechua*, Nick jumped when somebody grabbed his buttocks sharply from behind. He abruptly turned around and looked down to see Colel innocently standing there, gazing away but giggling under her breath.

For the love of Pete, he thought. *It's going to be a long night.*

He was right. Lying in bed much later and reflecting on what had played out, Nick had found himself spellbound by it all, with so many different peoples gathered under the boundless nighttime sky, a cacophony of languages in the air. He had observed a common pride in the past, angst of the present and fear of the future that seemed to bond the various tribes together. They certainly had their divisions and internecine rivalries, just like the countries they inhabited. But by and large seemed to be on the same noble endeavor of attempting to save their cultures from oblivion, before it was too late.

Up before the dawn, Nick took Nanook out to do his usual morning business. Standing there in the dark, he saw the lit tips of cigarettes, and heard two truckers talking about their cargos, destinations, and best whorehouses along the route. When he heard one say he would end up in Guatemala to deliver his load and pick up another, he listened harder.

Yes, a region that rich in recently discovered archeological sites would be believable, Nick thought. *This would be perfect if I can pull it off. It might keep them off my trail in Mexico City, if only for a little while.*

Nick's eyes followed the trucker as he went back to his rig and noted the make and license plate. After he brought Nanook back in, he grabbed the blinking black box out of his truck and hid until no one was visible and all was perfectly quiet. Just to be safe he forced himself to wait another five minutes, then stealthily crept inside the back-cargo bin of the tractor trailer. Pulling up a canvas tarp, he quickly unstacked several crates, then placed the black box deep under the machine parts that were in it and restacked the crates. Pulling the tarp back over, he slipped out the back, the only sound being his own muffled breathing and the beating of his own heart, ever louder in his ears. Back in his room and safely under the covers he tried to get back to sleep, but it was useless. He quietly made coffee and read his phone in the dark, letting Soba get a little more rest before they hit the road.

"I lost you for a few days there," Soba observed as the scenery flashed by her open window. "Are you always so obsessive when you catch a scent?"

"Hmm, yes. I guess so. I think I got that from my dad. He used to joke that the road to nowhere was to become a jack of all trades and master of none, just like him," Nick reflected. "But when he wanted to accomplish something important, it always got his complete focus. Mom, she could keep all the balls in the air at once, but not Dad. He was kind of like the absent-minded professor type when he got into a project. I guess that's why they made a good team."

"Well, we've got some time to kill on the ride," Soba added. "You've been immersed in my world the last few days, how about you bring me up to date on yours?"

Nick turned and smiled at her. "OK, but remember, you asked

for it. I've been on a bit of a roll since we got to Cuernavaca, it is pretty amazing what can be found online. Not the conspiracy stuff or alien theories, but solid academic research. When you are in the field like me, you get keys to virtual doors that aren't open to the public. And I have contacts all over the world who also give me *their* keys. Add in the fact that institutions are methodically digitizing their collections, and it's pretty incredible what you can find by applying sophisticated search algorithms."

"I love it when you talk technical to me. So that sets the stage, but what did you find? Or maybe better yet, what couldn't you find?" Soba asked.

"Spanish conquistadors made trek after trek up through the Desert Southwest, into the Great Plains, and down into the jungles of Central America." Nick replied. "All of that independent of Pizzaro looting the Incas and starting a frenzy of exploration in South America."

Soba frowned for a moment, trying to get things straight in her own mind. "Tell me of the myths, I keep getting them confused."

"It's interesting. There were different legends in different places. The *Seven Cities of Cibola* was based initially on stories told by a shipwreck survivor of a failed expedition to Florida. His name was Cabeza de Vaca, and he wandered the Gulf and the Southwest all the way to the Pacific, until he reached Mexico City. The cities he was told about were supposed to be unbelievably rich, like Tenochtitlán was. And another survivor who was with him named Esteban told embellished stories too."

"I remember that one. What was the other famous one I kept hearing you talk about?" Soba interjected.

"The myth of *El Dorado* was set in South America and was about a chief who covered himself in gold dust every morning and washed it off every night. They called him the gilded man, and if he could wash gold dust off daily, his kingdom had to have been incredibly wealthy. Like any good story, both legends grew with the retelling."

Nick sighed before continuing. "Narváez, DeSoto, Coronado, Pardo, Oñate, they all put together well armed and financed expeditions, obviously approved based on some type of intelligence. Maybe myth crept into it, but the Spaniards were too pragmatic, too cruel, to just chase anything. They could torture the truth out of anyone. But they, and innumerable other searches over time, turned up nothing of consequence."

Now that they were headed to Mexico City with the conference behind them, Soba found herself relaxing and getting caught up in the excitement of Nick's quest too.

"Do you think your modern resources will turn up something they didn't?" she inquired. "You have more completed research to draw upon, better tools they could never have dreamed of, right?"

"Hopefully. I'm looking for the threads of what they were chasing, what led them to risk not just their fortunes, but their very lives. And I'm hoping to find other expeditions that may not have been as well documented or fell through the cracks of the historical record. Who knows, maybe some of those that didn't come back actually got close to finding something or did find it and were then lost to time. But as they say, hope isn't a strategy."

The drive was only about 90 minutes, and they worked their way back through the El Tepozteco National Park, northward to the outskirts of Mexico City. The traffic congestion grew and the clear air gradually gave way to the hazy pollution of Mexico City. Nanook stuck his head in through the back window and whined slightly, indicating he was not at all happy about where they were going. Soba made a pout face and gave his snout an affectionate rub.

"There there boy. I know, it smells even worse than Nick," she commiserated.

As they got on the outer beltway, the *Anillo Periférico*, they were immediately slowed down in the noisy, diesel scented traffic. Nick eventually turned off to head toward the National Museum of Anthropology, which was nestled among other museums and public attractions on a surprisingly expansive green space. This was familiar territory to Nick but not to Soba, and she was surprised to find the large, beautiful oasis within the city.

"Do you know what the nickname of Mexico City is?" Nick

inquired, almost to himself. "*The City of Palaces*. In the late 1700s, everyone who made their fortune tried to outdo everyone else by building the most palatial home. The ultimate game of one-upmanship to flaunt their wealth. Kind of like the mansions in Newport during the Gilded Age. Ostentatious, but still beautiful to look at. If we have time, I'll give you the nickel tour later."

Nick pulled in on the outer edge of the parking lot, in the shade, and let Nanook out. After the wolf eagerly marked his territory, he and Soba took him for a walk through the park and around a small lake, past the Chapultepec Zoo, the Chapultepec Palace, and the Museums of Modern and Contemporary Art. Looping back to the parking lot of the Anthropology Museum, Nick fed Nanook, then put him in the back of the truck and opened the windows.

"See you soon big fella. Be good, and don't eat anyone."

Pulling out his cell phone Nick sent a quick text, then walked with Soba over to *El Paraguas*, an iconic tower covered in native motifs in the center of a massive covered courtyard. Water streamed from the top in a deafening cascade, splashing in a circle around the base and giving off a cooling mist. Tourists took selfies in front of it while their children gleefully ran in and out of the torrent, splashing happily. Nick held Soba's hand and glanced around, taking in the familiar sights.

"Good to be back," he smiled at her. "Our personal guide should be here soon."

Soba reached around his waist and pulled him close as they walked slowly around the tower, leaning her head on his shoulder. The mist felt good, and their minds wandered as the sounds of children laughing echoed in their ears. Suddenly their reverie was interrupted by a harried looking man in a white lab coat, closely followed by two assistants. He stopped abruptly in front of them, stood straight and formally offered his hand.

"Señor LaBounty, my name is Dr. Carlos Lòpez, I am the Director of the Museo Nacional de Antropología. Bienvenido to you and Señorita. Your mentor, Dr. Storm, informed me you would be coming. I have worked with the good doctor since before you were born, a brilliant mind. He has been a significant contributor to this institution over the years, we are eternally indebted to him."

Introductions were made all around, and Carlos briskly led them inside the main museum entrance. There directly ahead sat the most famous known Aztec sculpture in the world, the massive Aztec Sun Stone. Discovered in 1790 during repairs to the Mexico City Cathedral, it had sat buried for centuries on the orders of the Archbishop of Mexico. He wanted to eradicate any memory of the ancient practice of human sacrifice and was determined to hide this very prominent reminder. Weighing over 27 tons, its intricately carved surface fascinated the world ever since. Nick couldn't help himself and walked directly to it, touching it and the pendant on his neck simultaneously.

Carlos smiled at the young Americano, impressed at the sincerity of his passion for antiquities and native history. And he had been highly recommended by Dr. Storm, quite an endorsement.

"You and señorita Soba may wander the exhibits at your leisure, but please allow me to provide you access to what isn't on exhibit. Unfortunately, that would be only for you señor Nick."

Soba and Nick agreed to meet later in the day, when he would walk her through the museum personally. Soba was happy to have time to explore the other museums in the area, and to let Nanook romp in the park. As she walked out, Soba paused and marveled at a large tapestry of the origin myth of the Aztecs, of the founding of their island city of Tenochtitlán. It was a myth which had seared itself into the psyche of the Mexican people and was proudly at the center of the Mexican national flag. It showed a magnificent eagle perched upon a cactus, a struggling snake firmly clenched in its beak and talons.

Carlos and his two assistants led Nick through a maze of air-conditioned corridors, back into the bowels of the complex. Upon reaching a locked secure area, Carlos informed Nick that the archives he sought were inside. One of the assistants, Raúl Concepción, would always be with him to provide admittance and aide in his research, as *no one* was allowed unmonitored and unfettered access. With a quick handshake, Carlos turned on his heel and left with the other assistant, their shoes clattering down the hallway.

Nick watched them walk away, and then turned and gave Raúl's shoulder a pat. "Well Raúl, it looks like it's just me and you. What say you show me the lay of the land, so I can get my research rolling? I've got some gaps to fill in amigo."

Over the course of several hours Nick was shown the backbone of not just the museum, but of all its affiliated institutions whose collections and digitized information he would be able to access across Mexico. Raúl was obviously proud of not just the impressive museum he served, but of his heritage and his role in preserving it. As he gained an understanding of what Nick was looking for, he provided useful insights of where to look and how to navigate the Byzantine labyrinth of resources and the archaic systems to access them.

After having comprehended at least a rudimentary understanding of what was available, Nick decided to not launch into research that day. It was a lot to digest. He wanted to ponder a game plan first, and sometimes he thought best when he didn't directly think about something at all. *Time to see Soba.*

"Raúl let's meet tomorrow at 8 a.m., if that works for you. I'll plan on a full day of digging for information. I really appreciate all the help."

When Soba showed up back in the main entrance at the agreed upon time, Nick was eager to provide a personal tour. While there were a fair number of people milling about for a Thursday afternoon, Nick knew from experience it was nothing like on the weekends. They took their time and wandered the seven regions covered by the museum, with Nick interpreting highlights such as the Aztec Sun Stone, Pakal's tomb, huge Olmec carved heads, and Montezuma's throne and headdress.

"That's absolutely stunning, the colors are so vibrant," Soba commented, looking closely at the quetzal feathers of the headdress. "It's amazing how they could use gold thread to secure them. What craftsmanship!"

"And you know what's even more amazing?" Nick inquired with

an exasperated expression. "The original is in Vienna, and how it went from the Aztecs to the Spanish to the Austrians is anyone's guess. The best they can do here, in the land it is actually from, is show a reproduction. It's like you have to go to the British Museum to see the statues that graced the Greek Parthenon. Unfortunately, with colonial exploitation, to the victor go the spoils."

With little fanfare, Nick then showed her his one piece on display, from when he had spent a summer digging through Toltec ruins. His Magnum Opus, he liked to joke. It was an elegant and remarkably well-preserved jade carving of *Quetzlcoatl*, the plumed serpent god. One of the pantheon of Mesoamerican gods, Nick said it was just luck he discovered it, and not one of the other students. But he felt the real credit should really go to Dr. Storm, who arranged everything and put the students in the ruins in the first place.

They took their time looking at the sculptures, stonework, pottery, ceramics, and textiles. Soba marveled at subtle similarities in Aztec and Mayan clothing with those of her Navajo ancestors. But it seemed to her that some things were missing from the collection or were underrepresented. She lingered in front of a display of beautifully wrought gold jewelry, dazzled by the skill of the craftsmen to create even the most subtle detail.

She turned to Nick, a quizzical expression on her face. "It just struck me. This seems mostly a collection of stone and sculpture. Why so little gold in the museum? Or the feather work for which they were so famous? Or more of their pictographs and stories?"

"As always, you ask the insightful questions," Nick replied. "What the Spanish didn't destroy outright or couldn't find, time and humidity did. They wanted to stamp out the old order and religion, to leave the populace nothing to rally around. They went to great lengths to eradicate an entire culture. Like the Nazis burned Jewish books, the Spanish burned Aztec codices. Very few survived. And it was a lot easier to transport gold and silver when it was melted down into ingots and stamped with the royal seal."

They wandered back toward the entrance, and Soba paused under the tapestry of the Aztec origin myth, deep in thought. Nick looked at her, ready to move on, but she lingered. "Read it to me again, that passage from Alexandre's letter about looking for a sign. And read it exactly as he wrote it."

Nick took out his phone and pulled up a photo of the letter. "OK, here it is. Bear with my pronunciations."

> *Sed ifin I ever git back ere, to look fur the sign of the outsa nd a taleys nd eyeteden in the peeblo.*

"The sign of what again?" she asked, excitement rising in her voice.

"The sign of the outsa and taleys and eyeteden in the pueblo?" Nick quizzically replied.

"Outsa taleys eyeteden. He couldn't spell well and the languages are jumbled, that's why I didn't see it. *Atsa, Tliish, Iteedin*, now it's so obvious! Atsa is Navajo for eagle, like Bidzii's good friend's name. Tliish is Navajo for snake. And Iteedn is Apache for cactus," she whispered loudly, trying not to draw attention, and pointed excitedly to the tapestry. "Look for the sign of the eagle, snake, and cactus in the pueblo!"

"That's it!" exclaimed Nick, as he gave Soba a hug that lifted her off her feet. "You rock! I couldn't get past that clue, it had me stumped. That's another door unlocked in this whole mystery!"

Nick suddenly realized where he was, and gently put her down and whispered in her ear. "My gypsy shaman of many tongues evidently gets as excited as me in solving old mysteries too. Now we've just got to find the right pueblo that's hidden out there somewhere."

Another critical tumbler had fallen into place, the lock on the complex riddle one step closer to being opened. As they were about to exit, Soba caught a glimpse of Nick intensely looking around one last time, mentally cataloguing every artifact that was visible from here, with a last lingering gaze of the tapestry.

"This is your church, isn't it, your sacred place? Any museum, any archeological site, any new discovery?" she stated, more than asked. "The history of humanity is your religion, isn't it?"

Nick nodded, she knew him all too well, and she had known him only a few weeks. But what an intense few weeks it had been. He knew he had no secrets that the mystical woman in Soba couldn't see through, her green eyes laid his soul bare, so why bother trying?

Walking out the main entrance door they passed a row of newspaper racks, and something made Nick pause and look closer at one. An image had managed to catch his eye. He wasn't sure he understood all of the words of the headline, but upon closer inspection he immediately recognized a photograph of a person on the front page.

"Soba, what does this say?" he suddenly implored.

She paused, not sure why he was suddenly so upset about what had happened to some stranger.

Soba cleared her voice and said, "Francisco 'Chico' Martinez of Department of Antiquities found dead of apparent suicide. Why? Did you know him?"

CHAPTER 29 – JULY 3

Sitting in the courtyard in the middle of his sprawling mansion in the wealthiest part of Mexico City, Eztli casually flipped through the journal of Albert LaBounty. He took another bite of his imported Beluga Sturgeon caviar he was having for breakfast and washed it down with chilled Cristal Brut champagne. True, when in doubt he always got the more expensive option, and certain vintages of Dom Pérignon cost more. But he found he actually preferred the taste of the Cristal, so for once the hell with appearances. It was just him this morning after all.

The journal he held was the key, of that he was sure. He smiled at his own cleverness in obtaining it, how easy it was to have a wide network of informants on the payroll, constantly with their ears to the ground to do his bidding. This Albert LaBounty evidently had been on a quest that coincided with his own. And when Albert had written certain archivists and research scientists requesting information on very specific Spanish expeditions, word filtered back to him that perhaps someone had a piece of insight he lacked. His minions had dug into everything they could find out about Albert, and it indicated that there was some type of historical link that had led to his obsessiveness. Eztli smiled, this was a display of fanaticism he could fully relate to. Albert had dragged his whole family around the

Southwest every summer, and in one particular year, had come close to something Eztli coveted.

A servant discretely approached Eztli and said a guest had arrived. "Yes, yes, by all means show him in. And get the damn girls out of my bedroom right now, you know I never want to wake up with them. Don't ever let that happen again, or you will be shown out too. Way out."

The servant bowed and silently left, and a short, heavily muscled man with extensive tattoos sauntered in and sat down in front of Eztli, dropping a cloth bag loudly on the table between them. He grabbed the bottle of champagne and clinked it with the glass held by the Boss of Bosses, and took a long, deep swig. "Cheers! You know you look like fucking Al Capone sitting there in your robe," he exclaimed.

"Capone, ha, that's a good one. And salud to you too Miguel. You really should work on your manners, your decorum. You want to lead a bigger part of this empire, you need to exude a certain persona, have some gravitas," Eztli said, smiling across the table.

"Screw that brother, I'm your general for what you don't want to get your hands dirty with," Miguel replied. "You know, you lie down with dogs, you get up with fleas."

"Oh, I've had my share of fleas, and you more than anyone know I'm not above getting my hands dirty. But what we are doing is something I could only trust to family—to you. And I need you to think bigger with me, more steps ahead. We have a larger agenda to accomplish, and I think this journal still holds the key. Tell me what you have learned."

Miguel got up and walked around the courtyard. He had too much nervous energy to sit long, and nursed the large bottle as he spoke. "We did as you asked. We took the one journal and photographed the rest so as not to arouse suspicion and covered our tracks. We disposed of the body so that it looked like an accident." He then let out a large belch to show he did in fact have a certain gravitas, at least in his own mind.

"And it was well done, but what has the son been up to?" Eztli asked. "He seems to be on the trail of something."

"We know he went to Zuni and the Gila Cliff Dwellings. And we picked him up again when he crossed the border, one of our border agents planted a tracker on his pickup. He and the girl then went to Cuernavaca. A cop on our payroll saw him there, and now the GPS tracker says he is headed further south."

Scratching his chin, Eztli pondered his next move. "There are any number of sites further south, but it seemed to me the real trail leads north. That is where his father took him, where the journal leads us. Follow him closely Miguel, get eyes on him. I want to know what there is south of Cuernavaca that has his interest."

Reaching into the bag he had brought, Miguel pulled out a life-sized carved jade head of an Aztec Eagle Warrior. "It turns out Chico was holding out on us. He knew the best pieces were to go to you, not to some national museum for the peons. That didn't show much gratitude for you sponsoring him Eztli."

"I know, but still it pained me to have you kill him. He has been most useful to me over the years. But examples must be set, people must be kept in line. I saw from the headlines you made it look like suicide, well played hermano. I'm going to clean up. I'll meet you back in the war room."

Miguel watched his brother walk back inside and pulled a cigar out of his pocket and sniffed the length of it. He sat heavily and picked at the caviar, bit the end off the cigar, and lit it.

Fine champagne, caviar, and cigars. If he hadn't had the girls hustled out, I could have spent this time more productively, he thought.

An hour later Eztli took the elevator down to the unmarked lower level of the mansion, the access of which was granted only through an optical iris scan. Miguel was already there, impatiently waiting for him, one of only three who had access to the inner sanctum. The motion activated lights automatically went on as they walked away from the vast underground private museum to the discrete door of an even more heavily constructed room, a safe room to which Eztli alone had access. Another scan of his eye, and they entered.

"Ah, the appropriately named War Room. I haven't been in here since you sent me to Michigan," Miguel commented.

Before them on one entire wall were a series of screens, the largest of which was of all of Central America. This was flanked by smaller screens for individual countries, each with color coded indicators which showed specific types of activity. Blue indicated older, already explored archeological sites, yellow were suspected yet unverified sites, orange meant discovered but unexcavated sites, and red was reserved for excavations currently in progress. White lines, from infrared, LIDAR and satellite imagery, outlined the heavier trails, footpaths and trading routes. A confluence of intersections of these white lines was a solid indicator of a rich potential site, especially if it sat hidden under a canopy of tropical foliage. Under this, certain areas had been set aside by the government for indigenous tribes, who didn't take kindly to looters traipsing across their lands. But experience had taught Eztli's underlings that most tribes were easily outgunned.

Further off to the sides, additional screens also covered known ocean trading routes, and outlined actual or suspected shipwrecks from the Spanish Main in a similar manner. The left side was for the Pacific Ocean, the far right the Atlantic.

Eztli smiled as he spread out his arms toward all the screens. "All these scattered, random, ill-financed expeditions out there tripping over each other. They are barely aware of one another, much less the larger picture. This is how I manage my business brother, a single War Room to track *everything* that is taking place, to put it all in context. That is how I beat everyone to the punch, to only let them discover what I want them to. National Geographic can kiss my ass," he laughed viciously, exposing the jade inlays in his teeth.

The Blood Prince walked briskly over to the screen for Guatemala and touched a red indicator about 20 miles southwest of Tikal. Immediately a photograph of the lead archeologist popped up, images of the site before and after, what was discovered there so far, who was funding it, links to related information, and who on site was on Eztli's payroll.

"Not so bad, eh, Miguel? We have been adding layers of information to this. Knowledge is power brother! Nothing ever happens in my domain without me knowing it."

Eztli turned and sat in back of the conference table facing the screens, put his feet up, and hit the remote. Immediately the screens changed and showed color coded routes of known expeditions led by Narváez, DeSoto, Coronado, and Oñate, as well as other lesser known explorers, right up through modern times.

"Did I ever tell you the story of draining the lake, hermano?" Eztli asked. Miguel shook his head no, so Eztli continued and put a slide show up on the big screen.

"The conquistadors heard of a golden man called El Dorado. The legend said he was a chief of the *Muisca,* in what is now Columbia, and used to coat himself in gold dust every morning. In the evening he would wash it off in the lake, while his servants threw precious objects into the lake to appease the gods."

A photograph of a golden barge popped on the screen. "This is in a museum in Bogotá and shows the ritual in gold metalwork. See the Chief in the middle, the attendants around him? I have to admit, I have had my eye on this piece, maybe someday," Eztli commented, with a gleam in his eye.

"Eventually the Spanish found where they thought it was, at a place called Lake Guatavita. This was a big lake, but the Spanish, they were determined. So in 1545 they used slaves and formed a bucket brigade, and managed to lower the lake about 10 feet, and found gold worth about $100,000 today. In 1580 another attempt was made, by cutting a notch, which dropped the lake about another 65 feet. They found about $400,000 worth of gold. Now look at this photo, in 1898 a last attempt was made, and the notch was cut deeper. But all it did was leave four feet of muck, which hardened like concrete when exposed to the sun. They never really found anything more."

Miguel pounded the table. "Ha, that's a good one, all that work for just peanuts. Why do you tell me such a sad tale? We make ten times that getting one shipment across the border for the Norteamericanos to choke on."

Eztli leaned forward and held Miguel firmly with his gaze. "Because that took vision, it took big balls hermano. You need to think bigger if we are to accomplish grand things."

"Yeah, grande cajones, I know you've got those," Miguel sneered.

"Yes, and tonight I will use them, just wait and see. Draining a lake is child's play. I would drain an ocean if it got me what I wanted, if it helped to reincarnate the Aztec empire!"

Chico's death had left Nick in turmoil, and he spent a sleepless night pondering the implications. There was no way he would have killed himself, not from what he saw and learned the one evening they spent together. Too much passion, too much commitment for Chico to leave his dreams of bringing Mexico's ancient history to the people unfulfilled. But add in the warning he received from the policeman that evening, it all seemed too much of a coincidence. Nick and Soba had spent the night in a cheap hotel on the outskirts of Mexico City, and as usual he paid cash. He felt safe for the moment and thought that sending the black box tracker on the tractor trailer to Guatemala would buy him some time. But it was time to come clean with Soba, she was now intimately involved in this too.

As usual he was up before her, so he took Nanook out and followed his nose to a small neighborhood cantina. There was a short line, but when people saw Nanook they stood aside and waved him ahead. Nick ordered two cups of *champurrado*, a thick traditional Mexican chocolate drink, and some *churros*, tube-shaped deep-fried pastries. Soba awoke smiling from the fragrance wafting in the air and sat up for her cup.

"To what do I owe this pleasure, big spender? We didn't even ruffle the sheets last night," she cooed. She smoothed a spot on the bed covers and patted it.

Nick sat, passed her a drink and some churros. "I told you I didn't believe Chico killed himself, right? He just didn't seem like the type, had too much going on, way too full of life. When I left him I got warned off by a cop, like he was a bad hombre to avoid. That struck me as odd, to single out the lone American in the crowd. Then Chico turns up dead of suicide, I'm just not buying it."

Nick paused and took a sip of his champurrado and smiled in surprise. "Wow, a little bitter and spicy, nice. Where was I, oh yeah. It just seems too coincidental. I was just talking with him and then this happens."

Soba stopped nibbling on her churro, her eyes widening as she digested the implications. "That means if somebody warned you off, and he turns up dead, then they know where you are? Like right now?" she asked.

"Wait, it gets even better. Or worse. Remember when we spent the night in El Tepozteco Park, where we drove up the arroyo? That night after we made love and were lying on the ground, I rolled over and saw a blinking red light under my truck. I checked it out, and it was a tracking device."

Soba set down her drink and pulled her knees to her chest. "And your truck is right out front. Should we get out of here? Should we call the police?"

Nick reached out and put his hand on her shoulder. "We're OK, at least for the moment. Let me explain. I think they placed the tracker when we went through customs, I remember an agent crawling underneath when they brought the dog out, that could have been when they slipped it on. Before we left Cuernavaca I found a trucker headed to Guatemala, and I hid it deep in his shipment. That should put them off our trail, at least for a little bit. They think we're headed south right now, not here in Mexico City. But there is no telling how deep their tentacles go, I don't know who to trust. Especially not the police."

"So what's our next move?" Soba asked with a raised eyebrow.

"Get you safe. Time for you and Nanook to go to ground."

They finished breakfast, gathered their things, and Soba made a phone call speaking the Nahuatl language of the Aztecs her father had taught her as a little girl. It was a relatively simple matter for her to reach out to a trusted contact, as she had many scattered about Mexico. They decided the best place for her to disappear for a while would be to melt into one of the tribal communities away from Mexico City, where she would blend in and anyone looking for her would stand out.

Nick drove her to an agreed upon pick up spot deep in the *Nezo-Chalco-Itza* slum area, one of the largest in the world. It was easy to get lost in the crowd, his rusted pickup truck certainly gathered no attention here. The man they met was solemn looking but with kind eyes. His little daughter squealed when she saw Soba and ran to her. He gave Nick a set of local license plates from a nearby broken down junker and bent down to rub Nanook behind both ears.

"Well, this is it for a little while. I can only do what I need to do if I know you are well out of harm's way. And you're a little too tall, and Nanook is a little too noticeable, for you both to hide around me," Nick said with a frown. He didn't even know exactly where she was going. They had agreed he shouldn't know. Just in case.

Soba leaned into him and put her head on his shoulder, with the little girl still wrapped around her leg. "Where I am going I can disappear, we are ghosts among these people. Get word to me when you want to head north and be careful."

Nick held her tightly, gave her a single, long kiss, and walked toward his truck. As he opened the door, he looked back, smiled and waved.

"Come back to me Nick LaBounty. You don't want to make me chase you in the next life," Soba said with a grin, though her eyes betrayed something else.

Nick slowly drove through the maze of streets in the slums, eventually making his way to a major road, and back toward the National Archeology Museum. Before reaching his destination, he pulled off and discretely changed the license plates, putting the old ones behind his driver's bench seat. Upon arrival at the museum he walked into the entrance and saw Raúl chatting with the people working behind the counter. Raúl waved and came over and offered his hand and guided Nick back to the secure archives.

When Nick was sure they were completely alone, he decided it was time to feel Raúl out. He needed to know if he was among friend or foe, so he could react accordingly. It would dictate what he felt free to research, or not, under his supervision.

"Raúl, what drew you into this field, why make a career out of it? It's obviously not for everyone, and frankly doesn't pay all that well."

Raúl sat on the edge of a table, contemplating this gringo he had to babysit for who knew how long. He didn't think he was being bribed, more like subtly challenged somehow. He decided honesty would be the most direct route to cut through whatever bullshit game the Americano was playing.

"I'm Aztec. Not descended from nobility or anyone special, but that is my lineage. I'm sure we got watered down over time somewhere and I am part meztizo, but I am proud of my roots. And I'm proud to be part the greater tribe called Mexica. In my youth my grandfather used to take me looking for artifacts, not to sell, but to treasure. He told me stories, and it got in my blood, the insatiable curiosity. You know how impressionable a young boy can be. No, it doesn't pay much señor, and there are many who would pay well for some small favor or bit of information, but I don't want to be owned, or insult my ancestors. Is that any different from why you got in this field?"

Nick looked him squarely in the eye. "No Raúl it isn't, but evidently helping me can put people in compromising positions," he replied, not yet willing to mention his connection to Chico. "I just need to know that what you are going to see me investigate remains confidential, and not just for my own sake. But for yours too."

The discussion convinced Nick that Raúl could in fact be trusted, that he looked up to and was mentored by Carlos Lòpez, the museum director. And Carlos had been recommended by Dr. Storm, there was no better endorsement. When Nick asked about the internal video surveillance cameras, Raúl had laughed aloud. He explained that at this time they were a deterrent, but not even actually hooked up due to tight budgets, as he demonstrated by pulling a camera cable out of the wall that clearly wasn't connected to anything. "That is why you have been blessed with me. I *am* the camera on you."

The day was spent digging deeper into the archives, Nick methodically researching each expedition in his spreadsheet, filling in the blanks wherever he could. Some were well documented, some only partially, and some not at all. At times Nick would pull up original Spanish documents and get stuck on a phrase or word. Raúl demonstrated his native fluency in Spanish more than once, translating passages. It also turned out he had an excellent eye for deciphering the flowing cursive handwriting, and the older, more formal Spanish prose used in these types of documents. They agreed to meet the next day, a Saturday, to continue the work. All Raúl asked was that they take the Sunday off so he could be with his mother.

Walking out to his truck, Nick noticed a voice mail notification pop up that he hadn't been able to receive in the bowels of the museum. He also realized he needed to find a place to crash for the night, somewhere inconspicuous. Plopping down in the well-worn seat of his Chevy pickup, he listened to the voicemail, which was coincidentally from Dr. Storm.

"Hi Nick, I received your package. Fascinating stuff young man, simply fascinating. Per your note I will keep this short. I put detailed information on the secure server at the University, you know how to privately access that. The short answer is the rope is actually hemp from the nineteenth century. The scrapings are calcified tar, a type naturally occurring in the Four Corners region. We could tell from pollen imbedded within it that it was about 400 years old, give or take. The photos of the item are very intriguing, I won't comment on them here. Remember Nick, *alia vis servare secreta ipse prior*. And please give my best to Dr. Lòpez."

Nick hung up his phone, pondering the Latin phrase Dr. Storm had used. He was having a hard time translating it, he had too many bits of Spanish and Aztec and Navajo rattling in his brain, so he plugged it into a translator on his phone. *If you wish another to keep a secret, first keep it yourself.* He sat back and grinned, pithy advice as always from his mentor. Time to get to a cheap hotel somewhere and log into the university server and see what the good doctor really had on his mind.

All the preparations had been made meticulously for the opening ceremony this evening. Right in the heart of Mexico City a new *Ulama* ball court had been constructed in exacting detail. Measuring 30 feet by 120 feet with hand hewn stone walls on either side, it was a perfect replica of the courts that had graced nearly every pre-Columbian town in old Central America. Vertical stone rings were affixed to the walls opposite one another, and the Olmecs, Mayans, and Aztecs had all played versions of the popular sport. The object of this bruising game was to move a hard rubber ball using only elbows, knees, hips, and head. There were variations of play and ways to score points, but the game would end if a player actually managed to put the ball through one of the stone hoops. For certain ceremonies, the losing team would be sacrificed to the gods, providing plenty of incentive to play with a religious fervor.

Ulama had been banned by the Spanish nearly 500 years before due to religious and ritual aspects, just one more facet of the old ways eradicated forever. A recent surge of interest in reinvigorating indigenous cultural traditions across the region was now taking hold, as the masses tired of incompetent politicians, ever escalating drug violence, and perpetual poverty. Nostalgia for the simpler and more prosperous ways of the ancestors was growing, and this new ball court would also serve as a venue for other resurrected games and practices, a sort of ancient town center. Other such ball courts had been popping up recently across Mexico, Belize, Guatemala, Honduras, Nicaragua, and even as far south as Costa Rica in recent years. But the one in Mexico City, right near the seat of traditional Aztec power, would be the show piece.

Farseeing in his ambitions, Eztli had been discretely funding them throughout the region via a series of untraceable shell companies. The planting of seeds of political unrest and the cultivation of a sense of unifying Mesoamerican patriotism also served his ultimate interests. The gala tonight in Mexico City, however, was meant to garner attention on the world stage. It was time for the man behind the curtain pulling all the strings to make his presence known.

A long, jet black Mercedes pulled up to the red carpet, which had been set up to ceremoniously showcase each arriving luminary. As an elegantly dressed servant opened the rear door, Eztli emerged in a black tuxedo with a gold hilted walking cane, the round handle of which was crafted in the image of a skull, of Huitzilopochtli, the Aztec God of War. Smiling gracefully as the paparazzi snapped photographs, he slowly made his way to the grand stand, shaking hands and exchanging pleasantries along the way. A second man had emerged from the same car and accompanied his boss, with two more men with earpieces from a second car walking discretely behind them both.

Finally breaking away from the crowd, Eztli turned to his companion and spoke in a hushed tone. "Bread and circuses Javier, bread and circuses, just like the Romans did to keep the masses happy. Now that we've got some misdirection working, we'll stir up some pre-colonial nationalism. That'll really get things riled up. Always remember, chaos is our friend." He smiled deeply, enough to show the jade inlays in his teeth.

Javier Hernández nodded silently to Eztli, betraying no emotion. Javier had risen through the ranks of the drug empire alongside the Blood Prince, always slightly more in the shadows. Where Miguel managed the muscle and enforcement side of the business, Javier's talents lay in laundering and investing the obscene amount of wealth accumulated and executing Eztli's far reaching plans. He cast a veneer of respectability over operations, and divested investments across a wide variety of legitimate enterprises. Lately he made sure Eztli was shown as the benefactor to schools and hospitals, charities and orphanages. In the parlance of business, he was laying the groundwork and building the brand.

Javier had seen the advantages of utilizing digital currencies such as Bitcoin well before they had become mainstream in popularity, realizing the untraceable firewall they provided for moving vast sums away from prying eyes. Like Miguel he had Eztli's complete trust and was a confidant of high IQ who could conceptualize and execute complex stratagems. Their unique skills complimenting one another, the triumvirate efficiently and ruthlessly ran an ever-expanding empire that directly employed thousands, and indirectly employed tens of thousands more.

Eztli and Javier were the last VIP's to arrive, the timing orchestrated to the second. Everything about tonight had been carefully choreographed and practiced. They worked their way to a platform full of politicians, celebrities and business moguls, each trying to burnish their own star by being affiliated with the dedication of the premier Ulama ball court in the land. Being associated with the masses was both good politics *and* good business. The Mexican Minister for Cultural Affairs gave an address to the gathered crowd, which was well beyond capacity, thanking many for their contributions and efforts. At the end he made sure to acknowledge the foundation so generously spearheaded by Eztli, nodding to him, without whose efforts none of this would have been possible.

The speech concluded, a video showing how the game would have been played in ancient times was cast onto a huge screen in behind the podium, to the accompaniment of a line of drummers in traditional Aztec war dress marching out onto each side of the field. In the film, as soon as the ball finally went through the vertical stone hoop, a lingering image of Tenochtitlán in all its glory filled the screen, and then faded to black. The drumming abruptly ceased, and all spotlights immediately shifted to the center of the field, where Eztli stood alone with a microphone.

"Fellow countrymen, I am but a humble businessman who has been fortunate enough to help in these proceedings in some small way. I know firsthand of your struggles, these are difficult times we are living in. The outside world is ever less embracing of us, and we have our own petty internal squabbles and rivalries. But we can—and must—take care of our own house and be independent as a people again. Independent of those who would exploit us, who would harvest our labor, our natural resources and our creative minds. All to their own benefit, not ours. That is why I have set up the foundations I have, to benefit the people like you who make up the backbone not just of this great nation, but that of our neighbors, our kinsmen, our blood relatives. I tell you we can be an economic powerhouse, prosperous, independent, and culturally vibrant, with a great future for *all* our children. It is within our own power to become the envy of not just Central America, but of the world."

The gathered crowd hung on his every word, the excitement and anticipation building. When they heard exactly what they needed to hear, everyone exploded in a mass outpouring of pent up frustration, turning into a frenzy of national pride. Eztli let them work up to a crescendo, then raised his hand until it was quiet and continued.

"All great things start with small gestures. This Ulama court, so like those that graced the villages of our ancestors, is one such small gesture. It is also why I am dedicating myself to a program to honor the old ways. I hereby pledge to build 100 more of these courts from Mexico to Costa Rica and set up leagues with instructors to teach our young people to honor and play the traditional games of our ancestors. And in four years' time, we will host here in Mexico City, in the seat of ancient Tenochtitlán, athletes competing in each of those sports. We will welcome the world to the first Mesoamerican Games!"

At that the spotlights went off, and the drummers started beating in cadence again. Powerful black lights around the court came on, and two teams, elaborately costumed in body paint, colorful headdresses and warrior gear, stormed the field. A glowing red ball rolled to the very middle, and the players, outlined in bright neon as two teams of skeletons from the black lights, took their positions to the chanting from the crowd.

Eztli smiled broadly in the shadows and raised the microphone to his lips.

"Let the games begin!"

CHAPTER 30 – JULY 4

It certainly didn't feel like a typical Fourth of July. Nick woke up slowly, the sounds of someone down the hall in the communal bathroom rousing him out of his slumber. God, the guy was even more brutal than Charlie had been growing up, better give it a little time to air out. He had found a cheap room near one of the factory sections of the city, catering to migrant workers. With no internet, cable or air conditioning, it was off the beaten path and discrete, exactly what he needed to hide in plain sight.

He had walked to a nearby internet café late last night, full of workers video chatting, texting or reading the local news back home. He had paid cash for access to a computer and logged onto the private university server to see what additional information Dr. Storm had left him. As he lay on the rickety bed, he replayed in his mind what he had learned. Dr. Storm had examined the images of the gold link of the necklace Nick had provided on a digital card, and confidentially shared it with a trusted colleague who specialized in Mesoamerican precious metalwork. They thought it was definitely a part of a larger piece as exhibited by the linkage and wear marks, and displayed an advanced craftsmanship found in few surviving Central American artifacts. The three intricate teardrop inlays appeared to be jade, obsidian, and possibly some type of emerald, but it was impossible to definitively tell via a photograph.

Frankly it was nothing he didn't already suspect, but it was good to get confirmation from an expert in the field and someone he trusted. Knowing the rope was hemp from the nineteenth century, and the tar that covered it was from the Four Corners region of the Southwest, also confirmed his suspicions.

Nick wondered how Soba was doing, he missed her already, but knowing she was safe put his mind at ease. Her gift of tongues had solved the cryptic letter from Alexandre, and his mind wandered to where he might find the sign of the eagle, snake and cactus within one of the hundreds of pueblos scattered across northern Mexico and the Southwest. He needed to narrow down the field to make this a realistic quest. It was time to get back to the research and better his odds.

He gathered the few things he had brought into the room and went out to his pickup truck. As he sat there for a moment, he looked closely at the worn photograph he'd stuck to the dashboard when he first left Michigan on this trip. *Kind of like a fighter pilot with a picture of his family on the instrument panel before he goes into battle*, he thought. Old and faded, it showed a nine or ten-year-old version of himself, Charlie, Mom, and Dad in front of the old station wagon. A deserted highway stretched straight out into the distance, an occasional cactus on either side. Mom must have asked some other wandering tourist to snap it. *What intuition did you have Dad, what did you learn, what kept bringing you back? What the hell was in that missing journal?*

The traffic was lighter on a Saturday morning, and he made good time to the museum. Arriving a few minutes early, Nick waited outside by the beautiful El Paraguas tower, the mists from its cascading waterfall giving him the closest thing to a shower he would have today. He was daydreaming when Raúl walked up next to him with two cups of coffee, offering one.

"Buenos días señor Nick. What do you think we will uncover today?" he asked with a smile.

"Hopefully the right clue amigo," Nick said, taking a cup and breathing in the fragrance of the steaming coffee. "The right clue."

Nick had already read and reread every published account of

any related Southwest treasure expedition he could find. His dad had kept a collection of books in the old steamer trunk at the foot of his bed that stirred the imagination of any young boy. Nick had added to the collection himself when he went to college and had been expanding it ever since. He was to a point where he considered himself an expert on the topic, at least within the geography he was targeting. There was a large body of research already done, much of it excellent and meticulously researched. He had spent a good deal of time verifying the annotated bibliographies for resources, and in turn researching the original resources themselves. He even investigated theories which were not so conventional, including the Lost Tribes of Israel wandering North America, or shipwrecked Egyptians building Aztec pyramids, or aliens using superior technology to advance Mesoamerican civilizations. Not that he bought into any of it, but they had their own original resources which were worth reading and might in turn lead to something credible if properly interpreted.

The morning was spent drilling into the Mexican digital resources and doing every key word search that might yield any related documents. Nick and Raúl brainstormed every relevant word they could think of. Raúl helped with the more complex Spanish translations, which they plugged into the computer queries. A few more documents came to light, which upon examination yielded little useful information. Most of what they disclosed was already known and had already been written about and documented by noted scholars, archeologists or adventure novelists looking to cash in on a sensational topic. A smaller portion of undocumented resources yielded a few tantalizing details, but no linkages to anything concrete. So far it had all been a frustrating dead end.

The afternoon concentrated on cross referencing resources, and it soon became apparent that there was much information the Mexicans had which wasn't digitized or even catalogued. In the tumult of violent times and ongoing drug wars, the various government administrations struggled to find the funding to make it priority. It made the search cumbersome, and Nick and Raúl reviewed what other sources existed elsewhere across Mexico. The only saving grace was that the majority of it seemed to be in and around Mexico City. But a top down examination of descriptions of the catalogues led Nick to conclude that there was little that might be useful to him, not unless he wanted to devote a lifetime to pawing through massive troves of non-catalogued documents. He had hit the proverbial brick wall.

"The right lead could be hidden somewhere in here Raúl, I just don't know if there is a way for one gringo to uncover it in one lifetime."

Just then a door closed to the room they were in, and they both looked up to see Dr. Carlos Lòpez had walked in and listened to the end of their conversation.

"Or it is simply not here. As might be expected, there are deeper resources held by the conquerors than the conquered. After all they got to write the history that survives. Maybe you need to turn your search around and approach it from the other end."

The three of them sat watching the large screen television just off the inner courtyard of Eztli's mansion, gauging the public's reaction to last night's performance. A servant silently poured more Dom Pérignon all around, after all Eztli had an audience to play to today.

"The Mesoamerican Games, the press seems to be eating it up," Javier commented. "I like it, it transcends petty arbitrary borders."

Eztli grunted, having to constantly disguise his real intentions to the outside world grated on him. "I should have named it what it really is, the De-Colonization Games. The press would have had a field day with that one."

"True," Javier replied, "But Mesoamerican puts the right spin on it, it's marketable. All a means to an end."

Eztli walked by Miguel, whose boots were up on a fine linen tablecloth. He swept them off the table and fixed him with a stare. "Decorum brother, if we want to meld competing countries into a single empire, we need to exude class and leadership. And that's not something one simply turns on and off."

"You're in a mood today," Miguel retorted, sitting up. "Who pissed in your champagne?"

"Today the games to reinforce the ancestral ties between all our countries. Tomorrow unrestricted free trade and immigration zones to tie us all closer together. Then a real Central American coalition that is economically strong and independent. And finally a single, unified country, from Mexico to Costa Rica, the way it *always* should have been," Eztli said, his voice rising.

"Yeah, with you leading it. Why not have some real cajones and roll Panama into it too?" Miguel teased. "Don't you want to really stick it to the Norteamericanos?

"Yes I do brother, but they won't let their influence over the Panama Canal out of their grasp that easily. It is too vital to their strategic interests. First we need world opinion on our side, and that requires playing the long game. Dominos fall one at a time, not all at once hermano. Be patient, we'll show them what Montezuma's revenge really is."

By early afternoon, Eztli had sent Javier and Miguel off to carry out very specific orders. He was expecting a visit from someone and wanted no one around when that visitor arrived. Shortly after 2 p.m. the guest was announced, and Eztli walked him through the vast mansion to his library, where he closed the door and they sat across from one another.

"Tell me Professor, what exactly do the test results reveal?" Eztli inquired. It was obvious he was not a patient man and wanted to get straight to the heart of the matter.

Dr. Rojas shifted uncomfortably in his chair. His background was as a forensic biologist, and he was widely noted in Mexico for his experience in DNA analysis. He had been recruited directly by Eztli both for his expertise, and for his discretion. After all, he had been well financed by Eztli over the years, and several prominent cases had hung on his testimony. Fortunately for Dr. Rojas, the outcomes of those cases had coincided with Eztli's business interests. So far it had been a successful, symbiotic relationship.

"Well, I can confirm without a doubt you are descended from Aztec blood," Dr. Rojas replied, clenching a rolled-up document tightly in his hands.

"Good, good. And does it tell us anything else? Is it perhaps from a royal bloodline?" Eztli inquired. Because if he had a link to Aztec royalty, even a tenuous one, it would lend great credibility to his ultimate aspirations. He smiled, thinking of the spin Javier could put on that one.

Dr. Rojas nervously cleared his throat. "No, it isn't royalty, at least not to Montezuma's lineage. But definitely Aztec, yes Aztec. Although there is one more thing."

"Jesús Cristo, out with it man, can't you see I'm busy?" Eztli bellowed.

Dr. Rojas squirmed slightly in his seat. "It isn't *pure* Aztec. It would appear there are mixed, err, there are other, bloodlines within it. Spanish blood, sir. Catalonian to be exact," he said, handing the document over with a trembling hand.

His face turning red, Eztli grabbed it, the rage silently building within him. It simply couldn't be, this was not possible! He examined the document page by page, and saw the probabilities and permutations, the maps which highlighted areas of common ethnicity, the paths of migration, and where relations might live today. Including some distant ones that were in Spain.

Breathing slowly and deeply to regain his composure, he turned and smiled at the doctor. "We are sure of these results? There is no room for error?"

"No, I ran and reran them myself. As you asked I did not share this with anyone, and I knew you would want the results double checked. It is as accurate as current science allows. I would stake my professional reputation on it," Dr. Rojas replied, finally showing some semblance of a backbone.

"Good, good. It is important that this be as accurate and unbiased as possible. The truth will always serve my purposes. After all, are we not a nation of many ethnic groups? Aztec and Mayan, Zapotec and Mixtec, Otomi and Totonac. Certainly the Spanish left their footprints here, as we all have. Tell me Doctor, how far back does my Spanish blood line go?"

Dr. Rojas pointed to the lineage path on the maps. "This shows that a distant relative of yours likely came over around the time of the conquest. You have traces of some of the oldest Spanish blood in the country! But as you can see from the percentages, your lineage was pure Aztec before that, and Aztec ever since."

"Outstanding Doctor. I think good work like this deserves some insight into a very confidential project I have been working on, for the benefit of the whole country. I want to show you an exquisite collection that very few have seen. Please come with me, it's down in my basement."

It was one of those obvious ideas which in hindsight made him think he had blinders on. Dr. Lòpez had been talking with Nick's old mentor Dr. Storm, and they had been down this path of creative thinking before, of taking a complex problem with multiple variables and turning it on its head. *Yes, dummy, approach it from the other end.*

Nick squinted and peered out the small window, nothing much to see but a few wispy clouds and the wide cobalt blue Atlantic Ocean below. At least he had a window seat and didn't have to worry about people crawling over him to get out to the bathroom or stretch their legs. Better yet the flight wasn't sold out, and there was an open seat next to him. If you have to fly in economy, you might as well have a little elbow room.

Before he had left the museum on Saturday, they had formed a plan of action. The Spanish were meticulous record keepers, as the King always wanted to insure he received the *Quinto Real*, or royal fifth, of all treasure found or precious minerals mined in the New World. Royal blood money, which provided the means to fund the religious wars he so zealously prosecuted. There were troves of these records scattered across the world, from Mexico City to the Library of Congress to the Vatican, but the most promising for his immediate purposes seemed to be in the belly of the beast, in Spain. Dr. Storm would meet Nick in Seville on Monday to help open institutional doors, provide his expertise and also a little good old-fashioned moral support. His native level fluency in Spanish wouldn't hurt either.

Nick had spent Sunday packing and rushing to the airport a little hung over from his 4th of July celebration, which had spontaneously happened when he bumped into some ex-pats out at a cantina. All he was after was a burrito and a beer, but sometimes evenings have a way of taking on a life of their own. It had felt good to vent a little steam from the pressure that had been building, and things seemed to finally be falling into place, so why not celebrate a little? Viva América!

He had been surprised there was no direct flight from Mexico City to Seville and would have to change planes in Madrid. But the well-traveled Dr. Storm had made all the flight arrangements for him with frequent flyer miles, and here he was, flying the friendly skies. With the layover, it was 14 hours to Seville, so once Nick had his fill of cramped sleep, he dug back into his research via the in-flight wifi. The place he and Dr. Storm would initially search would be at the *Archivo General de Indias*, or General Archive of the Indies, which housed the important documents from the Spanish Empire in the Americas and the Philippines. The archives had previously been scattered across Spain in places such as Simancas, Cádiz and Seville, but in 1785 had been consolidated to the single Seville location by royal decree. Nick assiduously studied what was available online to get familiar with what resources would be available, as he wanted to maximize his time on the ground.

In Madrid he never left the airport, so when he finally touched down in Seville, he was excited to see the architecture and people of the city. He had been to Barcelona once, but never to Seville, and being in a new place always made his pulse quicken. On the cab ride the jet lag inevitably set in. The length of the flights and flying against time zones made him a bit upside down by the time he arrived at the hotel early Monday evening. As he checked in at the front desk, an immaculately dressed older gentleman with a neatly trimmed gray beard walked briskly from the bar across the great room and pumped his hand in a firm handshake.

"My how good it is to see you, young man. This is quite the adventure you have me on," Dr. Storm enthused. "You do look like you rode in the overhead bin. Why don't you freshen up a bit and meet me back at the bar and we'll conspire on our next steps!"

Slowly getting his bearings back, Nick firmly gripped the proffered hand. "Doc, I am flattered you would drop everything to help me out. I don't know how to thank you."

"Oh nonsense old boy, what I was doing can wait. An old hand like me lives for the accomplishments of his students, especially the exceptional ones," Dr. Storm replied, clapping Nick on the back. "I am most excited to have you fill me in on the details, we'll get you on the right track in no time."

An hour later Nick wandered down to the bar, refreshed from a shower and an energy drink. As he approached, he saw Dr. Storm holding court with the bartender and a group of guests, spinning a tale in Spanish that had them all laughing. He caught the good doctor's eye and wandered to a seat off to the side with a little privacy. Finishing to his little crowd with a flourish, Dr. Storm walked over and sat with Nick, his eyes dancing with the joy of being in a foreign city with interesting people, on an interesting adventure, with his young protégé.

"You're looking rather more human my good man, are the accommodations to your liking?" he inquired.

Nick smiled as he faced Dr. Storm. Always such a bundle of optimistic energy, he possessed that unique persona which always managed to make you feel better about yourself, regardless of the topic of conversation. It was a gift his mother had as well, and he found himself unconsciously drawn to those types of personalities.

"Yes, quite nice, thanks Doc. Frankly this is a bit higher end than I am used to. You know, the starving archeologist type."

"Outstanding. Let's grab a bite, my friends over there told me of just the right quaint place. We have a lot to catch up on."

They walked over and through the expansive and elegant town square, the Plaza de España, to an obscure restaurant tucked on a side street with only a few empty, scattered tables out front. "This is the place," Doctor Storm said, and he talked with the maitre d' and was led through a narrow doorway into a sprawling room filled with raucous locals and flowing pitchers of Sangria. He turned to Nick with a cocked eyebrow. "Does this meet the palate of the starving archeologist?"

Nick grinned and uttered a one-word reply. "Heaven."

The next morning they were both up early and made their way to the nearby General Archive of the Indies building, an impressive edifice of Spanish Renaissance architecture. Designated a World Heritage Site in 1987, it was adjoined by both the Seville Cathedral and the Alcázar of Seville. Nick stood with his mouth agape as they worked their way to the main entrance, for here was contained the journal of Christopher Columbus, autobiographical material of the first conquistadors, Pope Alexander VI's *Bull of Demarcation Inter Caetera* that divided the new world between Spain and Portugal, and the general archives that revealed the intricate workings of the vast machinery of the Spanish Empire. In short, everything that had historians and treasure seekers making pilgrimages to Seville for centuries.

Nick was feeling intoxicated by the mere proximity of so much history and couldn't help feeling a bit giddy despite the jet lag, even with such a daunting task in front of him.

Dr. Storm smiled at Nick as he saw his youthful-self reflected in the boyish enthusiasm and shook his head and tut-tutted to himself.

"The information you seek may not exist, or we may not be able to find it in the mountains of information here. But I'm all about us rolling up our sleeves and giving it our best effort. Let's see if lady luck chooses to smile upon our endeavors," he proffered, silently rubbing a medallion in his suit pocket of St. Anthony. The Patron Saint of Lost Things, his own mother had given it to him long ago at the start of his illustrious career.

The good doctor made his way to the front desk, where he signed in and said he had an appointment. They were immediately escorted, by two armed guards, deep within the labyrinth of hallways to the office of the Minister of Culture, where Dr. Storm was warmly greeted by an old friend.

"Ah, Philip, so good to see you, it's been much too long," said Juan Ramirez, planting a kiss on each cheek of Dr. Storm, then heartily embracing him in a bear hug with a laugh. "Too long my friend!" He nodded to the guards, who saluted and turned on their heels and left, their footsteps in perfect synch echoing away.

"Let me introduce to you my colleague, Nick LaBounty. Nick is about to finish his PhD, if he can clear up this little mystery he has on his hands first," Dr. Storm confided.

Nick reached out and felt his hand encompassed in a huge mitt and was given a hardy handshake.

"Pleased to meet you señor Nick, welcome," replied Juan. He closed the heavy door, sat behind an immense mahogany desk and motioned for them both to sit. "Now tell me all about what it is you so determinedly seek."

An hour later Dr. Storm and Juan were reminiscing and laughing about past fond times, adventures and acquaintances. While they talked, Nick wandered about the office, looking at a wide variety of interesting artifacts laying about, and framed photos of Juan with dignitaries from around the world. There was one that caught his eye in particular, in front of the pyramid of Chichen Itza. Juan stood proudly with his arm around what looked like the past President of Mexico, and someone of Aztec or Mayan decent, judging from the jade inlays of his teeth.

After bidding adieu and walking with an escort to the archives, Nick looked at Dr. Storm and asked, "Is there anyone in this field you don't know, Doc?"

"The longer one stays in a specialty, and the more one travels for expeditions, research, and conferences, the smaller the world gets. There is a camaraderie, an esprit de corps, and frankly a closing of ranks, among those who want to do the noble work of bringing the light of the past to the present. Because make no mistake, there is a darkness out there, an evil which confronts us. It is in those who would destroy the treasures of the past like ISIS recently did, or selfishly hoard stolen artifacts in private collections that never see the light of day or seek to pervert the past for their own disingenuous ends," Dr. Storm reflected, a deep, creeping sadness upon his face.

"Ah, it reminds me of Archeology 101 with Dr. Storm," Nick laughed, trying to break the mood. "Because those who cannot remember the past are condemned to repeat it."

"Indeed they are, and it is up to us to break the vicious cycle my friend."

So began a systematic search of the General Archive of the Indies, much in the same manner as Nick had conducted in Mexico City. The systems here were better financed, which allowed for more accurate cataloguing and cross referencing. The stability of the government also helped, although Spain was experiencing its own share of turmoil, as the Catalonians and the Basques were each seeking greater autonomy or outright independence. Several hours were spent familiarizing themselves with the rudiments of how to navigate the vast holdings, and then with the structure of the actual archives.

"Remember, the Spanish were exacting in their record keeping. The shipping manifests will tell what was shipped from where to where, and what was lost in transit. It was such manifests that led Mel Fisher to the mother lode of the Atocha off the Florida Keys. But manifests will never tell us what *wasn't* shipped, or what was shipped but never declared. And what you seek was supposedly never discovered, and therefore never made it to Spain," Dr. Storm reflected. "So we are looking for rumors and innuendos of the treasure that wasn't, of any Cibola or El Dorado or other myth in northern Mexico or the Southwest USA."

Nick smiled, it was always good to have the clarity and perspective of his respected mentor and friend. "Which brings us back to Cabeza de Vaca traipsing across the Gulf of Mexico to the Pacific and telling those in Mexico City what he saw," Nick replied. "And Fray Marcos, who claimed to have sighted the Seven Golden Cities of Cibola in the distance after being led there by someone from Cabeza de Vaca's party, and Fray Marcos then leading Coronado on a later expedition. And all the rest, ad nauseam. Numerous expeditions chased this, even to recent times. But even if it were based upon myth, there may be an underlying kernel of truth. Somewhere in these archives there must be breadcrumbs that will lead us to it."

Dr. Storm grinned as he noticed Nick rubbing the pendant of his necklace. "Let's hope the mice haven't eaten all the crumbs. Time to get to work."

CHAPTER 31 – JULY 8

The three of them were safely ensconced in the War Room in the basement of Eztli's Mexico City mansion, laying out elaborate plans for their ever-expanding empire. Montezuma's Mission Control for Mesoamerica, Eztli liked to joke. Miguel simply called it the Führer Bunker, never missing a chance to poke fun at his brother. Javier ignored them both, as it provided an impenetrable sanctuary and was a technological marvel, able to effectively manage their diverse holdings and monitor friend and foe alike.

"We have received unprecedented coverage from the opening of the Ulama ball court, very positive feedback. This is nicely positioning you in the public eye as someone who gets things done, cuts through the bullshit of red tape and bureaucracy. A benefactor to the common man," Javier commented.

Eztli smiled knowingly, many disparate things from years of planning were steadily and stealthily coming together. "Now that I have come out from behind the curtain, it is important to keep a steady presence up, and only in the most favorable light," he said, seated at the head of the conference table. "Work our contacts in the press, ensure that we slowly build this to a crescendo across all media. I want the timing to coincide with our other plans."

"Will do, Tlanahuatihqui," Javier replied, respectfully calling Eztli the word for leader in the Aztec language. "We will build and polish your image in the public eye. And I will also get the press to keep sowing discontent among the agitators. That will keep pressure on the government to stamp out fires, which will continue the backlash for the current administration. Revolution in the air and blood in the streets, that should have the people looking for a leader to straighten things out. They will look to a real patriot, a savior, to better their plight and make them proud once again."

Miguel had been sitting impatiently, and got up and walked nervously about, irritated at the formal way Eztli and Javier conducted business. He had known them both since they were nothing, street rats and peons, no better than he. But they had grown and flourished in their roles, thrived in the growing complexity of the drug empire, while he seemed stuck in his. He hated deferring to his younger brother, having never really accepted him in the dominant position of telling him what to do. And Javier, he needed to be taken down a peg or two, hard. After all, he *wasn't even family*. But despite it all he had to admit, running the enforcement and being the muscle appealed to his ego and his sadistic side. Perhaps they were playing to their innate strengths after all. He too could play the long game, as long as it ultimately benefited himself.

"Hey, I've got something you can polish too," he spat out. "We just lost a fricking tunnel under the border, and this one was no decoy tunnel. The goddamn DEA found it, and I don't know how. They either upped their technology, got lucky, or we have a fucking rat."

"I don't believe in luck," Eztli immediately retorted. "And with what we did to the last rat we found, I'm not sure anyone would risk it right now. If they have new tech, we need to know so we can take the proper countermeasures. This next year is critical, we need that revenue stream uninterrupted. Find out what you can Miguel."

Miguel stopped pacing and stared at the large video screen on the wall outlining their drug routes leading into the United States, and the amount of traffic and revenue carried on each. "Tunnels are getting too risky anyway, we need other methods. We can't fly it in anymore, haven't been able to do that effectively in years, they shut that down damn near cold. We've increased our shipments by truck and ship, hiding the drugs in everything imaginable, but the seizure rate is climbing, despite our best efforts."

"Yeah, in fresh fruit that one time, that was a great idea. The trucks got held up, the fruit rotted, and the drugs were exposed. Could have seen that one coming," Javier wryly commented.

Miguel shot him a look. "We have to be creative, we have to try all new options. The drones are working, but their capacity is limited, and the border patrols are now constantly on the lookout for them. The mules we use work well, but they can only carry so much. People are getting desperate, we have no lack of candidates, but the border is flat out getting tighter."

Calming himself, Miguel attempted to turn his anger to charm. "Funny, we lost another mule when the rubber busted and the drugs got into his system. He had one nice trip, then went bye-bye. We need something bigger, something harder to detect, something that can move tonnage."

Eztli sat patiently listening, and then toggled the control panel. Suddenly the image on the large screen in front of them changed, and a photo came into focus. It was of a conning tower of a small submarine cutting through the sea, with two sailors crowded tightly together sharply saluting toward the camera.

Miguel smiled broadly and looked at Eztli, then laughed aloud. "Are you telling me what I think you're telling me? Because if so that's big cajones, game changing cajones if you are!"

"Recently decommissioned by Venezuela, destined for the scrap heap. Their oil revenue is in shambles, they are so pathetically broke they couldn't even afford the upkeep. You grease the right palms in Caracas, we make their problem go away, and it magically becomes our asset. Poof!" Eztli said, making fireworks gestures with his hands for emphasis. "Comes with a crew too, only too eager to get the hell out of there. We pay them very well, they take care of their families back home, everybody wins."

"Originally built by North Korea, Yugo-class, diesel-electric, four-man crew, displaces 100 tons," Javier added. "Designed for coastal infiltration, perfect for drug running. Tell him the best part Eztli."

Miguel looked at his brother questioningly. "Well, out with it!"

"If we like how this works out, they have a second sub waiting on death row for the scrap heap, ours for the right price. Think of it, we could run one out of Baja and one in the Gulf, a two-ocean fleet. That's why it pays to think big!"

A servant discretely brought lunch, and the triumvirate toasted to the success of their new nautical endeavor while laughing and making pirate growls to one another. Eztli even posed as a jaunty Captain Morgan, his foot on a chair and his glass raised high. They ate and discussed more mundane business, before turning to the one matter still pressing on Eztli's mind.

"What do you mean you lost him? Lost him! I said I want eyes on him, was I not explicitly clear? He couldn't have just disappeared. I need to know what the hell he is up to, and I need to know now!" Eztli fumed, staring hard at his brother.

"We had him, we tracked him through customs, down to Cuernavaca, and our cops on the take leaned on him a little to see what they could learn," Miguel replied defensively. "We can't control where he fucking goes if we want him to lead us to something."

"Well maybe they leaned a little too hard, and now the rabbit runs, all the way to Guatemala! He could be anywhere, there are literally hundreds of archeological sites scattered down there." Eztli angrily stubbed out his half-smoked cigar, and he wasn't one to leave a fine cigar unfinished.

Javier noticed it and raised an eyebrow. His boss wasn't just mad, he was starting to boil, and Miguel would only escalate things like the jealous older brother he was. Miguel almost seemed to take a perverse joy in baiting Eztli, perhaps because he was the only one who could get away with it. But that would lead to an unproductive meeting, and they had much to accomplish. Javier tried to rein things back in and pointed to the large screen which showed the exact path the tracking mechanism had traveled, now sitting idle in Guatemala City.

"Perhaps this Nick now knows he's being watched. That was inevitable, he's no fool. But a gringo with a tall Navajo girlfriend and an oversized white mongrel mutt can't remain unseen for long.

Too much baggage. We have eyes and ears all over, they will turn up. They can't go off the grid forever. Be patient," he counseled.

Eztli had been about to go at it with Miguel, put him in his place, but slowly reflected it would accomplish nothing. He would address it, but now was not the time. He stood up from the conference room table and went through the ritual of clipping the end of his cigar and relighting it, puffing deeply, all the while slowly regaining his composure.

"Maybe he didn't plant it in the tractor trailer in Guatemala. Maybe this is all a head fake. He could have planted it while he was in Cuernavaca to get us off his trail, and if that is the case, he could still be there, or he could be anywhere. And now he will be more discrete. Like you said, he is no fool," Eztli reflected.

"We'll up the ante with our sources, make it enticingly rich for our feet on the street," Javier said as he nodded to Miguel, who finally nodded back. "He can run, but he can't hide. Not indefinitely."

"Alright, keep the pressure up and keep me informed. I want to know what he's up to, and this time let's not let him know we are back on to him. Let him think he has lost his tail. We'll let the rabbit do the heavy lifting and lead us to this treasure cache of Cibola, if it really exists. Am I perfectly clear Miguel? Comprende hermano?"

"Clear as a bell. And once he leads us there, his ass is mine," Miguel replied through clenched teeth, a hard gleam in his eye.

She reached the top of the small mountain and sat, catching her breath, looking back down on the broken trail she had climbed from the east. She squinted at the wide horizon stretching out before her and enjoyed the cooling morning updraft. The exertion had felt good, the knots in her tense shoulders working their way out from the strenuousness of the climb. She couldn't see the ocean from here, it was still a bit too far away, but she thought perhaps she caught a scent of salt water carried upward on the thermals, or maybe it was just her imagination.

Still breathing deeply she got up and looked westward, the sun no longer in her eyes, the gentle mountains tumbling down into brown foothills, and finally surrendering themselves to the arid plain stretching into the distance. The land there was definitely harder, crueler, less forgiving to those who tried to eke out a meager existence working its parched soil. That was the direction Soba had originally come through, and about one hundred miles southwest was Mexico City, with all its congestion, traffic, and pollution. And Nick.

The closest town to where she was staying in this sparsely populated region was Tulancingo, visible on the plain below. There were no real indigenous reservations per se in Mexico as there were in America, things had evolved differently here. Ironically, when Mexico finally achieved its independence from Spain in the nineteenth century, much of the land that had been set aside for the indigenous tribes was instead absorbed by large haciendas. It wasn't until after the Mexican Revolution of the twentieth century that most of the large commercial estates were forcibly broken up into *ejidos*, tracts of land worked by peasants who didn't own the land but had certain use rights to it. There was still a lingering conflict in the Chiapas region over that very issue, but the noise from the drug wars tended to drown it out on the world stage.

Soba gazed at the scattered ejidos on the plain in the distance, and ruefully reflected that neither system, the reservations of North America nor the ejidos of Mexico, ever really benefited those they were designed to protect. *What was the proverb Nick had said to me about it?* she thought. *The path to hell is paved with good intentions*, he had said, only half-joking.

Suddenly her quiet reverie was broken by a loud beating in the bushes off to her side, and two wildly flapping turkeys frantically emerged and ran past her, Nanook playfully nipping at their heels. She whistled once, a short, shrill note, and the lathered wolf came to a halt just past her, crouched and looking back over his shoulder for permission to continue the chase.

"You've scared them enough for now boy, let them go and raise their young and make the earth rich. You have already brought plenty of game home the last few days."

Nanook turned and faced her and huffed once, then twice, to make sure she wouldn't change her mind. When she didn't, he dejectedly came back and sat next to her, panting heavily. Nanook had not been quite himself since they left Nick behind, but he diligently kept his vigil of protecting her, while patiently awaiting his return.

"Hang in there *Tlācanēxquimilli*, I miss him too," she absentmindedly cooed to Nanook, calling him ghost in the native Nahuatl tongue of her Aztec ancestors. Nanook cocked his head at her when he heard that, it was a moniker she used rarely for him, only when her mind was somewhere else or troubled. Instinctively and protectively he leaned closer in.

Soba had found it was easy to blend in and disappear among this tribal community. The rhythms of their life were familiar and comforting to her, not all that different from her Navajo upbringing. Most were bilingual between Spanish and Nahuatl, but she noticed that while the elders only spoke Nahuatl among themselves, the young favored Spanish. It was the same everywhere. She sighed. The assimilation had been easier mentally than physically for her, as she stood a head taller than even the men, and Nanook, with his large size and bright white coat, didn't exactly blend in. But Nanook had found a companion, a beautiful female Husky raised in the little village, a favorite pet of all the children. And Soba had been openly welcomed in this land of perpetual drug wars and class discrimination, no questions ever asked.

Upon arrival she had decided to forego speaking any Spanish whatsoever, both to ingratiate herself among the tribal elders, and to refine and practice the Nahuatl language of the Aztecs her father had taught her. It wasn't hard at all, as immersion was always the best teacher, and she found herself easily slipping into it, like putting on an old favorite coat. The elders loved visiting with her, as an outsider's perspective and news was a welcomed diversion from their routine existence, although she was careful what she divulged about herself. And certainly not just for her own sake.

Some of the terms the elders used and their pronunciations, the subtle voice inflections, took her back to the days of her youth, with her father patiently teaching her the language that no one else used on her Navajo Reservation. She had never understood then why she had to master three languages, Nahuatl, Navajo, and English, not when all the other kids spoke mostly English and were actively rejecting Navajo. Now she found she wasn't just mastering contemporary Nahuatl but was getting a refresher course in the ancient Aztec dialect of Nahuatl of her ancestors.

The eldest of the elders was fondly nicknamed *Huehue*, for ancient one. Nobody really knew her age, but she would always grasp Soba with her bony, weathered hands to have an intimate talk in the whisperings of the old ones. Soba was now so fully immersed in the language she even found herself dreaming in it. It all had come full circle, and she silently offered a prayer to the memory of her father, and felt closer to him, among these simple, gracious people.

Soba ate an apple and venison jerky, peeled off a piece for Nanook, and took one last look at the vista spread all around her. *There's a cruel beauty to it,* she reflected, as she thought of all the history and turmoil that had taken place over these lands in the last five centuries. Snapping back to the present, she jogged back down the trail, Nanook trotting out in front of her. It was time to get back to the tribe, as the elders had something they had insisted they wanted to show her today.

Arriving back at the settlement tucked inconspicuously in the forest and foothills to the east, Soba had a sense of calm and peace. She felt safe here, she was accepted. Immediately a pack of children descended on Nanook, petting, rubbing, and laughing. When he crouched down and wagged his tail, they ran in all directions squealing and giggling as he pounced and nuzzled from one to the next, knocking them over like ten pins. Soba pulled a bucket up from an antiquated well and splashed herself to cool down. A smiling elder heard the commotion and saw her, motioned to follow, then disappeared.

Ducking, Soba entered a small dusty hut and paused a moment

to let her eyes adjust to the light. Four of the elders were sitting on the floor in a circle, looking at rolled scrolls made of deer hide. Two were talking to one another, and one was chanting. The other was Huehue, hunched over and silently painting brightly colored figures onto a hide with a steady hand that belied her age. When she saw Soba, she smiled and patted the empty space next to her. Soba sat carefully, tuning into the conversation and the chanting, and finally felt Huehue's hand on her knee.

"These are the lost art of the old ones. Their writing, their stories, their wisdom," Huehue softly intoned. "Time has been unkind to us, but we have our oral traditions and our memories. The art of producing these was handed down over the generations to a select few. Sadly, now hardly anyone wants to learn the craft. I am afraid that like so many of our customs, this may fade away with us."

"These are beautiful Huehue, simply beautiful! The art of producing them is timeless, priceless really. I am familiar with them, the outside world calls them codices. The only ones I have ever seen were produced *after* the conquest, when some learned Spanish men realized they must preserve the writing before the knowledge was lost forever," Soba replied. "But unfortunately the originals, those made before the Spanish arrived, like much of the feather and metal work, were simply destroyed." She purposely neglected to say she had learned much of this from her father and Nick.

"It seems we know similar things, just from different times and places," Huehue said, looking up at Soba through kind eyes. "You have an old soul dear, you could have been me many years ago." She concentrated back on her painting and started humming.

A thought suddenly occurred to Soba, and she hesitantly reached for her phone. She turned it on and flipped through some photos until she found what she was looking for. They were images of Aztec petroglyphs etched into the back of the collapsed room Lonan had shown them in Zuni on their trip south. "Huehue, you don't per chance think you could read these, do you?"

Huehue smiled and nodded yes, then joined in the chant, and time seemed to drift away on the dust of the light that filtered through the dull windows. Soba closed her eyes and had a strange sense of déjà vu, that she had heard this chant before, that she had been among these people before. That while she had a Navajo mother, these could have been part of her Aztec family. The rational, college educated linguist in her knew it wasn't possible, but the shaman in her wasn't quite so sure.

A little later, she went over to the worn-down community building, which had an old computer for everyone's use. It was slow and dated and smelled like ozone when you turned it on, but at least it had a spotty internet connection. Soba had turned off her phone and kept it off, despite the temptation to use it. She and Nick had agreed no using their phones, not under any circumstances, and kept it in airplane mode. No tracks. After all, that was why she was out here in the first place.

It turned out Nick liked to fancy himself as an amateur cryptologist. After all, wasn't an archeologist simply someone who liked solving complex puzzles of the past? Originally, he had come up with an elaborate coded system to communicate with Soba but abandoned it when he realized it was too complex for her. "Don't dumb it down for me," she had defiantly objected, but that was exactly what he had done. Instead, he had set up a series of unique, unrelated email addresses, each to be used for one simple message on one day only. And after Soba read the message, she was to delete it, and further to empty the email trash bin and never reuse that email address. Leave no footprints. Low budget and low tech, but hard to trace.

Any communication was to be in a simple series of code letters, signals from Nick to Soba. "A" meant all good, things are progressing. Any number after the "A" indicated how many more days Nick thought he needed, a question mark meant he didn't know yet. "B" meant someone was on to him and he had to lay low, again the number after indicated the number of days until he thought he was safe. "C" meant he was ready to come get her and for her to respond with coded GPS coordinates, because, for safety, he didn't even know where she was now. "D" was a signal that they were both in imminent danger, and that they would each make their own way to sanctuary at a predetermined rally point north of the border.

There were similar codes in case Soba needed to communicate with Nick in an emergency, otherwise the communication was to be one way only. Nick wouldn't even let her write the codes down and made her memorize them. She concentrated and mentally went through the sequence one more time to further burn it into her brain. "A" was all good, "B" was being careful, "C" was coming for you, and "D" was danger, run.

Soba nervously booted up the computer and logged into today's email address, which had one new message waiting for her. Anxiously she clicked on it and waited for the computer to slowly form the pixilated message on the screen. It simply read "A?", all good, the number of days yet to be determined. Well, no news was good news. She let out her breath in relief, then grinned when she saw Nick had included an emoticon below it, :-). Low tech indeed.

Still, she couldn't shake the increasing feeling of foreboding she was starting to experience. Ill portents were making her uneasy. Not with her being sequestered with the tribe, or with Nick doing research in Mexico City. It was something else, something bigger, something darker that seemed to be hovering off in the distance, menacingly gaining strength. Their last conversation kept replaying in her mind. She didn't like to rely on her intuition, but with her shamanistic upbringing she had tended to be unerringly prescient.

"Come back to me Nick LaBounty. You don't want to make me chase you in the next life," she had said, and now wished she hadn't.

An ocean away, unbeknownst to Soba, Nick was still diligently researching through the archives in Seville with Dr. Storm. They had approached the task in a scientific manner, much in the same vein as when Nick had conducted his research in Mexico City. The volume of available material was staggering, and the initial assault began with a series of computer algorithms to query the vast database of documents. Brainstorming together, they had come up with a list of key words and phrases that slightly expanded on the queries Nick had already used in Mexico. For their purposes, it was a richer trove of documents given the Spanish disposition of meticulously documenting everything. But that also meant going down the proverbial rabbit hole, again and again.

"This one is a dead end too," Nick groaned. "Just another tease."

Dr. Storm, lost in his own research, turned and looked over the top of his glasses at Nick. "Remember what Thomas Edison said my young friend. 'I have not failed. I have found 10,000 ways that won't work,'" he replied, smiling.

Nick chuckled. The good doctor always knew how to put an optimistic spin on any situation. After all, patience and persistence in research, the vital precursor to actual field work, were the hallmarks of any truly successful archeologist.

"Well, that leaves only 9,900 to go Doc!"

As one day faded into the next, they both settled into a routine. First thing each morning when they arrived, coffee in hand, they reviewed if anything promising had turned up and was worth investigating further. If not, they divided up the leads the search algorithms had produced and separately burrowed into them. Where possible, they reviewed images of the documents online since it made the process quicker, but if they hadn't been scanned, they had the original source materials delivered to them for a white glove review. The private room that had been set aside for them was typical of any such institution, no windows, harsh fluorescent lights, and stale recycled air. Throw in a cryptic ancient puzzle to solve and the company of his mentor, and Nick was in his element. He loved it.

Friday afternoon Juan Ramirez, the Minister of Culture, stopped by and inquired how they were progressing. "Only 9,500 stones left to turn over," Nick replied without looking up, banging away at a computer. When Juan raised an eyebrow, Dr. Storm explained to him the inside joke. Juan let out a hearty laugh, he had been skeptical of their finding any new useful information, but he was also rooting for their success.

"Don't mind him, he's just living the dream," Dr. Storm added, nodding over at Nick. "You remember how it used to be Juan, to be young and idealistic and full of piss and vinegar. When one could bend the world to their view of it and prove the unprovable because they were just too ignorant to know it couldn't be done."

"Ah yes, let the dreamers dream. We will all be the better for it. Keep me posted Philip, and let me know if there is anything this institution or I can supply to aide your efforts," Juan replied, and shook Dr. Storm's hand and patted Nick on the shoulder. Nick smiled and gave him a look of thanks and watched him leave the office.

"Good man, good friend," Dr. Storm commented. "How are things going over there, Nick? Anything interesting turning up yet?"

"Maybe, kind of. I found a reference of information about 'items' being secretly taken out of Tenochtitlán, but it dead ends. It doesn't say who provided the information, it's just a passing reference from a low-level priest to his superior, a kind of 'thought you would like to know.' The crux of the letter has to do with conversions of the heathens, the struggle to get them to reject their gods and accept the Christian faith. There isn't even a date that I can make out."

Dr. Storm thoughtfully rubbed the beard on his chin. "Hmm. Can you make out the name of his superior?"

"Not in this scan Doc. I already requested the original, should be here in a bit."

Later that afternoon an attendant dutifully wheeled in a cart, full of carefully arranged bound volumes, dusty manuscripts, and individual letters. Each had a small slip of printed paper sticking out of it, the computerized request form from either Nick or Dr. Storm. Nick thanked the attendant, put on his archival white gloves, and parceled them out.

"I have to admit, they are really on the ball. Even the paper they are printing our requests on are on acid-free paper, so they won't damage the originals." Nick and Dr. Storm then got lost in their own little worlds of going through their requested items, this time of the day being the most exciting part of the routine they had fallen into. Their chance to actually touch the history they were seeking to unravel.

Nick carefully pulled the letter the priest had written out of its clear plastic envelope. He then unfolded it with metal forceps, swung a brightly illuminated magnifying glass over it, and carefully examined it. He couldn't make out the date it was written or the name on the salutation, they had faded to nothing, and not even a trace of the indentation from the quill pen that wrote it survived. *That isn't unusual,* he reflected, as a quill pen wasn't typically pressed down very hard, since it would result in a thick flow of ink. One wouldn't do that unless it was on purpose, in which case you could probably just read the denser ink and not need the indentation in the first place.

The letter was one sided, and Nick flipped it over to examine the back. Nothing there either, just faded coloration marks and faint imperfections. He folded the letter and was about to put it back, when something caught his eye. It was the fold itself, it was odd. Upon closer examination the fold he had opened it from was relatively recent, from when someone had probably scanned the letter and then put it into the plastic sleeve. It wouldn't fit the sleeve they had, so they refolded it differently, smaller. But Nick now saw the older original fold and restored it to that format. And there on the back of the letter, which was folded into itself, in the very middle, was barely perceptible, faint lettering. The name of who this was addressed to, perhaps the name of the priest's superior.

Professor Storm jumped and bumped his forehead on his own lit magnifier when Nick broke the deafening silence with a 'woo-hoo' of excitement.

"We've got a live one Doc!"

CHAPTER 32 – JULY 10

In archeology, it often took just one barely tangible link to unravel a far greater mystery. One tenuous thread, so easily damaged or erased from existence, could be the singular link that led to a series of clues that in turn led to the hidden entrance of the tomb of King Tutankhamen in the Valley of the Kings, or to the buried time capsule of Pompeii in the shadows of Vesuvius, or even to the fossil of Lucy, our oldest human ancestor, in the deserts of Ethiopia. And both Nick and Dr. Storm innately knew it.

"Hey, take a look at this, what do you think?" Nick anxiously asked.

Dr. Storm bent over and squinted, holding the lit magnifier closer, and then farther away. "Hmm, there is definitely something there. But I can't make it out. The edges of some of the letters are visible, but then it fades. And the coloring is odd, not really black, hard to distinguish."

"I know, I think it was the ink he was using. At first I couldn't put my finger on it, but now it makes sense. This low-level priest didn't have imported ink to use, it was something he probably concocted himself off wherever he was, likely a berry extract," Nick surmised. "That is why the text of the letter itself is so hard to distinguish too."

Dr. Storm put the clear plastic sheet the letter came in on top of the folded letter to protect it and grabbed a higher magnification jeweler's loop out. He then leaned down so close his nose touched the plastic and squinted harder at the text.

"No good, we need an imager," he said, and dialed up Juan. Within 15 minutes, the same dutiful attendant was back with another cart and an expensive looking device on it, some cables and a remote control. He hooked the device up to a large display on the wall and handed the remote to Dr. Storm.

"Yes, I know my way around one of these pretty well. Thank you son," he replied as the attendant left.

"We really should get both him and Juan a good bottle of Scotch before we leave, remind me please Nick." He then placed the folded letter on the high-resolution document imager, and zoomed in. Nick walked over and turned on the display on the wall and stepped back.

"Ahh, let's have a look at what we can see now," Dr. Storm said as he zoomed in and sharpened the focus. A large, sharply defined image popped up on the wall display, surprising in its detail. Even the porosity and fabric of the paper itself were clearly visible. A bit more of the lettering could now be distinguished, but it still was mostly faded and illegible. He then flipped it over to the letter side and moved it to the beginning, and then to the end, but to no avail. "Damn, we are so very close."

"That's great resolution of something that isn't there. Too bad we didn't have a . . ." Nick said, as the doorknob turned.

Someone cracked open the door and backed in, bringing another cart in behind them. Once fully in the room, Juan turned around and with a laugh said, "I saw your first request, thought you might be able to use one of these too."

"Ha, welcome friend. You read our minds," Dr. Storm replied in greeting.

Juan had brought down an ESDA, or *electrostatic detection apparatus*, used to uncover indented writing below the original page, a very sensitive device used in espionage, and in the forensic archeology of ancient documents. Juan was now caught up in the chase too, and eagerly jumped right in. First, he plugged the ESDA in while Nick connected it to the wall display. Juan then put on cotton gloves and carefully placed the open document flat, letter side down, over a porous metal plate, then placed a clear Mylar sheet over it.

"Here we go," he grinned, and flipped the switch on. A little motor whirled to life, and an internal vacuum pulled the Mylar and letter tightly against the metal plate, creating a perfect, tight seal.

"Your honors señor Nick," Juan added, and handed a small metal wand to him.

Gingerly taking the wand, Nick slowly waved it back and forth over the area on the back of the letter that appeared to have the indistinguishable name on it. The wand was designed to produce static electricity, which would be greatest over the indentations. Nick then carefully sprayed a type of toner onto the Mylar, which collected where the static charge was strongest. Right along the imperceptibly light scratching of a quill pen 500 years ago.

As Nick stepped back, Juan zoomed the camera in, and everyone looked at the image on the wall display.

"Voilà gentlemen," Juan said. "I hope this is what you were looking for."

There, in barely discernible script, were letters interspersed with some still unreadable blanks, 'A_to_io__e Ci__da_ Rod_ig_.'

Nick walked over to the display screen and touched the letters lightly with his fingertips, deep in thought. Juan raised his eyebrows and looked at Dr. Storm, who was staring at the screen, stroking the point of his beard.

"I wonder . . ." Nick mused and went over to his computer and started typing furiously. He then jumped up and went back to the screen, and slowly spelled out the name with the missing letters, pointing to each in turn.

"A-n-t-o-n-i-o de C-i-u-d-a-d R-o-d-r-i-g-o. Don't you see? Antonio de Ciudad Rodrigo, one of the original twelve!" he gleefully yelled, dancing a little jig in a circle.

"One of the twelve!" Dr. Storm joined in, and slapped Nick on the back. "We've got a real trail!"

Seeing Juan's perplexed expression, Dr. Storm explained its relevance. "Antonio was one of the original group of twelve Franciscan missionaries to arrive in New Spain. Cortés had requested them to convert the indigenous population, to give himself a degree of legitimacy in the eyes of Charles V."

Nick, sitting back down at the computer, looked up and added, "Because the Governor of New Spain, seated in Cuba, hadn't wanted Cortés to go off on this expedition in the first place. He recalled him, but Cortés knew he was about to be stopped and slipped away anyway, and the rest, as they say, is history."

Juan still wasn't connecting all the dots and looked to his friend Philip. "This letter, likely written off in the hinterlands somewhere, is from a priest complaining about how hard it is to convert the savages to Christianity. But he makes mention of hearing about things being snuck out of Tenochtitlán. Why pass this information along to his superior Antonio, unless he was being asked to keep his ears open for it," Dr. Storm patiently explained. "And the time he was there was shortly after the conquest. So if it went to someone as important as Antonio Rodrigo, there is probably more of a paper trail to follow. It may be nothing, or it could be something, or it could be everything. But it's our first new solid lead that someone else hasn't already chased to ground and disproven."

As they talked, Nick flipped the letter over and tested it to see if he could find out who the author was. Even the ESDA couldn't pick up anything legible, which was unfortunate as his name would have been most useful. Alas, the priest would have to go unnamed.

"This calls for drinks on me. Cava it is, I'll meet you tonight at eight," Juan joyfully informed them.

"Drinks on you, this must indeed be a most special occasion," Dr. Storm joked as he walked Juan out. "I think you bought a round once, but I can't seem to remember when."

Nick didn't even hear them, he was already putting in a request for information on the computerized inventory system. "Materials on Antonio de Ciudad Rodrigo. Everything you've got."

The following day a comprehensive listing of resources came back. Nick and Dr. Storm immediately dove into the electronic documents that weren't held right there within the General Archive of the Indies to get an immediate start. Late in the afternoon, each was so engrossed in their own private paper chase that they didn't hear the door open. Two carts arrived this time, overflowing with a variety of original source materials. Sergio, the attendant, had thoughtfully placed slips in each wherever Antonio Rodrigo was mentioned or authored.

"Ah Sergio, you are much too kind to us," Dr. Storm said. Nick sat up as he remembered something, and reached into his backpack and produced a bottle, which Dr. Storm in turn passed along. "Muchas gracias our friend. Your diligent work is very much appreciated."

Sergio bowed slightly and blushed, unused to such a show of gratitude for merely doing his job and left mumbling his thanks.

"I think we made his day Doc," Nick commented.

Looking at the piles of documents on the carts, Dr. Storm sighed happily. "Yes. Let's hope he makes ours too."

No such luck. The days started blending, blurring into one another in the increasingly claustrophobic basement room. Nick and the good doctor even stepped back for a strategy session, objectively wondering if this might be a dead end, or if they should redeploy their limited resources and have one look for entirely different clues while the other continued to pursue the trail of Antonio de Ciudad Rodrigo. But there was only about a half cart of materials left, and they decided to dive in and see this lead through to its end before reevaluating.

The next morning, before he had even finished his cup of coffee, Dr. Storm abruptly stood up and walked a loosely bound manuscript over to Nick. He pointed to a passage written in Antonio's own hand and read it out verbatim as he translated.

"As you instructed, all our laymen have been listening most eagerly for tales of efforts by the Aztecas to hide their sacrilegious and precious objects. It is my fervent desire to turn their evil and heathen idol worship into that which may aide our most holy Charles V in his quest against the infidels who would oppose the sacred teachings of our Lord."

He paused and swiveled over a magnifier to better read the faded text. Nick sat motionless, now hanging on every word.

"I have received a second communication from Fray Garcia, who is converting the simple savages down in Chiapas. There he witnessed the forced confession of a native who said he was on a caravan from Tenochtitlán before the city was subdued by Cortés through the many blessings of our Lord. Before he died from the rigors of the queries put to him, he said this had been a false caravan, like several others. It was filled only with sand and rocks and sculpture to make the weight appear real. When they reached their destination, the worthless items were buried and the porters sacrificed to their heathen gods."

Nick and Dr. Storm's eyes met for a moment, the implications sinking in. The unknown priest in the hinterlands who provided the original letter to Antonio Rodrigo had to have been this Fray Garcia.

"Before leaving they had been blessed by their own priests, who said they were going on a pilgrimage, and making a holy sacrifice. He said he had wanted to go on the one true journey but wasn't chosen because he had never killed a Spaniard." Concluding, Dr. Storm set the document down.

Nick sat dumbstruck, the myths and rumors of all the years suddenly coalescing into proven fact. Slowly gathering himself, he looked at the document and let out a long, slow breath.

"Whew Doc, this is written in Antonio Rodrigo's own hand. This is irrefutable proof that there had been an actual expedition mounted before the fall of Tenochtitlán, the *one true journey*! And that the Aztecs sent out other caravans to throw the Spaniards off the scent. To have done that at this time of catastrophe, when their world was completely crumbling around them, meant it was absolutely vital to them as a people to pull it off. Think of the resources they must have poured into it, the commitment they made, they staked everything on this, one final roll of the dice!"

Dr. Storm had sat down, with a look of contentment Nick had seen only once or twice before on his face, and only after unlocking an exceedingly difficult and timeless puzzle.

"Just ponder it," Dr. Storm said. "How those other false expeditions may have given rise to other myths over time. Picture it, all the gold crazed Spaniards and treasure seekers down through the ages, who have been lost chasing ghosts on unnamed rivers and in impassable jungles, in terra incognito. Even real, well-funded scientific men were swallowed whole by their lust. It beggars belief, yet now all makes perfect sense."

Nick rummaged through his backpack again and proudly produced another bottle and poured a generous amount of bourbon into their empty coffee cups. "Well, now we have an official name for our quest. The next piece to unravel is not just what route this one true caravan took, but where it ultimately ended. Because that is where all my questions will be answered."

Dr. Storm took the offered cup and stared into it, swirling the brown liquid. "There is no denying one thing, that your father was onto something, and it was something very real. He started this quest, and I suspect you'll finish it young man. He would have been proud of you Nick."

Raising his cup he looked Nick in the eye, then toasted, "To the *one true journey*!"

As Charlie took his usual drive in to work from his home in the suburbs, Nick was on his mind. He hadn't heard from him at all in quite some time, and it was making him nervous. Usually he was good at keeping in touch or was at least accessible. But his calls and emails to Nick had lately gone unanswered. He was worried enough that he even reached out to Soba, but no reply from her either. That either meant Nick was off grid investigating a lead, or perhaps something more sinister was afoot. It didn't sit well with him.

When Charlie arrived at his office on the 59th floor of the Willis Tower in downtown Chicago, he noticed there were several voice mail messages. He distractedly listened to them in turn, and immediately perked up when he recognized Nick's voice on the last one. *Finally.*

He looked out at Lake Michigan, digesting the lengthy message Nick had left him. Shaking his head in disbelief, he listened to it one more time, jotted down bulleted notes from it, and then erased the recording as instructed. The global hedge fund he worked for was cutting edge and hyper vigilant, security across voice and data networks here was bulletproof, it had to be. His brother wasn't one to be spooked easily, but if it made him feel safer, so be it.

Nick had brought him up to date on a burner phone he had picked up, which he used once and discarded. Come to think of it, Nick had never even mentioned where he was calling from. He said Soba was safely hidden somewhere else that even he didn't know, just as a precaution. He was making progress, had a solid lead and was hoping for a breakthrough soon, more to follow later. But most importantly, he wanted to leverage the investigative resources Charlie had at his disposal with the hedge fund.

There had to be a direct connection between the missing journal, the death of their father, and now the tracking mechanism he found hidden under his truck, Nick explained. He also mentioned the conversation with the Mexican cop who leaned on him in Cuernavaca, and meeting Francisco 'Chico' Martinez from the Mexican Department of Antiquities in a bar, who turned up dead just after.

"I just don't believe in coincidences," Nick had said. "But I do believe it means I'm getting close to something very valuable to someone. Maybe too close."

Well, we can either keep dancing to someone else's tune or try to get in front of it, Charlie thought. They obviously know a lot about us. Time to see what we can find out about them. He tapped his pen on the pad and underlined the last bullet he had just written down.

Find the SOB that killed Dad.

Things started progressing more quickly now, at least in terms of how deep archival research typically unfolded. Refining their search parameters, Nick and Dr. Storm started looking for mentions of the name of the lonely priest far off in the jungle, who was the original source that heard the tortured utterings of an Aztec mentioning a false expedition he had been on. And the one true journey he *wished*

he had been on. That a priest was there to witness it and not just the treasure blinded conquistadors, and that his letter documenting it even survived. Serendipity indeed, as the fates finally seemed to be smiling upon them.

They refined their search algorithms to pick up any mention of Fray Garcia, Friar Garcia, Padre Garcia, false caravan, true journey, etc., and within a few days uncovered several documents that mentioned him, and one that also used the phrase the one true journey. A cheerful Sergio brought that and several other documents down to the research room, where Nick anxiously greeted him.

"Ah, it's our good luck charm Sergio, let's see what possible discoveries he has brought to us today," Nick said in greeting. Again Sergio blushed, but he was getting used to good natured kidding and now actually looked forward to it.

The number of documents were so few and so specific that Nick and Dr. Storm examined each of them together. The first documents that mentioned Garcia contained questions he posed about matters such as if there should be single or mass conversions of the heathens, how much work they were required to do, who would be free or slave, and how to collect taxes. Insightful information to have gleaned, but not what they were ultimately looking for.

Then Dr. Storm placed the last letter, carefully preserved in a plastic envelope, out on the document imager. It was the single surviving document that had the words 'Fray Garcia' *and* 'one true journey' within it. They had purposely kept it for last. He fiddled with the positioning of the salutation until it was under the lens and came into focus on the display on the wall. They hesitantly looked at each other before turning to look up to see if it was legible.

When they read silently to themselves and grasped the significance, they both let out an audible gasp.

Nick took a photo on his phone of the letter, and without saying a word they excitedly shook hands and headed upstairs, to the office of Juan Ramirez.

When Dr. Storm rapped on the door frame, Juan looked up and immediately waved them in. "Welcome gentlemen, what fair tidings do you bring?" Juan inquired in his deep baritone voice.

Closing the door behind them, Dr. Storm and Nick seated themselves, mentally exhausted and yet elated, a strange juxtaposition of the senses. Juan sat behind his desk, waited a moment, then opened his palms questioningly. "Well?"

Dr. Storm cleared his voice. "We found another related document, written in the hand of one Marcos de Niza. In it he talks about the interrogation Fray Garcia witnessed, and about the one true journey out of Tenochtitlán. This document provides the linkage we sought. Nick, you know the history better than anyone, enlighten my good friend."

Nick sat up and leaned toward Juan. "Marcos was just another Franciscan missionary, one of many now pouring into the New World. But he earned his stripes for the order first in Peru on the heels of Pizarro conquering the Incas, then in Guatemala. His star was on the rise. In 1537 he is summoned to Mexico City by the Viceroy of all of New Spain, Antonio de Mendoza, and all the while is privy to the information the Franciscan Order is accumulating. Their purpose is to convert the conquered, protect them from the cruelty of their new masters, and to see that the crown gets its royal fifth to spread the faith.

Remember Cabeza de Vaca? He was shipwrecked in the Gulf of Mexico, and wandered around the Southwest to the Pacific, and eventually made it back to Mexico City along with several others, including a slave named Esteban the Moor. They claim to have seen fabulous things, and the story of the Seven Cities of Cibola takes root in the New World. With me so far?"

Juan nodded eagerly, caught up in the tale that was so intertwined with the archives he oversaw, just outside his door.

"In 1539 Fray Marcos is sent under orders from the Viceroy on an expedition to verify Cabeza de Vaca's reports and find Cibola, and the party is accompanied by none other than Esteban the Moor to help guide them. They make a long journey and ultimately Esteban is killed, but Fray Marcos claims to have seen Cibola off in the distance, and the survivors return."

"So Marcos never actually went there, but only saw it in the distance?" Juan asked.

"True, but that was good enough to launch a *second* expedition, but this one more seriously outfitted, and led by none other than Francisco Vásquez de Coronado," Nick replied. "Fray Marcos went with them, and what he saw in the distance from the first expedition turned out to be the Zuni Pueblos of New Mexico, which Coronado now ransacked in frustration. They are led further on a wild goose chase, all the way to Quivira, in Kansas. They never found what they sought, and Fray Marcos was sent back in shame.

But now we know Coronado was actually on the right track. The confession from a tortured Aztec that was witnessed by Fray Garcia, who wrote about it to his superior Antonio Rodriguez, which was mentioned verbatim in *this letter* by Marcos de Niza. Marcos was then summoned by the Viceroy of New Spain to Mexico City, and then accompanied Coronado on the quest for Cibola," Nick summarized.

"But how does that narrow down what route that one true journey took, or where it ended up?" Juan pondered. "Coronado wandered far and wide, and never actually found it. That's a lot of ground to cover."

"It is, unless your dad spent every summer of your youth narrowing it down. And I now have all the clues I need to make perfect sense of those wanderings." Nick concluded.

"*Excepcional*, I'm happy for you. It is not often the gods favor us with revealing their secrets," Juan replied. "It does the soul good to see righteousness occasionally illuminate the darkness."

Dr. Storm stood up and offered his hand to Juan. "I appreciate all your help and the access you so generously provided. Nick and I have a little token of our appreciation for you." With that he put a bottle of Macallan 25-year-old scotch on his desk and was hugged by his old friend.

On the ride back to the hotel, both of them a bit emotionally drained, Dr. Storm looked over at Nick questioningly. "You never told him the whole story, of the key clues you left out. You don't completely trust him, do you?"

"I have no secrets from you Doc, I trust you with my life. And it's not that I don't trust Juan, I just may not trust all those around him. You can tell from the photos in his office that he attracts cultural groupies and political wonks like a dog collects fleas. I've got to step carefully, there are a lot of people who are important to me involved now, you included. There's more at stake here than just solving a mystery."

CHAPTER 33 – JULY 18

Stepping off the plane back in the Mexico City International Airport, Nick looked over his shoulder for Dr. Storm out of habit, as they had just spent so much time together in Spain. But his old mentor wasn't with him on this flight and had instead gone off to visit other colleagues while he was in Europe.

"Overdue debts to pay," he had joked.

"More like royalty being fêted," Nick had countered.

They had departed with a warm embrace and a promise by Nick to discretely keep the good doctor up to date on events as they unfolded.

Before leaving the airport, Nick found an internet café and rented time on a computer, as he was still in black out mode with his phone. He logged into the appropriate one-time use e-mail account, and found Soba's reply awaiting him, which consisted of two long strings of numbers, which would appear as gibberish to any prying eyes. It was the coded latitude and longitude GPS coordinates of her location.

"Which one should I list first?" she had asked when they were coming up with the code for this single most confidential piece of information, where her exact hidden location would be.

"Well just like Occam's Razor says, simplicity is always better than complexity," he had replied. Seeing her puzzled look, he realized she had never heard of this age-old theorem of problem solving. "The simplest solution is always the best. Just list them alphabetically, latitude before longitude."

To get the deciphered coordinates, he dropped the first six and the last six digits from each string of numbers. He then subtracted the six digits of Soba's birthday from the remaining latitude number, and the six digits of the day they had met back on the summer solstice from the longitude. He found using rhythms helped Soba remember key instructions. Everything in sixes to keep it simple, sixes for Soba he had joked. He smiled that she had insisted they use her birthday within the code.

"Easy for me to remember, and it is important you memorize it anyway. Because you know, it's customary to give a gift then, even among white people," she had laughed.

Finished, Nick proudly looked at the resulting coordinates, this is where he would now find her. He deleted the email message itself, and then emptied the electronic trash bin too. *Good luck to anyone tracking that one,* he thought.

He quickly went to the long-term parking lot where he had parked his pickup truck, not immediately recognizing it due to the switched license plates he had put on. He had forgotten he had swapped them out, the flight and time zone changes having thrown him off. Pulling out onto the highway, the familiar sights and sounds of Mexico City filled his senses as he headed northeast, away from the city, to a destination on a map in the wilderness beyond a small town named Tulancingo.

The drive was through increasingly barren country, which eventually gave way to more fertile foothills. Nick motored past the scattered communal ejidos, with workers toiling in the fields, the occasional one waving a hat to him. He rechecked the coordinates he had plugged into his portable GPS and made his way up an increasingly steep and desolate roadway. Reaching the crest he briefly took in the panoramic view, then worked his way down the back side. The location on the screen was not on any marked road, so he drove slowly, looking for an unmarked roadway or trail to angle in toward it.

"It would be so much easier just to call her," he found himself saying aloud out of frustration, after he turned back around to try again. But he absolutely wouldn't do that now, not after having maintained radio silence with his phone for this long. And she wouldn't have her phone on in the first place. At least she better not.

He almost missed it, the turn off partially obscured by the old growth of draping tree limbs, impinging scrub brush and a decided lack of traffic. He carefully turned in, a scratching sound trailing along the length of his truck as branches clawed at it. Slowly he followed the rutted road, really more of a trail, wondering if he had made the correct turn off. The increasingly dense canopy overhead obscured any GPS signal, so he resolutely ventured onward, starting to worry if he could even find a place to turn around as the trail closed in ever more tightly around him.

Finally forced to put the Chevy into four-wheel drive, Nick drove on over the bumps and ruts, until he finally came to a sharp corner and turned. There in front of him the trail opened into a meadow, a field and small buildings and huts scattered along the far edge. He suddenly tensed as he saw the tall grass move in the distance, parting, something large coming at him, gaining momentum and thudding on the ground, then abruptly jumping up and putting two muddy paws on the hood and looking directly at him. Nanook. Just as suddenly another dog jumped up and did the same, his female Husky running mate.

Nick pulled off the trail over to the side, where a couple of other beat up, older vehicles sat, his well-worn pickup perfectly blending in. Nanook nuzzled Nick and pranced about him until he relented and got on his knees and returned the affection. At which point the Husky worked her way in, sniffed Nick, and leaned in for a rub too. "Whatcha got here boy, a girlfriend? About time, you old dog you!"

He gathered his things, and Nanook and the Husky eagerly led the way, bounding back across the meadow. Hearing Nanook bark once, Soba stuck her head out of a hut to see what he wanted, her eyes immediately meeting Nick's.

"My *mą'iitsoh nahat'ín*," my wolf whisperer, Soba said in her sing song cadence as she slowly walked toward Nick. Looking eye to eye for a moment, she suddenly jumped up on him, wrapping her arms and legs around him, making him drop everything he was holding to hold on to her. Nick burrowed his face into her hair and neck and breathed deeply, inhaling that familiar, calming scent that was Soba and slowly twirling her about as Nanook and the Husky ran circles around them both.

"We're safe as long as we're together. And we're not going to be apart until you see this thing through," she whispered in his ear, holding on tight.

They both looked up when they heard laughter and giggling, as two children held each other mimicking them by making kissing sounds, and people started gathering about from the sudden commotion. Nick smiled broadly as he looked at the little crowd, and back into Soba's deep green eyes. "I've been to Spain, and have much to tell you, but we can catch up on the drive north. First, why don't you do the introductions to your new friends?"

Soba gazed out as the scenery drifted by her open truck window, then looked sternly over at Nick. "So you were actually in Spain? In Seville? Living it up at a luxury hotel and fine dining with Dr. Storm? All this time I was feeling sorry for you being holed up in some hostel in Mexico City, or worried you were being abducted by some drug cartel," Soba fake pouted, unable to conceal a grin.

Nick checked his watch, then looked up. "Hey, we should be to customs in El Paso in only about 20 hours," he joked. "Hardly any time at all to catch up or enjoy the pleasure of your company. Did I mention I missed you?"

He then meticulously outlined everything that had transpired in Seville, what he had learned, and the trail he believed the clues put him onto. It didn't solve everything, but he believed it put him on the right path, and he was excited to dive into it.

Finally caught up on each other's lives, Soba sighed and leaned into him, and started to doze off contentedly. As sleep finally began to calm her tortured imagination, Nanook nuzzled his head between them both through the open window to the back, looking for some attention. He gave Soba a loud huff in her ear and Nick a sloppy lick. It was going to be a long drive.

The sun slowly set, and dusk settled on the horizon to the west. The drive turned monotonous, the adrenaline rush of seeing Soba and wanting to start the search wearing off, and Nick found his eye lids getting heavier in the increasing darkness. After having driven for nearly 12 hours he finally gave in, the jet lag catching up and overpowering him. Looking for a place to pull off and crash, they entered the *Mapimi Biosphere Reserve*, a National Park just off their route north. After parking off the road, they crawled into the back of the truck, Nick fast asleep and gently snoring before Soba could even say good night.

She was up before the dawn with Nanook, foraged for a few items, and prepared a quick breakfast. Nick heard them through the fog of deep sleep and arose and shook off the hangover from the time change. Rummaging in the back of his driver's seat, he pulled out his American license plates. He would need these to get through customs and swapped them with the Mexican plates he had been using to stay incognito south of the border.

The remaining drive was uneventful, but the tension steadily built as they got closer to the crossing at El Paso, Texas. When they slowed and then finally stopped behind a long line of vehicles to enter the states, Soba reached over, rubbed Nick's shoulder and smiled nervously.

"Yeah, I'll be glad to get through this too. Keep your eyes open, last time around they put that tracker under the truck," Nick nervously said. Nanook sensed the tension and sat with his head resting through the window between them, alert and on watch. "Be suspicious of anyone approaching the vehicle from any side. That means you too Nanook," he said, giving him an ear rub.

Time slowed, and the big rigs around them belched smoke and diesel as they inched toward the border crossing. Kids in a station wagon one lane over caught sight of Nanook and called and whistled to him, but he was indifferent, stoic. The clogged lanes parted into two groups, tractor trailers heading off to the right, and smaller vehicles staying straight ahead. They crept up a ramp over the border wall dividing the two countries, and then back down. Nick drummed his fingers on the dashboard, trying to appear nonchalant. Finally they pulled up to a booth, where they were greeted by a trim US Customs Agent standing outside of it. The agent leaned over and glanced around while asking Nick to see identification and took their passports. He opened each, and carefully looked at and evaluated Nick and Soba in turn.

"Anything to declare?" They both nodded their heads no, and Nick was given the passports back. "Well then, welcome back to the United States folks," the agent said in his Texas drawl, and promptly snapped his fingers and motioned for the next car to pull up.

Nick drove quickly away from the border crossing and zoomed up to speed on Interstate 10 North. Finally he let out a long breath and looked over at Soba. "Free and clear baby, free and clear. I didn't see a thing on my side or in back. How about you?"

"Nothing at all, there was barely time for anything. I guess we didn't look as suspicious coming back as we did going down," Soba responded hopefully.

"That, or whoever was tracking us had someone in Mexican Customs on their payroll, but no one on the US side. That was so quick I don't see how they could have put anything on us while we were there."

"So where to now?"

"Back up to Gila, we've got a date with my buddy Killian tomorrow. I feel we are getting close," he smiled to Soba, and patted her knee affectionately. "The plot thickens, the adventure continues!"

"You would have been better off lying to me, don't you know honesty kills?" Eztli said, as he carefully placed the freshly cleaned skull of Dr. Rojas on the top row of the skull rack. The rack was placed strategically near the centerpiece of his underground museum, the solid gold Aztec Sun Stone, created in tribute to the glory that had been the Aztec Empire. And would soon be again.

He stood back to admire his handiwork, the empty eye sockets of 61 skulls, of those who had dared cross him over the years, staring back blankly in mute testimony to his single minded and ruthless determination. He still had plenty of space to add more, whatever it took to achieve his goals. Certainly the ends of Mesoamerican pride and reunification justified the means.

The geneticist had dared tell him the truth, that Eztli's blood line contained the Spanish blood of the conquerors, and that while he was predominantly Aztec, he wasn't a pure blood. *Mestizo*, mixed blood, he wouldn't even deign to speak the word. No one must ever know this secret, it would undermine everything he was strategically building toward, the premise of the empire he had made his life's purpose to resurrect.

"Ah well, Dr. Rojas, dead men tell no tales."

There was much to accomplish today. He checked his watch and realized that his deputy Javier and brother Miguel would soon be here with their trusted lieutenants.

He wandered over to the elevator and looked back upon his museum, the rows of display cases of Aztec artifacts, elegantly displayed figurines, sculptures, precious metalwork and rescued treasure, and felt pride in his quest. The apogee of pre-Columbian civilization, acquired over many years by any means necessary, lay before him. And if he could add the rumored riches of Cibola to this, it would place Aztec heritage on a par with the other great civilizations of the past. Beyond them even.

They all sat out in the courtyard of the mansion, lunch and niceties dispensed with, ready to get down to business. Eztli nodded to Javier, who summarized the latest political unrest, the fallout from the ongoing drug wars between the cartels, and the pressure it was building on the current administration. "Perhaps an opportunity to be exploited," Javier suggested.

"It is, and we should take advantage of the timing," Eztli said, addressing the whole group. "Javier has informed me that the Minister of Defense has recently reached out, via backwater channels. He is not ignorant of our business interests. But he also knows it is impossible to simply cut the head off the hydra, more will only grow in its place."

He pulled out a cigar, and carefully went through the ritual of lighting it. "I believe he would like to deal with fewer heads, perhaps only one. So I have let it be known to him, via the same discrete backwater channel, that perhaps we could come to some type of mutually beneficial accommodation. That I would be willing to get rid of some heads of the hydra for him, if we were granted certain exclusive privileges." He paused and took a long puff on the cigar and exhaled it slowly.

"His administration and his Presidente will look like they are winning the drug war, we get rid of much of our competition, and they agree to recognize the importance of our 'contributions' to the good of the nation. Another step in our gaining recognition and legitimacy, and one step closer to my ultimate goals."

"You are a patient man brother," Miguel interjected. "You know I have always favored a shorter path. Perhaps an accident and then a coup, seize power quickly and decisively rather than tiptoe with these baby steps."

"Miguel, it is not just legitimacy we seek in the eyes of the Mexican people, we are steadily gaining that. It is in the eyes of neighboring countries and on the world stage. Otherwise the grand design will be stillborn," Eztli said, carefully looking at everyone gathered in turn. "I need all of you to play the long game with me, great glory ultimately awaits not only each of us, but all of *Aztlán*," Eztli said, invoking the mythical homeland of the Aztecs.

He rolled up his sleeve and showed a tattoo for emphasis, and heads nodded. After all, part of their initiation was to have that very image branded on the right bicep, sort of their secret handshake to one another. It also served another darker purpose, being easy to hide with a t-shirt, but readily visible when pointing a gun at someone so they would know who was delivering the killing blow.

Other business was discussed in the same way any board meeting would have unfolded, with updates of the cartel's business and a final summary by Eztli himself. It was an honor for the lieutenants to have been invited to the great man's home and was a signal they were part of the trusted inner circle. They were all made men and were being groomed for greater things.

Once the remaining business was concluded, everyone was

dismissed, except for Miguel. Eztli nodded to him, and they went inside after all the others left, and took the elevator to the basement. Miguel noticed the new addition to the skull rack and raised an eyebrow as he smiled at his brother.

Eztli shrugged as if to say, 'these things happen.'

"What news do you have of the rabbit," Eztli asked as they walked into the conference room and sat.

"The rabbit evidently has been busy. It seems this Nick went to Seville, did some research and returned. He and his Navajo whore went through customs at El Paso and are headed north," Miguel replied.

"Interesting, that means he found something, and he is on the trail. He is tenacious, I will give him that. He doesn't suspect we are tailing him? No? Good. If you don't mind my asking, how did you find out where he went?" Eztli inquired. After all, one didn't survive in this cutthroat underworld without having your finger on the pulse and *always* knowing the details.

"As you taught me, find the weak spot. The man who assisted Nick here at the National Archeology Museum has only one parent, his mother. We showed this peon photographs of the inside of her home with her asleep in bed, so he would know we could take or kill her anytime we choose. After that he became most cooperative, and that is how we found that gringo went to Seville to do further research. And we also have a well-paid Americano on the inside at customs, it was a simple matter for him to check the database to catch the license plate coming through. Nick is being tailed now, very discretely."

"Nice work hermano." Eztli got up and clapped him on the shoulder, then paced as he thought, as was his habit when he was on the cusp of making a critical decision.

"I have a very important task I need you personally to take care of. Keep eyes on him, but he can't know we are on to him, not yet. Take four of your best men and go through the border separately, then pull your team back together. This is what I want you to do to gain me the leverage I need over our wandering gringo treasure seeker."

Eztli grinned and gestured animatedly as he outlined his plan to Miguel, whose face betrayed an increasingly satisfied and sinister glare.

Driving well into the evening, the closest lodging Nick could find was nearly 20 miles outside of the Gila Cliff Dwellings. He pulled into an inconspicuous motel with a vacancy, decided it didn't look too decrepit, and paid cash. Heck, it even featured a continental breakfast, pretty high living according to Soba.

The next morning they were up early and arrived at the Gila Trailhead Museum as it opened, where they were greeted by Nick's good friend Killian. Soba giggled as the boys exchanged some sort of exotic secret college handshake from their past days together and gave Killian a hug and greeting. They wandered down the trail toward Cliff Dweller Canyon, seeking space for a private conversation away from the early morning tourists and hikers. They stopped at a scenic overlook and admired the timeless view of the cliff dwellings off in the distance, with the Gila River winding quietly below.

"Did I tell you that four mummies have 'officially' been found here over the years, not including the one I showed you? But who knows how many others were found and looted, they were a pretty big deal to private collectors," Killian said as he sipped a cup of coffee in a beat-up travel mug.

"The initial rumors were that an extinct race of dwarf cliff dwellers used to inhabit the area, and a small mummy was supposedly in a glass display at a general store over in Silver City. That was according to an 1892 newspaper account I came across. But no photos ever surfaced and that mummy mysteriously went missing. Finally, in 1912 the fourth one was found just over there and was sent to the Smithsonian. Turns out it was an infant, as the others likely were as well."

Nick smiled at his friend. "Of course they were infants. But dwarf mummies make a better story, better for tourism and business. I suspect the best mummified remains from this area are long gone, like you said. Tell me, what became of the 'Misplaced Padre' mummy you found and showed us?"

"After I stabilized him, he was taken up to Albuquerque, examined by a forensic archeologist. They did a detailed examination, including a CAT scan and then an MRI. Turns out he was remarkably well preserved. It's not like he had his internal organs removed as the Egyptians did, it was just the natural drying process of this arid part of the country. About what you would look like if you crawled in that cave over there, and we found you 500 years later."

"Thanks for that visual, remind me not to hike with you," Nick joked. "What about establishing provenance, did anything else come out about when this was, or where he came from?"

"Yes, some interesting details have emerged. First off, he had no eyes."

"No eyes?" Soba said, somewhat taken aback. "How can anyone have possibly survived in this country with no eyes back then?"

Killian paused as a well outfitted older couple trudged by, their hiking poles clicking in rhythm on the hardpan surface of the trail.

"Well, he had no eyes, at least not then. Evidently they had been burned out, the sockets were cauterized, healed over. I don't know, maybe he was a prisoner or a slave of some sort, but that doesn't jibe with him being buried with a silver cross and chain. And he was shrouded and carefully positioned, I suspect that whoever put him where I found him went to great lengths to pay him respect and carefully hide him."

Nick looked up and down the path to see if anyone was coming. "Yeah, that doesn't sound much like a slave to me, why go through the trouble, much less leave him with anything of value like that large silver cross he held. You kill or trade captives here, this wasn't exactly a land of plenty. Anything else?"

"Yeah, follow me, I think you'll find this intriguing." Killian led them back to the museum, and to the same room where he had shown them the mummy. He unlocked the door and went over to one of the file cabinets. Digging around, he pulled a box out from the very back recess of one of the drawers.

"After they took the mummy away to examine, I went back to where I had found him, and did a thorough examination of the area. I found some artifacts buried in the dirt right around where he was. Here, take a look. Obsidian arrow heads, a broken sword, two gold rings, and what looked like part of a broken Spanish breast plate," Killian replied.

Nick carefully examined each item in turn and took detailed photographs of them. While he was doing this, Soba touched an arrowhead, then picked up the broken sword. She closed her eyes in quiet contemplation, and then slowly opened them.

"Two worlds," she said.

They both looked at her with puzzled expressions.

"Don't you see? They paid him honor by the way they consecrated him," Soba observed. "He may have been a Spanish Friar or priest or whatever, but he earned the respect of those who brought him here, at no small effort. Perhaps, even without his eyes, he had vision that was helpful to them."

She paused for a moment, slowly turning over the sword in her hands, and then continued. "They didn't bury him, animals would have dug him up. They didn't burn him, that would have been against *his* religion. So they did the best they could to honor him in their own way, to preserve him and prepare him for his spiritual journey. They symbolically put things from the worlds he inhabited to be with him in the next life. Things from both the Old World and the New. Two worlds."

Killian and Nick stared at her for a moment, then looked at each other. "I told you she was a voodoo shaman Kill Devil. Never question her intuition," Nick laughed. "Hey, you didn't per chance find any petroglyphs near any of this, did you?"

Dinner that night was out at Killian's trailer, nestled off a remote road on the edge of the Gila National Forest, overlooking the Apache Reservation to the west. Killian lived there with his two brothers, one who worked for the Park Service, the other as a professional guide.

"Somewhere my tribal elders are cursing me, entering the home of a Chiricahua Apache," Soba softly laughed as Nick led her in.

"My brothers, let me introduce my colleague Nick, and the nicest Navajo I have ever met, Soba." The brothers shook hands and introduced themselves, and then headed out for a little late-night hunting. They both stepped warily around Nanook on their way out, not quite sure what to make of him. Killian took the offered gift of a large bottle of wine from Soba and poured all around.

"Hunting off season and at night, that's called poaching back where I'm from," Nick teased, looking into his glass as he swirled the deep red liquid around.

"Around here we call it survival. Or at least supplemental. Believe me, we eat what we kill. I had to get my brothers off the res, life is no good there. Our parents are gone, but we still have lots of relatives living there. We'll stock our freezer and bring the rest to them."

"Cheers to that," Soba toasted. "Same as it ever was."

Wine flowed, stories followed. Killian and Soba started bonding at Nick's expense, his idiosyncrasies laid bare to their mutual amusement. They found they shared much more than just their native roots.

Nick took it all in good fun, even when some of the joshing hit a little too close to home. "Hey, I've got feelings you know," he finally exclaimed, to much laughter.

Nick's frailties eventually exhausted, the conversation drifted back to the day's events. Nick explained to Killian that a similar hidden cache of items had been found further north on the Zuni Reservation.

"But why no pieces of eight in either?" Killian wondered aloud, feeling a little buzzed. "If they were leaving them talismans from the Old and New World, that would have seemed appropriate."

"It would have, if they had any with them, and perhaps they didn't," Nick replied, frowning. "Or, depending on timing, it might have predated the minting of coinage here in the New World. The Spaniards didn't start stamping coins in Tenochtitlán until well after the conquest. Which means, if both these caches are at all connected, they might be from the same, pre-conquest journey."

Taking his time, Nick explained what he had uncovered in Seville, and how he believed Coronado received information that put him onto something, although eventually he had lost the actual scent. A scent Nick was now hot on the trail of.

Saying their goodbyes late into the night, Killian walked them out, and gave Nick a bro hug and Soba a heartfelt embrace. "Ah, my favorite Navajo, so tell me, why do you put up with this knucklehead?"

"Same reason as you, my now favorite Apache," she smiled warmly. "The fates seem to have ordained it."

Nick didn't drive far after departing with Killian, as it was pitch dark, he didn't know the roads, and the wine had settled in. He chose to stay within the friendly confines of the Gila National Forest and pulled over near Apache Creek. The fork on the road it sat on would provide options of which direction to head the next morning.

As they lay next to each other in the back of the pickup in the predawn twilight, Soba rolled over into Nick's arm. "Zuni is the next stop, right? I'm missing home, and it's just past there. It will be good to see everyone again. I have to admit I might be a little homesick."

Nick leaned up on one elbow and checked for messages on his phone. "It will be, I've got some catching up to do with Bidzii and the boys too. But first we have a little detour to make." He showed her the message on the phone, and she smiled and cuddled back into him.

They stood beside his truck, now at the Albuquerque airport, patiently waiting in the pick up zone. Soon they were able to see Charlie in a small crowd exiting the terminal and waved when he caught sight of them. As he approached, Nick reached out for his brother, who instead handed him his hiker's backpack, pushed him away and turned and embraced Soba.

"So you are the she-devil my brother can't stop talking about,"

Charlie said, and stepped back and looked at her appraisingly. "You overachieved here Nick, definitely out of your league."

Soba blushed slightly, happy to finally meet Charlie after all she and Nick had been through. "Nice to meet you Charlie, I've heard so much about you. I feel I already know you."

"Yeah, well lies, all lies I can assure you. But let me tell you some stories about my little brother, things you should know, things you can use." He grinned mischievously at Nick, and then finally grabbed him by the back of the neck and embraced him.

"Yeah, missed you too, you big lug," Nick mumbled in his ear.

They had two and a half hours to catch up on the ride as they headed due west to Zuni. Soba squeezed over to the middle of the worn bench seat of the pickup, while Charlie sat with his arm hanging out the window. Nanook poked his head in from in back and gave Charlie an approving sniff and lick. Charlie jumped at first, intimidated by the size of the head on Soba's shoulder, but calmed down and smiled when he heard Nick and Soba cracking up.

Nick pointed out the window as they whizzed past a turnoff sign to the Acoma Pueblo. "We whites call it Sky City, it's one of the oldest, continuously inhabited places in the country, for over 2,000 years. An interesting place, still looks much like it did when the Spanish first encountered it, isolated on top of a small mesa."

Soba noticed Nick was peacefully content on the ride and couldn't decide if it was because he was happy his brother was with them, or because he enjoyed showing her off a little, or because he was ever closer on his quest. Perhaps a bit of each she finally settled on, listening with amusement as the brothers good naturedly traded barbs and bantered back and forth.

"OK, I appreciate the update bro, you've covered a whole lot of ground and are hot on the trail. That's fantastic news, I'm excited as you to put this to bed, one way or another," Charlie said, gazing back out the window. "Oh yeah, per that message you left me, I've been doing some research of my own, and I've got to tell you what I've uncovered. Some of it's pretty gritty, sure you want Soba in on all of this?"

"No secrets here Chuck, she's as much a part of this as any of us. We're like the three musketeers now. All for one . . ."

"And one for all," Charlie rejoined.

He proceeded to reveal that he had utilized the sophisticated and yet discrete resources of the multi-billion hedge fund he worked for. Their expertise was in evaluating potential threats to their multinational investments from an economic and geopolitical perspective, taking into account transparency and accuracy of financial information, stability of government, political unrest, human rights record, key players, etc. He had first honed in on all of Central America, and then Mexico in particular.

"We handicap risk, and right now Mexico is trending poorly. Not like its Venezuela, which is imploding, but it's definitely getting dicey down there. The current administration is viewed as increasingly powerless and corrupt, and is losing the confidence of the masses, mainly due to its inability to control the cartels and mass killings within its own borders. That is scaring off needed investment, both foreign and domestic, so the standard of living further erodes, and it wasn't great to start. They are caught in a self-fulfilling prophecy that is hard to break out of. Ineffective government leads to social unrest, which leads to a change of regime, who line their own pockets as the expense of the masses, which leads to more social unrest . . ."

"Yeah, the more things change, the more they stay the same," Soba added.

Charlie looked at her and nodded. "You've got that right sister. But of all the power brokers behind the scenes, it's the drug cartels with the most to gain or lose. They are pretty fragmented, but one cartel has quietly risen in power the past few years by quashing then absorbing many of their competitors. They are called the *Texcoco Cartel*, and from what I've seen, are not to be messed with."

"Interesting name, Texcoco," Nick observed. "Back in pre-colonial times, that was the name of the lake that the Aztec seat of power sat on, the island city of Tenochtitlán. A modern spin with Tex, as in Aztec, and coco, as in cocaine. Clever."

"Yeah, well you don't want to be messing with these guys. They bribe, intimidate, torture, and kill to get what they want. Literally leave a trail of dead bodies in their wake. Rumor has it the head of this cartel brands all members with an Aztec symbol so they can never hide their affiliation, and puts them through a bloody initiation ritual, like making your first kill by cutting a heart out," Charlie said, wringing his hands. "The cartel makes more money than some countries. They launder it through a series of shell companies and then set up legitimate businesses with the cleaned money. Which ingrains and endears them to the locals. Pretty efficient when you think about it."

He looked over directly at Nick and continued. "It also turns out the Texcoco cartel is headed by a guy with political aspirations. With his cash hoard he comes across as a benefactor of the common man, a regular fricking Mexican Robin Hood. But here is what is really interesting. Turns out this cat is one of the biggest black-market buyers of pre-Columbian artifacts in the world, the kind of guy who would want what Dad was looking for, what we're now looking for. And be willing to kill for it."

"What's his name?" Nick asked.

"Esteban González," Charlie replied. "More commonly known as Eztli. He just might be the one behind all of this."

"Eztli," Soba slowly pronounced, with a Nahuatl accent. "Do you know what that means?" she asked, looking at each brother in turn. "It's Aztec for *blood*."

They drove due west on the interstate, eventually angling off to a smaller roadway and onto Zuni Reservation land. They met their friend Lonan as arranged near the Visitors Center and introduced him to Charlie as one of the respected tribal elders. Lonan lit up when he saw Soba, who gave him a big bear hug and a kiss atop his bald head. With one sniff Nanook recognized him and leaned into him, almost knocking him over. Lonan laughed and patted him on the head.

"Easy big wolf, I just old man. This one trouble," he said as he winked at Soba, and walked feebly over to his dilapidated jeep. He pointed to the passenger seat, and Soba jumped in front and Nanook in back, the two of them chatting amicably in the Zuni language as he drove away. Nick and Charlie got back in the pickup and followed, finally rolling up the windows due to the dust kicking up in front of them.

"He certainly took a shining to her, didn't he?" Charlie observed. "She knows his language too?"

"It seems she knows them all. She was raised speaking multiple languages, went to college as a linguist studying native languages, and definitely has the gift of tongues. Lonan likes her, he never had a daughter, and she can be kind of charming, right?" Nick laughed.

"What was the deal with this area, anyway, how does it all tie in?" Charlie asked.

"Coronado was led right here by Fray Marcos de Niza, who had supposedly seen these 'Seven Cities of Gold' off in the distance on a prior expedition. Turns out when they got here no fabulous seven cities, no treasure. Coronado then goes on a wild goose chase to the east, tribes just wanting to get rid of him. But he was onto something, at least up to this point. And this is where the other group of artifacts turned up that mimic what Killian showed us at Gila. More of the Two Worlds, as Soba so aptly put it."

They pulled into the same compound of buildings that Nick and Soba had visited last time, and went over to the nondescript collapsed wall, still marked off with nothing more than sticks pounded into the ground. Lonan pointed to the area and wandered off a short distance chanting to himself, Nanook trotting along beside him.

"So what are you hoping to find that you didn't last time?" Soba asked.

"Insight," Nick replied. "Insight into the context of why anything at all was put here. Behind an enclosed wall, which was purposely built to blend in. There was no mummy here like at Gila, just the artifacts and the petroglyphs. But the same type of artifacts." He wandered away and looked at the site from more of a distance.

"Killian said there were petroglyphs at Gila too when you asked him. Did they tell anything?" Charlie asked.

"No, too deteriorated, too faded. My best guess is there was another body in here at one point, but when the wall crumbled, wild animals probably dragged it away. Who knows how long ago that may have been. But the petroglyphs right there held up, if anyone could ever decipher them. So far, no luck."

Soba suddenly brightened. "Not true," she exclaimed. "When I was in hiding while you were gallivanting around Seville, I was with a tribe of Aztec descendants. There was an elder there, her name was Huehue, and she was still practicing the art of symbol writing. Not the tourist version, the real ancient, handed down generation to generation version. She was hoping to pass the knowledge of it down to someone, but there was little interest. I think she wanted me to learn, but we left too soon."

"So she could read the old symbols, even though so few exist?" Nick incredulously asked. He and Charlie walked over and hung on the answer.

"Yes, mostly. I showed her the photos of the glyphs you had taken here, on the off chance she might be able to pick up a meaning or two. She couldn't make all of them out, some were badly faded. But what she did read translated roughly as this. 'Go to cold. Follow old ones. Away from devil.' The rest she couldn't read. Does it make any sense or help?"

Nick went to the petroglyphs carved into the stone, knelt down and traced them with his fingertips. "Let's assume a caravan did indeed leave Tenochtitlán, before Cortés conquers it. They send out false expeditions at the same time to confuse anyone looking for it. We don't know the exact path the *one true journey* went, but let's role play that they eventually made their way to Gila, and left an offering with a carefully preserved mummy, and a hint in stone too faded to read. And then they come to Zuni, and leave another offering, and a body we can't find, but a hint we can read." He blew into the cracks of the etching, a small cloud of dust hanging in the tepid air.

"And the hint says, 'go to cold.' That means north. 'Follow old ones.' That could mean the old, pre-Aztec interconnecting network of ancient pathways and villages, just like here at Zuni. And 'away from devil.' Away from the Spanish, away from Cortés. You know where the path of the ancient ones, the Anasazi, leads from here?

Along a well-built pathway north, dotted with villages and warning pyres on the cliffs, right to Chaco canyon, the epicenter of their world. And you know where the pathway north from there leads? To Mesa Verde, all of them on a nearly perfect celestial axis."

Nick got off his knees and turned to them. "They were right here, I know it, I feel it. And they wanted what they left behind to be found, but not for a long, long time. It was just like Alexandre said in his letter."

"It had to be," Charlie excitedly said, pointing at Nick and quoting the letter. "Many years from now, when there is peace between us, have good people put the souls of the Mexica in a safe place forever."

Suddenly they heard one person behind them slowly clapping, walking toward them from behind the corner of a wall of the ruin. Behind him came two men carrying the collapsed body of Lonan, and two others with guns aimed at them.

"I hope you can now solve this mystery, for all your sakes," Miguel González sneered. "Because your lives depend on it. My organization seeks the treasure of the Aztecs that the Spanish never found, the lost treasure of the Seven Cities of Cibola."

His men roughly herded Nick, Charlie and Soba together, and dumped the unconscious body of Lonan on a large rock right in front of them. Nick made a move toward him, and was pistol whipped across the back of his head. He slowly staggered back to his feet, dazed.

"What the hell have you done to him? What do you want with him?" Nick asked aghast, looking down at Lonan. "He's just an old man, he has nothing to do with any of this."

Miguel nodded, and guns were leveled at each of them. He pulled a tranquilizer dart out of the back of Lonan's shoulder and held it up. "He is simply a means to an end, that's all. We didn't want to interrupt that little speech you were making, it being so very insightful. Now this dart just turns out to be merciful."

Miguel pulled out an obsidian blade, and shifted Lonan around, chest up. "Let me be perfectly clear. If you don't do exactly as we ask, this is what I will do to her," he said, staring at Soba.

Nick and Charlie both made a move toward him, but were hit with the butts of the guns, and despite struggling were forced to their knees, their heads held straight ahead by their hair. Miguel held the blade aloft for a moment, then plunged it deeply into Lonan's chest, whose eyes opened wide, then slowly closed. Miguel cut deeper, then reached in and pulled hard, and held a dripping heart aloft.

Soba looked on in disbelief and screamed, as two of the men held her tightly by the arms and roughly led her away. Miguel put a boot on Nick's chest and stared deep into him. "Do as instructed, or this will be the last piece of her you ever see." With that he contemptuously tossed the heart on the ground in front of Nick, the blood spattering up all over him. Miguel then nodded to the men holding Nick and Charlie, who swung down hard with the butts of their guns.

Charlie came to first. He rolled over and got to his knees, then saw Nick lying next to him, blood all over his shirt. Thinking that he had been executed, Charlie cried out and shook him, until he came to. Nick moaned deeply and cautiously sat up, clutching the back of his head. Gaining his senses, he stood, and immediately started yelling out to Soba. He glanced over at the crumpled figure of Lonan, and ran around the corner to the road, Charlie trailing him.

No one was there, just his pickup and the jeep, but he noticed another set of vehicle tracks coming in and leaving. He glanced at his watch, they had both been unconscious for over an hour. Suddenly Charlie motioned for him to be quiet, and they heard a slight whimpering. They cautiously walked toward the sound, and found Nanook lying on his side, two broken tranquilizer darts sticking out of his ribs, and one imbedded in his neck.

Nick knelt down gingerly next to him, and carefully pulled each one out. He noticed kick marks all over him, and pooled blood around his mouth and snout. "I know, you tried boy. Nothing you could've done, not with these in you." He checked Nanook's eyes carefully, the pupils fully dilated, still half drugged. The two of them carried the large canine over to the pickup and set him in the back on unrolled sleeping bags. They then reverently gathered Lonan and his remains and wrapped him in a tarp and put him in the back of the jeep.

"We'll have to tell the tribe, they need to know what happened here, on their sacred land. But they can keep it quiet until we figure out what to do. I suspect there are some who will want to avenge him," Nick said, still shaking his head in disbelief. "I have to get her back Charlie, whatever it takes. I can't lose Dad *and* Soba over this."

Charlie walked over and started the jeep, while Nick got in his pickup. On the middle of the seat, where Soba had sat just a short while ago on the ride out, was a small bag. He opened it and pulled out a phone and his dad's missing journal. A folded note was tucked inside, along with a long lock of jet-black hair, bloody at one end. He read the message with shaking hands:

I thought you could make better use of this journal than I, as you are apparently so close to discovering the hidden treasure of my great Aztec ancestors.

We could not decipher this, I trust you can. Perhaps it provides the missing clues to that which has proven elusive for so very long. If your dad had simply chosen to have been more cooperative, it would be him concluding this search, and not you. Such are the fates which have brought us together.

Do not think to involve the authorities. If we suspect anything, parts of your Navajo mistress will be shipped to you, one at a time. We know how to make life linger, for her sake do not doubt the sincerity of my intentions.

Keep this phone on you at all times. It will allow me to contact you, and always tell me exactly where you are. If you attempt to disable it, or I can't contact you, or I don't know where you are, body parts will start to arrive. And then I will personally deliver the last one.

You are now on the clock, run rabbit run. Find the treasure of the Aztecs, find Cibola, before it's too late.

Nick sat in stunned silence, unable to come to terms with Lonan's death and Soba's abduction, right before his very eyes. He turned the letter over, it was unsigned, and the men who had accosted them never mentioned who they were. But he had seen the distinct brand mark on their arms, it was the unmistakable image of *Miquiztli*, the skull-like Aztec symbol of death. The badge of honor of the Texcoco cartel. The calling card of Eztli.

CHAPTER 34 – JULY 22

They drove slowly back to the Zuni Visitors Center, where Nick had first met Lonan just over a month before. Lonan had been so helpful and cheerful back then, and now here they were delivering his dismembered body back. A crowd slowly converged around the center as word spread. Both Nick and Charlie had clearly been assaulted, Nick still slightly dazed and in the same blood-spattered shirt. They were led inside, where a couple of kind Zuni women who worked there got them ice packs and tended their wounds. A few phone calls were made, and other tribal leaders started showing up. They were then led to a back room, where only Zuni elders were permitted to enter, while some of the younger Zuni men stood as informal guards outside. The elders sat in a circle on the floor, silent, looking at them, questions on their minds.

Nick stood and addressed those gathered. After all he was the one who had gotten Lonan involved in the first place, had brought this pestilence down upon them, and felt it his duty to be as forthcoming as possible. He explained how the local discovery on their land had drawn the interest of the scientific community, how it tied into the personal quest he was on, and who he thought the killers were. The same evil men as who had killed his own father. He also explained that Soba, the tall Navajo who had accompanied him and spoke their language so eloquently, had been abducted, her life now at stake. He asked for their silence to give him a chance to recover her, or at least until things played out one way or the other.

The elders talked amongst themselves in their own language for a few minutes, a sort of consensus reached, and one arose to speak for the rest.

"Lonan explained to us of your visit and showed the artifacts you had uncovered. These were not Zuni things, but of our southern cousins the Azteca, and of the Spanish. Talismans of a fight that we Zuni soon joined when the conquistadors came here looking for gold we never had. They were cruel, and killed many of us, and we never forgot. Today evil men come again from the south, for something we still don't have, and kill our brother. Greed echoes through time here. We will respect your wishes, just as Lonan respected you. But now we must mourn our dead. Go, find what you seek, and may it bring back that she that you truly treasure."

The brothers went back outside, the crowd larger now, agitated. The elders worked their way through the crowd, carefully lifted the body of Lonan, still wrapped in the tarp, and led a procession along a narrow path that led away from the Visitors Center, away from all vestiges of civilization. The sounds of chanting and crying drifted back toward them on a slight breeze.

Nick went to the back of his truck and opened it, Nanook seeing him and woozily trying to sit up. Nick pet his head, leaned him back down and rubbed the fur around his neck until Nanook's breathing fell into a regular rhythm, deep asleep. He felt Charlie's hand on his shoulder and turned to see him nodding toward a group of younger men, one of whom stepped forward, who he recognized as the informal leader of those standing guard inside the center not long before.

"My name is *Ahaiyuta*," he said, whose name meant Morning Star. "We heard what happened, I mourn for Lonan, and am sorry for your friend." He paused, gathering his thoughts. "Someone coming here, on our sacred land, and doing that to a respected elder," he tailed off, lost in his anger, clenching his fists. "It simply cannot be, it cannot go unavenged. Tell us who did this."

"Ahaiyuta, I understand your anger, I feel it too. There is a time and a place for that, for justice. But first I must find something for them, or I have nothing to bargain with to get my friend back," Nick reasoned. "Be patient, you will hear from me when the time is right. Tell your warriors to be ready."

Charlie slid into the driver's seat of the Chevy, he was in the better shape of the two, and Nick wanted to dig into his dad's missing journal as they traveled.

"Wow, I haven't driven this in years. I see the clutch is still a little soft," Charlie said with a touch of nostalgia, getting used to shifting the gears again, since in one of the reworks they had been installed upside down. "So where to bro?"

"North, towards Mesa Verde. Somehow it and Chaco Canyon were tied together in dad's mind, but I don't yet know how. This journal wouldn't have come up missing if it wasn't vital, and Dad wouldn't have had us scatter their ashes in Chaco Canyon if he didn't suspect something there. There is something hidden in this," Nick said, tapping the journal for emphasis. "I just have to get in his mindset to figure it out."

Charlie drove along silently, off the Zuni Reservation, past Fort Wingate, northward towards Sheep Springs. Nick was buried in the journal, writing furiously as he worked to decipher their dad's cryptic annotations. Albert had kept detailed notes, but not all were written in a straightforward manner. Some were his musings, brainstorming possibilities and probabilities, and some were purposely archaic and coded. Waiting for the day someone would unlock their secrets, someone who understood exactly how he thought.

"Interesting, he goes into great detail on what I always guessed was just a paper weight," Nick commented, and reached under his seat and held up an old, heavy piece of metal. "Remember this? Something in my head told me to bring it when his journal went missing. In his notes here Dad says it's a bracket to hold an axle to a wagon, a very old, hand forged one. He sent photos to various museums that had early Spanish artifacts, to see if it possibly matched anything. One museum in Guanajuato replied and sent him a photo back. They look identical, and they show it on a wagon they reconstructed from the early 1500s, with some of the original parts."

"So how did he find it in the first place?" Charlie asked. "I always remember it on his desk, but I don't remember the story of where it came from."

"Neither did I, until I read it here. It says he bought it at Mackenna's Trading Post, up near Shiprock. Said there was a newspaper article on the wall that he read, that made him interested in it. There was a photo of the article, but I don't see it in here. How far to Shiprock?"

"About an hour," Charlie answered. "Remember seeing Shiprock for the first time with Dad? Wild looking rock formation, kinda looked like a butte."

"Actually the throat of a volcano, the softer rock around it had eroded away."

"Thanks Mr. Geology. Catch a few winks, you look like you could use them. I'll wake you when we get there."

Nick was about to argue but saw the wisdom in it. He would need a clear head to work through things soon enough. After what seemed like five minutes, he awoke with a start, Nanook licking his ear through the window to the back of the pickup. "Good to see you up ol' boy, how you feeling?"

He went around to the back and let Nanook out, who seemed to be showing no ill effects from the tranquilizers, although he favored his ribs on one side. Maybe a couple were cracked from the kicking, but Nick marveled at the toughness of the creature. *Good,* he thought. *I'm going to need you to help track Soba with me. Because if I can't actually find the treasure, we're going to have to fake it to get her back.*

He looked up at where they were parked, and saw it was at a dated sort of roadside general store, emporium and apothecary, the kind that would have been popular in the 1950s and '60s. In those heady postwar years when interstates were being built across the country and veterans were buying cars, starting families, and taking them on road trips to places just like this. He glanced around and saw it hadn't been updated in a long while, had fallen on hard times, the fast-paced modern world moving past it. Mackenna's Trading Post.

He walked in, the creaky screen door slamming several times behind him, and saw Charlie was the only customer, chatting amicably with the owner at the counter. He was a disheveled looking older man with wild hair pulled into a ponytail. Evidently a holdover from the hippie generation who apparently preferred alternate tobacco judging from the distinct odor of pot wafting in the air, and still believed in the righteousness of flower power, sticking it to the man, and dark conspiracy theories. Nick vaguely heard their conversation, but drifted back deep into the old shop, past the rows and shelves filled with outdated merchandise. It was dimly lit and musky, and sensed he had been here before a long time ago. As a child.

Nick smiled and felt déjà vu when he recognized a trinket his dad had bought him, the exact same one, dusty on a shelf. He picked it up, blew it off and examined it, then wandered further toward the back. Past old faded movie posters on the walls, along with some yellowed newspaper articles, falling out of kilter in their frames, the deteriorated scotch tape relinquishing its grip many years ago. One article in particular grabbed his attention, and his pulse quickened as he read the headline:

Native Remains, Spanish Artifacts Found in Ravine

The article was dated November 24, 1960. It was from a small regional newspaper that had ceased to exist a long time ago. Nick read and reread it, fascinated. He was startled to feel a hand on him and turned to see Charlie silently reading over his shoulder.

"They interviewed my Pappy for that," the proprietor said, standing at the end of the aisle. "Long time ago, yep. He was a regular bone collector, that one was. Spent his time traipsing 'bout these here parts, always sniffing for rumored treasure and artifacts. Found some too, and would sell 'em right here, at the store. Those were good days."

"This is Don Mackenna," Charlie said, introducing him. "His

father owned this place, built it up, and passed it on to Don, back, when was that Don?"

"Round bout '93. Yes siree, Pappy fancied himself an amateur archeologist, a regular rockhound he did. He got all swept up in a rumor of a gold canyon round these parts, it being called Adam's Diggings. Many folks did back then, and more than a few died looking 'bout these here parts for it. Daddy never did find it, but he found lots of other things, sure nuf. Adam's Diggings, you can look it up."

As Don and Charlie walked to the front, Nick took a photo of the yellowed article and joined them at the counter. "So what kind of things did he find?" Nick asked.

"Well, he found himself dinosaur bones, old burial grounds, abandoned mines, Injun relics, even stuff the Spanish left behind from their exploring. And their dying, seems they did a lot of that. Course he found some gold and silver too. Never enough to get rich, but he made himself a living, kept a roof over our heads and kept us all fed."

"What about from that article in back?" Charlie interjected, trying to keep him on track. "What did he find related to that?"

"Oh that, a bunch of bones and some metal fixin's and gear in an old stream bed wash, just like that article said. He thought the parts were Spanish, 'cause they included some sword handles, bits of helmets and such. And a fellar from some university come and look at it all, and said the bones were natives since he'd seen same ones elsewhere, but no exact way to tell how old. That professor took the bones with him, but my Pappy went back out and found more scattered further downstream, brought 'em back and sold 'em here in the store. Made good money too, for way back then."

"Wow, no kidding. Our dad bought a part here too, probably from the same cache. You don't know where he found them, where that creek bed wash was per chance, do you?" Nick felt compelled to ask, not really expecting an answer.

"Nope, way too long-ago sonny. Pappy used to take me out with him all the time to look for stuff, and he took me back to that gulch once or twice too. But this old noggin couldn't find it if you dropped me off there," Don laughed. "But come to think of it, he didn't sell everything. The old man would never throw anything out, always thought he might get some coin for it someday. I wonder if? What the heck, follow me."

Don led them to the very back of the shop, past the restroom with a steadily dripping toilet tank, past stained curtained windows with marijuana plants reaching for sunlight. He leaned heavily into an old door with squeaky hinges that protested his intrusion before finally yielding. Stepping into the dark he reached blindly for a string, found it and yanked downward. A single bulb illuminated old metal shelves with boxes of every shape and size. He grabbed a flashlight off the floor and beamed it into the recesses of the racks, looking for something in particular. He rummaged around, bumping the racks and swearing gently, until he found what he as after.

"Aha, there she is," he said in triumph. He squeezed between the rows, and came out with a deteriorating banker's box, proudly holding it out to them. "Hundred bucks for the lot of it, boys, if'n you please."

Nick put the box down on his tailgate, finally with enough light to evaluate what they had purchased, somewhat sight unseen. Nanook sniffed the box, sneezed, then put his head in and proudly came out with a femur bone in his jaws. "Whoa boy," Nick said as he pried it away from him. "No eating dead people, these will need a proper burial."

Charlie dug underneath as Nick lifted out the bones on top, and found a small cross, spurs, a helmet crest, a horseshoe and hand hammered nails. And a fire tarnished bracket exactly like Albert used as a paperweight. Nick examined each and raised an eyebrow to Charlie.

"OK, continuing conjecture of a possible scenario. Our one true journey expedition starts off in Tenochtitlán, wanders up to Gila, goes through Zuni, and finally to here. Latest evidence pointing to this, human bones and Spanish wagon parts and artifacts. I can't prove the bones are Aztec, and I can't date the artifacts, we simply don't have the time. To my trained eye, I find them pretty compelling. But I need something more concrete to get us to the end game, or Soba is dead." Nick paused, composing himself.

"I'm not going to chase my tail here around Shiprock Charlie, we have no hard location data to dig into. Don couldn't find his ass with a map and a flashlight, much less lead us back to that creek bed. But everything in this box suggests our caravan went through somewhere near here, and maybe lost a wagon or two. Who knows, perhaps a fight with the native tribes in the area. But Dad knew something was just beyond here, in Mesa Verde, his journal is leading us there, and the circumstantial evidence is building too. I've got some deciphering to do, you drive."

Charlie jumped in the driver's seat again and drove past the imposing Shiprock rock formation just off to the west, through the Ute Mountain Reservation, and toward the town of Cortez, on the edge of Mesa Verde National Park. Nick sat unspeaking, lost in the journal of riddles, codes, whispers and half spoken dreams for over a half hour. Charlie finally broke the silence.

"Hey Rain Man, come up with anything yet?"

"It's interesting, Dad kept these journals chronologically, one for every year he took trips out west. This one is from the last time he took us all to Mesa Verde, but there are more recent notes in the back of it, like he was planning to get back there," Nick replied. "He kept adding notes to this, he was working it out. Most of these make sense, I can understand his thinking, he was slowly triangulating in on something, or someplace, within Mesa Verde itself. And then the whole back of the journal is just gibberish, it must be some kind of code."

"That doesn't make sense," Charlie reflected. "Why code notes to himself? Notes in a journal buried in a steamer chest that no one knew about. Unless he was already suspecting bad things."

Nick looked at him, distraught, trying to keep it together. "Yeah, someone knew about it. Dad was probing, reaching out to resources across the country and in Mexico, asking questions to fill in the blanks, to put him on the right trail. And that bastard head of the cartel, what the hell was his name? Eztli? He must have somehow gotten wind of it. And here we fricking are."

"Hang in there, bro, we're both frazzled, let's find a hotel to crash and get our heads on straight. Things will be clearer in the morning."

Charlie heard something vaguely in the background, paper rustling, a pen scratching, Nanook pacing, then finally huffing in his ear. He opened his eyes and glanced at his watch. It was just after 4 a.m., and Nick was at a rickety table. He was using his laptop computer for light, alternating between reading the journal and writing on a cheap pad of hotel stationary. Nick saw him and nodded.

"Couldn't sleep anymore, but I got to thinking about the gibberish in the back of the journal. I realized there was a two-word title above the body of text. It was so obvious, I should have known. The title was in a simple substitution code, the first one Dad ever taught us when we were kids. Cryptology 101. He knew we would figure that one out, but all the rest is in a much deeper code. Something meant for our eyes only."

"So what does it say Sherlock?" Charlie drowsily asked, starting to wake up.

"Sullivan Ballou."

"Sullivan Ballou? That Civil War letter he copied and gave to Mom? The one she framed and kept on her bed stand? What the hell does that possibly have to do with anything?"

"The code to the gibberish in the journal is in that letter," Nick replied, like it was obvious.

"Well, that's great, except the letter is back home in Michigan."

"No, in fact it's not. When Dad died, I needed to keep a part of him with me. I took that letter out of the frame and have kept it in my wallet ever since." With that Nick passed him the well creased and dog-eared letter. "Look at the back of it, I never paid it any notice."

Charlie took the letter, carefully turning it over to look at the back. "Wow, that's definitely Dad's handwriting, but why in pencil?

Looks like he kept changing parts, erasing things. Reminds me of a word search, just a page full of random letters."

"And because they are random it is virtually unbreakable. It's called a onetime pad, basically a handmade encryption key just like the CIA and KGB used, Cold War level stuff. No one can read the coded message, unless they have the one sheet in existence that can decipher it. You're holding it."

Charlie shook his head in amazement. "Seriously? Dad sure went to a lot of trouble to keep information away from someone."

"Yeah, and he went to just as much trouble to make sure we were the only ones to find and understand it. He wrote it in pencil because he was working the code out to get it perfect. It took me over an hour to get this, check it out," Nick said, as he handed him the just deciphered note on hotel stationary.

Boys if you are reading this I met my end. Don't mourn long, I am with your Mother now by the grace of God. Get busy and finish the quest, that will be my salvation, your legacy, and our joint contribution to humanity.

I was recently approached by a phone call to help solve the mystery of Cibola and was threatened. I refused, these are not honorable people, and I fear their intentions. I write this to you just in case they find me or force my hand.

My Mother had a rare moment of lucidity just a few weeks ago, revealing a critical new clue. She passed along an oral history supplementing Alexandre's letter home. There was second letter from him before he was killed, but it was lost to time. She said in it he was told there was a key to the mystery, at the biggest palace hidden under the table. Behind a wall where there is food forever. The key will show you where. Then she faded, you know how it goes.

Live a long and fulfilling life boys. Make your mark, make us proud. Mom and I will see you when you are done.

Love, Dad

It took Charlie a few minutes to get his head around it, to digest everything he had just learned. He was still shaking off the cobwebs, whereas Nick had already been up doing research, deciphering the letter, and was sharp and ready to go. Nick gave Charlie a few minutes to gather himself, made some brew in the hotel room's cheap coffee maker, and handed him a cup.

"The biggest palace hidden under the table. That's an easy one." Nick observed. "Mesa Verde is Spanish for green table. The biggest pueblo anywhere around here is called Cliff Palace, right under the lip of the mesa. I was there not too long ago. But behind a wall with food forever. That's going to be a tougher nut to crack."

"Food forever, yeah, you got me on that one," Charlie replied. "Hey, the sun will be up soon, we can't just go digging around with Park Rangers and tourists everywhere. Peak season, a bad place for tomb raiders. They let you camp out here a while back, didn't they?"

"Yeah, and I'm sure they will let us again, professional courtesy and all. Let's see if we can narrow our search and pick up the right gear to do some midnight prospecting. And I've gotta make a call later to Soba's brother, not looking forward to that one."

Nick went online with his laptop and a frustratingly slow internet connection, to private access university and research web sites, pulling up various diagrams of the layout of the Cliff Palace, its orientation to the sun at different times of year, the sizes of the rooms, excavation results, photos from various angles, etc. It was taking far too long, so he turned on his smart phone. There was no sense in not using it anymore, the bad guys already knew where they were. But the signal was weak, he needed to get to a different location. Having access to the online documentation was crucial.

They checked out of the hotel, drove around until he got a solid signal, and pulled into a nondescript diner in the center of Cortez. Grabbing a booth in the corner, he watched a black Escalade drive by, slow down, and then drive around the block and park down a side street, facing them. The windows were so heavily tinted he could barely see into it, but Nick thought he saw two people in the front seats. That meant there was at least one other vehicle lying low somewhere with the other three men and Soba. Unless she had been taken back to Mexico. The very thought of it made his heart sink and his stomach nauseous.

"Eyes on us," Nick nodded to Charlie, looking out at the Escalade. "We need to show them only what we want them to see. Bear in mind if we find any kind of treasure, that is our *only* leverage. And if we don't, we'll have to fake it, and I don't think they will be easy to deceive. We need to get a step ahead of them."

Charlie ordered lunch as Nick did a deep dive on his cell phone, downloading photos, topo maps and detailed diagrams of the floor plan of the Cliff Palace. He also grabbed satellite photos which showed current and ancient trails, all the access points in and out. Quizzing Charlie, he made an inventory of what they had and what they would need, things to help with the search and to better the odds stacked so heavily against them.

"It has over 150 rooms, and we're looking for something behind a wall with food forever. Gotta narrow it down. Food forever," Nick said out loud to himself.

Charlie looked up from his plate, raising an eyebrow. "That would be a lot of food. So where would they store it? What kind of food did they even eat?"

"Beans, squash, pumpkins, amaranth, wild plants, small game, they even raised dogs and turkeys. When the season was right they could eat the pads of prickly pear cactus. But corn was their money crop, their world revolved around it, and they could store it for winters and lean times. There was a famous find near here in a cave, an elaborate ceremonial jar full of corn, over 800 years old. It had an upside-down bowl over the top to keep mice and insects out, perfectly preserved. A little time capsule of their most valuable commodity, that which gave them life. An offering to the gods."

Nick turned back to a detailed diagram of the Cliff Palace, reviewing it in minute detail. "It had to be a granary, that is the only thing that makes sense. They had granaries interspersed throughout the whole complex, so losing any one or two wouldn't be fatal. We have to find the single, right one. But I don't see any that stand out as being overly large. This is going to be challenging."

"That's why you earn the big bucks, bro," Charlie joked. "Oh, that's right, archeology students are indentured servants, I almost forgot. You're in it for the love of it, not the money. It's your big brother who makes the big bucks." Nick just looked at him and shook his head.

Lunch finished, the brothers hustled over to a hiking and hunting outfitters store on the edge of town and bought gear they needed to supplement what Nick had already brought along. Fresh strap on headlamps, glow sticks, high intensity flashlights, extra batteries, a pickax, foldable shovel, rappelling rope with stop descenders, extra carabineers, high grip gloves, hunting knives, two compound bows, a night vision scope, two pistols, ammo, scent eliminators, face paint and camouflage gear. In short everything needed to get in and out of a difficult location in the middle of the night, and to protect themselves. Charlie took the owner of the shop aside, told him he appreciated his discretion, and paid him in cash, along with a five-hundred-dollar tip.

Nick walked into the Mesa Verde Park Center and saw the same Ranger who had arranged his previous overnight stay. Exchanging pleasantries, he introduced Charlie, and explained he would like his city slicker brother to experience the same stunning view, if it wouldn't be too much of an imposition.

"Always happy to accommodate someone with as much expertise and interest as you," the Ranger replied as he wrote a pass. "We don't get many people who understand Mesoamerican history nearly as deeply as you. Maybe the occasional aspiring author or research archeologist, but heck, you could give the tours here. Look us up if you ever want a second career."

Late in the day they pulled into the parking lot closest to the Cliff Palace and watched the last of the straggling tourists filter out into the fading twilight. They showed their pass as the Rangers closed things down and drove away, then waited until dark to make sure no one was coming back. When they were confident they were alone, they grabbed their gear and walked down the trail. It eventually became more challenging, the path constricted in spots by the rock walls, with thick, sturdy wooden ladders and natural steps up and down at certain points. The night was dark and the moon obscured, so the normal view of the pueblo off in the distance wasn't visible at all. Nanook led the way, sometimes off path to get around the ladders, and they followed more cautiously with heavy loads, seeing only as far as their headlamps allowed. Finally they came upon a partial tower, dark and foreboding, guarding the narrow footpath in, easily defensible.

Rubbing his hand along the seams of the stones of the tower, Nick looked up, impressed. "This was well thought out, they carefully controlled the access points. A handful of determined warriors could hold off a much larger force, indefinitely if they had enough food and water." He grinned at Charlie. "Let's find where they hid that damn food."

They walked carefully along the path to the complex, past the Northern Quarter and the Old Quarter, to the approximate center of the Cliff Palace, an area called the Plaza Quarter. Nick pulled out two diagrams, one a view from above looking down with rooms labeled by function, and another looking at the face of it, showing how things stacked on top of one another.

"I've highlighted the granaries, you can see them interspersed about, with several up there," Nick said, pointing far up into the dark recesses. "They have all been extensively explored and excavated over time, the remains are what tell the story. No space wasted at all here, they were very efficient in how they laid this whole place out. It evolved over several iterations to what we're looking at now."

Charlie fingered the front view diagram, with several highlighted storage rooms tucked high up in back. "Tell me we don't have to get way up into those."

"We might, but that's not where I'm starting. Remember the quote from Grandma Ingrid, that the key is behind a wall with food forever. None of the marked granaries on here fit that description, none stand out as something that large." Nick pulled out another map, similar to the top down view, but the back area was enlarged. "See how the buildings butt up to the very back edge of the cavern? They don't exactly fit, and they leave two large gaps behind. One is here, in back of the Old Quarter, and the second one is here, in back of the Plaza Quarter."

Charlie leaned in for a closer look, adjusted his head lamp and tapped the diagram. "But they say refuse space. They just dumped their garbage back there? These were already explored, right?"

"This place was abandoned 700 years ago, and it is likely that some people may have hung on a little longer than others. I'm betting as an extended drought set in, order eventually breaks down, and in the chaos of people leaving, what was once their largest granary was emptied. Those who were here last treated the empty space as a refuse heap. We archeologists come along, dig into the layer of trash, and label the space a dump. I'll bet if we dig completely through the trash layer, we'll see the bottom and sides were finished in a kind of plaster, to protect it. You wouldn't do that for a trash pit."

"OK, decision time. There are two refuse spaces, which one do we go after?"

"I'm thinking this one, in the far back of the Old Quarter. It is the larger of the two, and the access is better, easier. If their lives depend on their largest granary, I gotta believe it would be where it was well protected, yet still easy to get at. Let's do this."

They carefully worked their way back into the complex, feeling as much as seeing their way, ducking under low doorways, their headlamps playing off the walls and casting eerie shadows. Nick stopped to orient them in what appeared to be a small courtyard, and then led the way to the final row of rooms tucked the furthest back. They were shorter in height then those closer to the front, constricted by the angle of the cliff. Searching through the rooms they found several backwards facing windows, and two different doorways into the very back edge of the cavern itself.

"The windows would allow them to dump grain from several vantage points to level it, and also provide air circulation to keep it dry. And the doorways allow people to get down into the cavern, to fill baskets that could have been brought up by rope," Nick commented as he felt a subtle groove in the center of a window, sloping toward the cavern. "This wasn't designed as a garbage pit, it only became one when things broke down." He cracked and tossed several glow sticks into the cavern, gauging its depth.

Charlie got out two high intensity flashlights and set them on stands in two of the windows, which illuminated a surprising amount of the cavern. Nanook sniffed around and peered over the edge, then wandered back to the courtyard. Huffing, he planted himself facing outward, protecting the only access point to where they were working.

The depth appeared to be about twenty feet, and Nick descended on a secured rope, with Charlie then relaying some equipment down to him. Nick stepped carefully, seeing grids and test pits on the floor from prior excavations, digging down into the detritus of the years. He started on the far-left hand side of the cavern wall, closely examining it by tapping with a prospector's hand pick in one hand, while feeling the grooves and rock surfaces with the fingertips of the other. He smiled when he saw the wall had been lined with a sort of plaster, up to a height of two or three feet above the bottom of the test pit. Maybe this wasn't a trash pit after all.

He worked his way to the right, listening to any change in the sound of pick on rock, which echoed dully in the cavern. Bats started flying about disturbed by the intrusion, and headed out through the windows and doors, Nanook jumping up and snapping at a few that flew over him. After about fifteen minutes Nick was about three quarters of the way around, and the sound of the pick suddenly made a different, hollower, sound. He looked up at the ceiling, now only a couple of feet above his head, and thought it stopped sloping, which would indicate it should further indent, but the wall did not. He tapped the pick again. Hollow.

"Hey Charlie, come join the party," he called out.

Nick meticulously photographed the area, and then carefully chipped away at seams in the plaster, which revealed the same sandstone construction used in the buildings above. But this little section was built slightly differently, the workmanship not as practiced, but well concealed by the finish on the outside. Without warning a section of false wall gave way, tumbling inward, and Nick and

Charlie stared at one another for a startled moment. Nick stuck his head into the opening, his headlamp illuminating the interior.

"C'mon man, what do you see?"

"Wow, unbelievable. Two time travelers, and maybe a map on the wall," Nick replied. "Let's take this apart carefully, because I'm going to want to leave it exactly the way we found it."

Nick worked methodically, Charlie stacking bricks in the order they were removed, until there was an opening just large enough to squeeze into. Nick wormed his way in with his headlamp and a bright flashlight, while Charlie held another at an angle. Two mummies were on the floor, seated, legs crossed, facing one another. The male looked like he had been very old and was wearing the traditional garb of the Aztecs, dusty and cobweb covered, while the woman appeared younger, and dressed as an Apache or Navajo. The sealed tomb was perfectly dry and serene, and small items were on the floor around them, some that looked to be Aztec, perhaps from Mexico, and some that appeared Spanish. *Items from two worlds, the Old and the New.*

Nick took photographs from every angle, careful not to disturb anything, and then examined the walls carefully. There was what appeared to be a rough map etched into the stone, tracing a meandering route. Toward the top there was a symbol on an intersection of the trails, the figure of a throne, and then several larger panels of codices next to it. One looked vaguely familiar to Nick, but he couldn't quite place it. He took more detailed photos of the etchings and slipped back out.

"We've got our key brother, hidden where there is food forever! That little throne, where the trails converge, is where we will find it. And I can tell you from reading every ancient map on the area in existence, that location is Chaco Canyon." Nick pointed the flashlight to the etched codices. "And those are the markers that will help us find exactly where."

Charlie stuck his head in for a brief look, and then they put the wall back together. They sealed the cracks as best they could with the dry mortar they had displaced mixed with a little water from the water bladders in their backpacks. Finished, the brothers made their way back out, taking all their equipment and brushing over their tracks. Nanook thumped his tail when he saw them and followed until they stood on the ledge of the Cliff Palace, looking outward, as the predawn sky slightly brightened. They hiked back to the pickup truck and stowed their gear before the earliest tourists or rangers showed up. Nick led Charlie to an overlook, and they sat and watched the sun rise over the mesa, just as it had for countless millennia.

"You look lost in thought," Charlie said to Nick, clapping him gently on the shoulder. "I know you're thinking about Soba, you holding up OK?"

"Yeah, she's on my mind. But I gotta tell you, seeing those two mummies, and knowing her back story of being raised as a tribe within a tribe, it gives me an eerie feeling. Like somehow this is all tied together. Maybe it's just the exhaustion talking, but first things first. We've got to find what we came for."

Exhausted from their all-night expedition, they found a shady spot and were both soon fast asleep, Nanook alert at their feet. They knew their ultimate fate, and Soba's, would soon be determined in Chaco Canyon. One way or another.

Nick called Bidzii while Charlie drove south to Chaco Canyon, and nervously filled him in on the details of Lonan's death and Soba's abduction. After getting over the initial shock, Bidzii made plans to meet them at Chaco, which sat on Navajo Reservation land. It was only a short drive for him, in an area he knew intimately from growing up nearby. Nick asked him to bring a couple of specific items along, to better their odds in any sort of confrontation. No firm plan yet, but he was hoping something would coalesce soon enough. *One crisis at a time, hottest fire first,* he thought as he hung up.

They drove due south a little over an hour to Farmington, grabbed a quick bite to go, and immediately got back on the road. Charlie was puzzled by something he had seen the prior night with the mummies, in particular on the etched map on the wall.

"You said you recognized the 'map' on the wall, that the trails converged at Chaco Canyon. There was a symbol there in the middle of it, looked like some kind of seat. What does that signify?"

Nick looked up from his cell phone, busily downloading maps and data about Chaco Canyon. "I can't be sure, but I have a theory. I think it's the symbol for a throne, the seat of royalty. It bears a resemblance to the stepped Throne of Montezuma, which I just saw at the National Museum in Mexico City. It was a spectacular find, discovered in 1831 under the city, covered with relief carvings. If that is really what it was meant to symbolize on the map, then Chaco is the right place to be looking."

The phone that Nick had been given by the cartel suddenly vibrated. He tapped Charlie and pointed for him to pull over. There, staring back at Nick, was an image of Soba, hands bound, looking terrified. There was also a text message:

You better be making progress, I am not a patient man. Update me.

Nick paused, composing his thoughts. He needed to buy time, some separation. He didn't know if he was being followed now, and frankly wouldn't be able to tell given the mix of ethnicities of tourists everywhere during peak season. He had to assume there were eyes on them. But he also needed to bluff a little, to test how much rope he would be given. As long as that rope wasn't around Soba's neck.

Making progress but leads imperfect. Searching hard, eliminating false trails. Need some time.

After he pressed send, he panicked when he realized he would be in and out of cell phone coverage. Had this Eztli even considered that? He quickly added to his message:

This search necessitates being in and out of cell phone coverage. Please don't do harm because we can't reach each other.

The reply came quickly:

Be careful rabbit. Time is what you don't have much of. Send progress update every 24 hours and await my reply, miss it and parts will follow.

He waited for any additional information, but there was none. Passing the phone to Charlie, he saw his hands were shaking. This was becoming all too real, the image of Soba etched in his mind. The pressure gnawing at the back of his brain rushed to the front, the black dog of depression overpowering him, a migraine forming. Not now, not with so much to accomplish, there was no time for this. He rushed to the back of the truck, his vision constricting into a tunnel, the daylight suddenly blinding him, and fumbled in a cooler for a high caffeine energy drink and chugged it. He grabbed a second one, and stumbled back to the front seat, and drank that down too.

Charlie knew what was happening, had seen this hit his brother before, back when they found out their mother had fatal cancer. He reached over and covered Nick's eyes with his own baseball cap. He knew Nick needed two things which were diametrically opposed, caffeine and sleep, and slowly drove on ever smaller roads, until they were within the Chaco Canyon Historical Park itself.

As they approached the Visitors Center, Charlie recognized Bidzii standing outside with three others. He looked over at Nick and saw he was still sleeping, waved at Bidzii, then put a finger to his lips, be quiet. He parked and walked over, shook Bidzii's hand and gave his condolences on the situation, and explained Nick needed to sleep off an intense migraine. He let Nanook out, who happily bounded around Bidzii and his friends, Charlie now realizing they were his band mates. Blues to the rescue.

Finding a place in the shade behind the Visitors Center, Bidzii and Charlie talked intensely while the others looked on, catching up, as Nick slept in the pickup. After about a half hour, Nick wandered over to them, still slightly dazed but his mind coming back into focus. Seeing Bidzii he stumbled over and hugged him, apologizing over and over.

"Not your fault Nick, not your fault. Others took her. She knew what she was getting into. But we gotta get her back man, unharmed."

Nick stood straight up, the last vestiges of the migraine dissipating. He took off his sunglasses and now saw Atsa, Yas, and Tahoma standing in the shadows, and a grateful smile crept across his face. Fajada Butte was just off in the distance behind them, and something about it made him drift off for a moment, some relevant memory he couldn't quite get his mind around. He looked back at Bidzii and slapped him on the shoulder. "We'll get her back pronto, Tonto. But first we gotta go find something for leverage."

They grabbed a camp site as a base of operations, one of the few left that no one wanted, which was ideal as it was rugged and out of the way. Yas and Tahoma found shady spots to keep lookout, while Nanook habitually positioned himself on the main access point in. Nick, Charlie, and Bidzii reviewed maps and brainstormed about possible places something could have been hidden, as Atsa listened in.

"Don't underestimate what we are trying to achieve here gentlemen," Nick cautioned. "This is something that has been missing 500 years, and fortunes and lives have been lost in its pursuit. History has shown that the more valuable the treasure, the more elaborate the deception. Take Genghis Kahn and his treasure. Supposedly anyone who witnessed where he was buried was killed, and the killers in turn killed by those who didn't know the location. That location was purportedly under some unknown river, which had been diverted to allow burial, and then redirected back to its original path."

Bidzii stared hard at Nick, his look said he'd do anything to find it to get Soba back.

Nick nodded at him. "What we seek may very well be here at Chaco Canyon, but we're going to have to earn it. And if we can't find it, we'll need a plan B."

"This is a big area, we have explored much of it over the years. Pueblo Bonita, Casa Rinconada, Penasco Blanco, Tsin Kletsin, it could be anywhere. Does anything you learned help narrow it down?" Bidzii asked.

"The petroglyphs of the codices where we found the mummies in Mesa Verde are our best bet. There was a map of sorts, and what had to be other hints with it," Nick replied, as he showed them the images. "That is the riddle we need to figure out."

"What about that woman Soba was with, the one who could read an original Aztec codex?" Charlie suddenly thought.

"Huehue, yeah she might be able to help. But unless we completely strike out, I don't want to involve her, not yet. I have a feeling that would be the end of her little tribe down there. I've spread enough pain around already."

They all ate a simple meal and talked softly late into the night. Atsa, Yas, Tahoma, and Bidzii rotated guard duty, two always on, so quietly that Nick never noticed the rotation. Finally admitting defeat for the night, he crashed in the back of the pickup while Charlie simply tossed a sleeping bag on a mat and slept on the ground.

A couple hours later Bidzii heard Nick mumbling in his sleep, thrashing about, and then finally quite again. He assumed it was worry about Soba giving him nightmares, but he couldn't have been further from the truth. And then he heard a scream.

Nick dreamed deeply, his mind overwrought from the stress, knowing at least one life, and probably more, hung in the balance. The dream started off as his migraine had, his vision fading around the edges, turning into a narrow tunnel, until pure white blinding light appeared and searing pain eclipsed everything. Then just as suddenly the pain subsided, and he had perfect clarity. He saw a bird's eye view of Fajada Butte, with himself down below, taking pictures at sunrise on the summer solstice. The view shifted, and he now saw through the camera lens, the sound of the clicking of the shutter sharp in his ears, as he slowly turned and took a series of photos along the horizon. When he had turned completely to the west, he saw an image of the sun's rising rays hitting a mesa wall on the west side of Chaco Canyon, briefly illuminating a narrow crevice within it. That image froze in his dream, and then he saw a similar outlined image, of an etched codice on a wall, the wall in

Mesa Verde where they discovered the two mummies. That outline faded to a tattoo of a ray from a barely risen sun near a butte illuminating a cleft in a cliff. A tattoo that had a bite mark around it, the only clue a drowning man under the ice could leave, the tattoo on his dad's arm.

He was caught in the dream, knew he was dreaming, and saw it fading away, breaking apart, turning to mist even as he tried to grasp it. Wake up, wake up, wake up he yelled in his head, biting his tongue in desperation. WAKE UP!

He screamed, so loud he sat straight up, hitting his head, and Charlie came running to check on him.

"What's going on? You OK?"

"Quiet!" Nick yelled. "I can't lose this, I can't let it fade. Remember this, the tattoo is the clue, it's in the codice on the wall, it's in the camera. The summer solstice, it all aligns, remember it! Swear you'll remember it!"

Trembling, he dug into his backpack and took out his camera. "Repeat it to me Charlie. Repeat it!"

Charlie nervously recited it back, word for word, as the others gathered around from the commotion. Nick turned the camera on, looked at the viewer on the back, and scrolled to the photos he had taken on the summer solstice, the very day he had met Soba. Starting to sweat, he clicked through until he came to the series of shots of the sunrise and the butte, of the rays creeping up the west mesa wall frame by frame, until he saw the single shot of the light illuminating a slight crack within it. He zoomed in, and at the bottom saw a small dark opening. The photos taken an instant before and after showed nothing on the wall, no crevice pointing to an opening, it was a single ephemeral moment in time, visible only at sunrise on the summer solstice.

Nick looked up and smiled. "That was almost like the damn Vision Quest you had me on Bidzii. I know where it is."

"We need to do this tonight, before sunrise. It's a restricted area due to the fragile artwork on the walls of the cave leading in to where we want to go," Nick said, stabbing his finger on a topographic map of the west mesa. "It's called Atlatl Cave, named for a spear-throwing lever that was found there. Whatever is back there was so well hidden that people came and went for centuries without ever knowing. This has to be it."

"It's just after midnight, do we have enough time to pull this off?" Charlie asked.

"I gotta text the cartel tomorrow afternoon, I'd rather know what I'm up against here first. And if we do find it, maybe I can string them along for one more day, to let us plan how the hell to handle them, if they aren't already here. We can drive close to the cave, there is a service route here. From there we're going to have to hike in. Bidzii why don't you come in there with Charlie and I, and the rest of you provide cover while we're there."

They drove away from the camp site in Bidzii's truck, three in the front and three plus Nanook in the back, wanting to keep it to one vehicle to draw less attention. There was also less chance it had been bugged. Bidzii kept the headlights off, and he and Nick each had a high intensity flashlight they would flash on out their windows briefly when needed. After coming down off the mesa, they linked up with the service road, and drove to a spot closest to Atlatl Cave. Atsa stayed with the truck, and Yas and Tahoma spread in opposite directions, keeping lookout. Everyone had the two-way handheld radios Nick had bought the day before, perfect for dead spaces with limited cell phone coverage. Nick, Charlie, and Bidzii grabbed their gear, and worked their way across the valley floor utilizing their headlamps, Nanook circling in a wide arc around them. A faint deer path led the way, which zigzagged to the foot of the west mesa. They finally approached the cleft in the mesa, which they could only see when they were right on top of it, that descended to a large, arch shaped alcove under the cliff face at ground level.

"I've been here, we all have, when we were kids. I didn't recognize it at first, this type of arch formation is pretty common around here. But those," Bidzii said, pointing a flashlight at painted figures and handprints on the walls, "I've definitely seen before."

The ground right in front of them sloped upward, the loose rock scree underfoot making them slip as they scampered up into the alcove.

"Let's try to leave it as we found it," Nick advised, as they carefully picked their way back deeper. The back of the alcove gradually transformed into an ever-narrowing tunnel and followed a meandering path with several false dead-end passageways off to the sides. With limited room to maneuver, Bidzii stopped and walked back out to the main entrance, acting as lookout. He tested his handheld radio, all was good with the others, and gave a thumbs up. Nick continued until only one person could fit and took off his pack and handed it back to Charlie. Charlie took off his too and started removing the gear they would need.

Nick worked his way deeper and deeper in, and came to a sharp turn to the right, then another to the left, and finally to a constricted spot too narrow to pass. There were bones from small animals on the ground and bits of broken pottery. It was the end of the line, simple offerings made, several handprints on the wall. The ceiling was black, torches had been used for light back here. There were outcroppings on either side directly in front of him, nearly touching, and he chipped away at one with his pick. It rang true, hard stone, unyielding. He then did the same on its facing companion, and the pick stuck in it, sandstone, or some type of mortar mixture. Looking at the ground there was a pile of powdered residue, the softer outcropping eroding over time. He then felt a slight draft, faint, barely moving, and holding his breath lit a match to see if it was his imagination. The flame flickered for a moment, then went straight up again.

"Charlie, pass me that folding shovel, and hold open a garbage bag. I've got to do some digging. Time check?"

"One thirty. And Bidzii says all still clear outside."

Nick used the sharp edge to chip the outcropping, it flaked away easily, and he scooped it into the bag. He continued until he could contort his body through the opening, and directly in front of him stood an unnaturally smooth faced wall. He chipped it with his pick, and the same material as the outcropping easily crumbled, revealing an artificial wall. The workmanship was crude, eerily reminiscent of the back of the granary at Mesa Verde. Working eagerly now, he chipped and dug quickly, filling several garbage bags, which Charlie pulled back out of the way. Finally an opening emerged at eye level, and air first came out of it, then went back into it, almost as if the mesa itself was breathing. *Just the pressure normalizing, this was sealed pretty damn tight,* Nick thought, anxious with anticipation. He made the opening big enough to peer into and stuck his arm in with a bright flashlight.

"Oh my God," was all he could utter.

The crevice, barely visible on the outside as an imperceptibly slight crack in the face of the mesa, in fact opened into a large triangular shaped fissure as it ran deep under the mesa, wide at the bottom and perhaps a hundred yards in length. Visible just in front of him were crudely carved sandstone stairs that descended into the cavern. Nick contorted himself to squeeze in, getting a head full of chalky mortar in the process, and finally stood on the top step. He cracked several glow sticks and threw them about and played his flashlight around the walls and ceiling of the perfectly dry interior, finally to the floor and center area, not believing his eyes.

The cavern was overflowing with objects of every description, the wealth of the vanished Aztec empire, tribute from its vassal states, piled high and dense in the middle and tapering to the edges. It had all been carefully arranged in a sort of ancient chorography. In the very center was an elevated throne, a figure upon it, the face and chest covered in some type of large, shimmering mask. Metal work of gold, silver and precious gems lay about, feathered headdresses and cloaks, textiles, tapestries, gilded furniture, shields, war clubs and spears, and overflowing chests. Three carefully placed mummies were at the back edge, looking inward toward the throne in the center.

Nick walked about dazed, no logic to his path, until he found himself in front of one of the mummies and saw a pile of what looked like deerskin at its feet. He knelt, and unfolded a part of one, and realized they were codices. The handwritten history of the Aztecs, thought to have been lost forever.

Suddenly he heard Charlie calling him from above, asking what he saw, and trying to enter with his slightly larger girth. He heard a shovel thudding, heard grunting, then saw Charlie emerge dust covered, standing on the top step, the same incredulous look on his face.

"This," Nick said, spreading his arms out wide. "This is what we've found, what Dad so carefully led us to, the treasure of Cibola! Step carefully brother, this is sacred ground."

Charlie worked his way down, wandering about in the same stupefied manner Nick had, until they stood side by side. Slowly they tiptoed around things to the center of the cavern, careful not to disturb anything that lay about, and approached the throne. A mummified figure sat regally upon it, the face and torso hidden by a large mask with sparkling chains dangling downward, only the hands and feet visible under spun gossamer garments of gold interleafed with silver. Nick approached it closer, the flashlight reflecting brightly off the gleaming golden mask, intricately inlaid with precious gems, which extended part way down to the chest, and then became a series of links, one connected to the next, golden teardrops of emerald, obsidian and jade cascading all the way down past the lap. He took his own necklace off and held the link against a strand in the middle of the mask, a piece missing at its end. A perfect fit.

"Grandma Ingrid, you've been holding out on me," he whispered aloud to himself. The old family legend, the letter, the necklace, his father's obsessive search, it all came together. It all perfectly fit, right here, at this singular moment in time.

"Who could it possibly be?" Charlie asked, his voice trembling.

"When there is peace between us, have good people put the Mexica souls in a safe place forever," Nick replied, quoting the letter Alexandre penned so long ago. "This is Montezuma, emperor of the Aztecs. They smuggled his body out, and those of his forefathers over there, and all the collective history they could gather, before Cortez returned, conquered, and razed Tenochtitlán. Someone brought it all the way here, into this shrine, perfectly sealed in the desert, preserving everything."

One hand of the mummy held a ceremonial golden dagger with an obsidian blade, the other held a folded deerskin codice. Nick removed the codice, and gently opened it and looked at the first panels. He shook his head, looked at Charlie and smiled.

"And this, this will tell us the story of how they managed to make their journey all the way to here."

CHAPTER 35 – JULY 25

They quietly drove away from Atlatl Cave, still with the lights off, trying not to draw unwanted attention as night faded to predawn twilight. Yas and Tahoma were left off at key vantage points along the way, each with a two-way radio, a backpack of supplies, and food and water. They would watch and ensure no one had followed them, and that no one would approach the cave.

Bidzii saw the concerned look on Nick's face. "Don't worry, if there is one thing we Indians can do, it's disappear into the landscape. We grew up here, this is our home court man. Bring it on."

Pulling into their campsite, Bidzii and Atsa watched as Nick and Charlie carefully removed the heavy golden mask that had covered Montezuma from the back of the truck. The golden links clinked as they swayed under the sleeping bag wrapped around it.

"OK, one quick look before I photograph this, then we have to bury it for insurance," Nick said, still stunned by the beauty and craftsmanship of the piece. They all gawked while he took a series of meticulous photos, capturing it from every angle. Turning it over for the first time, he noticed on the inside were two inlaid eyes that faced Montezuma's own, some type of white precious stones with real jade green pupils. The rest had a detailed etching of the Aztec's view of the cosmos and their pantheon of gods within it, a view that Montezuma would gaze upon for eternity. The only thing Nick could remotely compare it to, in his trained archeologist's mind, was the burial mask of King Tutankhamen from the Valley of the Kings in Egypt. But this was larger, more intricate, decorated inside *and* out, the most beautiful thing he had ever seen created by the hand of man. He noticed his own hands shaking slightly as he held it, the excitement of beholding such a piece of history palatable.

They wrapped it carefully in the sleeping bag, and slipped it into a hidden sandstone fissure, covering the opening with stone and sand, and erased their tracks. Time to make plans.

Nick, Charlie, and Bidzii huddled around, with Atsa and Nanook keeping watch a short distance away. They inventoried their weapons and strategized, what they would do in different scenarios, how they would communicate, and what kind of a welcoming reception they could prepare. Bidzii would reach out to other trusted Navajo friends nearby, while Nick would contact Killian, and then Lonan's Zuni kinfolk. They had all earned that right. It was likely the cartel would send people out tonight, but somehow they needed to get Soba back before they gave them the treasure. And the now hidden Mask of Montezuma was their last line of insurance.

Nick and Charlie drove back toward the Chaco Canyon Visitors Center, where he hoped to pick up enough cell phone signal to make a call on one of several unused burner phones he still had. This time with Charlie keeping watch, Nick wandered around on a small hill until he finally got a useable connection. He told Killian, his Apache friend and classmate, and then Ahaiyuta, the Zuni who knew Lonan so well, what had transpired and the predicament they now faced. Both said they would get there quickly and discretely, Killian with a bit longer of a drive.

It was now close to noon, and Nick would have to call the cartel in three hours. That was three more hours to prepare, and they hustled back to their camp site. When they arrived there were four more Navajos already at camp, grim expressions on their faces, two of whom Nick recognized from hanging out with Bidzii and the band back in more innocent times. When Nick asked Bidzii if they should synchronize their watches, they all laughed, and Bidzii simply pointed at the sun. Atsa called Tahoma and Yas on the two-way's and got the all clear and led the new recruits away to predetermined locations back along the footpath to Atlatl Cave. The countdown had begun.

"A lovely hacienda, with all the comforts of home, don't you agree dear?" Eztli asked, sitting in a rustic chair on the porch of the lodge, smoking a cigar and enjoying the panoramic view.

Soba didn't reply, she was still horrified that they had so casually gunned down the owners, a lovely older couple, so trusting and trying to be so helpful, under the pretense of being lost in this rugged no-man's land. There was still blood on the porch steps, where the bodies had been dragged out.

This lodge had been carefully chosen, a single road in and out, well-guarded, with a view that ensured there would be no surprises. There were thirteen of them, she had taken pains to notice, with three vehicles including a black Escalade, a gray Chevy Suburban and a dark green Ford Expedition. She had heard one of them saying they didn't want the same trucks so they didn't look like a caravan, not wanting to draw attention, but still needed the cargo space. They hadn't abused her, at least so far, because Eztli had seen to that. The others deferred to him, even his brother Miguel, who scared her more than anybody. But she had zip ties on her wrists, a rope that hobbled her around her ankles, and a gag they used if she became too hysterical. She sat motionless and unspeaking next to Eztli, who continued to expound on his future plans.

That means Mr. Master of the Universe is either planning to keep me or kill me, because this information isn't going anywhere, she dejectedly thought. She had let on that she could speak Spanish, English, or Navajo, but acted ignorant when they slipped into the Nahuatl language of their joint Aztec ancestors. There was useful information to be gleaned there.

"You more that anyone should appreciate what I am trying to do. Free the people from the bondage of oppression, both colonial and now self-inflicted by useless politicians. Like the recent Arab Spring, that tried the same thing and so magnificently failed. This isn't for my glory, or for Mexico's glory, it is for the right of all the oppressed peoples of Central America to live as they were meant to live. Free, with pride in their heritage, and pride in their place in the world. It is all there for the taking. All it needs is a little guidance, a little encouragement. And restoring our lost identity with the treasure your boyfriend so feverishly seeks, will rally us all together under one banner, a Mesoamerica jihad that will lead to unification."

Javier walked up on the porch, and he and Eztli wandered a short distance away, talking. She hadn't figured that shadowy figure out yet, but it was obvious Eztli was top dog, and Javier and Miguel his key lieutenants, and everyone else professional muscle. Javier's expression had betrayed sympathy, maybe even compassion, perhaps there was an angle there she could exploit. Miguel now joined them, and she quickly looked away, but not before she had caught his eye. She couldn't place if it was lust or cruelty, but his mere presence chilled her to her very soul.

"You shouldn't even be here brother, why take the risk of all of us being on Norteamericano soil? Don't you trust me to get this done?" Miguel asked Eztli.

"It isn't a matter of trust, I just couldn't miss out on this. I've devoted years of my life to finding proof of anything significant to illustrate Aztec dominance, and now it is so very close. Yes, I know it's risky, but we have plenty of security, and after all I have you looking after me!" Eztli replied, hugging Miguel hard around the shoulder.

"Yes you do, and we have more men I can bring here from the safe house if needed. You said keep a low profile, so only three vehicles for now."

Eztli wandered back toward Soba when his phone dinged with a text message. "Ah, right on time, the gringo reaches out," he said, smiling so broadly she noticed the jade inlays of his teeth for the first time. He stared at the message on his phone, unbelieving, then held it triumphantly aloft.

"Jesús Cristobal," he suddenly exclaimed so loudly everyone in the lodge could hear. "They've found it! They actually found it!" He showed a photograph to Javier then Miguel. "I knew it, we could never be denied, our legacy exists, it exists!"

He peered more carefully at the photograph, it was of a cavern, full of treasure and artifacts that even his expansive imagination had not dared to dream of. As he gaped, a text followed.

Found near Chaco Canyon. Can't access during daylight, area too exposed. Can lead you there at night. How is Soba, how do we exchange?

Eztli had a quick conversation with Javier, Miguel, and another armed man, and formulated plans. Soba tried to overhear them, but they wandered too far away, the conversation muted. Finished, Eztli walked over to Soba, indicated for her to lift her head, and snapped a picture. He sent it with a text.

Send coordinates, will arrive at midnight. Deliver me to the cave, I will give you Soba once in it. Do not cross me, we are many and heavily armed.

When he received the coordinates back, they went into the lodge, and spread maps out on a table. Soba was brought inside and forced onto a couch in the corner, away from any doors. They all switched to speaking in Nahuatl, as was their habit when discussing important things, and she concentrated and tuned in, while trying to look disinterested.

Eztli was about to point to the map, then paused and clapped his hands, unable to contain his excitement. "Can you believe it? It's real, it's more than I imagined. From the picture, I can tell we can't take it all, not tonight. We'll remove the key pieces, document everything, and come back as many nights as it takes. We'll leave armed guards there tonight, make sure they have enough food and water."

"What about her, and what about this Nick, and whoever else might be there?" Miguel asked. "They might try to pull something."

"He's no fool, but we have her, he has no choice. Once we get the treasure, do with her as you like. But make sure Nick and whoever else is with him never leaves the cave. This can't come to light until after we are finished, but I prefer it never comes to light at all. If I didn't know brother, I would suspect you were a little jealous of her, being so much taller than you," Eztli teased.

"Yes, she is now, but we'll see when I get done with her." Miguel looked at Soba and smiled, and she tried to shyly smile back and then look away. It wasn't easy.

"Javier, we will take everything to the safe house," Eztli commanded. "It may take us three or four nights to clear out the cave, we'll know better once we are there. I want the cross-border shipments to be split up, we can't risk losing everything in one or two large batches. Do whatever it takes to bring our legacy safely home."

"I'm used to sneaking things north of the border, not south," Javier joked. "But consider it done, I will make the necessary arrangements," he said, stealing a glance at Soba, fear for her in his eyes.

It was later afternoon when the Zuni called Ahaiyuta showed up with two others. Nick could see that he was angry, and evidently not just at Lonan's death. Ahaiyuta looked apologetically at Nick, and firmly shook his hand.

"I thought we would be more, that everyone who talked so loudly about avenging the death of Lonan would join us. But suddenly everyone has a reason not to come, they turn to squaws, the death of an old man not so important to them. It may be just us three here now, but we carry fury in our hearts."

"And we shall put it to good use," Nick replied. "Numbers aren't what's important tonight, coordination and planning are. This is Atsa, he knows exactly what needs to be done. Follow him, he will explain everything and show you where to go."

Later, when Atsa and the three Zuni had settled into their positions, Nick used his radio to ask everyone to try their cell phones one more time to ensure that they were in a dead zone. No one, from their camp site to the access road to the route to the cavern, could pick up anything.

"Good, we can communicate by the two-way radios, maybe they aren't as prepared. But let's assume they will be," Nick said, as Bidzii and Charlie gathered around a map of the area. He was about to continue when they all saw another truck driving toward them, a cloud of dust in its wake, and he smiled when he finally recognized it. The odds were heavily tilted against them, it would be a good night to have an Apache on their side.

"Guys, this is Killian, we went to school together. Irish name, Apache heart, a story for another time," Nick said, grabbing him by one shoulder. "Huddle in man, we're making our final preparations."

Bidzii pointed to the access road. "They will have to leave whatever vehicles they bring in about here, where Nick will meet them. They will probably leave someone behind there to guard them."

"I'm guessing they will cover the entrance to the cave with someone too," Charlie added. "But there is no way any electronic comm system is going to penetrate into that mesa, the cave is too far back. If we can break them apart, string them out, get those in the cave isolated from the others, I like our odds a whole lot better."

Nick studied the topographical map, looking at elevations and lines of sight. "Bidzii, you know how I want you positioned. Charlie, you're going to be at the entrance of the cave, I'll signal to you with a flashlight when I am with Soba. Morse code, password 'Shaman.' No signal, no Soba, and you stay hidden. At that point assume I'm dead, and then it's up to you guys."

Nick turned and looked at Killian. "We need someone to run things from the east edge of the mesa, looking down on the valley, across to Atlatl cave. There are the remains of an Anasazi great house here, called Tsin Kletsin. Go there by this route and work your way west to this ridge. You will be the one person who can see everything going on, at least up to the cave entrance under the alcove. You should have a good view from up there."

Nick explained in detail his role, how he was mission control if things went awry, and what to do in every scenario he could think of. "You're the one guy who is ex-military out of this whole crew," Nick said, knowing Killian had served in the army after they had met in college. "If it hits the fan, help them keep it together man."

Killian nodded, and walked to the back of his truck. He carefully opened a long industrial looking case and pulled out what looked like a sniper's rifle. He screwed in a scope, threw ammo into a backpack, and patted the gun.

"Now you will see how my brothers and I got so good at poaching," Killian chuckled. "A little insurance for tonight." Nick smiled at him gratefully.

"OK, radio silence from here on out everyone, use your earpieces only," Nick broadcast to the team. "Killian will be up on the ridge overlooking everything. He is the only one who will communicate from here on out. I can't thank you all enough for being here. Hunker down, eat something and stay hydrated, then stay concealed. Good luck, you know what to do."

The sun set in its usual spectacular fashion on the canyon, some of the tourists cheering and applauding as it finally blinked completely out, the horizon of the west mesa fading to orange then deep purple. A curtain of stars started to emerge as the view to the east turned darker, the headlights of the last day trippers leaving the park scattering like fireflies in the distance. Killian could see a few fires and lanterns at camp sites a little north of him from his concealed vantage point. He stayed alert, concentrating on the service route in front of him parallel to the west mesa, and the cavern hidden within it. As the night turned to black the moon slowly rose, and elongated shadows crept silently across the valley floor. It was close to 11 p.m., and he used his night vision scope to search up and down the route, looking for any early arrivers or a possible scouting party. So far, nothing.

Nick stood alone on the service route opposite Atlatl Cave, nervously pacing, checking his watch. He looked up and down the service route and avoided glancing where he knew Killian was stationed. He was unarmed and had no radio on him. He knew he would be searched, there was no sense in it. He had to put his faith in the others, and to the hand of fate, there was only so much they could plan for. "What was it that Prussian von Moltke had said?" Nick mused. "No plan survives contact with the enemy." He looked down the road and heard a noise. "The enemy cometh."

Killian spied a single vehicle slowly working its way down the access road from the camp sites to the north, only its running lights on. *Of course, they must have come in with the tourists, and hidden and mingled with the crowd. That would be their scout,* he thought. He followed it through his scope and reached for the two-way.

"One vehicle approaching," he let the team know.

He couldn't hear the vehicle, it was too far off, but it made steady progress toward where Nick was stationed. A faint whirring sound far off in the distance to his left briefly distracted him, and he shifted his scope to see if he could see anything. There was nothing, and the sound faded as quickly as it had come. He looked back at the vehicle, it was a little further down the road now, and saw that Nick was looking in that direction. The soft sound started again, it seemed to have shifted in front of him, below the crest of the ridge, carried up on air currents. A jarring realization hit him and he jumped up with his rifle just as a black drone rose directly in front of him. As he turned there was a single muffled shot in back of him, the last thing he ever heard, and a bullet entered the base of his brain and tore out through his forehead.

The black Escalade stopped for a moment, as though indecisive, and then continued on toward Nick. He squinted in the darkness, unable to make out anyone within it. Finally, it pulled up to him and turned off the running lights and motor. Four heavily armed men emerged, saying nothing. Two approached him, one putting a pistol to his head, the other frisking him heavy handedly from head to foot. The other two spread out, examining the area through the night vision goggles they wore. They nodded back to the one who had frisked Nick, he in turn touching an earpiece. "He's clean, only a phone and a flashlight."

A gray Chevy Suburban and a dark green Ford Expedition now

made their way along the same access route to where Nick waited. He had zip ties put on his wrists and was forced to his knees. The two guards watching Nick lit cigarillos and talked quietly, flicking the matches at him for amusement. When the other two trucks finally pulled up, they cut the chatter and came to something close to resembling attention. Three men piled out of the Chevy, the one named Miguel evidently in charge. Miguel pointed to the hood, and one of the men put a computer tablet there and they both looked at its screen and then looked up, as a whirring noise flew over them, toward the cave. Miguel walked over to Nick and grabbed him by the hair, looked into his face, then spit on the ground.

Three more men emerged from the Expedition, and automatically took up positions on the perimeter. Finally Soba and one other man stepped out of the truck and approached Nick. Nick got off his knees, and Soba ran to him, sobbing. They both had their hands tied, so she leaned into him and put her face to his ear.

"Thirteen of them, they plan to kill us in the cave," she whispered, then started fake crying again.

Miguel immediately pulled her off Nick, and roughly pushed her away. Nick had been discretely and carefully tallying the cartel members and came up with eleven between the three vehicles. That meant there were two jackals out stalking in the night, and they had eyes in the sky.

For God's sake, be careful, Killian, he thought. *We need you.*

The figure with Soba now walked over to the tablet and stared at it, talked with the men, and looked hard at Nick.

"I am Eztli. Thank you for finding this most precious legacy of my ancestors. Our drone shows someone at the cave entrance, who is it?"

"My brother. We have been guarding the treasure since we found it, awaiting you. And Soba."

"Yes, well I can tell you we captured your friend on the ridge over there. Try anything else, and you will be an only child. One without a girlfriend. Miguel here is only too anxious to take you apart, let's not give him a reason, shall we?"

Nick tried to keep his poker face, but already his plan was disintegrating. "OK. Can I signal my brother that Soba is here, that we are coming? Because if he doesn't get that signal, explosives are rigged to bring the face of the Mesa down, and not only will it seal the cave, it will draw a whole lot of unwanted attention."

Eztli pondered for a moment but decided against making threats. Time was ticking away, and there was no telling what measures desperate men might take to deprive him of his destiny. He had to give them hope, at least until he fully controlled the situation, and had the treasure within his actual grasp.

"Agreed," he replied.

Eztli then turned to Miguel, and in Nahuatl told him to scout ahead, verify the treasure was there, and then signal for the rest to follow once the coast was clear. When they were all in the cave, they could figure out how many nights it would take to evacuate it. Miguel nodded, pointed to two men, and grabbed Nick by the scruff of the neck and pushed him toward the mesa. After Nick had blinked his predetermined signal to Charlie, he led them along the faint deer trail, toward an unknown fate.

Arriving at the entrance to Atlatl Cave, Miguel eyed Charlie, and waved him down. He then put a gun to his head, and waited while one of his men frisked him, and then put zip ties around his hands. His two men then checked all around the edges of the cave, but could find no detonator, explosive devices or wires.

"Just as I thought, a bluff, so pathetically predictable. You, wait here with this gringo, we're going in to check it out. If we're not back in twenty minutes, kill him, then tell Eztli to kill the Navajo whore," he said, and turned to Nick. "You lead, rabbit. The clock is ticking."

Miguel, Nick and one other man went into the far back of the alcove, to the small tunnel opening. Nick then led the way with a flashlight, proceeding as fast as he could, stumbling occasionally, conscience of the countdown he was up against. Working his way up and down the narrow tunnel and finally zigzagging through the last turns, he squeezed through, onto the top steps of the cavern. Miguel came next, sweating heavily, the other man left to stand guard from above.

"Que mierda," Miguel exclaimed as the light of their flashlights slowly illuminated different parts of the cavern. He wandered briefly, reaching out and touching a few relics, then came back to the stairs.

"I never really believed in it, but it is so. Pablo, stay here with this one and guard him. I'll get the others. If he gives you any trouble, kill him."

Nick checked his watch, 11 minutes in, and looked at Miguel anxiously. Miguel tapped his earpiece and tried to communicate with the man he had left outside with Charlie, but only got static, the walls of the mesa too thick to permit any electronic communication. Miguel frowned, then worked his way back to the entrance as fast as his out of shape legs could carry him. Charlie finally breathed a sigh of relief when he heard him coming and saw that the man who had been guarding him, nervously fingering his gun, finally back down. Miguel emerged winded, waved his flashlight to the trucks, and called Eztli.

"The explosives were a ruse, the entrance is clear. But in the cave, it is as he said, as the photograph showed. Simply magnificent brother, I can't even begin to describe it."

"Then it is as I thought, as we all hoped. We will take key pieces with us tonight, and then finish in stages to avoid suspicion. We'll leave guards in there like we discussed. I am on my way to you, destiny awaits us all."

Eztli instructed men to remain with the trucks, both to stand guard and to move them if needed, even to four wheel over to the cave entrance in an emergency. But that would be only as a last resort, for it would reveal their activity and leave an obvious path that something serious was going on at Atlatl Cave. He gently pushed Soba ahead of him.

"Let's get to your lover, señorita. He awaits you at Cibola."

Miguel flashed his light again, and the party headed over toward it, slowly picking their way along the unknown route. They kept in single file, not wanting to leave any more of a trail than necessary. Eztli heard the faint whirring of the drone fly high over them, his eye in the sky, ensuring no surprises. Over the comm system in his earpiece the drone operator said, "All is clear, except for some type of large animal circling the perimeter, probably a wolf."

No worries there, Eztli thought. *Target practice.*

They all scrambled up the loose scree to the entrance of the hidden cavern, tucked so discretely under the mesa. Eztli wasn't sure they could have even found it at night without the signal from the flashlight.

Miguel embraced Eztli, overjoyed at what he had seen. "It is real brother, I have seen it with my own eyes," he exclaimed. "The comm system doesn't work in there, the walls are too hard, the cave too deep."

Eztli pondered that, a wrinkle in his planning. He wasn't one to take unnecessary chances. "Let's post two men here, they can talk with the men at the trucks and up on the ridge. The rest of us will go in, we can use runners to communicate back to here if needed. How long to get there?"

"Eight or nine minutes if you hustle, there is a lot of climbing up and down through small spaces," Miguel replied, still sweaty from his own exertions

Two men were left stationed at the entrance, while the rest of the group started into the tunnel, Soba and Charlie carefully guarded in the middle of the group. The air was dusty, the space confining, and there were false fissures off the sides. Miguel had already been there and back and led the way. Soba and Charlie bumped their heads several times, having no head lamps and standing taller than the others. Miguel squeezed through the last outcropping and stood on the steps, Eztli emerging immediately behind him.

Without waiting for the others, Eztli wandered down the steps, spellbound, mouth agape, taking in the enormity of what his mind struggled to comprehend. He almost tripped over Nick, sitting at the bottom, his guard standing at attention to the side.

Nick was pulled out of the way, and Charlie and Soba were herded over to him, two guards now watching them, while a third stood as a lookout above. Eztli, Miguel, and Javier walked around the cavern as if in a stupor, the cavern silent except for the relics rattling as they grabbed them and showed each other.

Soba looked at Nick and Charlie for some type of signal, even fear, but their faces betrayed nothing.

After ten minutes of exploration and disbelief, Eztli walked over and stood before Nick, smiling widely.

"I underestimated you, gringo. I hoped if we possessed this one," he said, glancing at Soba. "We would at least give you incentive to try your best. I don't know if I truly believed you would ever find it, or if it even really existed. Yet here we are, and I have you to thank. Tell me, what's your professional opinion of all of this?"

Nick stared hard into Eztli's eyes, his voice firm yet composed. "It defies belief, but I have had a day longer than you to get my mind around it. It's not just the value of the precious metals and objects, it is the historical significance of everything here. The history of the Aztecs, in their own words, are in those codices. That alone is priceless. This is all more complete and better preserved than anything ever found in ancient Egypt, Mesopotamia, or China. No looters ever touched it, the desert air perfectly preserved it. They meant it as a time capsule to be found eventually, a microcosm of their entire heritage. And that is the great Montezuma in the center, the other mummies are his forefathers, all escaped destruction at the hands of the Spanish. It is truly a treasure for the ages."

Eztli listened with interest, this was the view the outside world would have, and it played into his plans perfectly. "Very well said, I will have to use that in one of my future speeches. But unfortunately, it's time for you to join your father, and for us to get to work."

Eztli motioned to the guards, who pushed Nick and Charlie away from Soba and leveled their guns. Miguel walked up behind her and grabbed her forcefully and looked around the cavern for a private place away from the prying eyes of the others, where he could satisfy his lust.

"Kill us," Nick said in the same controlled tone, "And you'll miss out on the greatest treasure of all."

Eztli held up his hand and nodded to the guard, who roughly forced Nick to his knees. The Boss of Bosses felt his blood suddenly start to boil, could feel the heat rising in his face. On the cusp of his greatest accomplishment he was being disrespected and delayed by this Americano, by this mere academic. He grabbed Nick firmly by the hair and sputtered at him. "What treasure?"

"The mask of Montezuma."

It all suddenly dawned on Eztli, that in the original photograph Nick had sent him of the cavern, the mummy in the very center was wearing a magnificent mask covering his face and torso. He turned and stared at the mummy, regal in pose, now covered only in some type of linen shroud, golden greaves on the arms and wrists, one hand holding an ornate golden dagger, the other a codice. He hadn't noticed the missing mask in the excitement of seeing everything else piled throughout the cavern.

Nick saw the look of realization on Eztli's face. "Check my phone." Eztli grasped it, the home screen immediately showing a close-up of the mask laid out on a sleeping bag on the ground, stunning in its craftsmanship and grandeur. It was a singular piece encapsulating the essence of the Aztec civilization. If he were to rally all of Central America to his banner, this would be the iconic centerpiece, a tangible reflection of the glory that had been, and would soon be again.

Miguel dragged Soba back over and threw her to the ground next to Nick, tearing out an earring in the process, and pushed his brother aside and held Nick's head between his shaking hands.

"First I'll kill your brother, then I'll rape and kill her before your eyes, and then I'll take you apart piece by piece until you tell us where it is. We *will* get that mask, and you *will* tell us where it is."

Eztli forced himself to breathe deeply, trying to regain his composure, and motioned Miguel to the side. This was a time for rationality and not emotions to rule, the clock was ticking, for the first time against them.

"My brother speaks the truth. There is no way you will ever leave here alive, it is simply an impossibility, a loose end I cannot allow. Tell us where it is, and your deaths will be quick, merciful. I will even kill her first, to prove she won't suffer," Eztli said, looking at Soba.

"That's not what we agreed to," Miguel fumed at Eztli, unable to control his rage. "We dictate what happens here, not bound peon captives!"

Eztli sadly shook his head and glanced at Charlie, and then stared hard at Nick. "You know this can only end one of two ways, quickly or painfully. But in the end, we will get what we want." He nodded to Miguel, who pulled out his pistol.

"The choice is yours, but we begin now."

Up on the ridge, two men sat on an outcropping with a panoramic view of the valley and the mesa across the way, one playing with the sniper rifle he had found next to the dead Apache, the other looking at a screen and controlling the drone with a joystick. He zoomed in the drone camera on the two guards standing outside below the entrance to the cave, one pulling down his pants and flashing him a moon.

"Ha, good one, I'll have to get him back," he said, laughing and showing the screen to his companion.

Suddenly that man yelled, pointing frantically at the screen. He clicked his earpiece and screamed a warning, but it was too late for the men at the cave. At nearly the same time two of the men guarding the trucks heard the warning in their earpieces and reached for their guns, a third one having wandered off to relieve himself, unaware anything was happening.

From up on the ridge they could see the flashes of gun shots near the trucks, going off in crazy directions, the sound delayed, distant across the valley floor. Distracted by the firefight below and trying to communicate through their earpieces, neither realized that the hunters were now the hunted, stealthily being stalked, until a large white animal leapt at the man holding the rifle and ripped his upraised hands apart until he dropped it. The second man let go of the bright screen and reached for his pistol just an instant too late, the powerful jaws clamping down, crushing his windpipe and severing the carotids. The pitiless nighttime eyes of the large canine then locked onto the screaming figure frantically trying to crawl away, paced back and forth while emitting a deep primeval growl, then leapt again.

Just moments before, Ahaiyuta lay buried under desert sand and gravel, carefully controlling his breathing through a reed. His two Zuni companions were similarly hidden nearby, enduring the same fate. The heat from the afternoon sun had dissipated, relieving the suffering of his temporary tomb. His mind had focused back on times of his youth on the Zuni Reservation, and the kind guidance the elder Lonan had always provided him in the ways of his people and their traditions, and of the discipline to control his mind over his body, despite physical pain and discomfort. Lonan had been a good man, a credit to his people. And he had been brutally murdered right on their sacred land. Not just killed, but had his heart brutally cut out. Ahaiyuta came out of his trance like state, alerted by footsteps nearby, felt the earth vibrate slightly, and heard muffled laughter. He felt the cold steel of the knife handle in his palm, and unconsciously gripped it hard. The time for vengeance was at hand.

Ahaiyuta emerged out of the ground shrieking like a demon, both to scare his enemy and to alert his comrades to join him, and saw a man staring wide eyed at him, disbelieving, his pants down around his ankles. He plunged the blade deep into the startled man's heart, a single powerful thrust, and saw the other two Zuni run down another man, both of them manically slashing him before he could even bring his gun to bear.

At nearly the same instant at the parked trucks, two of the cartel men were puffing cigarillos, the red tips the only thing visible in the dark landscape under a carpet of stars and a slowly arcing moon. They had taken their night vision goggles off to enjoy a quick smoke, their companion still wearing his so he wouldn't trip as he went to take a leak. Abruptly panicked yelling came over the comm system, and they instinctively looked toward the alcove in the face of the mesa. They both grabbed their Uzi's and hurried to put their night vision goggles back on. The first man heard something whiz by his head and land with a sickening thud in his partner, whose cigarillo cast sparks as it spun about in the air, his gun firing wildly as he fell. He glanced at what had hit his companion, some type of long arrow or spear sticking out of his chest and turned and began firing before he even got his goggles on, blinded by his own muzzle flashes. He heard something whoosh by him, missing him, and then heard the same hollow sound that had struck his partner, and heard it again, staggering backward, firing blindly into the sky as he collapsed to the ground.

Fifty yards away the third guard squatted down, and knew an ambush was unfolding. The firing was brief and wild, then abruptly stopped. At least one intruder had been hit, he heard the cry of pain, the fall of a body. Hell, his cartel brothers had almost shot him in their panic. His heart pounding, he carefully glanced around with his night vision goggles, and saw men creeping toward the trucks, toward his compañeros. He only had a pistol on him, but knew he had back-up on the ridge above, and circled around hugging the earth to ascertain how many there were. He whispered on the comm system, but there was no reply from anyone, just static.

So be it, if he had to do it himself, he would. He had trained for this moment his entire life, if he pulled it off he would be richly rewarded. If he didn't, he was as good as dead anyway. He now had the advantage of surprise, and crawled closer. He saw there were three men, he could take one down with the first shot, charge and shoot the second before he could react, then take his chances with the third. He drew a bead with his pistol, but something was in the way, a large cactus. He carefully inched to the left to get a better angle for his shot, his nerves steady. Without warning he suddenly felt himself airborne, his pistol spiraling away, a snare around his ankle, the tightly sprung cottonwood flinging him heavily into the cactus, a hundred needles impaling him upside down. His goggles still on, he watched as a lone figure walked slowly toward him, the glint of a blade in his hand. He tried to call out but couldn't, the fear caught in his throat, until he was grabbed by the hair and the knife sharply sliced his scalp away.

Outside of Atlatl Cave, in the timeless landscape of Chaco Canyon, the quiet of the night was broken by the victory chant of a

Navajo warrior holding a grisly trophy aloft, and the haunting howl of a lone wolf in reply.

Nick was frozen with indecision, he had to buy time before they started pulling triggers. Javier didn't seem to have the stomach for any of this and was discretely working his way up the stairs. Nick glanced quickly around, one guard on the stairs with Javier, two guards behind him, Charlie and Soba, and Eztli and Miguel right in his face.

"Enough!" Miguel said aiming his pistol at Charlie, and pulled the trigger and shot him, Charlie reeling heavily to the floor from the impact. "I killed your dad. I will kill your whole fucking family. It will be as if you never were!"

"Last time, easy or hard?" Eztli asked.

Miguel aimed the gun at Nick and made sure he noticed as he looked at Soba and licked his lips. He then stared back at Nick, tapping the trigger.

Nick was about to speak when the guard on the steps above fell to his knees, swatting at his neck. Foaming from the mouth he tumbled down the steps, landing with a sickening thud. All the cartel members immediately looked around with raised guns, but there was no movement anywhere, the prisoners all zip tied and on their knees except for Charlie, who writhed in pain on the floor.

One of the guards behind Nick now reached for his neck, pulled out a small dart, and examined it with curiosity until his eyes rolled into the back of his head and he collapsed.

Eztli knew a trap was being sprung and leveled his gun at Nick and fired. Nick saw it coming and attempted to roll away, the shot hitting him squarely in his arm. Miguel quickly grabbed Soba as a shield, and looked around for something, anything, to shoot at. He instinctively sought cover and dragged Soba in front of him over to Montezuma's mummy on the throne in the center, backing against it for protection.

In taking the bullet Nick fell and rolled his legs around hard, knocking down the other guard behind him, who fell on top of him. Nick wrestled with him for his gun with tied hands, while Eztli fired at them both, not caring who he hit, and heard the satisfying thud of at least two rounds hitting flesh. Eztli's attention was then suddenly distracted as the three mummies in the back, Atsa, Yas and Tahoma in disguise, dropped their blow guns and started firing back with their own pistols, the sounds filling the cavern with gun blasts and ricochets.

Javier dodged a shot and sprayed fire with the Uzi he picked up off the top of the stairs, hitting Tahoma and forcing the others to dive for cover. Nick rolled the dead body off him and took careful aim at the distracted Eztli and shot him in the stomach, knocking him to the ground. Miguel leaned against Montezuma, one arm choking Soba, the other aiming at Nick's head, about to pull the trigger. That was when he felt the arm of the mummy behind him suddenly move and draw the gold handled obsidian blade deeply across his throat. He fell to his knees, shock on his face and grasping at his neck while choking on his own blood, as Montezuma arose from the throne and looked down upon him. The last thing Miguel saw as the life gushed out of him was Soba leaning into Montezuma's shoulder, Bidzii removing the mummy's shroud and holding her tightly. As he breathed his last, Soba glared at him and rolled him off the throne's landing with her heel.

Nick slowly got to his feet, holding the gun shakily with both his zip-tied hands, and walked over to Eztli, who was doubled over and holding his gut. Eztli saw movement off to the side with his peripheral vision, and stealthily reached over for his own gun. Just as he was about to grasp it, a boot stepped firmly on his hand and ground it into the dirt of the cavern floor. Nick then kicked the gun away, cocked his own trigger, and pressed the still warm barrel against Eztli's temple.

"Like you said, to leave here alive would simply be an impossibility."

Seeing there was no hope in the cavern, Javier fled down the tunnel. He tried his comm earpiece, but no response, damn the walls. He just needed to reach the entrance, gather the men together, regroup. After all there was only one way in and one way out. He had seen Eztli and Miguel go down, probably killed. If he played this right, he would now be the Jefe de Jefes, the Boss of Bosses. No one knew the operation better than he did, he practically ran it while Eztli played collector and politician. He alone knew all the finances, had set up all the offshore accounts, and laundered the money. If anyone knew the inner workings of the Texcoco cartel and was prepared to run it, it was him. *Just rally the troops, kill everyone in the cave before morning, and come back another time, live to fight another day. This could work, it will work, just get to the entrance now.*

He looked up, finally concentrating on where he was. This part of the tunnel didn't look familiar, he pointed the flashlight around, he must have taken a wrong turn somewhere. He turned around, would double back, and work his way out. With one hand on the wall he stumbled forward, the flashlight beam toward the floor, so he could be sure of his steps. The walls narrowed and he raised the flashlight, and jumped back, stifling a scream, aghast. Staring at him was the face of a mummy, stuffed into the crevice. He stepped back and laughed at himself. *This is what the gringos did with the actual mummies, when they cleverly substituted assassins in their place.* Turning he paused, and heard a deep growl echoing down the tunnel, toward him. He reached for his gun, fumbled for it in the confined space and dropped the flashlight, which went black as it hit the floor. The ominous growl was much closer, and he thought he caught a glint of two reflective eyes bounding toward him as he fired, again and again.

Atsa and Yas checked the bodies laying about the cavern, making sure no one would play hero, and walked over to where Nick stood. He was looking down at Eztli, who was holding his abdomen. Charlie pulled himself up for a better view, as Soba stanched the bleeding of his shoulder. Bidzii stood over Tahoma, tears welling in his eyes. He then made his way over next to Nick, and nodded no,

Tahoma hadn't survived. Nick's jaw clenched, a pistol in his hand pointed at Eztli's head.

"Don't do it, Nick," Charlie said. He's the head of the snake. Let's give him to the authorities and let them stamp out the whole damn cartel."

Eztli defiantly glared at Nick, uncowering. "Good advice, listen to your brother. This is bigger than simple revenge, I am much too valuable to silence forever."

Nick pondered the ramifications, and what would ultimately be the greater good. The death of one versus the unraveling of an entire drug empire, he could literally save thousands of lives, prevent who knew how many people from becoming addicts, spare untold destroyed families and anguish. It was over, he had done his part, and slowly lowered his arm down.

Eztli saw the change in demeanor and grinned, there might be a way out of this yet for him. Payoffs in the right places and he would be extradited back to Mexico, where he knew people in key places, people who would look out for his best interests, for their nation's best interests. A delay in his plans, yes, but it need not thwart his ultimate long-term ambitions. He had perfect calm and clarity, the bullet hadn't hit any vital organs, and if he had survived the mean streets of Ciudad Victoria as an abandoned orphan, he would survive this as well. Survive, then thrive, and finally rise again, like the remnants of the Aztec Empire now all around him.

Sounds started coming toward them from the tunnel, faint at first, then increasingly louder, footsteps and commotion, and everyone trained their guns on the entrance. Suddenly Javier emerged, stumbling and holding the tied off pulp of a bloody arm, followed by Ahaiyuta and the other warriors from outside the cave.

"We bring you this one as a gift. We found him trembling in a side passage," Ahaiyuta said. "The white wolf was locked onto his arm, dead."

Nick felt a jolt at the news, and looked at Soba, her tear-filled eyes meeting his. First Tahoma, now this. And who knew what had happened to Killian. Shaking it off and concentrating on the matter at hand, he stared at Javier. What was it about him he knew? He then remembered the dossier Charlie had reviewed with him about the cartel, that Javier was the number two man, the finance and logistics wizard, the brains behind the operation. He looked back at Eztli, and his emotions hardened.

"I'm not going to give you to the Feds so you can cut a deal, you don't get to hide behind the protection of our legal system," Nick said, glancing over at Javier. "He does."

"But you can't. I own Mexico," Eztli blurted out, feeling his control slipping away. "I have billions hidden, precious archeological treasures you wouldn't believe, let me tell you what I can do for you, for all of you . . ."

"Tell it to my dad."

A gun fired, echoed briefly, and the cavern went silent.

CHAPTER 36 – JULY 26

The Park Service arrived first, alerted that some type of disturbance was taking place near Atlatl Cave. Finding bodies scattered outside and seeing survivors coming out of the cave, they quickly alerted the authorities, sealed off the area and closed all access to the ridge, the valley, and the mesa. State and federal authorities arrived shortly thereafter, and as soon as it became apparent an international drug cartel was involved, the Drug Enforcement Agency took charge of the situation. The media wasn't allowed immediate access, and the only information to trickle out was from a DEA spokesman who provided a few carefully chosen, yet purposely vague remarks.

"Now, let me make sure I've got this straight, a distant relative of yours was given a single gold link of a purported treasure, clues to its location, and this was handed down over time, ultimately to your father. He spent summers looking for it with you, your brother, and mother, and was killed this past winter by someone interested in this treasure, but you had no definitive proof. So you went west to scatter your parent's ashes and picked up on the search from there. Right so far?" Robert Sommers, Director of the DEA, asked. William Bashant, Acting Director of the Department of the Interior, also awaited the answer.

"Yes, sir," Nick replied. He had told this story repeatedly to a slew of officials, to those in progressively higher offices, until he finally sat across from the head of the DEA and the Department of the Interior. The DEA wanted to neutralize the Texcoco drug cartel, capture and incarcerate its leadership and seize its assets, while the Department of the Interior would ultimately decide on the fate of the Aztec treasure found hidden within the confines of an American National Historical Park at Chaco Canyon. Mexico would want to deal with the drug cartel in its own way, and would no doubt claim national sovereignty over the treasure. Complex decisions and negotiations awaited both Directors, so they wanted to hear the unfiltered original story, directly from the horse's mouth.

"So you and this Navajo girl you met, Altsoba, together worked your way down to Mexico, where you uncovered more clues," continued Director Sommers. "You then went to Spain, were met by one Philip Storm, evidently your mentor and PhD Advisor, and jointly uncovered more leads on the trail of this treasure. Back to Mexico you came, where you picked up Miss Altsoba, went back to the states, were joined by your brother, and together went to Zuni, New Mexico. Where an elderly gentleman of your acquaintance named Lonan was killed, and Altsoba forcibly kidnapped." He paused, looking at his notes.

"You know, this is simply incredible, the whole journey," Director Bashant interjected, picking up the story. "You then decipher the clues your dad left you in his journal and on the back of a letter, follow them to find a treasure of the Aztec people that defies belief in a sealed cave in Chaco Canyon, enlist the help of three regional tribes to prepare an ambush, and take down the most ruthless cartel in the western hemisphere in a single night. Does that pretty well summarize it?"

"Well, yes, I guess it does. But that cartel left a trail of bodies pursuing their goal, both north and south of the border. And good people gave their lives that night in Chaco Canyon bringing them down. None of this was accomplished without tremendous costs."

"We understand and sympathize with the sacrifices made. But if there is a silver lining in any of this, it is the fact that Javier Hernández survived," Director Sommers interjected. "He may be minus an arm, but that's the price he paid. And he's already singing, he knows everything, and actually seems to show a little remorse. We'll bring the Texcoco cartel down from the inside out."

"That's great news," Nick solemnly replied. "But if you need nothing more from me gentlemen, I have funerals to attend." Both Directors offered their condolences, and he was shown out.

The drive to where Killian was being buried on the Apache Reservation was somber despite Soba accompanying him, as they were both still licking their wounds, figuratively and literally. Charlie had been transported to Albuquerque, his shoulder gunshot wound serious but not life threatening. He would have the better story to tell, he could hear it now, as Nick's was just a clean flesh wound through muscle only. But not only would Nick have to get through Killian's funeral, he knew another awaited him after it, on Navajo land.

Nick and Soba were met by Killian's two brothers as they attended the ritual service on the Apache Reservation. It was a simple yet poignant ceremony. Nick could see life for those on the reservation was hard, the value of traditional ways fading, opportunities scarce. The youth had few role models here that valued the past, but certainly Killian was one. His parents had passed, but there were a number of other relatives and friends about, and Nick was spontaneously asked to say a few words, to try to put meaning behind such a loss.

"Killian was a good friend, a good colleague, and most importantly a good human being. He always saw the best in situations, in people, in the world. And he treasured his heritage and wanted nothing more than to have a hand in discovering it, in nurturing it, and passing it along. That is why he chose the career path he did, and why he chose to help me. Because he didn't just belong to the Apache tribe, he belonged to the human tribe, and found our collective history just as important as his own. That is why he gave his life to protect it for future generations." Nick found himself speaking about his friend expansively, about the choices and sacrifices he had made, and his fierce determination to do small acts that made a difference. About why he had joined the Army, why he went to college, and ultimately chose to come back and serve his people. He spoke extemporaneously and sincerely, about the loss of a dear friend.

Feeling despondent and doubting he did any good, Nick made small talk with Killian's brothers and Soba outside the meeting center. But he felt better as people left and offered condolences to Killian's brothers and their thanks to him, and as several young people asked exactly what it was Killian went to school for, and if Nick would perhaps provide some guidance.

"I think you gave exactly the message they needed to hear," Soba said on the drive out. "You explained sacrifice for a cause greater than oneself, and you gave them a modicum of hope."

"I didn't know I would be speaking, I hadn't prepared anything. But when it's about a good friend, you just speak the truth from the heart."

Soba leaned into him and sighed heavily. "You know, I don't care what Colel says about you. You really aren't half bad for a white guy."

They drove northward along familiar roads, through the Zuni Reservation, up towards the Navajo Reservation and home for Soba. As they got closer, they both girded themselves to say their goodbyes. It was particularly hard on Soba, as she had grown up with Tahoma and the other young Navajo who gave his life on that desperate night.

Both were given the traditional burial of the *Diné*, or simply The People, as the tribe called themselves. Four people to mourn the deceased were chosen, including Bidzii, who prepared the body for the funeral ritual, carried it to the burial site led by a horse, and communicated only by a type of sign language. All passersby knew to avoid the path they took for four days, the official mourning time. The elders believed that the *Chindi*, the ghost left behind with the body's last breath, contained the residue of everything that was bad about the deceased and must be avoided. Following the burial, many took part in self-purification with sage smoke.

After the four days of mourning a non-traditional gathering was held, to commemorate the lives lost. Colel and several others from various tribes showed up to pay their respects and to support their dear friend Soba. The gesture genuinely touched her, and in her grief meant more than she could adequately express. Colel, her wild spirited alter ego, stoically stayed by her side, the mere presence of a kindred spirit providing a calming influence and unspoken support.

Soba, the tribal outcast shunned in her youth, was now honored as the woman of the hour. The discovery in Atlatl Cave had brought prominence and pride upon the Navajo, that some of their own had such a hand in its unearthing. And the acts of heroism of their young men echoed past days of dignity and honor, when they were still a powerful, free nation.

Bidzii, Atsa, and Yas struck up the band and played under the stars for all gathered, purposely leaving an empty chair on their makeshift stage. Nick and Soba heard the music drifting toward them on the wind, as they sat on a small westward facing peak. This particular spot had an uninterrupted view of the festivities below, of the entire Navajo Reservation. It had seemed an especially fitting place to bury Nanook, who had always loyally stood watch, their ever-vigilant sentinel.

"I feel better knowing he is watching over my people," Soba softly said, her voice trembling. "They will be safer for all time with him here."

The back to back dedication ceremonies went off without a hitch. In Mexico City, the former estate of Esteban "Eztli" González, head of the notorious Texcoco drug cartel, had been confiscated, then turned into a beautiful museum devoted to pre-Columbian Mesoamerican history. Not surprisingly, the current political administration had seen the discovery of Montezuma's treasure, as it was being heralded in Mexico, as a boon to both their credibility in the drug war, and to the tourism dollars that would inevitably follow. Alejandro Diaz, the humble Mexican patriot Nick had met at the Palace of Cortez, was elevated to its Director, his many years of dedication being recognized and rewarded. Eztli's vast private collection of bought, stolen, and looted antiquities, hidden from the public's eyes for so many years, at last saw the light of day. The holdings of his drug empire were liquidated, a portion going to funding the museum and sponsoring Mesoamerican historical research and preservation in perpetuity. Nick wryly commented that Eztli's empire had indeed expanded, just not in the way he had envisioned.

Nick and Dr. Storm were named to the Board of Directors and had an active hand in the orchestration and presentation of the exhibits, helping decide what should be given special prominence. The solid gold Aztec Sunstone was moved upstairs, into the courtyard, now covered with a Louvre like clear pyramid that was based on the Hueteocalli Temple, allowing the sunstone and accompanying silverwork to be brilliantly shown as the tears of the sun and sweat of the moon. Stairs were added to the basement, with much of the collection still kept there, as well as the inner workings of the cartel's information systems. Dr. Storm had joked that attending this would be like going to the Egyptian Museum in Cairo and the Spy Museum in Washington at the same time, a veritable Disneyland for the whole family.

Nick was pleased to hear a wing of the museum had been named the Francisco Martinez Gallery. It had been in honor of his friend Chico, who he met in Cuernavaca while doing research and had been assassinated by the cartel. Another wing of the museum was devoted to the newly discovered codices, which filled in a gap of knowledge in the historical record, told for the first time from the Aztec perspective, but most importantly from those who had actually lived it. There was also a living history segment, as Huehue now spent a few days per week explaining the codices and painting new ones for the exhibit. The craft of creating a codice was suddenly in vogue, and Huehue herself now seen as a national treasure.

Soba, Bidzii, and Charlie joined Nick and Dr. Storm for the grand opening ceremony, feted as rock stars and trailed by the paparazzi, roles they all tried to avoid. The museum immediately became Mexico's must-see tourist hot spot, so popular access had to be restricted, a lottery system instituted until demand diminished.

An especially solicitous rumor was making the rounds in the tabloids, that Eztli's skull rack, the one containing the heads of so many of his enemies, now contained his own. Wisely the new Director of the museum refused comment, fueling both speculation and gawking foot traffic.

A week later they were all back at Chaco Canyon, an impressive museum having been created there as well. This one was purposely built from the ground up on the site of the old Visitors Center, with a dedicated museum and learning center, and a special glass encased walk through in Atlatl Cave itself, preserving the original native history and much of the treasure, left in situ. Permanent bronze memorials had been set up where Tahoma, the other young Navajo, and Killian had each fought and died. There was even a bronze of Nanook up on the ridge, next to Killian's, the nose already rubbed to a shiny gloss by sympathetic visitors, especially the children.

William Bashant, Director of the Department of the Interior and never one to resist good publicity, shared the ribbon cutting with Nick and Soba. While Nick and Dr. Storm were again named board members, this was especially poignant as Soba had been named Special Counsel for Legacy Preservation and Living History of the newly established museum. Her vision to preserve the languages, oral histories and traditions of native peoples was now her professional charter. Her first act was to fast track a program to video record interviews with tribal elders across the land, before they took their stories away with them forever. Soba then set up a series of internships to give those interested in the field some real hand's on experience. She joked she was actively grooming the next generation.

An agreement had been struck between the Mexican and American governments to periodically rotate key artifacts between the two museums, although ownership of what was found in Atlatl cave was never relinquished by American authorities. Cibola, as the treasure was known everywhere but in Mexico, suddenly became the most sought-after tourist destination in the country despite its somewhat remote location. Access was carefully managed, lest the popularity of the new museum diminish the land and people it was meant to celebrate.

Renewed interest in the story of the discovery of the New World, of its conquest, of the treasure of Cibola, provided an economic boom to the tribes of the Southwest, and provided a deeper understanding of their struggles and enduring legacy. As did the liquidation of cartel assets and the subsequent programs they funded, on both sides of the border.

Dr. Storm was pleased by the appearance of his good friend and colleague Juan Ramirez, the Spanish Minister of Culture, who flew in especially for the dedication. "I think the Mexicans are still mad at us Spaniards, so I came to this one instead of Mexico City," he half-jokingly said.

Moments before giving his dedication speech, Director Bashant informed Nick and Charlie that the central part of the new museum, the one which would display the breath taking and timeless Mask of Montezuma, was being named the Albert LaBounty Gallery in honor of their father. Overcome with emotion, Nick took a moment to compose himself, then stepped to the podium.

"I want to thank all of you for coming here today, as we dedicate something that was waiting so very long to be discovered. There was wisdom in how and where the Aztecs hid it, as they wanted it to be found, but not until the world was ready for it. I think today the world is finally ready.

This carefully hidden time capsule of an entire people's history had a story to tell, beyond simple conquest, greed, or man's inhumanity to man. It is the story of that quality that makes humans strive, explore and endure, that makes us wonder at our place in the universe under the vastness of a nighttime sky, that makes us ache with every molecule of our being at the transcendence of our existence. Whether it is building the Great Pyramids of Giza or planting our flag on the surface of the moon, it is that great urge, that very instinct, to say we existed, we were here, we did great things, and we did not go gentle into that good night."

The crowd in the auditorium, in a festive mood and bursting with anticipation at seeing the newly revealed treasures, broke into spontaneous applause. Nick smiled and waited a moment for it to die down.

"Codices of the Aztec version of that story somehow miraculously survived, in the only place they could have, away from the Spanish who would have burned them, away from the moisture that would have destroyed them, away from the looters who would have scattered them. They tell us of a great people that were, and of an epic journey that took place. Their author was a man named Asupacaci, the sole surviving son of Montezuma. He was the Aztec version of Odysseus, wandering after a war, looking for meaning in this world. But instead of trying to get home, he is trying to preserve what was home, for the ages. Leading his brethren, he transports the legacy of his people through jungles, across deserts, through friendly and hostile tribes, to here, to this very place. He completes his odyssey, and prepares to lay down his life, the last survivor of the expedition he led.

But the codices tell us he is found, and in a profound moment decides to live, to leave more than a simple treasure behind, to also leave a living legacy. He takes a wife, starts a family, and instructs his son to always carry on, to pass down to his descendants the secrets of his people, to prepare them for the day they can again take their proper place in the world. One of his descendants met my great, great, great grandfather, and passed along a talisman of Cibola, and that led us all to be here, today.

A pretty reporter in the crowd yelled, "We love you Nick," which led laughter and to another round of applause.

"That story you all know, I well realize it's been impossible to avoid in the media. But now for something you didn't know. While Asupacaci left the treasure here, he spent the remainder of his life up near Mesa Verde. His body was found there, well preserved, still bearing a Spanish cross bolt in its shoulder. His father Montezuma, also well preserved, was found in the cave just behind us. DNA tests recently conducted on both mummies have conclusively proven that the new Special Counsel for Legacy Preservation and Living History, standing just over there, is the last living descendant of the house of Montezuma."

An audible gasp filled the auditorium, and the reporters and photographers could be seen scrambling for a better view of her, camera shutters clicking. Nick grinned and motioned for quiet.

"While we can't tell what eye color the mummies had, the codices indicate that some of the royal descendants had green eyes, an indelible mark of their royal lineage. And if you look at the *inside* of the Mask of Montezuma, you will notice it has green jade inlaid into the pupils. For those of you who haven't had the pleasure of meeting her, that green eyed woman over there is named Altsoba. Which means 'At War' in Navajo. Let's all hope that this now means she can do her good works, and finally be at peace."

Later in the evening when the dedication was concluded, Nick and Soba made their way out. An unexpected crowd had gathered waiting for them, and they were bombarded by people wanting to write their story, looking for movie rights, asking for endorsements. A few even wanted autographs, or to take selfies with them. The Paparazzi started taking photos, shoving microphones in front of them.

"Good people," Nick said, pulling Soba close and waving the crowd back. "The bodies of our friends who gave their lives for this aren't even cool in their graves yet, let's let the dead rest a bit, shall we?"

Nick was touched by the gift, having been lost in the hectic life suddenly thrust upon him by his fifteen minutes of fame. He had flown into Grand Rapids with Soba, to show her around his old stomping grounds. Sophie and the kids had some time off and were up at the old camp, and Charlie picked his brother and Soba up at the airport. Walking out of the terminal to the parking lot, Charlie tossed him the keys to his old truck, indicating for him to drive. When Nick looked up and saw his 1972 Chevy pickup truck, he didn't recognize it. Charlie had quietly had it completely restored, and it looked factory new. But it was even better, because it had all the latest technology installed as well. And a killer sound system for all those blues tunes on road trips.

"You know, I've been managing your accounts for a while, we both inherited a few bucks, and we've parlayed your fame to good use," Charlie said. "You're financially set man. But I know you, you're so tight you squeak, so I thought it might be a good idea to finally take your first communion money and upgrade your ride."

A bro hug shared, they put the luggage in back, including a piece that was making a lot of noise. Nick had one stop to make before he went to the cabin on Lake Charlevoix, and he was anxious to get there. It took him a few minutes to get used to the restored pickup, the gear box didn't shift upside down like the old one, and the new clutch and brakes were tight, but he had to admit, it was one smooth ride. His dad had bought the truck used, even he didn't get to ride it in this condition.

After walking down the hallway, he gently rapped on the door and let himself and Soba in. The old woman looked asleep, but Nick leaned in and kissed her forehead anyway. Soba caught sight of the dream catcher turning lazily in the window, the very one that had played such a part in linking everything together. The woman slowly opened her eyes and smiled genuinely when she saw Nick standing there.

"Hello, Grandma Ingrid, I've missed you."

"Why, don't be silly, Albert, you were just here. But so kind of you to say so," she said, habitually mistaking Nick for his father in her slightly confused state, with a sense of time that meant little to her anymore.

"I wanted to introduce someone to you, Gram, her name is Soba, and she is Navajo."

Grandma Ingrid perked up when she saw Soba and grasped her hand tightly. Her eyes came into sharp focus, and a glint of recognition came to her.

"Why that means you finally finished the quest, didn't you dear?" Grandma Ingrid said, never taking her eyes off Soba.

"We did, it was quite the adventure. It was all everyone thought it was, and more," Nick replied.

Grandma Ingrid was listening but seemed more interested in Soba. She patted Soba's hand gently.

"And you my dear, just where have you been hiding all these years?" she asked.

"Why I've been out on the reservation," Soba said, blushing slightly.

"Of course you have, where else would you be after all? I've been waiting for you so patiently all this time, for my family to finally find you. You know a quest can become quite an obsession if you let it, I was quite afraid they might never find you. But here you are now, safe and sound. I'm afraid I'm a bit tired, so nice to see you again," Grandma Ingrid sighed, closing her eyes.

Soba looked at Nick and raised her eyebrows, still holding Grandma Ingrid's hand.

"I swear I've seen her before. I feel I know her," Soba said.

Grandma Ingrid faintly smiled, and then nodded off. Nick and Soba walked down the hall, digesting what had just taken place.

"How does she think she knows you when you have never met? You must remind her of someone."

"No, I don't think that's it at all. We did know each other, just not in this lifetime," Soba replied, smiling her mystical shaman smile.

Nick shook his head. "She talked like your fore bearers surviving were what was important, like *you* were the real treasure."

Soba smiled and squeezed his hand. "Sometimes it takes the blind to see."

When they pulled into camp, Charlie and Sophie were out on the deck, the kids splashing about in the water. Nick took the carrier out of the truck and opened the door, and two rambunctious puppies tumbled out, one a husky-like gray color, the other bigger and pure white. Nick and Soba followed them as they yelped and ran to the kids.

"Julien and Yvette, I talked with your mom and dad, and they said you could have a dog. That little gray fuzz ball is now yours, the big white one is Soba's," Nick joyfully told them.

"For real, Uncle Nick? Really?" Julien squealed.

"Yes, for real. It turns out Nanook had himself a girlfriend when Soba was staying with Huehue," Nick said, winking at Soba.

"Does he have a name?" Yvette asked.

"He's a she. Make sure you pick a good name," Soba said.

"What did you name yours?" Julien asked.

"Diné, because he will watch over my people," she replied. "Like yours will watch over you."

Charlie walked back to Nick's truck and brought some luggage in and came down off the porch toward the lake holding a guitar. "Is this the one Bidzii gave you bro? How about a tune?"

Nick took the guitar and smiled, thinking of all they had been through, how this was the one place he truly felt at peace, felt connected, and reflected on all their parents had given them. Most of all unrequited love. He looked out at the familiar and tranquil view of the sun setting on the lake, dragonflies darting down to the water surface, and started strumming a song by one of his Dad's favorite musicians, Bob Seger, from downstate in the Detroit area. He winked at Soba as he softly sang.

Out past the cornfields where the woods got heavy
Out in the back seat of my '60 Chevy
Workin' on mysteries without any clues
Workin' on our night moves

The song eventually finished. The kids started giggling and clapping, liking the melody but having no inkling of the meaning of the lyrics. "Sing us another one Uncle Nick," they shouted, which he obliged as the sun finished its downward descent, the cicadas and bull frogs providing the background accompaniment.

"Hmm, nice. I've missed that. Where does the time go?" Sophie said, mostly to herself, as she watched her children. "So, what's next for you two, now that the dust has settled a little?"

"After I enjoy some time with all of you, I'm back to my new job, so exciting for me," Soba said, casting her deep green eyes at Nick. "I truly feel this is what I was meant to do, every day I get a chance to change the world a little, help people to remember from whence we came, and capture some of our collective history before it fades away."

Nick smiled and thought for a moment while he held Soba's hand, and looked around at his brother and wife, the cabin on the lake, and the kids and dogs happily splashing about. "Now that I got my PhD, some financial independence, sit on the boards of a couple museums, and have a little momentary fame, it affords me the opportunity to chase down the next big mystery. Which one that is going to be I haven't decided yet, it's percolating in the back of my mind. But as Dad would have said, there's a whole lot out there that needs finding and explaining."

"Like old times," Charlie said, handing Nick a highball of bourbon and putting his arm around him. "There's nothing like a good quest to get the blood pumping and make you feel alive."

The brothers slowly meandered down to the water together, and each poured a little of the bourbon into the lake, to the spirits of their parents, and clinked their glasses and downed the rest. Nick put a hand on Charlie's shoulder and let out a contented sigh.

"Cheers to that, brother. Cheers to that."

EPILOGUE

CORTEZ THE KILLER

And the women all were beautiful
And the men stood straight and strong
They offered life in sacrifice
So that others could go on

Song & Lyrics by Neil Young

SEPTEMBER 12, 1578

He was a weary, scarred old man now. And while time had worn down his body, he still carried himself with a regal dignity, his mind sharp and alert even yet. He sat cross legged in front of his teepee, somewhere between dozing and daydreaming in the gentle warmth of the midday sun. A shout from a young man riding a powerful white stallion caused him to crack open his pale green eyes and squint out upon him prancing on the plain.

Asupacaci had survived an incredible journey of distance and hardship in this life, and from the toll it had taken he knew he would soon be joining his ancestors. He had spent his twilight years preparing as best he could and found himself looking forward to his final journey. The calls were stronger and more frequent now, the time was finally upon him.

"Come here *Tlanextic*," Asupacaci called out to him, motioning with his one good arm. Despite having been befriended by the Navajo tribe and having taken a Navajo wife, he had bestowed a name upon his son that meant *Light of Dawn* in the Nahuatl language of his people, the Aztecs. His son was indeed the light that would carry on after he was gone and survive as a tribe within the tribe. The bloodline of Asupacaci's people would be perpetuated forever more while cocooned within the safety of the powerful Navajo nation. That was the sanctuary the tribal elders had granted him and his descendants for all time, for the knowledge and leadership he had provided that they might survive the inevitable encroachment of the Spanish. He had proven himself to them, time and again, and had earned that asylum for his descendants.

The Navajo thought of his foreign knowledge as a sort of magic, and so cast him as a shaman, one who learned their language, but who also spoke the odd language and practiced the strange rituals of the Aztecs. While he was an honored part of the tribe, for the most part they left him alone to his dark arts.

Showing off his skill, his son rode the horse expertly in a wide circle, and just as he was about to pass he nimbly jumped off and slapped his horse on the flank, allowing it to graze nearby. He had grown taller than the other Navajos, with a physical strength and self confidence that belied his eighteen changings of the seasons. Tlanextic sat down stoically next to his father, unflinching, used to long periods of silence before his father might deign to impart some few words of wisdom.

Asupacaci smiled inwardly with pride at having his son by his side, and softly hummed a chant in thanks. He unconsciously rubbed the scar of the imbedded Spanish cross bolt near his shoulder, its poison eventually crippling the arm, a constant reminder of those who destroyed his world.

He had sat in the sweat lodge for a long time yesterday, usually it provided him some relief from the dull, throbbing ache, but not anymore. This pain would be with him until the end.

He hadn't intended to live this long, and after having delivered the treasure of his people to its final resting place, had been ready to offer his life as one last gift to the gods. But he had decided against it, for the simple fact that he wanted to make sure the Spanish never picked up on the trail, and that the treasure and legacy of his people would be safe for eternity. That meant surviving a little longer in this life and watching until he could be sure the danger had passed and the trail had grown cold.

After having sat together until the sun started on its downward arc, Asupacaci finally spoke. "It is time. Tell your mother we will go to the place of the Old Ones. I have a need to be there now. It is easier for my old ears to hear the spirits there and talk where the winds can carry my words to the gods one last time."

As early evening descended, they said their goodbyes to the tribe. Asupacaci was seated on the back of the same horse as his son, holding onto him with his one good arm. The chief of the Navajo reached out and put a hand on Asupacaci's knee and looked at him through knowing eyes. They had been through much together these past years, and each in his own way had protected the legacy of his own people. They were both proud leaders and warriors, and knew the world was inexorably changing around them. Nothing was said, nothing need be said, and after the two old men gave a brief nod to one another, Tlanextic coaxed the horse slowly down the dusty path.

They worked their way away from the camp onto the broad mesa, toward the canyons, the cries of warriors and lamentations of women fading with the distance. Despite all their differences, they had grown from the same great tree, and would be missed. His faithful wife followed on a smaller dark horse behind them, ever devoted to the last. Her Navajo name was *Kaya*, meaning Wise Child, and was appropriate for her gifts. Kaya was intelligent and perceptive and had greatly aided Asupacaci in his integration into the larger tribe, while also keeping his Aztec customs and traditions alive. She had the gift of tongues and had learned the Nahuatl language of the Aztecs fluently. He took comfort that she would accompany him on this last journey as well. Tlanextic was now of age. Asupacaci could continue no further. It was time for his son to carry on the legacy.

The mesa abruptly ended, revealing a wide gash in the earth, a broad valley looming below the sheer cliff edge. Tlanextic helped his father down from the horse and led him to a faint path along the very edge of the cliff. He gathered his things, and slowly started the descent, with his father shuffling behind with a hand on his shoulder to keep his balance. Kaya silently followed, carrying blankets, food, and water. They expertly worked their way down, intuitively knowing every step and hand hold from years of making their pilgrimages here. Eventually they went down below the silent stone buildings built high into the cliff face, over to the only route back up to them. Tlanextic found subtle indentations in the rock face and scrambled up. Once there he found the hidden coil of rope and lowered one end to his father. Kaya looped it under his arms, and Asupacaci was slowly pulled up by his powerful son.

Reaching the top of that level, he paused for breath. "It is a good thing I do not weigh what I used to son."

"Your body has gotten lighter, but your soul is still full father. You chose the right night, the omens are good."

They stood there, side by side, for a moment, gazing at a brilliant full moon just rising over the other edge of the canyon, illuminating the broad mesa that stretched away far into the distance. A lonely wolf howled somewhere on the opposite ledge, and another further away answered. Tlanextic lowered the rope again and brought up the supplies, then his mother.

They followed an ancient foot path, which funneled them to an easily protected point where stood a guard tower, and tread carefully on the narrow ledge past it. Finally they were all standing in front of a stone palace masterfully built into the cliff, the barely visible and well protected home of the old ones. This was a well-chosen place that could be easily defended by but a few determined warriors. It contained innumerable rooms, tucked into every crevice, some three or four stories high. No space was wasted. There were hundreds of such stone dwellings hidden in cliffs throughout the area, but this was the largest and best preserved.

As a fire was made and a last meal prepared, Asupacaci finally spoke. "I choose this place because the Spanish never found it. The old ones left long before even the Navajo came here, so it is sacred and a good place to rest our souls. You will prepare us in the traditional way I have taught you and hide our bodies deep within. And then you must never return."

Asupacaci paused, wanting to make sure his directions were perfectly clear and completely understood. Tlanextic nodded at his father, looking back at him across smoke of the fire, through his piercing green eyes. Asupacaci continued. "I am going to tell you our story one last time, that you may remember it and tell your son, who may tell his."

His brow furrowed in concentration, Asupacaci recounted how his father, the great Montezuma, had ruled a fabulous empire from the throne of their island city of Tenochtitlán far to the south. That the strange foreigners called Spaniards had come, and through duplicity, magic weapons and disease, had killed his father and family, and were about to topple the Aztec empire. That was when his uncle Cuitláhuac sent Asupacaci on his sacred mission to preserve the legacy of their people. To throw the Spanish off the trail his uncle wisely sent out other false expeditions and did not even know or want to know where Asupacaci would ultimately go.

In a soft voice and with a laugh Asupacaci told of the warrior general Cipactli who accompanied him, and how his large head reminded him of a crocodile. How Huitzilin, the flitting Hummingbird leader of the scouts, provided intelligence to keep the expedition safe. He told of the friendship he formed with Friar Rodrìguez, how he had learned from him, and that while not all Spanish were evil, gold drove them mad. And finally how Xicohtencatl, the Angry Bumblebee, had caught a wild pony and gifted it to Asupacaci, and protected him to his very last breath.

"That wild pony was the grandfather of the horse you now ride so proudly. The same color, the same strength, the same intelligence. Keep the bloodline of that horse going, just as you must continue mine."

It was Tlanextic's turn to smile, of the many tales his father had regaled him with over the years, some over and over again, he had never heard the one about the pony. He sat in rapt attention, as there was no telling what other final secrets might be revealed tonight.

The story shifted to the treacherous journey north, through the lands of the Chichimeca, the Coahuiltecan, and finally of the fateful encounter with the Chiricahua Apache, when Asupacaci feared all was about to be lost.

"We were surrounded in a valley where the walls had closed in, at a place they rolled boulders down the hills to block the trail. We could neither go forward nor back, and so prepared to die, to give our lives dearly, and waited for them to attack. The air was stifling, we had little water or shade. But after being harassed for two settings of the sun, they suddenly stopped. A procession came down from the hills, with our Coahuiltecan guides in their midst. One was carried dead, one dragged barely alive. We had thought the guides were traitors and had led us into a trap, but we were wrong. The guides had been taken captive by the Apache because they could speak their language, and the Apache tortured them to learn the truth of our intentions."

Asupacaci paused and coughed, he wasn't used to talking this much anymore, his strength steadily ebbing away. Kaya wrapped a blanket around his shoulders and brought him a gourd of water, which he sipped and then continued.

"But what was the truth? That a terrible storm was coming that would sweep up everything before it as leaves before the wind? That an evil god would blow pestilence and disease in advance of their cursed warriors? The Apache Chief believed he had heard truth from the mouths of the tortured guides. They could not lie with what they did to them. And he examined the few Spaniards we had left, their pallid skin, their strange beards, the horses that pulled the wagons, and the Spanish weapons we brought. He saw the truth in it and knew that he must prepare his own people. We gave him tribute and the last of the Spaniards except for the Friar, and he granted us safe passage."

Despite his failing body he was caught up in the tale, the passion building in his voice, as he knew this was the last time it would be told by one who had directly experienced it. He must pass the story on orally with as much detail as possible and do so accurately. The codices he had painstakingly left behind only told so much of the story. He paused to catch his breath and took another sip of water.

"Northward we went, staying away from any rivers the Spanish might use. We followed footpaths and trails, and even found some ancient walkways. Over time we learned these were made by the old ones, the ones who built places like this palace hidden in the cliffs. None of the tribes we encountered knew who the old ones were or what had become of them, but they left behind great stone houses and monuments, worn down by time. We traveled on for months, our numbers dwindling the further we advanced."

Tlanextic nodded at his father, concentrating hard to etch the tale deep into his memory. Asupacaci paused, gathering his thoughts and the strength to continue.

"We passed through a place named *Paquimé,* then eventually came to a large area of many cliff dwellings called *Gila.* That is where Friar Rodrìguez died, worn out from the journey. I hid him deep in a cliff palace much like this one, but smaller. While I curse what his people did, he showed me there were honorable men among them. Perhaps that means some measure of hope for the future."

"We went further to a place called *Hawikuh.* The distance we could go was dependent on the strength of the horses, and we were lucky to find good grazing along the way. We buried our dead in unmarked graves, left no offerings or trinkets that would betray our passing."

"Finally, we came to what was the center of the world of the old ones, that the natives called *Chaco.* They had great houses of many rooms made of stone, but on flat ground, not in the cliffs as here. They had large round rooms the Navajo called Kivas, which was where they honored their gods. It was a magnificent place, and our horses were worn out and our number few. So we searched until we found a deep cave, and inside the air was dry and still, with only dust and old bones on the floor. The omens said this was *the* place, that it was safe, that it would preserve all we had. We put all that was valuable deep within it, and then sealed the entrance and covered our tracks so none would ever find it.

"With empty carts we continued on, further north. I wanted to leave nothing that could point to where we hid our people's history. The distance and journey took their toll, until finally we could go no further. There was a single strange shaped mountain right here, with a long ridge, almost like a tail. I took it as a sign from the gods telling me to stop, the trail ends here."

"We scattered what horses remained except for my pony, and

stacked the wagons and all our possessions into a funeral pyre in a dry riverbed. Only a few of the strongest warriors were still with me. One by one they lay down their lives as I offered their hearts to the gods, until only my loyal Bumblebee was left.

We put all their bodies on top of the pyre, and then Bumblebee lay across them and handed me his obsidian blade. I made a final offering, of my most faithful warrior, and cried. I couldn't remember the last time I cried, I must have been a child, but I cried for him, for all who made the journey, for the people of Tenochtitlán, for the souls of our ancestors. And then I lit the pyre and knew that the spring rains would eventually flood the river basin and wash the ashes away, and it would be as if we had never been."

"I sat there by the ashes for days, waiting for the gods to take me too. Time stopped for me. I no longer knew where I was. I don't even remember the Navajo finding me. They said that I talked in a babbling language they couldn't understand, that the gods must have touched me. They looked at the great pile of ashes and bone and said I had to possess big magic to burn down the desert and all my enemies. They took me in and brought me even further north. When I regained my strength I decided to survive a little longer, to ensure the Spanish never found the treasure of our ancestors. They accepted me, and I lived with them for years as a shaman, an odd holy man who had knowledge and magic they did not, who worshiped other gods."

A deep racking cough interrupted Asupacaci, and as he gathered himself, Kaya rested her head on his good shoulder. Tlanextic could still see the fierce pride in her eyes, her belief in the soul mate she had and the life she had lived.

"One day a group of traders came through, and one of their slaves threw himself at my feet. He was Aztec, and called me *Tlanahuatihqui*, great leader. It had been so very long since anyone called me that. He had escaped from Tenochtitlán by fleeing north, was captured, and traded from tribe to tribe. He recognized me as belonging to the royal family and told what had happened. A great battle had been fought, with Cortés and his allies coming back and besieging Tenochtitlán after I had left. They built strange, large ships to sail and surround our city on Lake Texcoco, our war canoes no match for them. Like an anaconda they slowly strangled the survivors into smaller and smaller spaces, until there was none left. Many thousands died on both sides, but in the end our people were massacred and enslaved. Our great place of sacrifice, the Hueteocalli Temple, was destroyed, and their house of worship built on top of it. My uncle, Cuitláhuac, the last leader of the Aztecs, was executed." Asupacaci took a moment to regain his breath.

"The slave died soon after he told me this. It was as if he had survived all his hardships only long enough to pass the tale to me, his sacred duty finally fulfilled. I went south, back to the place of the ashes, to check that all was safe and undisturbed. The ashes were gone, washed out, only bits of metal and bone remained. These I buried, and I fasted that I might know what destiny the gods now held for me. I finally had a vision from our ancestors showing me the way, what must be done. And what I saw was a son, who would live with the Navajo, but always keep the language and the old ways of his ancestors alive. That would be our legacy, that the Spanish might not stamp us completely off the face of mother earth, that our royal bloodline would survive forever more. I told the Navajo Chief of my vision, and he gifted me his only daughter so I would not have to live alone, so that my bloodline could go on."

Tlanextic looked at his mother and smiled.

"Kaya taught me their language, their customs, how to survive in this land, and finally gifted you to me. I in turn taught them the Aztec knowledge of crops, horses, warfare, and much about the Spanish who must surely come this way some day."

He paused, his voice now barely a whisper, and with great effort took an object off from around his neck with the shaky hand of his one good arm.

"Take this necklace and wear it always, as I have done. It is a talisman, a reminder, of the glory from whence we came. You, son, are now the last of the house of Montezuma."

Passing along what looked like a single gold link on a thin rope, Asupacaci sat back, utterly exhausted. Kaya still leaned against him, a faint smile on her lips, a single tear trickling down her cheek.

Fighting back his own emotions, yet proud of all his parents had been through, Tlanextic reverently put the necklace around his own neck. He then gave each of them a long drink of the bitter tasting poison that had been carefully prepared for this night.

Asupacaci and Kaya sat contentedly in silence, holding one hand together, the light of the full moon giving them a ghostlike appearance, as if their spirits were about to drift away in the breeze. Time passed, the fire faded to a glowing bed of embers, the brilliant moon edged across the sky, and Kaya slowly closed her eyes, and breathed no more.

Asupacaci looked at her, unwilling to let go of her hand and sighed heavily, then nodded to his son, closing his own eyes for the final time. The warmth of the embers seemed to penetrate not just his wrinkled, leathery skin, but the very soul of his being. He felt his mortal body melt away, he was light as a quetzal feather drifting in the wind, drifting far to the south, over deserts and canyons, mountains and rivers, to territory so familiar it made his heart ache, finally descending toward the sacred Lake Texcoco.

He saw his father seated on a magnificent throne in his regal headdress smile and nod at him, ruling in the heart of the world, in Tenochtitlán. Nobles in fantastic colored robes surrounded Montezuma and paid him homage, bound captives bowed before him, while slaves served him drinks cooled by the snow from distant mountains. Colorful parrots flittered about as the sounds of animals in the nearby zoo could be heard over the din of the crowd. He felt his mother's hand, Queen Teotlalco's, on his shoulder, smelled her favorite perfume, could taste on his tongue the banquet feast that had been prepared, and heard his brothers' familiar voices calling out and teasing him. It had been so very long since he had been here, yet every detail came back to him like it was only yesterday, vivid to all his senses.

He slowly breathed it all in before exhaling one last time, a slight smile of contentment upon his lips. He was home at long last having completed his odyssey to save the soul of his people, forever.

Asupacaci's One True Journey

PRINCIPLE CAST OF CHARACTERS

PRESENT DAY

Ahaiyuta – Zuni for *Morning Star*, guard to tribal elders
Albert (Al) LaBounty – Father of Nick LaBounty
Alexandre LaBounty – Distant relative of Nick LaBounty
Atsa – Navajo for *Eagle*, musician
Bidzii – Navajo for *Strong One*, leader of Navajo blues band
Charles (Charlie) LaBounty – Nick's older brother
Chico (Francisco) Martinez – Mexican Department of Antiquities
Dr. Carlos Lòpez – Director of National Museum of Anthropology
Dr. Philip Storm – Nick's mentor in college and PhD Advisor
Dr. Rojas – Pioneering Mexican DNA specialist
Eztli (Esteban) González – Nahuatl for *Blood*, Cartel Boss of Bosses
Huehue – Nahuatl for *Ancient One*, Writer of Codices
Javier Hernández – Right hand of Cartel Boss Eztli González
Josephine LaBounty – Mother of Nick LaBounty
Juan Ramirez – Spanish Minister of Culture
Lonan – Zuni for *Cloud*, respected tribal elder
Miguel González – Brother of Cartel Boss Eztli González, Enforcer
Nanook – Inuit for *Master of Bears*, Soba's domesticated wolf

Nick LaBounty – Aspiring Archeologist and PhD Student
Raúl Concepción – Student Assistant to Dr. Carlos Lòpez
Robert Sommers – Director of the Drug Enforcement Agency (DEA)
Soba (Altsoba) – Navajo for *At War*, Tribal Shaman and Linguist
Sophie LaBounty –Wife of Charles LaBounty, Registered Nurse
Willard Bashant – Acting Director of the Department of the Interior
Tahoma – Navajo for *Water's Edge*, roadie for the band
Yas – Navajo for *Snow*, musician

TIME OF THE CONQUEST (1521)

Álvar Núñez Cabeza de Vaca – Survivor who walked across Southwest

Antonio de Ciudad Rodrigo – One of New World's first Missionaries

Asupacaci – Third son of Montezuma

Bartolomé de las Casas – Bishop who championed Indigenous Rights

Charles V – King of Spain, Castile and Aragon, Holy Roman Emperor

Chimalpopoca – First son of Montezuma

Cipactli – Nahuatl for *Crocodile*, Warrior General

Cuitláhuac – Last Ruler of the Aztecs, younger brother of Montezuma

El Capitán – Conquistador leader who accompanied Cortés

Francisco Coronado – Conquistador and explorer seeking Cibola

Fray Garcia – Franciscan priest in Chiapas region

Friar Rodrìguez – Spanish Priest who accompanied Cortés

Hernán Cortés – Spanish Leader, conqueror of Aztec Empire

Kaya – Navajo for *Wise Child*, wife of Asupacaci

Huitzilin – Nahuatl for *Hummingbird*, Warrior Leader of the Scouts

La Malinche – Interpreter and courtesan of Cortés

Marcos de Niza – Franciscan priest who claimed to see Cibola
Montezuma – Emperor of the Aztecs
Pánfilo de Narváez – Led ill-fated expedition to La Florida
Queen Teotlalco – Wife of Montezuma, mother of Asupacaci
Tlaltecatzin – Second son of Montezuma
Tlanextic – Nahuatl for *Light of Dawn*, Asupacaci's son
Xicohtencatl – Nahuatl for *Angry Bumblebee*, Jaguar Knight
Xólotl – Leader of the Chichimeca

ABOUT THE AUTHOR

A graduate of the S.I. Newhouse School of Public Communications and the Whitman School of Management at Syracuse University, Jay LaBarge spent his professional career growing companies in the networking, telecommunication, and consumer electronics industries. A businessman by profession but historian by passion, he and his wife Sandy raised their daughters Ashley and Kara in the Central New York area, with frequent trips to his childhood home in the Adirondack Mountains.

He continues to pursue his love of history and travel with his wife to out of the way places both domestic and abroad. His lifetime of curiosity and wanderlust ultimately led to the creation of Aztec Odyssey.

You can find him and more Nick LaBounty stories at jayclabarge.com